Finding Her

—for Ann Smith, in memoriam

Finding Her

SJ

The back door to the deck opened. It was Gert. "Dinner's ready, you two." She watched Reece laughing, Kristin frowning. "Everything okay?"

"Yeah, thanks, Mom," said Kristin.

Seeing Gert sobered Reece, and he brought his laughter to a stop. "Stuffed bell peppers." The words sounded ridiculous, and he burst out laughing again.

"Whatever," said Gert. "But it's ready. Kristin, your dad is at the table to say the blessing." She let the storm door slam behind her.

"Reece. If I tell them what you've told me about Cindy and Emma, they won't let me marry you. And why should they?"

Reece pinched his thigh and reined it in. "Don't tell them everything you know. We should go in and eat. I don't want Edwin going hungry."

"Stop," said Kristin. She stood and waited for him to follow. "Come on."

"Leave the dog out?"

"Yeah, he'll just beg at the table. Come on, playboy."

"Hey, that's not fair." He followed her inside to the warm smells of stuffed bell pepper. He tousled his hair, mahogany-chestnut as he liked to call it.

Kristin took her place at the table, and so did Reece. He looked at Edwin and knew that he would ask him to say the blessing. Besides the bell peppers stuffed with hamburger, there were green beans and garlic toast.

Edwin looked somber. "Reece, would you say grace?"

He bowed his head and closed his eyes.

Reece could only think about the guy who had been excommunicated from their church. "Dear Lord, we thank you for this day and for loving each and every one of us. Bless this food and this family. Amen." He hadn't bowed his head or closed his eyes.

Both Gert and Edwin said, "Amen," exchanging glances.

Reece steeled himself, expecting Kristin to spill the beans about seeing Cindy's boobs or that he had admitted to bonding with Emma. He waited for everyone to serve themselves.

"This is delicious, honey," said Edwin. He chewed with precision.

"Thank you, dear," said Gert.

"Smells and tastes good." Reece took a bite of buttery garlic toast. He felt kind of sick.

Kristin took small bites, staring at her plate and then glancing at Reece. Soon, to break the silence, Reece asked Edwin how things were going at work. There wasn't much of interest to report, except that the city was cracking down on dog fighting, which got Kristin's attention.

"That's just awful. Those poor dogs."

Reece spoke up. "In Godo, the dogs would fight at night and kill each other. Sometimes I couldn't sleep because of it."

"Did they keep them as pets?" asked Edwin.

"Not really. Mostly wild, just hanging around. We had several dog bites at the clinic. I usually carried a rock, just in case."

"Reece, those poor dogs," said Kristin. "You didn't hit

one, did you?"

"It was enough just to act like you were going to, and they'd run off growling. There were hyenas, too. Killed mules at night. I saw one on the path, half eaten—"

"Reece, stop," said Kristin. "What a horrible place. I can't believe you were even there. How did you talk me into letting you go?"

"Sorry." He remembered doing a book report in front of class in seventh grade. He'd been sharing a gory scene about plane crash survivors eating human flesh. The teacher had said, "Reece, that's enough," and made him sit down.

Gert was shaking her head. "Yes, please stop." She ate as if each forkful were pure gold.

"Well, it's certainly another world over there," said Edwin. "Sometimes I wish I had traveled, but maybe just to Europe or somewhere like that."

Reece felt something like sympathy. "I'd like to...to go back some day."

Gert coughed. "Even with what happened, being shot like that?" Her face registered a profound disbelief, like he had just told her the moon was made of crackers.

Kristin worked to cut the bell pepper with her fork, silent.

"Yeah, travel is good," said Reece. "Makes you appreciate the small things, like this good dinner." He felt Kristin's leg brush his, as if she was on the verge of forgiving him everything.

"You certainly showed some courage going over there, but I would have to question your sanity if you went back. You wouldn't expect Kristin to go, would you?" asked Edwin.

"Never in a million years," said Kristin. "Visiting him in the hospital was enough. Everything was so dirty, people begging in the streets."

"The people are really nice, though," said Reece. He felt a lump in his throat. How better to explain?

"There are nice people here, too," said Kristin.

"People are people," said Reece. It's all he could think of.

"Do you still want to be a missionary?" asked Edwin. "After what happened? It sounds like the people could use more than food and medicine."

Reece thought. "That is exactly what they needed. They've been Christian since the fourth century AD. Well, there are the Muslims too, but they seem to be just fine, except they get hungry just like the Christians."

"I wonder why Jesus or his disciples never went to Africa?" asked Edwin. He postured as if revealing a deep web of mystery.

"Didn't one of the disciples travel to North Africa? Philip?" asked Reece.

Edwin's breath caught, and he looked to Gert for help. "You're the missionary, I suppose. I'll have to look that up."

"Carthage. I believe he went to Carthage, in North Africa." Reece felt like he'd gotten a free play on a pinball machine. "The ticker's still tickin' and the clicker's still clickin'."

No one quite knew what he meant, forks hitting plates, Walter scratching at the back door.

"Maybe you should teach Sunday School," said Gert. She was enamored of Bible knowledge.

"Maybe not," said Kristin. "He's been looking at other girls' boobs." She nudged him under the table.

"What's this?" asked Edwin. His plate was clean. Gert looked disgusted as if she expected the worst.

"Brother," said Reece. "You have to understand the circumstances. It just happened. I had nothing to do with it. I looked, but then I looked away. What can I say?" He then explained in detail how Cindy had pulled down her tube top on the pier.

"Well, what a hussy," said Gert. She was frowning, trying to digest this surprising news. Reece just seemed to attract trouble.

"That's never happened to me," said Edwin, with a lilt of humor in his voice. One glance from Gert, though, and his tone changed. "She needs the Lord."

"I think Reece needs the Lord," said Kristin.

Gert smiled at that one. She played with the sugar bowl, a souvenir from Gatlinburg.

"Okay, I looked. I'm sorry. Jesus has forgiven me, so how about you?" He wondered if his neck was red. He felt hot and bothered. Hell, he couldn't get the vision of Cindy's breasts out of his head, nor did he want to.

"Honey, he's right," said Edwin. "I know you're upset, but you do have to forgive him."

"Oh, the guys are of one mind," said Kristin. "Mom, you gonna throw in the towel too?"

Gert laughed a soft laugh. "Honey, settle down. Men do have one-track minds. At least she didn't try to rip his clothes off."

"He also said he had bonded with Emma over there. Just now. On the deck. Is this the tip of the iceberg that flips over?" A tear appeared in each corner of her eyes. "I give up." She stood and walked into the den with her arms folded. She glanced back once, headed to her room.

"Uh, hold on," said Reece. He stood. "Should I go back there?" He needed help.

"Yes, you should," said Gert. "She wants you to."

"Just as long as she doesn't shoot me." He laughed, but cut it short.

Emma remained on the toilet with her pants down, while the rest stood ramrod straight. Sally held the pregnancy stick behind her back. Heather announced the seconds as they passed.

"One minute," said Heather. She loved her Movado watch, but had trouble reading the time on the numberless dial.

"Don't we just take the cake?" asked Sarah. "Jesus, I'm a nervous wreck."

"Well, what about me?" asked Emma. "It's my pee you're all swooning over." She reached behind and flushed again.

Sarah rubbed Emma's head. "Baby girl, you bring us so much joy."

"One minute, thirty seconds," said Heather. "Gosh, my heart is just beating up a storm." She kept her eyes glued to her watch.

The tiny bathroom was getting warm, and a trickle of sweat ran between Sally's shoulder blades. "I'm a nervous wreck. Emma, if it's positive, what're you gonna do?"

"I wish I knew," said Emma. "I wish someone knew."

"One minute forty-five seconds." Heather stood on her tiptoes, her finger on the rim of her watch.

Emma sang. "Amazing grace, how sweet the sound..." No one joined in. "What? Sally, look at the damn stick."

Heather went into the countdown. "Five, four, three, two, one, blast off!"

Sally got rattled and dropped the stick. "Dammit to hell. Y'all stand back so I can pick it up." It was face down on the dirty tile. She brought it into the light and didn't speak.

"Sally!" said Emma. "Tell me!"

"It's a blue line. You're negative. Thank God!" She held it out for everyone to see.

Emma felt a rush of normalcy, as if she'd been cured of a giant facial birthmark. "Yes, thank you, Jesus. Sally! That nearly killed me. My leg's gone to sleep. Somebody help me up."

"You want to save this contraption?" asked Sally. "Or should I toss it?"

Heather and Sarah helped Emma to stand. She pulled up her pants. "I don't want it. Why would I want it?"

"Okay, simmer down now." Sally dropped the stick into the trash can. "Let's tell Sammy the good news."

Someone knocked on the door. "Y'all okay in there?" It was Emma, the waitress. Once, a homeless woman took a bath in the bathroom. Anything could happen.

Sally pulled the door open. "Hey, just us girls, doing girl things."

Emma, the waitress, looked as if she disbelieved. "Well, okay then. Y'all have a good night."

"We will, honey," said Sarah.

Sally led the way out and pushed into the warm September evening.

"What the hell have y'all been up to?" asked Sammy. "I was going to call the fire department." He was sweating.

"We had to check and see," said Sally.

"To see if I was pregnant," said Emma. "But I'm good to go." She felt royally weary.

Sammy was putting two and two together. "Yeah, right.

Sorry. Emma, Sally told me what happened. I didn't want to bring it up." He burped fried fish.

"No harm done," said Emma. She slid into the back-seat. "Let Momma sit up front."

"No, I want to be by you, baby girl. I know that was hard."

Sally took the front seat. "Anybody want ice cream? Sammy's got his wallet out tonight."

"Not me," said Emma. "I'm too full. I think I would puke."

"Me too," said Sarah. "Let's just get her home and relax. I need a cigarette."

"I think we all need a cigarette," said Sammy. "Y'all had that waitress worried. She came outside and asked me if somebody got sick." He laughed and put on his blinker.

"Y'all are the craziest damn people I've ever met," said Emma. "But I guess I love you."

Sarah kissed her hair. "You too, baby girl."

Sammy tuned the radio to Rock 99.5. It was the chorus of "Sweet Home Alabama," and Sally joined in, followed by everyone but Sarah, who didn't know the words. They sang with gusto, giving Emma an official welcome home.

Back at the two-story house wrapped in vinyl siding, they gathered on the driveway, passing around a can of mosquito repellent. Sammy had to call it a night, having to work early the next day. Emma stood and hugged him.

"Night, y'all!" and he was off.

"I missed old Sammy," said Emma.

"Yeah, he's kinda queer but in all the right ways," said Sally.

"Hold on a minute," said Emma. "I'll be right back."

"What you need, baby girl?" Sarah puffed her cancer stick.

"Nothing." Emma went into the living room where the phone and answering machine were. The light was blinking, and her heart skipped. She hit the play button and listened to the message, about a minute in length. It was a collection agency asking about the mortgage. "Shit."

The screen door slammed behind Emma, and she took the empty chair on the carport. Her mom worked a full-time job at the barbecue and collected social security, but maybe that wasn't enough. She thought about her bastard dad living in a trailer, paid for. She wondered if she should call Reece.

"Emma, we missed you, girl," said Sally. "It just wasn't the same without you. Don't you ever go off like that again. You hear?"

"I hear," said Emma.

"Aunt Emma, tell us a story," said Heather. "About working in the clinic over there. I'm thinking about being a nurse. Did Momma tell you?"

Emma sat up a little straighter. "You'd make a great nurse. You're very patient, which is a gift." She thought about a story to tell. *Where to start?* Her mind was just a blank, but then she spoke.

"Well, this is pretty typical. There would be a line of folks up the hill at least thirty or forty deep to start the day, sometimes more. I always felt bad that they had to squat and sit in the sun. A few would bring an old ratty umbrella. It's a higher elevation there, and the sun burns you quicker, plus it takes water forever to boil." She leaned forward, looking at the cement as if gazing into a small fire. "But, Jesus, I have to describe the smells first. The women all smelled like smoke and milk. The men just smelled like heavy sweat. No one ever took a bath because there was very little water, just enough to cook and drink with. What I missed most was a hot shower. But you don't sweat much there, just kind of dry age like cheese maybe." She glanced up, and all eyes were on her. She felt that glee of safety, of being surrounded and protected. "Where was I? Oh yeah, the clinic. And you have to understand that Afewerki was there. He was our interpreter. I was cleaning a leg wound when a little boy came in with his father. Reece asked him what the problem was. I always kind of listened to him, and he listened to what was going on with me. It was much quicker seeing two at a time. So, anyway, the father said his son had gone deaf. The poor little boy looked scared out of his mind. It took some doing, but finally, the boy let Reece look into his ears, and it was just a royal mess in there. So, Reece took some peroxide and, injecting it into one ear, let it bubble like crazy with pus and bits of dirt boiling out."

"You can do that?" asked Sally. "It won't hurt your ear?"

"My word," said Sarah.

"The little boy was moaning and squirming. Reece could see something, and he asked me for my forceps. He cleaned them off, and I had to look. He reached in and grabbed at something. It broke off, and he went in a little deeper. And out came a gooey plug of wax, pus, dirt, and two dead flies."

"Gross," said Heather. "What about his other ear?"

"So, by now, the little boy was crying, and the dad was grinning. Reece did the other ear, and it was sort of the same thing, a glob of junk."

"And could he hear?" asked Sally. She was sitting on the edge of her seat.

"What do you think? By now, he was still as a mouse and gripping his daddy's ripped shirt. His daddy said something to him, and the little boy mumbled. We could tell by Afewerki's expression that the little boy could hear, and then he told us. Cured with peroxide." Emma loosened her grip on the aluminum armrests. "There, how's that?"

No one spoke for a few seconds.

"I'm glad there's a happy ending there," said Sarah. "But how can you just let a fly die in your ear like that?"

"The flies there are different. They'll fly up your nose and down your throat if you're not careful. Once they're in, they're in. I hated those dang flies." A hundred other stories flooded her mind.

"That's so gross," said Heather.

"But the little boy could hear again, right?" asked Sally. "Tell us about the mean guy who ran the village. You wrote me about him."

Emma laughed. The Hyena had at one time represented everything she hated in a person, but now he seemed harmless from so far away.

"In the end, I kind of feel sorry for him. He was a serious alcoholic and drug addict. He chewed qat, which is a narcotic leaf. He would always walk around with his guns and a couple of young guys with AK-47s. Nobody liked him in the village that I could tell. He would steal from us and arrested Afewerki at least three times while I was there. One day, he made this pregnant woman get off her mule so that he could ride it out to see one of his girlfriends. That really got me." She was clenching her fists. "He was a bastard for sure, but maybe not the worst of the lot...He used to be a soldier. Afewerki told me that he'd been sent to Godo as a punishment. Never did find out why."

"Didn't he attack you one day?" asked Sally. "I'd like to wring his neck."

"Yeah, him and his two thugs. I was out walking one day by myself. But this old monk heard the commotion and scared them off." Her head drooped just a bit. She hoped Sally wasn't going to ask her about the rape, especially with Heather and her mom listening.

Reece pulled close to Kristin's bedroom door and listened—nothing. He knocked three times. "Kristin?" The door was locked. "Kristin? Open up." He waited for an eternity.

The door opened. "What? Did they send you here?" Kristin's face was a blank framed in curls. She let the door open a little wider.

"No, they didn't. Can I come in?"

"If you want." She retreated and sat on her bed.

"Look, I'm sorry about what happened with Cindy. It was totally out of my control. She just did it."

"And nothing else happened?" She stood and arranged a small music box on her dresser.

"No. Nothing." Reece felt like cotton seeds, buried in a fluff of deceit. Where would it end?

"Okay, I forgive you for that. But it all adds up, right? You can see how I would be upset. And then you told me you had bonded with Emma. That's even worse than seeing some girl's breasts. A bond is something special, like what we have. Right?"

Reece sat on the bed. "Yes, yes, but how to explain? We only worked together for a month or so. It's not like we knew each other's secret wishes or could finish one another's sentences. The place, Godo, is just so harsh. You have to stick together to survive. No room for being at odds with someone. Maybe that's the better way to put it."

"What, that you weren't at odds? That sounds strange, not anything like bonding." She walked to the small window in her room, which overlooked the driveway. "Today's Wednesday. You want to go to this party that Brad invited me to? Maybe that'll take a notch out of his belt."

"So, you're not mad? Just want to be sure." He stood near her. He had no desire whatsoever to go to Brad's party.

"No. I'm sorry that I'm so bitchy sometimes. I just started my period, if that means anything." She blushed.

Reece paused at that. That was new. He'd never had anyone he'd dated talk about her period before. "Yeah, no problem. Maybe the best thing is for us to go out and not go to this party. What kind of party is it again?"

"Pool party at some doctor's house. I'm sure there'll be lots of alcohol, but I won't make that mistake again. I was just so mad at you that night."

"Ugh, a pool party, probably with bad, loud music. I've never cared to socialize with doctors, anyway." He eased up to her and put his arms around her from behind.

"Would you just do it for me? I'm not happy about it either, but Brad needs to see us together. Maybe you'll punch him on the diving board." She laughed.

"Oh God," said Reece. "And there'll be doctors I'll be working with in ICU, doctors I've worked with in CCU. Brad is a tiny nail." He laughed and squeezed her.

"Can you rub my tummy? It hurts and needs some love." She moved his hands there. She squirmed. "Don't tickle me, silly."

"Like this?" Her skin felt hot under his hands, and he was getting aroused. He massaged her belly with both hands, wanting to let them drop lower. The door to her room was open.

"Yeah, like that. Ooh, that feels good. Here, let's do this." She disengaged, closed her door, and lay on the bed. "Straddle me and keep rubbing. You lucky boy."

Reece could hear the TV in the den. At least Edwin was occupied. He did as told and straddled her legs. He pushed up her shirt a bit, but her jeans were in the way.

"Easy fix," said Kristin. She unbuttoned and pushed them down below her belly button. "That's all, though, buster. Mom's liable to barge in."

Reece took a deep breath. His erection was tangled in his underwear, and he contorted to try to straighten things out without touching himself. He could see it poking into his jeans at a bent angle. He put his hands on her belly and rubbed with his thumbs.

That feels good." Kristin closed her eyes. "Just a little harder."

Reece knew he was in trouble, but there was no turning back. He pushed in his thumbs, circling down to the top of her panties. His erection was fierce and throbbing. He leaned down and kissed her on the lips.

"Kiss me again."

It hurt his back, but he leaned down, somewhat bowed, and kissed her on the neck, working his way to her ear, trying to stay balanced and rub her stomach. Just as he was beginning to pitch forward, she pulled him down on top of her, his chest in her face. He pushed up and slid down, his erection poking her in the groin.

"We have a visitor," she said. She laughed and mumbled, arching into him.

Reece put his mouth on hers, giving her deep kisses. He could feel his belly next to hers and reached to push her jeans down farther. He took deep, regular breaths, his hand squeezing her butt.

"Hey, be careful," she whispered. "I've got girl things down there." Reece pressed into her, kissing her ear as she moaned.

"Okay. God." He pressed into her again and finally had to reach inside his pants to adjust his manhood before he exploded.

She ran her hands under his shirt and drew her nails down his back. He grunted his approval, and then it was beyond his control as his hips began to jerk and he came.

There was a knock on the door.

"Crap." Reece bolted upright, a darkening circle on the front of his jeans. Kristin turned on her side, fumbling with her zipper.

Another knock. "Kristin? We have apple pie." The door opened.

"Hey," said Kristin. She had a big smile. She glanced at Reece, who pretended to be looking out the window.

"Uh, we have apple pie," said Gert. "You guys okay in here?"

"That's one steep driveway," said Reece. "I wonder if I put the parking brake on." He half turned and gave Gert a guilty glance.

"Mom, apple pie. That's our favorite. Give us a minute, and we'll be right out. Just making up is all. Reece said... well, we'll be out."

"Okay," said Gert. She left the door open. The six o'clock news was on, into the sports. Then came the weather.

"Christ Jesus," said Reece.

"Really steep driveway?" Kristin laughed and popped

up, buttoning her jeans. "You naughty boy." She inspected his pants. "You might need the bathroom before I do."

"Jeez, does she just walk in like that? Scared the living crap out of me. I guess the sooner we get married, the better, huh?" He inspected his pants, pulled his shirt down, and shook his head. "Feel like a damn criminal."

"Silly, just go to the bathroom. Keep a straight face, and you'll be fine."

"Yeah, right." He passed into the hall and ducked into the bathroom.

Kristin adjusted her look in the mirror and went to the den. Gert was whispering to Edwin. He looked solemn.

"Where's the pie? Reece'll be out in a minute," said Kristin.

"On the table," said Gert, as if using the last of her breath.

"Okay." Kristin plopped onto the couch.

"Did you get it worked out, honey?" asked Edwin. He went from full recline to three-quarters.

Kristin giggled. "Oh, we did. It wasn't his fault. I think we're good. How was work?"

The front door opened, and it was Robyn. "Smells good," she said from the stairs. She bumped into Reece in the hall. "Hey."

"Hey." Reece tried not to look down at his pants. The shirt covered most of it. "You working today?"

"Nope, off today. Been to the gym." She left him in the hall and made her way to the kitchen.

Reece came into the den and mustered a smile. He couldn't decide whether to sit or not, waiting for Kristin to make a move. She stood and led him by the hand into the dining room, to the pie on the table. He went along like a little boy. Robyn was in the kitchen, making herself a plate.

"Here, have a seat, excitable guy," said Kristin. She glanced at Gert in the kitchen, who was frowning.

"Yum, apple pie," said Reece. "With crumbles on top. See the crumbles. The crumbles on top."

Gert put two paper plates on the table.

"Thank you," said Reece. "Looks great. Apple pie."

"With crumbles on top," said Kristin.

"What are you babbling about?" asked Robyn, still wearing her black unitard.

"The pie has crumbles on top," said Reece. He took a bite. "Delicious pie with crumbles on top."

Robyn dug into her stuffed bell pepper. "Well, whatever. Crumbles on top yourself."

Reece and Kristin laughed.

"Maybe Robyn would like to go to Brad's party," said Reece. "She can take my place." He leaned forward to glance at the clock on the stove.

"What?" asked Kristin. "I thought you said you'd go."

"We were talking about it, but that's all." He ate some pie. He just couldn't stomach the thought of hanging out with a bunch of doctors.

"Is it that Brad guy from work who won't leave you alone?" asked Robyn.

"Yeah, he's like the little train that could. Don't you agree that Reece should go to protect me?" asked Kristin.

"Should you be going places where you need protection?" asked Robyn. "You got wasted at the last party. That's no secret."

"My words exactly." Reece pointed his fork at Robyn.

"I don't mean protect like that. You know what I mean. To protect my honor. I'm his fiancée and not some piece of candy in a candy store. I'm taken."

Gert was listening, cleaning the sink for the second time.

"Reece? What say ye?" Robyn savored a bite of green beans with some of the bell pepper meat filling. "And save some of that pie for big sister."

Reece sighed. "Okay, I get it. But he hasn't invited me anyway. We could do something else, maybe go hiking at Oak Mountain. What about that?"

"I would go with you," said Robyn.

"Those parties sound like bad news to me, honey," said Gert. She was wearing her pastel dishwashing gloves.

"He would say you're invited. Of course, you can go. With you there, it might be fun. I'm sure they'll grill stuff and swim." Kristin dabbed the corner of her mouth with a paper napkin. She seemed determined to go.

"You know they'll have the football games on, probably be sacked out in front of the TV." Reece didn't much care for football, although he was an Auburn fan.

"He's probably right," said Robyn. "I've got to get out of this outfit." She tugged at the underwear beneath her unitard and kicked her tennis shoes beneath the table.

"Robyn, your stinky shoes. Take them to your room." Gert walked in a tight circle, looking for the scrub brush.

"Maybe they'll just have the radio on. What's wrong with that? Reece, maybe we could go hiking on Sunday, after church. Am I going to have to beg you?"

"No. It's just that doctors and nurses don't mix very well. Maybe I have short-man syndrome. Who knows? I tolerate them at work, but then I'm done. That's what was so great about the clinic in Godo, no doctors."

"Just you and Emma, right?" Kristin frowned, exaggerated it into a pumpkin face. "I bet if Emma were at the party, you'd go."

Reece examined the last slice of apple pie in the tin. "No, that's not the point here." He wanted just to leave and go home and maybe sit on the pier or read *National Geographic,* the ones he'd missed while he was gone. Plus, hadn't he promised Emma that he would call her? He wasn't exactly sure. He imagined what would happen if Emma called him at Kristin's.

"Reece, just give in and go," said Robyn. "You'll never hear the end of it otherwise."

Reece felt he was being cornered. He tapped his fork on the table. "Let's go hiking with Robyn."

Kristin grumbled. "Now it's my sister. Everyone wants a piece of you." She pushed back from the table. "Reece, don't you understand I lost you, but you came back like a miracle? We have to do something...with us. The two of us. Is that too much to ask?"

"Don't drag me into this," said Robyn. She laughed. "Fine. Go hiking without me. Just thought we'd hang out. Reece is all yours, babydoll."

"Girls," said Gert, scrubbing the hide off the metal sink. "Just get along."

"Is the sink clean yet?" asked Robyn. She locked eyes with Gert for a hot second.

"Okay, I'll go with you." Reece wondered what it would be like to drown, to walk into a lake with a car battery tied around his neck.

Emma told the story about the pregnant woman who drank antiseptic because it was in a wine bottle, and then about the monk who was digging the church into the rock, about the recurrent staph infection on his face and neck. It had turned out that he was shaving with a razor that was over a year old.

The crickets and cicadas had joined in chorus, serenading the late evening heat. Above, spare white clouds moved along beneath a bright moon. A car was turning into the driveway, one headlight out.

"God dammit," said Sarah. She stood and knocked over the ashtray.

"What?" asked Emma, but then she knew by the sound of the old beat-up Beetle, painted a new color every few years.

"What the hell is he doing here?" asked Sally. She told Heather to go inside, but Heather shook her head no.

The engine cut, but rattled on for a few seconds before dying. The door creaked open, and out staggered Emma's dad, Daryl, shirtless and barefoot, wearing a pair of cut-off jeans. Sarah stood at the head of the carport like a stone, arms folded. She waited for him to say something, to measure how drunk he was.

Daryl stood in front of the one headlight, still on. "Well, hey, y'all! Heard my girl was back in these here parts." He squinted.

"Daryl, you're drunk, and I'll call the cops," said Sarah.

Emma nudged past her. "Hey...Daryl. Yeah, I'm back.

You should do like Mom says and go." Her mom kept two loaded pistols in the house.

Sally chimed in. "Yeah, go on and git. You're not welcome here, drunk or not drunk," her voice shaking.

"Don't mind me. I'm just the father of your precious… babies." Daryl took two big steps forward, tripped, and had to bend over to keep from falling. He retched and threw up liquid.

"For God's sake, your granddaughter is here!" said Sally. "Just you go."

Daryl looked surprised at his body revolting against him, as if he were being tricked. "Can I sit down? I'd like… to talk to Emma about her traveling to China."

Emma started to laugh and softened just a bit. "It was Africa, Daryl. Not China. You should sit in your car until you can drive back home. Need help?"

"Emma," said Sarah. "Don't you touch him."

"Africa! Hell, nobody told me that." He let loose with a colorful variety of words to describe Africans. "Goddamn porch monkeys. What the hell you want to get tangled up with such as that?" He laughed and spit, his head moving like it was in orbit.

"You go home and rest," said Emma. She stepped closer. "You're in a bad way."

"Emma, I'm calling the cops," said Sarah. "You hear me, Daryl? You're not supposed to come here. You know that."

He took another step and was within arm's length of Emma. She looked into bleary eyes, like shattered glass. His hair was a mess, and she could smell the alcohol and vomit. She stepped toward him.

"I'm gonna walk you to the car, Daryl." She took his

sweaty arm.

"Fucking hell, you are. And call me Daddy like you damn well should."

"Emma!" said Sarah and Sally. But it was too late.

Daryl reeled from Emma's shove and bent backwards over the hood of the Beetle. He gathered his wits, sitting on the thin bumper. "Fuck it." He pushed up and stood. "I don't need you cunts. You never been nothin' but goddamn trouble." He reached left as if grabbing a door and stumbled.

"Go!" said Emma. She looked back and saw Sarah slipping into the house. "You may think you're nasty and mean, but you're nothing. I've met your match three times over. So, just go." She heard the screen door open and close.

Daryl looked confused but determined. "Goddamn nigger lover." He took a step toward her.

A single shot, and Daryl nearly jumped out of his skin. Sarah had the pistol, a .38.

Emma ducked and turned back. "Mom, no. Hold on."

Daryl looked around as if a crowd might be watching. He lived alone in his trailer, the windows blacked out with spray paint. He found his way back to the open door and fell inside.

The women gathered in a group and watched him back into the yard right over the prized Hosta. The gears ground, and with the effort of a hundred tired giants, the car lumbered down the driveway onto the road.

"Why is he such a bad man?" asked Heather. She'd only seen him up close a handful of times.

"Born that way," said Sarah.

"He's sick, for real sick," said Emma. "Just a dead man walking." She remembered seeing him fight off demons with a plastic lawn chair, remembered him not sleeping for days, remembered his hands reaching into her pants. She shivered. "Maybe we should get inside. He might come back."

"Mom, you okay?" asked Sally. "You look good holding that pistol."

"I'm alright. Let's go inside." She was shaking.

Emma put her arm around her, and they gathered in the dim living room while Sarah put on a pot of coffee and chain-smoked.

"I don't know, Emma. You should have stayed back," said Sally. "But you sure got the best of him. I wouldn't touch him with a ten-foot pole. Heather, don't you ever go acting foolish like your Aunt Emma."

"God, he's so creepy. I about died when Granny shot off the gun."

"If you ever see him, just walk the other way. He'll always be too drunk to follow," said Sally. "Wait till Sammy hears about this. It'd be better if he didn't, though. He wouldn't be in his right mind."

Sarah joined them and paced in a circle, her arms wrapped around herself.

"So, how about another story?" asked Emma. She didn't wait. "Well, Reece and I went to the Saturday market. They have a little market on Tuesdays, but the big market is on Saturdays. People come from miles around, and it gets pretty crowded. The women hold chickens between their toes. Anyway, you kind of have to walk like you're on a balance beam between everybody squatting with their goods. Reece was wearing his clunky hiking boots and stepped on this old woman's foot. She kicked a pile of peppers and yelled at him, stood up, and shook her finger at him, which is a big insult. Reece didn't know what to do. I was laughing, which didn't help matters. Anyway, Reece wound up buying all of her peppers for thirty birr, which is about a month's wages. God, he was embarrassed as hell, but couldn't explain it to her." Emma beamed, her teeth framed in a big smile.

Even Sarah had stopped pacing and was laughing. "He does seem easy to embarrass. I bet he was more careful after that."

Sally was shaking her head. "I've got to meet this Reece. He sounds like a likable fellow."

"You will. He might even call tonight. He's got to meet you."

"The women hold chickens between their toes?" asked Heather.

"They do," said Emma. "They carry them upside-down when they're walking, which made me kind of sad. Their wings flopping. It's a different place."

Sarah sat in the recliner and reached for another cigarette, looking at her girls shoulder to shoulder on the couch. Their eyes turned to her, and a silence ensued.

"Look," said Sally. "Maybe one more story, and I've got to get this girl home and to bed. You got math homework, right?"

Heather frowned. "Yeah, my favorite subject. One more story, though, a long one, Aunt Emma."

Emma side-hugged her and kissed her hair. "Maybe not a long one. Let me see." She thought about the man with the inguinal hernia who had a loop of intestine in his scrotum. She remembered the woman who had claimed to have been pregnant for seven years. She could see the strips of pounded tree bark that the women used as sanitary napkins during their periods.

"Emma?" asked Sally.

"Oh, yeah." Emma cleared her throat. "We had a shelter in addition to the clinic where mothers could stay with their kids. They were usually widows and had no way of making a living, basically homeless. It was my job to visit the shelter at the end of the day and make sure everyone was okay. The guys on the team made sure there was food and water. There was a cookhouse where they took turns cooking, and an old guard to keep the men away. So, we had a shintabet there, like a big hole in the ground covered with poles and dirt with a hole in the middle. Everyone was supposed to use it, but they just kind of went everywhere, which made a huge mess and smell. All the women wear long dresses without underwear and just squat when they need to go, shit and piss, pardon my language. The kids were the worst, though, making little piles here and there.

"When Reece came, I had more time to think about the shelter, so we decided one Saturday to get the guys together and clean up the piles. But they said no way, and I don't blame them. So, it was just Reece and me. Reece had this idea that if the women saw us picking up the poop, they'd use the shintabet." She laughed.

"That's so gross," said Heather.

"Yeah, gross it was, but we had latex gloves. So, you can just imagine me and Reece picking up human turds and stuffing them into grain bags. The kids thought we were hilarious and just ran circles around us, laughing. The women mostly stood back and said God knows what about us, that we were crazy foreigners."

"I'd be in agreement with them," said Sarah.

"We spent an hour or so cleaning up the piles and then had these two bags of poop. We didn't have anywhere to put it, so we had to go into the shintabet and drop hand-fuls down the hole. The smell was something awful. We were squatting there, about finished, and Reece started to laugh. He said that the women would wonder why we were inside the toilet together for so long. That got me laughing so hard that I had to sit down. Our gloves were covered with shit, and we were howling."

"Dear God," said Sally.

"He stood up to keep from falling over and helped me to stand up. He was on one side of the hole, and I was on the other. I kind of looked him in the eyes, and before I knew it, he had leaned over and kissed me."

"You kissed in the toilet?" asked Heather.

"Yeah...And then I stepped into the hole. He caught me, pulled me up, and then that's when the serious kissing..." Emma took a deep breath. "And that's what happened...in the shit house."

"Holy cow," said Sally. "This just gets more and more interesting. You and this Reece."

Sarah looked dumbfounded, puffing her cigarette.

"Maybe there's more," said Emma. She put her head into her hands and looked around the living room. There were no pictures on the walls.

"Well," said Sally. "You save that for me tomorrow.

Come on, girl, gotta go before this gets too hot. Emma, I'm so glad to see you back. You gave old Daryl the what for, but I hope he stays away. He won't forget you pushing him like that."

"He'll probably wake up with a blank slate. He was sloshed," said Emma. She stood and hugged Heather and then Sally. "Y'all take care."

"You take care," said Sally, and they were out the door.

After the apple pie and agreeing to go to Brad's party, Reece had hung out with Kristin till ten and then headed home. He'd felt like driving fast and had run a red light in Trussville. He didn't even have a bathing suit that fit, his old one being baggy. At the pool at the lake, he usually wore cut-off jeans, but that wouldn't be good enough for the party.

Back at the lake, Horace was snoring, and Dora was sitting in bed reading a Christian romance, wearing an old nightcap of blue silk. She'd turned off her light after he came home, and Reece settled into Horace's recliner, skimming the August issue of *National Geographic*. He was drawn to the article on Uranus, but couldn't focus. It occurred to him he'd memorized Emma's phone number, and the seven digits with one dash played in his head. Should he? He put the magazine down, and a map of the Pacific Northwest fell out.

He took the cheap plastic phone and placed it on his lap, the cord full of tangles. Whenever it rang, Horace usually knocked it into the garbage can beside the recliner. Reece picked up the receiver and could hear the dial tone droning. Soon, the drone turned to an agitated beeping, and he let the receiver drop back into the cradle. The wind outside was rising, and a few small drops of rain hit the AC unit in the window behind the love seat. Maybe he would watch TV with the sound off, and he turned on the large console with a remote. The screen jumped to life, flooding the room with flashes of light. *The Tonight Show.* It looked like Bill Cosby was the guest host. It was Wednesday, and his CT scan was on Friday. The phone rang once, scaring the bejesus out of him. He picked up the receiver and listened.

"Hello?"

"Hey! I got tired of waiting on you to call." Emma was on the kitchen phone, the lights blazing, the curtains pulled with the blinds lowered in case Daryl came creeping around.

Reece felt his heart tilt toward his throat. "Hey there. I was just thinking about calling." He pushed back in the recliner.

"That makes me feel better. What's up? How was your day? You sleep late?"

"Yeah, and then Dora had me picking up pinecones to wake me up. I'll bet you slept in."

"I did. Sally and my niece came by and hung out. It was great to see them. Yesterday, her husband Sammy drove us all out to eat. The Seafood Box. You ever been there?"

"I've heard of it. They have those little hushpuppies." He examined his skinny legs, rubbing at a freckle.

Emma laughed. "That's the place. Man, it was good. And Sally brought a pecan pie with her. How's Kristin?"

"What? Oh, she's fine. I was over there tonight. We had apple pie, with crumbles."

"I like the crumbles," said Emma.

"Yeah, me too. Had stuffed bell peppers for dinner. That's Edwin's favorite, her dad."

"Speaking of dads, mine came by this evening drunk as hell. He made a big scene, but Mom came out with the pistol. She actually fired a shot into the ground."

"Holy...Did he leave? I guess he did after that."

"He did, but said some nasty things on his way out. Threw up in the driveway."

"Ugh," said Reece. "I wouldn't care to meet him. Sounds like trouble."

"He's trouble, especially when he's drunk. I told you about what he did, back in Godo, remember?"

The word Godo made Reece shiver. Her dad had molested the girls, beaten Sarah to a bloody pulp.

"Do you wish you were back there?" asked Emma. "It seems like it should just be around the corner, but already it's getting fuzzy in my head."

"I would like to go back. Kristin's nixed that idea, though."

"Yeah, as crazy as it sounds, me too. I miss the clinic and the women at the shelter. I feel guilty."

"I sort of feel the same." Reece crossed his feet, uncrossed them, moved the phone from one ear to the other. "You not tired?"

"No. I'm wide awake. I feel like I'm flying, though, that the ground is moving away from me. I'm still exhausted as all get out."

"I bet you are. Hey, Carraway called me today. I got a job in ICU on night shift. I know the head nurse there."

"I thought maybe you were thinking about UAB."

"I was, but Kristin wanted me to take this one. If I ever get on day shift, we can ride together."

"Huh. Yeah, that's true. But she's in CCU, right?"

"Yeah." There was a sound of something hitting the wall, and Horace staggered into the den on his way to the bathroom. He squinted at Reece and waved.

"Reece? Can I ask you a question?"

Reece sat up. "Sure?"

"Do you love Kristin?"

Reece hesitated and winced. "Uh, yeah. We love each other. She's a great person. We generally get along, you know. Her parents don't like me." He told her about the excommunication at their church, that he'd stormed out with Kristin in tow.

"That sucks. My mom likes you, and Sally is dying to meet you. Sammy, too."

"I'll bet your dad doesn't corner folks and talk about the Second Coming." He sort of laughed.

"God no. I doubt that he's ever been to church, not that I can recall. But he's out of the picture for good."

Reece nodded as if she were in the room. Horace was making his way back to bed, holding to the walls. "We kind of set a date for next spring, the wedding, you know." Reece listened to the silence, like an electric train gliding through a long tunnel.

"Well, congratulations. I guess. Reece?"

"Yeah?"

"Can I tell you something that you can't tell anyone else? I'm not even telling my mom."

"Sure. You can tell me anything." His pulse quickened just a bit. What would she say?

"After you were shot, I was so depressed and angry. Right? I mean, there was no justice, and you were just taken away. I mean, I missed you, having you in the clinic. It was just so much easier with you there. And I felt like we... bonded. You know?"

Reece knew. "Yeah, the clinic was hell, but we were a

team with Afewerki there. It kind of felt golden."

"But then, poof, you were gone. I thought you were going to die." Emma choked up. "Reece…"

"Yes?"

"I tried to kill myself after you left."

"Jesus." Reece moved the phone to the other ear. "But, you didn't?"

"We were in the helicopter. I jumped out."

Reece tried to imagine the scene but couldn't. "You're kidding?"

"We weren't that far off the ground, though. Terry saved my life, but I hit the ground pretty hard. Just bruises. But I wanted to die. I missed you so much, and it wasn't fair."

"Wow…I don't know what to say." He realized the TV was still on and turned it off.

"You don't think I'm crazy, do you? But I felt crazy." She was whispering, and Reece strained for the words.

"You jumped out? But, not really because of me, right? I mean, it was super stressful over there. I guess you were alone again…and that…"

"Reece, I cared about you. I was devastated." She began to cry. "God, am I going…going insane? Reece?" Her voice cracked.

"No, you were under a lot of pressure. Running that clinic was too much for just you. I couldn't believe that you'd been doing it for months before I got there. You were just overwhelmed. Please don't cry. Emma?" He listened to her snuffle and clear her throat. "You're home now. Everything's okay now."

"I just had to tell you. Everyone knew that I did it. I know they thought I was crazy, but never said anything, kind of swept it under the rug. I was so depressed. I've never been depressed like that before. I think in my heart I just wanted to come back when you did, but was ashamed of abandoning the clinic. God, I was just so jealous of Kristin when she left that I could have screamed."

Reece was sure he wasn't saying the right things. "I used to get super depressed in high school, maybe even middle school. We moved around a lot. The Army life, you know. I'm sure that doesn't help. I mean, there were times when I wanted to, well, you know, kill myself. I never told anyone. I think I thought it was normal."

Emma brightened just a bit. "Have you told Kristin that? I mean, it's just such a bad thing, so taboo. And now it seems like a joke. How can anyone take me seriously after I did something like that?"

"No one can ever know what you felt like. You're a special person. You're different, but in a good way." Reece wanted to tell her that he loved her, but did he love her? That he loved everything about her. Did he love Kristin? It just wasn't the same thing. He had met Kristin first. Was that the only variable that mattered here? What if he had met Emma first? He would never know, but there was an urgency to sort things out. "You are the bomb."

Emma hiccupped and laughed. "I guess that's a sweet thing to say. Unless I'm a bomb waiting to go off."

"No, no…"

"Reece?"

"Yes?"

"You're a great listener."

"Thanks. Just quiet is all. I love to hear you talk."

"Reece?"

"Yes?"

"I'm going to my church on Sunday. It's kind of got me freaked out. They're going to be focused on all the good they thought I did over there. There's no way to tell them the bad. I'm afraid I'm going to look like an idiot. Maybe you could go with me? I understand if you can't. I mean, what would Kristin say?"

"Wow, I want to." Reece felt squeezed, but he wanted to see her again. But Kristin had been there for him all this time, and she would be furious if he even suggested it. She had already let him know she wanted him to go with her to church on Sunday. And then there was the pool party on Saturday. He tried to imagine what it meant to be engaged, what that entailed. Was he not committed to Kristin, to meeting her needs versus getting in deeper with Emma? But he had to admit it. There was something magical about Emma, something otherworldly that he was drawn to. He tried to convince himself that it was just a sexual attraction. That, of course, he would always find other women attractive. And why not? He thought about his parents. They had been like two planets orbiting one another, completely cut off from the world. He had never wanted to be like them and felt guilty.

"Reece?"

"I'm here." He scratched his ankle, a mosquito bite, and made it bleed.

"So, maybe you'll see if you can come. I don't know if I can do it alone. I just feel so weak inside, like a failure. I suppose Mom would go, but I haven't asked her. She might have to work, and Sally doesn't go to church, but she wants to meet you."

"I'll let you know tomorrow. I would like to." Reece thought about dancing with Emma at the Waffle House. Had that happened? That would have never happened with Kristin, or maybe he was selling her short?

"That would be great! I mean, you get it. How can I ever explain that place to anyone and make them understand? I'm sure the preacher is going to want me to speak to the church, tell them about all the wonderful things I did. But I kind of want to disappear into a hole."

"I know how you feel. It's been so peaceful being back here at the lake. I just want to sit on the pier and watch the fish and turtles. Forget about everything." He thought about Kristin's pet squirrel in the baby pool. He thought about having sex with Kristin, that he wasn't a virgin anymore. A pang sharped his chest. He hadn't used a condom, had never even bought condoms before. Maybe he was sterile, unable to have children. He glanced at the bookshelf to his right. There was a cup there with German coins in it. When he was two, and his father was stationed in Augsburg, his grandparents came over, and they went on a long road trip through Switzerland and to Rome. He couldn't remember any of it, but Horace liked to tell stories about how he'd been hard to keep up with, always running off like a madman. That had been twenty years ago.

"Reece, you're a good person."

Reece smiled. "I don't feel like a good person. I think you've got me beat. You were there before me and after me. I just dropped in and then *bang*. I did survive that tornado, though."

"You haven't told me about that. You have to, okay?

Somebody's looking out for you."

"And you saved my life. Everybody knows that, even Kristin. I think my grandparents are curious to meet you. You'd get a kick out of them. And I liked your mom."

"Speak of the devil, she's in here getting a cup of coffee."

"Tell her, hey."

"Yeah, I will. Look, I think she wants to talk. She's giving me that look."

"Yeah, okay. I'll call you tomorrow, after I talk with Kristin." He felt he could talk all night.

"Okay, you're the best, and don't forget it."

Reece laughed. "Maybe you are crazy after all."

The day before, Friday, Reece went for his CT scan. Horace and Dora had insisted on going with him, and he'd let them, feeling they had an investment in his well-being. He was on his way now to pick up Kristin for the glorious pool party with a bunch of doctors, Brad included.

Kristin's steep driveway was full, and he pulled onto the grass. On the phone, he'd asked Kristin about going to church with Emma, and that had gone poorly. He braced for an in-person interrogation. He stepped out of the truck and shut the squeaky door. He'd decided to let Kristin drive her car. The day was dusky with bright white clouds but still warm and very humid. He looked up where the sun should be and guessed that it was past noon. He realized he'd forgotten his bathing suit and cursed, but he was in shorts. He decided to sit and dangle his legs in the water. *Good enough.* He could hear the piano from inside.

Edwin answered the door and greeted him. Reece was a good six inches taller than Edwin. Reece passed him and headed up the stairs, finding Kristin at the piano playing something classical. She glanced at him and kept playing, putting her shoulders into the keys. He moseyed up behind her and looked at the music, just swirls of ink to him. He sometimes felt badly about his ignorance of music, although he appreciated music, but more in the line of heavy metal and rock. While a nursing student at the community college, he'd discovered Christian heavy metal and had latched onto the likes of Rez Band and Stryper.

Reece stood, waiting for her to finish, and she did with a flourish.

"Hey," she said. "You bring a towel?"

Reece sat on the living room couch, which was covered in protective plastic. He grunted. "I forgot that and my bathing suit."

"Reece, but I wanted you to swim with me and protect me from all those doctors. Maybe don't sit there. Come into the den." She wore bright white shorts that rode a little high and an aqua scrub top, tucked in, that she'd pilfered from Robyn.

"Sure. You ready to go? Did he say to bring anything?"

Gert waved from the dining room. Reece waved back.

"He said to bring some drinks. I'm sure there'll be lots of beer and such."

Edwin perked up. "Now, honey, don't you be drinking. It's not good for you. I know they'll offer it to you, but you have to resist. Reece, you keep an eye out for her, okay?" He wore a button-up with thin, widely spaced maroon stripes.

"Oh, Daddy, don't worry. It's probably Reece we'll have to keep an eye on. You know he drank hard liquor over in Ethiopia."

Reece looked uncomfortable. "Just being polite is all. They make beer, a kind of mead, and some stuff like vodka called katikala. I never tried the beer." He was pondering the idea of buying beer for the party. Ethiopia had been his first experience with alcohol, and he considered that his abstinence was a thing of the past.

"Well, I'm just saying," said Edwin.

Gert came into the den. "Honey, don't drink, okay? It's just better that way." She patted her on the shoulder.

"Hey," said Kristin. "I should take my Bible. That would

freak them out."

Reece laughed.

"Well," said Edwin, "just remember that you are a witness for Christ in all things that you do." He sat in his recliner and touched his shaved face.

"We'll be good. I promise," said Kristin.

"Hey, can we take your car?" asked Reece.

"Why, ashamed of the truck? I'm not. Who cares what they think? Although Brad does drive that little sports car."

"With that stupid license plate, Dr2Be," said Reece.

"I'll drive if it makes you feel better. Let me get my keys." She went to her bedroom, brushed out her hair a bit more, and then remembered to grab a towel for Reece, but he'd forgotten his bathing suit. She frowned.

"You'll have to read the directions to me," she said.

"Sure." Reece took the directions from her, written on the back of a prescription slip, and they left.

In the car, they headed toward the interstate to make their way to the address in Vestavia Hills. The resident who owned the house was single.

"So, stop at a gas station and let me get some beer," said Reece. He had a twenty.

"No way," said Kristin. "I'm not gonna stoop to that. We can get some Diet Coke or something." She tuned the radio to the Christian station, WDJC, Amy Grant singing "El Shaddai."

"It's just beer," said Reece.

"It's still alcohol. Reece, you've changed in so many ways. It's kind of scary. I would have thought you'd, you know, be even more religious than before you left. Did the other missionaries over there drink? I'll bet Dr. Guthrie didn't."

"Well, they were pretty straitlaced as far as I could tell." Before he could catch himself, he said, "Emma drank a little, just to be polite. It would have been—"

"And there's our Emma. Did you drink with her over there?" She pulled onto 459 and accelerated.

"Maybe once or twice with the local folks. Don't forget to stop at a gas station." He wasn't wearing socks with his running shoes, and imagined he could smell his feet.

"You're not going to buy beer, are you?" She glanced at him and squinted.

"I'll buy it for them to drink, to be hospitable. We'll get some Diet Coke too, for us." He ran his hand through his hair. He hadn't bothered to shower that morning. Kristin smelled like soap.

"Reece, really?"

"Yeah. We're adults."

"We can set an example, that you can have fun without drinking."

Reece wanted to firm up the next day, whether or not he was going to church with Emma. He'd promised to call her and let her know. He just said it. "Not to bring Emma up again, but she'd like someone to go to church with her." A commercial for a window company played. He imagined a Christian window versus a pagan window.

Kristin rolled her window down just a bit, and the wind whistled inside the car. "What's next? Maybe you and her can have a private Bible study together. I thought maybe that you'd just let that go."

"She's nervous about what people will ask, if that

makes sense. She just wants...someone with her who understands. That's all."

"Why does it have to be you? Will it always be you, the understanding guy who's engaged to me?" She sped up and passed a cement truck.

"No, just this once. I promise. Heck, she even said that you could come." He opened the glove box, half expecting to find a gun.

"I told you that I wanted you to go to church with me. Does that not matter?" She pulled back into the middle lane, doing seventy-five.

"Yes, of course. And my grandparents want me to go with them too. Look, we can go to the evening service. I'll just do the morning thing with her. I'll even meet you for lunch after church."

Kristin drove without responding, glancing into the rearview mirror, turning up the radio.

Reece waited. "Where would you like to go to eat?"

"Whatever. You're going to do what you want to do. But, if you come back and say she wants to have a quiet dinner with you, because you understand her, I'll..."

Reece laughed.

"What are you laughing at? I'm being serious. One thing leads to another."

"Sorry. Just church tomorrow. That's it. I promise."

Kristin shook her head and glanced at him. "Why am I so jealous? She's just so, so, persistent. I would never intrude like that with someone's fiancée."

"It's a deadly sin."

"Well, you're right." She reached over and pinched his thigh, swerving.

"Ow!" He reached over and squeezed her arm.

They passed the Galleria and soon exited onto 31. She turned and pulled into a Shell station, much to his surprise.

"You want to go in?" asked Reece. She nodded no, and he pushed inside the cold convenience store. He gazed at the selection for what seemed a long time. At random, he picked out a six-pack of Miller Lite and then grabbed a six-pack of Diet Coke from a display. He waited in line and was surprised when the cashier asked for his ID. He fumbled in his little leather wallet and produced his driver's license, feeling that a great divide had been passed.

Back in the car, he settled in. "Done deal."

"Reece, no drinking, okay? You promised, or did you?"

"I might have one. They'll think I'm some kind of prude. Just to be polite."

"You sure are concerned with being polite." She turned back on 31 and followed the directions Reece gave her, leading them deep into the suburb.

Within ten minutes, she crept down a shaded road, looking at the house numbers.

"Thirty-four fourteen," said Reece. "Up on the left." He gazed at the two-story house with white pillars. The U-shaped driveway held five cars, including Brad's Porsche. A dread filled his stomach as he stepped out of the car. "Well, here goes nothing."

"Stay with me, okay?"

They walked to the front door and rang the doorbell. No one came, and Reece suggested they walk around to the back. He took her hand and walked them past a bird fountain, following a hedge to a tall wooden fence. He could hear splashing and music.

"Ready, my dear?" he said.

"I hope no one's wearing a Speedo." Kristin laughed.

"We'll leave if that's the case." Reece tried to figure out the latch on the gate and then pulled it open.

The pool was not so big and had a water slide but no diving board. Pink Floyd's "Money" was playing on a boom box. There were a few people standing in the pool, all with drinks, and a couple of women in bikinis in lounge chairs. Reece recognized the guy at a large silver grill, smoke pouring out, but didn't recognize the rest. One short guy in the pool was waving.

"There's Brad." She clung to Reece and waved. "Let's go say hi."

"Okay," and he half stumbled, following her lead, gripping the paper sack like a football to his chest.

"Hey, guys." Brad made his way to the edge of the blue pool. "Great to see you." He gazed at Reece and held out his hand. "Brad Phillips."

"Reece...Myers." He bent over and shook Brad's wet hand. "Brought some drinks."

"Yeah, great. The cooler's over there." He pointed. "Bring your suits?"

"I'm wearing mine," said Kristin. She laughed. "Reece forgot his." She frowned at him.

"That's no good." Brad's hair was freshly cut and still dry. He had a fraternity tattoo on his left shoulder.

"I'll be right back." Reece went to the cooler and opened it. It was all bottles of beer, and he wondered why he had brought cans. A tan woman in a pink bikini was walking toward him. It was Misty, Dr. Joiner's wife.

"Hi, I'm Misty. You must be Reece. I met Kristin at another party."

"Hey. Yeah, that's me." How did she know his name? He tried not to stare at her breasts surging in her top.

"You gonna have a beer or do you want a big boy drink? Margarita? I'll make you and Kristin one."

"Well, sure." Reece could tell that she was looking at the scars on his head. He shoved his beer in the cooler, left the Diet Coke in the bag, and made his way back to Kristin, who was talking with Brad.

"You an Auburn fan?" asked Brad. "Bama's not playing today."

"Well, I can be," said Reece.

Brad laughed. "That's a good answer. The game's on in an hour or so."

"Great," said Reece. He rubbed his belly.

"He doesn't watch a lot of football," said Kristin. "He's different like that."

Misty walked up with two red plastic cups. "Hey there, Kristin. I met Reece. He's a doll. Got your drinks."

Kristin took the cup and looked at Reece.

"Margarita," said Reece, taking his cup. "Maybe just one."

"Oh," said Kristin.

"Something wrong?" asked Misty.

"No," said Reece. He sipped the sweet and sour drink and licked his lips.

"You guys just make yourself at home. You need to say hey to Dr. List, I mean Dennis. This is his place. Hey, Dennis!"

Dennis, wearing sunglasses and a golf visor, pushed his

way through the water. He had thinning blond hair and a massive smile. He put out his hand for Kristin to shake.

"Nice to meet you," said Kristin. She took a sip.

"Brad's told me all about you. Best nurse in CCU. And who's this?"

"This is Reece, my fiancée."

"Fiancée? Well, welcome. Make yourself at home."

"Thanks," said Reece. He sipped his drink, looking around at the massive oak trees. "Lots of leaves in the pool come fall?"

Dennis laughed. "Yeah, it's a bitch to keep it clean, but it's worth it. Y'all get in. Bring your suits?"

"I did," said Kristin. "Reece didn't."

"Whatever floats your boat," said Dennis. He waded back to the middle of the pool.

Brad and Kristin continued to talk, and Reece pushed off his tennis shoes. He was surprised when Kristin pulled her top off and pushed down her shorts, revealing a two-piece suit that fit her just right. She handed him her clothes, and he looked around for an empty chair. He wished he'd thought to bring sunglasses, but he still needed his glasses to see anyway. With Kristin's clothes, he scoped out an empty chair near the table with the big radio and sat down, wondering what he should do next, wishing that it was time to go. He imagined having to watch an entire football game with these strangers, and a mild panic and urge to leave crept over him. He took a big gulp of his margarita and tried to relax, thinking about church with Emma the next day. He heard a distant rumble of thunder and asked God for a storm.

The storm came, and everyone retreated inside to eat and watch the game between Tennessee and Auburn. The living room was crowded, and Kristin sat in Reece's lap, giving him a two-hour erection. He'd managed to convince her to leave at halftime, and they did, slightly tipsy but not quite drunk. He stayed for dinner at Kristin's, baked macaroni and cheese with ham chunks, and then wound up watching TV with her in the den. Gert and Edwin had gone to bed.

Kristin snuggled into Reece, partially reclined on the couch. "That wasn't so bad, was it?"

Reece grunted, watching *Saturday Night Live* with the volume low. "Was okay." He struggled to keep his eyes open. "Nice enough. But those margaritas made me so sleepy."

"You're a bad influence, Reece Myers." She kissed him on the neck.

"Hey, it wasn't my idea to go." He could hear the cicadas cycling in the trees outside. They always seemed extra loud after a big rain, as if celebrating. He kissed the top of her head and put his hand on her stomach. "Oh, you're warm."

"And your hand is cold. Feels good, though. I'm still cramping down there." She put her hand on top of his. "Kind of push down."

"Like that?" He maneuvered so that she was between his legs, her head on his chest. He enveloped her and massaged her stomach with both hands.

"Mmmhmm."

"Should I close the door? Maybe the TV will keep them awake." He wondered if he was an oddball getting erections so easily.

"Don't you move. I'll close it. You're just worried they'll walk in on us." She did that and nestled back into his arms.

"Maybe. They're pretty strict with you, even though you're twenty-one."

"But this is nothing. Just wait until I get heated up." She giggled and tickled his knees. He jerked his legs.

"Hey, hold it. Sensitive." He tried tickling her stomach, but she wasn't ticklish there.

"Reece? Can I ask you a personal question?" She settled back.

"Uh, sure. What?"

"Have you ever had oral sex? I know you said you were a virgin before you know what."

Reece said, "Nope." He supposed that was something that one graduated to over time. It seemed much more graphic than just sex. "You?"

"No...Would you like me to...you know?" She put his hands back on her exposed belly.

He couldn't say no. Could he? "Well, if you were, you know, comfortable with it." He wondered if she would swallow his sperm, how it would play out.

"I think I'd like to."

Reece knew what he had to do. "What about you? You ever had oral sex? You know, done to you?" His mind raced to his anatomy and physiology classes. He wasn't exactly sure how to go about it. His dad never had a sex talk with him.

"No. I've been saving myself for you, silly." She massaged his thighs.

"Right. Yeah, we should try that." He let his hands drift

down beneath her waistband, just above her pubic hair. She arched, moaned, and turned on her side, reaching up to kiss him. Reece pulled his hands back and cupped her breasts. She'd removed her bra.

She turned to straddle him, his legs poking over the edge of the couch. He could see down her scrub top, her small breasts, the pink nipples. He pulled her on top of him, and they kissed deep and long, Reece's nether region throbbing with blood. He was wondering what it would taste like, how wet it would be, whether he'd be grossed out. He shoved his hands down the back of her shorts and gripped her soft butt.

"Reece. Hold on." She unbuttoned her shorts and unzipped. "There. Keep doing what you were doing. That felt so good."

Reece did so, massaging her glutes, pulling his groin back to relieve the pressure there. Her shorts were coming down, and his hands moved to the side of her hips. She was kissing his ear, tonguing him there, and a sharp thrill shot through his body.

Reece couldn't relax, though, worried that Gert or Edwin would catch them in the wild throes of sex, but he couldn't stop. He found her mouth again and felt that she would inhale him or that he could swallow her entire being. He tried as hard as he could to hold back his orgasm, thinking of grub worms, then loops of intestine.

In silence, to the low buzz of Father Guido Sarducci, they pressed into each other, then they were side to side, Reece holding her onto the couch. He ran his hand up her shirt and massaged her breast, one and then the other. She groaned and kissed him. They shifted, and he was on top of her. He sat up to catch his breath. Her top was up, her breasts exposed, her shorts around her knees. She was reaching to undo his pants, his cock throbbing.

"Can I see it?" she said.

"Oh, what if—"

"Who cares? I need to see him."

Reece unzipped and let her slide his pants down and then his battered blue underwear. It felt like an angry missile ready to explode. She took it in her hand.

"Oh," he said. He was ticklish, especially there, and squirmed and closed his eyes, holding off the inevitable.

"He's so red," she said. "And big. I can't believe that was inside me." She was pulling his hips toward her, and soon her mouth was there, her tongue moving over the sensitive end.

"God," said Reece. He thought he heard something, but didn't care. He was in her warm mouth, and then his hips thrust, coming into her, onto her.

There was a light knock at the door.

Reece said, "Fuck." He struggled to zip up.

The door opened.

"Mom!" said Kristin. She pulled her top down.

"Young lady! You two. Reece." She was in her housecoat, curlers in her short hair, with an astonished look on her face.

Reece slid, sitting on top of her legs. He couldn't bring himself to look at Gert. His heart pounded, but somehow he didn't care.

"She's gone." Kristin sat up. "Don't worry. She won't shoot you." She wiped slippery fluid from her face. "I think it went into my eye." She laughed.

Reece laughed too, feeling a desire just to curl up and fall asleep there on the couch. "What about Edwin? Should I leave?" He glanced back at the door, still open.

"No, stay. You can't go." She rubbed his groin. "All better down there?"

"Yeah. I can't believe we did that here, though. You okay? I mean, I didn't mean to, you know, come all over you like that." He kissed her cheek. "God, are you sure you've never done that before?"

Kristin gave him a naughty look. "No, mister. And I don't mind. That's what happens, right? The way it's supposed to be. I want you to remember that when you're at church with Emma tomorrow." She frowned. "Maybe you'll change your mind about going?"

Reece kind of slumped, adjusting his pants. "I promised. And, yeah, when the preacher's talking, I doubt if I'll be able to concentrate. God, you're...beautiful."

Kristin smiled. "Don't ever forget that. I do think I need to wash my face, though. Feels sticky."

Reece wanted to ask her what it tasted like. "I want to do the same for you...oral sex."

"Yeah, buddy. It's my turn, but maybe not right now. Mom's had enough shock for one night." She stroked his face, his hair. A commercial for mobile homes was on.

Reece let her snuggle under his arm and turned his attention to the TV. "I should be going soon, though." He looked at the clock, eleven-fifteen. "Getting late."

"So you can be fresh for Emma?" She pulled back and slapped him on the arm.

"No. For Pete's sake. We're going out for lunch after, right? Just me and you."

"I know. I just worry, is all. The connection you two have."

"Nothing like tonight, though. Right?"

"Better not be." She kissed him and stared into his eyes.

The service was at ten, and Reece woke up at eight, feeling exhausted. He only had thirty minutes to get ready and then make the hour's drive. He could hear Dora in the kitchen, could smell a vague odor of something cooked. He threw back his blanket, grabbed a pair of underwear, and headed to the shower.

"Hey, boy," said Horace, sitting in his recliner in dress pants and a t-shirt. "You going to church with us?"

Dora stepped in from the kitchen. "He's going to meet that other nurse from Africa at church. Got some biscuits and grits."

"Yeah, maybe next Sunday, though. Gotta hurry."

"You got gas in the truck? Need some money?" asked Horace. He was already reaching for his wallet. Reece had a hundred dollars or so in his checking account, and that was all.

"Well, maybe a twenty would be good. I'm taking Kristin out to eat after church." He watched Horace peel off two twenties and hold them out like a cracker.

"Thanks a bunch." He laid the bills on top of the TV and then went over for a quick bite of grits.

"Kristin knows you're going to church with that other girl?" asked Dora. Her hair was done, sprayed, every hair in place.

Reece swallowed. "Yeah, she knows. I told her."

"That's good," said Dora. "You came in late last night."

"Yeah, not too late, though, maybe midnight."

"Just watch your p's and q's."

Reece laughed, imagining the air full of letters. He ate and then showered, dressing in his only pair of Sunday pants. He fumbled in his tiny closet and pulled out a dress shirt, but it was wrinkled, and the collar was wonky. He grabbed a short-sleeved pullover and slipped on his brown Sunday shoes.

"Gotta go," and he was out the door and into the truck. He turned the ignition, and there was only clicking. "Shit."

He went into the garage and cranked the big riding mower, backed it out, and rummaged for the jumper cables behind the truck seat. It took about five minutes, but the engine turned over, and he was on his way, sweat on his face and soaking his back, his window down and vent fan blowing warm air.

Halfway there, he realized he didn't quite remember how to get to Emma's and strained at every exit to see a sign for the Waffle House. On a hunch, he took an exit, soon saw the Waffle House, and barreled down the boulevard looking for the left turn. There was no clock in the truck, and he worried he would be late. In vain, he looked for something familiar and slowed at every intersection. It couldn't be much farther.

A four-way with a light, and he took the left, worrying next about finding the house on the left. It was a long driveway he knew, but couldn't remember what the house looked like. Had it been white? Was it brick? He drove about half a mile and then slowed, a car tailing him. He slowed some more, and the car roared around him. He tried to remember the number of her house, sped up, and then slowed again. Soon, there was a long driveway bordered by azaleas, and on faith, he turned. There was the carport, and he breathed a sigh of relief.

He'd never felt more nervous and parked. He glanced in the rearview and saw that his hair was a mess from the wind. He brushed at it with his hand and hoped the sweat had dried on the back of his shirt. Before he knew it, he was on the carport knocking on the screen door.

"Hey!" It was Sarah, holding a cigarette. She wore knit pants and a sweatshirt. "Come on in. She's getting ready."

Reece nodded and stepped into the neat kitchen. The appliances looked old but clean. The linoleum was a dark green with a diamond pattern.

"Thought I was late," he said.

"You can never be late for church," said Sarah. "You won't miss much." She laughed and coughed.

Reece felt naked and laughed with her. "Is the church far?"

"About ten minutes is all. Want some coffee?" She was already headed to the pot on the counter. "You like cream or sugar?"

Just black is fine. Can I use the bathroom?" He put his hands in his pockets.

"Yeah, sure. Just through there on the other side of the stairs. Your coffee'll be here on the table."

Reece said, "Thanks," and headed that way. He guessed that Emma was upstairs, and she was. He nearly didn't unzip in time and let out a massive sigh as his nervous pee jetted into the pale pink commode. It was a half-bath with matching pink tile of tiny squares on the floor. He'd forgotten to lift the seat and wiped off the drops with toilet paper. Relieved, he went back into the kitchen and seated himself at the table. Sarah was still there, wearing a hair net. He could see bobby pins around her ears.

"You gonna testify at church today?" asked Sarah. "You know they want Emma to speak today. They love missionaries, those Baptists."

Reece frowned. He hadn't expected that. "I hope not. I'm not much of a speaker."

"Yeah, they'll be all over you like bark on a tree." She chuckled, leaning against the counter. "Drink your coffee. You've got time."

"Thanks." He took a sip and let the hot liquid trickle down his throat. He didn't know what to say. A cat was scratching at the screen door.

Sarah opened the door, and a black cat sauntered in, tail erect. "Here comes Sweetie." She reached down and scratched his back. The cat went under the table and rubbed against Reece.

"Hey, buddy," said Reece. He scratched Sweetie's ears, feeling some calm.

"He likes you. That's a good sign. Cats know people, not like a slobbering dog." She puffed and coughed.

"I like cats." Reece glanced through the door into the living room, and there she was, wearing a blue knee-length cotton dress. He stood, hit his thigh, sloshing his coffee.

"Well, look who the cat drug in," said Emma. She gave him a half-smile and headed straight for him with arms open.

"Hey," said Reece, hugging her. "Wow, you look great." She smelled like Dial soap.

"Thanks." Emma stood back and inspected him. "I guess you'll do," and she laughed.

"So, your mom said you'd be speaking today, at church?" He sat back down, wondering if that was the right move.

"The preacher called and asked me to. I guess I will. I wouldn't have done it, though, if you hadn't been coming with me." She adjusted her bra through her dress. "You look nice."

"Yeah, thanks." He wondered if she'd want to ride in the beat-up truck. "Should we go? Don't want you to be late." He took a big drink of his coffee and already felt like he needed to pee again.

Emma checked her tiny watch. "Oh heck, why don't we just skip it and go back to the Waffle House? Might be more fun."

"Probably," said Reece. "I felt sorry for the cook. He was kind of freaked out."

Emma laughed. "Yeah, maybe we can go there after church. Maybe Momma would come with us."

Reece looked dumbfounded and thought about his options. "I guess I can't. I mean, I promised Kristin," her name came out slow, "that I'd have lunch with her. But maybe...we could all go out together." He swallowed and nearly choked.

"That might not be so good," said Emma. "We can go another time." She looked disappointed.

"Yeah, maybe so. But you're welcome to join us. I think we're going to the Sizzler."

Emma leaned against the marigold fridge. "If you say so. I'd like to see her again. She's a sweet girl. You sure?"

Reece picked up the coffee. "Sure." He took a sip.

"Well, y'all can leave me out," said Sarah. "You'll have to come to the barbecue, though, one day. It's my second home."

"Sure," said Reece. He felt that a great mountain was rising in front of him.

"Let me get my Bible, and we'll go," said Emma. She twirled and headed into the living room.

"Don't get in over your head," said Sarah. "If you know what I mean." She laughed and stubbed her butt on the ashtray.

Reece nodded, and there she was again, black Bible in hand. He couldn't believe that they'd been working together in Godo. It seemed like yesterday. He felt the scars on his head, stood, opened the screen door for Emma, and followed her outside.

"Take the truck?" Reece went to open the door for her, reaching through the open window.

"Have to. I sold my car before I went over." She climbed in and admired the red vinyl seat, which had paint stains on it.

Reece closed her door and walked around to hop in. He turned the key, and the truck lunged in first gear. "Damn." He'd forgotten to push the clutch.

"Whoa," said Emma. "You sure you know how to drive? Let me buckle up." She was laughing.

Reece turned red. "Sorry about that." He took a look at her tanned knees.

Once on the freshly asphalted road, she gave him directions to Green Hill Baptist Church. They talked about the church in Godo, about the inner sanctum where a replica of the Ark of the Covenant was said to be held. As foreigners, they had not been allowed to enter the church, although their donations had been gladly accepted. Reece took a left and could see the church, a crowded parking lot. The front of the brick building held a large, round, stained-glass window. A white steeple was set farther back.

"Looks like we're here," said Emma. "I didn't have it in me to do Sunday school."

"I definitely can do without Sunday school," said Reece.

"Now get ready for people to swarm me, I expect. They haven't seen me in two years or so. I promise not to leave you behind." She half-smiled and smoothed down her dress.

Reece parked and jumped out, but she'd let herself out before he could get there. "You lead the way, missionary girl. They might have a record number of the saved today."

There were white cement stairs leading up to the front doors, and right away, Emma was spotted. A middle-aged couple was waving and coming toward them. The Spanglers.

"Emma Smith, you're back! Oh, we heard but didn't believe it. How are you?" asked Mrs. Spangler. She wore a red dress with a V down the back. Mr. Spangler just stood there, googly-eyed like he was meeting a movie star.

"I am back. Just been a week. It's good to see you guys. Reece, these are the Spanglers. This is my friend, Reece. He was over in Ethiopia, too."

Reece shook Mr. Spangler's hand. He was looking at the scars on Reece's temples. "Why, you're that boy with the funny name that Pastor Tom had us praying for." Little drops of spit.

Reece looked surprised.

Emma took his hand and held it. "Yep. I told them all about you, Reece, and what happened. I hope that was okay. They put you on the prayer list as soon as I wrote Pastor Tom."

"It must have worked." He didn't know what to do with Emma's hand, but she let go. "I appreciate it."

"Emma, you're so skinny. Did you have enough to eat over there?" asked Mrs. Spangler.

Emma laughed. "Yeah, plenty to eat, but spicy. Sometimes it was hard to eat." A group of high schoolers walked by, and Emma recognized a few of them. She waved and smiled. They hesitated, as if with one mind, and then moved on up the stairs.

"It's great to see you," said Emma. "I need to get inside and find Pastor Tom. He wants me to say something this morning."

"Oh, how wonderful," said Mrs. Spangler. She bent at the waist and gave Emma a top hug.

"Good to meet you," said Reece, and they headed up the stairs.

They passed into the curved vestibule filled with worshippers and deacons passing out bulletins. Several people approached and formed a kind of line to welcome her back. Emma shook hands and gave hugs. An elderly woman in her eighties grabbed both of her hands and just stared at her as if she were an apparition.

"Hey, Mrs. Stubbs," said Emma. "I'm back." Mrs. Stubbs had a firm grip on her.

"You are just a blessing, and we are so, so glad to have you back over here. You hear me? So, so happy." She let the words soak into Emma and kept on talking.

Emma looked around, smiling, wondering how to disengage from Mrs. Stubbs. Her husband had been killed at a pipe foundry. Reece just stood back and let the crowd take her.

"Pastor Tom!" said Emma. She managed to pull one hand free and waved.

Pastor Tom hurried over, and the crowd opened to let him pass. He wore a gray suit with a lavender tie. His jet-black hair was combed straight back. He was tall and towered over most there.

"Emma, my goodness, you look fantastic. Welcome home!" He gave her a top hug. Those gathered around smiled, pleased at the scene. "Can you sit on the front pew, Emma? I want to have you come up before the offertory and say a few words. We are pleased as punch to have you back."

"Yeah, sure, and glad to be back in the flesh. No more of my long letters."

"We loved those letters," said Pastor Tom. "Mrs. Stubbs, I'm going to borrow Emma from you. Emma dear, come with me."

Emma turned to find Reece. "Reece, come on!" and off she went with Pastor Tom, heading into the large open auditorium with the vaulted ceiling and exposed beams. The air conditioning was in full force, and goose bumps washed her arms. As she walked, she waved and smiled at familiar faces. Reece fell behind but caught up with her at the front.

"Pastor Tom, this is Reece. He was with me in Godo. I wrote you about him."

Pastor Tom's jaw dropped a bit. "Bless your soul. Rice,

it is so good to meet you. When we heard what happened, my goodness, we were just lifting you to the Lord for healing." He gazed at the scars on Reece's head as if to verify his identity. "Now you two sit right here and don't move." The organ began to play, and the choir was filing into the choir loft. He gave them a look as if admiring a fine painting.

"Quick, let's sit down before we get mobbed," said Emma. Her cheeks were flushed, and she pulled Reece by the hand.

"Wow," said Reece. "I had no idea." He felt exposed sitting on the front row and put his hand on a hymnal to anchor himself. "People here really like you."

"Baptists love missionaries. I'll bet he tries to take us out to lunch." She patted his leg and sat up straight, as if about to judge a pie at the county fair.

"Nice guy." Reece breathed in the cool air and gazed around the auditorium. Large stained-glass windows lined either side, flooding the room with light. He had a nagging feeling that Pastor Tom would ask him to open the service with prayer. He hummed along to the organ playing "Blessed Redeemer."

Emma opened her Bible and pulled out a photograph. She nudged Reece. He looked, and it was a picture of them standing in front of the clinic with Afewerki standing in the doorway. The image froze him. "From film I sent back to Mom," said Emma.

"Wow." He'd almost forgotten what the little tin-roofed building looked like, the rough poles, the crooked door. Afewerki had his cool look on, wearing his Exxon ballcap, as if waiting for a storm to pass.

Emma closed her Bible. "Thanks for coming with me. I think they took you on as a prayer project. You probably don't remember it, but Pastor Tom visited you in the hospital here."

"Yeah, I don't remember. Dora said that there were people she didn't know who visited."

Pastor Tom and the choir director mounted the stage that was covered in tan carpet, taking their large wooden chairs. The crowd settled in, buzzing with hushed talking as the start of the service approached. With the last organ strains, Pastor Tom stood and addressed the audience.

"What a beautiful, wonderful day to worship the Lord," he said. He spoke about how well the funding drive for the family life center was going and encouraged everyone to be generous in their giving that day. He then looked down and smiled at Emma. "And today we have cause to celebrate. One of our own has returned from the mission field, all the way from Africa." He paused to let that sink in. "We are blessed to have Emma Smith with us today." Several "Amens" punctuated the silence. "And with her is the young man that we so diligently lifted up to the Lord for healing after he was shot in that same tiny village where Emma lived and worked for our Lord. Let's give them a round of applause."

The auditorium erupted with clapping. Reece felt a chill run through him and stared at his shoes as Emma smiled, wiping at a tear in her eye.

"When I heard that Emma had returned to American soil, I thanked God. I praised Him. What she's done for this lonely planet is beyond words, and she's going to speak for a few minutes today. I know how anxious you all are to hear about the wonderful work she was doing over there, God's work. Amen?" Several "Amens."

"Reece, aren't they the best?" asked Emma. "I'm so nervous."

"You'll do fine. Just say what's on your heart." His words sounded foreign to him. His throat was dry, and he coughed. His back had begun to ache, and he crossed his legs. Church always made his back ache.

Pastor Tom finished, and the choir director, Brother Samuel, took over, having everyone stand for page 212, "Love Lifted Me." Reece held the hymnal for Emma, but they both knew the words by heart. Reece couldn't help looking at Emma in her trim blue dress, her smart loafers, mouthing the words. He felt giddy and a little bit sick. He wondered what Kristin would say. He wondered if he should tell her about the evident love that this church had poured into him.

Everyone sat and waited for the highlight of the service, Emma's speech. Brother Samuel spoke as the deacons arranged themselves for the offertory. He was a bulky man in a blue suit, with silvering hair and thick glasses. But, first, he said that Emma would say a few words and invited her to the stage.

Emma almost took her Bible with her, then turned and handed it to Reece. She mounted the stage and made her way behind the pulpit, which was tall enough to obscure her from the shoulders down. She gazed out at the Sunday faces and felt a gush of warmth in her bones. *How to start?* She hadn't been a missionary in the true sense, just a nurse working in a clinic. She made eye contact with Reece and then let the words come as they may.

"Well, I'm overwhelmed to be back. I was just a nurse, helping the people there and overseeing a feeding program. What I think of now are the smells, the wood smoke, the incense. Everyone kept a cook fire going, pretty much all day long. It seemed like a very strange place when I first went over, but it came to be my home. Now, I didn't preach or evangelize. Others did that, but I did what I know, treating the sick."

Emma felt a rush of confidence, and she stood a little taller. "There are no people more deserving than those in Ethiopia. I wouldn't take a million dollars for my experiences there. There was sacrifice, for sure. No running water. No electricity. Most people didn't even have shoes. The last few months were the hardest, and I don't think I could have made it without Reece there. He's sitting here in the front row. Like me, Reece is a nurse.

"You should have seen us working together in that tiny clinic. God sent him along when I was at my lowest, when I didn't think I had it left in me to treat a hundred patients a day." She choked up. "And he paid the ultimate sacrifice, nearly losing his life doing good for other people. Beside him, I'm just an onlooker, and I mean that. He'll never know what his short time there meant to me." Not a sound could be heard, just the gentle hint of AC blowing. "This church means so much to me...you all mean so much to me." She looked back at Pastor Tom and nodded. She felt like a flower wilting on the hood of a hot car.

Pastor Tom stood and raised his hands to the ceiling, then joined her at the podium, waiting for any final words, but there were none.

Kristin walked to the parking lot, placed her red Bible in the passenger seat, and rolled down her windows to let out the heat. She'd told a few people that Reece might come, and they'd been disappointed not to see him. She turned on her radio and the AC and drove onto the parkway to access the interstate. She was meeting Reece at the Sizzler in Center Point, but would stop by the house first to change into something more comfortable. The restaurant would be crowded, and she hoped he wouldn't be late.

In faded blue jeans and a simple white blouse, she backed down the steep driveway. Her mom had done nothing but frown at her, and Edwin had been strangely silent. She made her way to the four-lane, eager to hear about the service with Emma. She couldn't be so bad, being a Christian, and she chastised herself for giving Reece such a hard time about her. The visit to her church would mark the end of their socializing, and everything would finally return to normal.

Pastor Tom had indeed invited Emma and Reece out to lunch, but she had declined, telling him that Reece had plans. In his truck, she again asked him if Kristin would be okay with her joining them for lunch. Plus, he would have to drive her back to Hueytown.

Reece glanced at Emma in her blue dress, almost sick at what he was getting himself into. How could he say no? Maybe they would just become best friends.

"Hot enough for you?" he said over the noise of the engine and the air whipping through the windows.

Emma laughed. "I like riding with the windows down."

"No choice in this old clunker." Reece could feel the sweat beginning to dry on his back. He wondered if he should pay for Emma and Kristin, but ruled that out if things got that far. The closer they got to Center Point, the more tightly a knot in his stomach coiled. He could just see the look of surprise on Kristin's face and mentally cursed.

He pulled off 59 onto the four-lane and drove with one hand. The steering was loose, and he had to turn the wheel back and forth to keep the truck straight. Soon, the Sizzler came up on the left, and he turned, looking for Kristin's dark blue Toyota.

The parking lot was full, and he drove around to the back, and there was Kristin's car. "There's her car," he said, as if pointing out a giraffe.

"Gotta get me a car," said Emma. She wanted to say that she needed a man to go with it, but didn't.

A car was backing out, and Reece waited, then pulled in. "Here we go. She might be surprised at first, but..." He cut the engine. Why was life so damn hard?

Emma slid out and joined him, walking, drawing closer to the entrance.

Inside, Kristin had been waiting for fifteen minutes, standing just inside near the back of the line that snaked through a series of ropes. She was beginning to worry, keeping her eye on the door, and there he was. And he was with Emma. She recognized her right away, and her heart dropped. She folded her arms and waited for him to find her, wondering what she could possibly say.

Reece spotted her and waved. He glanced at Emma, who was smiling and leading the way.

"Hey, sister!" said Emma. She waited for a reply, looking back at Reece, who seemed glued to the floor. The inside of the restaurant was loud with conversation and hustle and bustle.

Reece made his move and approached Kristin, trying not to stand too close to Emma. "Hey, thought Emma could join us. You guys have met before, in Addis Ababa." He felt like he was chewing dry crackers and noted Kristin's hurt look.

"Oh," said Kristin. She held out her hand to shake Emma's.

Emma balked. "How about a hug instead?" She moved in and gave Kristin a full-body hug. "You look great. I wish I had my jeans on, although this dress is cooler. How are you?"

Kristin looked stunned. "I'm fine, and you?"

"Should we get in line?" Reece walked that way, then stopped and reached for Kristin's hand, but she didn't budge.

"Is it okay that I join you guys? I haven't had steak in forever. Just chicken, sheep, and goat." Emma smiled.

"Reece, I guess you should have told me," said Kristin. She turned and sauntered to the line, not trying to hide her frown.

Reece was thinking how long the meal would be, how he had to drive Emma back to her house. "I couldn't call," he said to her back. "I mean, you were at church." He surveyed the long line, which looked like something at Six Flags.

Kristin unfolded her arms and let them dangle. "I don't mean to be rude...Emma. I'm just surprised. That's all."

"Maybe I shouldn't have come?" said Emma. "I mean, you guys probably need to talk? Reece told me about the wedding in the spring. Are you excited?"

"Well, of course," said Kristin.

"Yeah, we're excited," said Reece. He looked from one to the other. The line moved forward just a bit.

"I bet you are," said Emma. "Congratulations and all that."

"Thanks." Kristin looked at her tennis shoes and then at Emma's smart loafers. The fact that Emma's dress was form-fitting did not escape her. "You buying? Reece?"

Reece hoped that his two twenties would cover the bill. "Yeah, of course. On me today."

"I have money," said Emma. "But it's in my purse, in the truck. Should I get it? I can pay you back."

"No worries," said Reece. "You can pay me back. No problem." Kristin inched forward, and he inched forward. "I can't wait for the salad bar."

They made their way through the line and within twenty minutes had their trays, silverware, and drinks. Kristin ordered water, and Reece and Emma sweet tea. Reece held his breath as the cashier rung him up. "Thirty-four eighty," she said. He recognized her but couldn't place her.

Emma spotted a table in the back, beyond the salad bar, and led the way. She sat, and Reece did his best to pull out a chair for Kristin, but she was too quick. They all sat there looking at each other. A waitress named Penny came by and checked the number on their receipt, saying the food would be out shortly.

"What did you get?" asked Emma.

Kristin looked at Reece. "Beef tips and a baked potato," she said.

"Reece?" asked Emma. "What did you get? I got the sirloin medium rare."

Reece stumbled. "Uh, the sirloin...medium rare." He felt that he should high-five Emma, do a cartwheel, or something. He gazed around at the humanity, people in their Sunday best, all gorging on food. He felt that he would leave his body and float above them, commenting on their plates. Kristin looked mildly disgusted, and she was. "Salad bar, anyone?" asked Reece. It came with their meals.

"Yeah sure," said Kristin. She stood and, without waiting, walked that way.

"She's not happy." He stood and hurried to catch up with her, followed by Emma. She stopped, though, to say hey to an old friend from high school with a new baby.

"You're upset. I can tell," said Reece.

"Oh, can you?" Kristin took a salad plate and tonged chopped lettuce onto it. "Reece, I'm at my wits' end with you. This has got to stop. Next thing you know, she'll move in with you."

"I couldn't just say no. Her whole church has been praying for me after I was shot. I felt like some kind of rock star. The preacher invited us out to lunch, but I didn't take him up on it."

"Well, that was sweet." She arranged three cherry tomatoes on her lettuce, then added shredded cheese. "Look at her. She's like Mrs. Popular. Does that turn you on? I bet everybody and his brother wants a piece of her. Little Miss

Missionary." She dipped into the French dressing and then added fake bacon bits. "Say something."

"How was church?" He added fake bacon bits to his salad and decided against the croutons.

"Reece, do you know that I could be pregnant with your baby? Have you even thought about that? I've done things with you that I've never considered doing with anybody else."

Reece followed her back to the table, trying hard not to see if Emma was getting her salad. He sighed and sat down. The thought had occurred to him, but he'd dismissed it.

"Reece, answer me." She looked at her salad, disgusted.

"I've thought about it, that's all. If it happens, it happens, I guess." He put in a mouthful of salad that was too large and wiped the dressing from his lips. "Ooh, that's sweet."

"What's sweet?"

"The dressing." He could see Emma at the salad bar and imagined her in her scrubs, a stethoscope around her neck. She'd kissed him, or had he kissed her?

"That's informative. And don't tell me that you've got to give her a ride back to her house."

Reece shoveled in more salad and nearly rolled his eyes. "I do. How else will she get home?"

"I've got a mind to get up and walk out." She hadn't touched her salad. "In fact, I think I will." She pushed her chair back and clutched her purse.

"Kristin, no, please don't. I'm sorry. It just happened. It was a bad idea. I take the blame."

Kristin made a low growl. "But this is it. No, Emma, ever

again. You will not see her again. Promise me that." She looked around, and the table next to them seemed to be watching, especially a woman with a large pile of red hair. "You know I don't have it in me to make a scene. I'm just too dang nice."

"I promise…"

Emma sat down with a heaped plate. "That was a friend of mine. She had no idea that I'd even left the country. Cute little baby. Her husband is in the Army, stationed overseas." She poked a cherry tomato and ate it whole. "I love tomatoes, especially in a salad." She glanced at Kristin.

"So, how was church?" asked Kristin. She ate a piece of lettuce and sipped her water.

"Emma spoke for a few minutes," said Reece. "Everybody was super glad to see her."

"I didn't say much," said Emma. "They want me to do a whole service some Sunday night. I've got some slides. Y'all should come." She ate a black olive paired with some red onion. "Mmm, this salad is so good. I'm as hungry as a horse."

"I'm sure Reece'll wind up speaking at his church, his grandparents' church. Right, honey?"

"I'd like to, although I don't have any slides or nearly as much to say as Emma. My little adventure was cut short." He pointed to the scars on his head and tried to laugh.

At that, Kristin choked up and stopped eating.

"What's wrong?" Reece reached over and touched her shoulder.

Kristin composed herself. "I nearly lost you, that's all. You were as good as dead." She knew Emma had probably saved his life and wanted to explode.

Emma wanted to say that she knew how Kristin felt. "That would have been a tragedy for sure. Anything can happen. Not just over there, but here too."

"Well, I'm not dead yet. As far as I can tell."

"Reece, don't be so...flippant." Kristin scooted her chair back to the table. "Don't you get it? What would your grandparents have done? I mean, your parents were shot, and then you were shot. My God, it's just horrible."

Penny arrived with their plates and gave the beef tips to Emma instead of Kristin, but then switched the plates. "Sorry about that. I'll be back with refills. Sweet tea, sweet tea, and water. Right?" She hurried off without waiting for a reply.

"Ugh," said Reece. "Horrible is right. It's just different when it happens to you. To me, I never thought I would die, at least as far as I can remember. I don't remember actually being shot or what happened right after." He had to say it. "Emma saved my life, so she's to blame." He laughed.

"I just did like I was trained," said Emma. The scene with the blood and the IV fluids played through her head. She got busy cutting her steak.

"I did thank you, didn't I, in Ethiopia, while I was there?" Kristin pushed a beef tip with her fork, mixed some rice in the gravy.

"Of course you did. I remember," said Emma. Her steak was underdone, but she didn't care.

"Let me thank you again, okay? I mean, truly."

"No need," said Emma. "I did what I had to do. But thanks. You got a spot of gravy on your blouse there."

Reece didn't look up during the exchange, chewing his steak and eating his fries, feeling that the storm had passed.

Reece pulled into the long driveway. Sally's car was there. The day was still warm, and the sun glared in a clear blue sky. He met Emma in front of the truck. He really should have just let her out, but she'd invited him in for a cup of coffee, and now he had to meet her sister Sally, who was a hoot, according to Emma.

"She's gonna love you," said Emma. "Come on."

"Well, okay, but not for long." Reece fell in behind her, watching her hips move beneath the dress.

Sally, Sarah, and Heather were in the kitchen, gossiping at the table. "Hey, Mr. Reece!" said Sally. In her tight jeans, she opened her arms for a big hug. Reece hugged her and smelled flowers. "And this is my daughter, Heather."

"Hey," said Reece. He shook Heather's hand. "Good to see you again, Mrs. Smith." Sarah moved in for a side hug.

"Nice to meet you, sir," said Heather. She was wearing one of her dad's NASCAR shirts.

"Sir!" said Emma.

"Yeah, just Reece." He put his hands in his pockets.

"Reece, Emma's told us all about you. We appreciate what you did for her over there, working with her and all," said Sally. "She's pretty special to us."

Emma was beaming. "Let's go to the living room. I told Reece he could have a cup of coffee."

"Let me make some fresh," said Sarah, dressed in loose jeans and an old plaid shirt.

"I guess I shouldn't stay long. I'm expected back in an hour or so." Reece followed Emma into the dim living room. Sarah opened the curtains, letting in some light. He waited to see where everyone would sit.

"Sit down, boy," said Sally. She patted the couch cushion between her and Emma and laughed. "Don't be shy." She was an older version of Emma, attractive but with curly hair.

Reece eased down and felt snug between them. Sally turned and hooked his arm with hers. "Tell us all about yourself." She winked at Emma.

"Not much to tell. I'm a nurse, like Emma. I'm staying with my grandparents in Palmerdale...I've been shot in the head." He laughed. He could feel her breast against his arm and smell her fresh breath, like she'd been sucking on a lollipop. He squirmed.

"Did it hurt?" asked Heather. She was in the recliner, twisting a braid of her long black hair.

"Not really. I never felt a thing. I get a headache now and then. I've had a couple of seizures."

"And you were with Emma when it happened?" asked Sally. She gripped his arm like he would float to the ceiling. "Emma's told us, but I want to hear what you remember."

"Yep. I was in her house. I was going to sleep on the floor. There was this other guy in my bed..." Reece was flushed. He felt a hand on his thigh, and it was Emma's.

"He was standing behind me," said Emma. "I'll never forget it. There were two shots. One ricocheted off the poles in the wall, and the second came clean through. I'm not sure if it was the first or second shot that hit him." She squeezed his thigh even tighter.

"I went down," said Reece. "Emma says blood was shooting from the entrance wound." He stopped and pointed to the scar on the right temple. His heart had picked up, and he took a deep breath. "She forgot to take a picture."

Sally laughed and slapped him on the shoulder. "God, you're funny. How can you joke about that?"

Sarah came back in. "Coffee's brewing." She pulled on her cigarette and smiled.

"You need a seat?" asked Reece. He started to stand.

"No, no, I'll get a chair from the kitchen. Stay where you are. Tell your story." She folded her arms.

"I don't know what happened next." He dropped his chin to his chest and looked at Emma. "Emma here saved the day."

Emma perked up. "I yelled for IV fluid, and Afewerki took off like a bullet. Isaac had to run after him because he had the key to the clinic. He was back in a flash, and I started a neck line."

"What's a neck line?" asked Sally

"An IV in the jugular," said Emma. "Over here, nurses aren't allowed to start neck lines, but he needed fluids fast. Of course, I was praying the whole time...the blood just kept coming. We stayed up with him the whole night, put him in my bed, and took a jeep to AK the next morning. Then it was in the helicopter to Addis." She licked her dry lips and took a deep breath.

Reece pitched in. "I remember some of the jeep ride." He wondered what time it was.

"I thought that bouncing around would kill you," said Emma. "There's a pothole every ten feet and huge rocks in the road. At some point, I used spit to clean his glasses. Afewerki held the IV bottle the whole ride."

"Thank God, you were right there," said Sarah. "Who was it that pulled the trigger. The Snake?"

Reece and Emma laughed, exchanging knowing looks. "The Hyena," said Emma. "Although he was a snake."

"Nobody saw him do it, though. Right?" He'd not had a thorough conversation about what had happened that night. Kristin didn't like to hear about it.

"Oh, he did it. People saw him on the path, carrying his pistol." Emma's eyes flashed. "Damn dirty bastard."

Sally laughed but shook her head. "And he got away with it clean and simple. Just like those other bastards..." She eased the pressure on Reece's arm and relaxed.

"As far as I know," said Reece. "At this point, I don't care."

"Holy cow, I'd have him arrested," said Heather, clutching her knees.

"I think he was trying to scare Emma. He had no way of knowing I was in there," said Reece. "I was in the wrong place at the wrong time. Just luck, his luck. He hated us."

"But why would he hate you, doing all that good work, helping those people?" asked Sarah.

"I think he was jealous. Nobody in the village liked him. He was so mean. The people there really appreciated what we were doing. Kind of felt sorry for him sometimes." Emma loosened her grip on Reece's thigh and gave him a pat.

"Yeah, me too," said Reece. "But, if he had hurt Emma, I would've taken him out." The words came out too forceful.

"An eye for an eye," said Sarah. She heard the coffee maker beeping and turned away.

"Good Lord," said Sally. "You're the better man. I'd want to see him locked up." She poked him in the ribs. "You're better looking than Emma let on."

Reece swallowed. "Did she say I was like the back end of a baboon?" He reached over and squeezed her knee.

"That's my tickle spot, my knees!" Sally was laughing and poked him in the ribs again.

"Sorry," said Reece, although he was smiling. He felt welcome, energized, and wanted to see the rest of the house. He watched Sarah come at him with a mug of coffee. "Thanks." He looked to make sure no one was about to poke him and took a hot sip.

"Cute as a bug," said Sally.

"A bug in a rug," said Emma. "Hey, you want to see my room? I've got some pictures, Mom developed for me. Come on."

"Well, I do need to go, you know."

"What's your hurry?" asked Sally. "Stay awhile."

"It's his fiancée. She's expecting him back," said Emma.

Reece prepared himself to leave on that note.

"Oh, come on up and see the pictures," said Sally. "Didn't you have lunch with her?"

"Yeah, the Sizzler. She wasn't too happy to see Emma, I'll have to admit." He ran his fingers through his hair.

"She'll get over it. You're just engaged, right? You're a free man, technically. Right?" She winked at Emma.

"It's hard to say. I've never been engaged before."

Emma stood and held her hand out to him. "I've got some pictures from the clinic. Come on. Just a few minutes."

Reece nodded and let Emma pull him up. "Okay, what time is it?"

Emma checked her tiny watch. "It's yesterday, so you have plenty of time." She laughed and walked toward the stairs. "Plus, I'll tell you what we learned at the Seafood Box." She winked at Sally on the couch.

Reece followed her upstairs, the stairs squeaking beneath the carpet. Emma's firm calves rippled. He paused at her bedroom door, looking in as if viewing Bathsheba in her tub. Emma held a packet of photos, sitting on the bed. He sat next to her, his feet just touching the floor. And then Sally walked in and sat on his other side, followed by Heather, who squeezed in behind them.

Emma held about twenty four-by-six color photos. "I took these after you came. Check this out."

Squeezed between them, he took a photo. In it, he was bent over a little boy standing between his mother's legs. He recognized it right away. "Oh yeah, another kid with clogged ears. I'm squirting peroxide in his ear. He looks terrified." He stared at the image, unable to believe that he'd been there and was now sitting on Emma's bed.

"Lots of those," said Emma. "Almost as common as diarrhea and worms." She handed him the next photo. He was sitting on a bag of grain with Afewerki and Mariam behind him. Behind them, he could see a woman covered in milk powder.

"Must have been ration day," said Reece.

"Yep," said Emma. "Everybody had to have the yellow card. Most of the time, the kids would eat the milk powder like candy. Must have been sweet."

"Right," said Reece. Heather was squatting behind him, her chin on his shoulder, looking on. He felt like a tightly wrapped sausage.

Emma brought out the other photos, each one conjuring a remembrance by Reece. He felt relieved that he could remember the scenes. The last picture showed Emma dressing a wound, a woman with ruptured lymph nodes in her groin. Sally and Heather groaned at that one.

"I've got more," said Emma, "but they're slides. Maybe you could come over and help me make the slideshow for my church."

Reece felt he should jump and run, but said, "Okay," relishing the idea of sharing more time with her. And then they just sat there in silence until Emma poked him.

"Hey!" said Reece.

And then Sally was poking him, too, tickling him. He didn't know what to do other than laugh and squirm, and then Heather joined in. Before he knew it, he was on the bed, fending them off as they hit him with pillows. They were all laughing, Reece sweating. An erection swooped in, and he panicked, wondering what he should do. They were all over him, and he found it hard to breathe, laughing so hard. Someone pinched his leg, and he sat up, hitting his mouth on the back of Heather's head. Right away, he tasted blood.

"Shit," he said.

"For Pete's sake, don't kill him," said Emma. She was on her knees, her dress nearly up to her waist.

Sally laughed. "He's a survivor. Can't kill him," and she gave him a final tickle on his stomach. "He's so cute."

Reece sat up, bewildered. "You guys are crazy. Gosh, I hate to leave, but I'll be in big trouble if I don't." He let his erection pipe down and dangled his legs off the bed.

"Oh well," said Emma. "I understand. Let's get you a tissue for your little booboo there."

Reece estimated his heart rate at 110 and stood. He

looked in Emma's mirror over the dresser at his swollen lip. It had cut on his tooth. "Man, you girls are rough." He tried to laugh, wondering if Kristin would notice. "Okay, gotta go."

They all stood and followed him down the hall and the stairs.

"Reece, I'm so glad to meet you," said Sally. "Any friend of Emma's is a friend of mine." She reined him in for a hug.

"Yeah, me too. You're a great bunch." He wondered what he'd done with his coffee.

"Here, I'll walk you out," said Emma. She led the way into the kitchen and onto the carport. The cicadas were buzzing in the September heat. Sarah was in her chair, smoking.

"Come back and see us, okay?" said Sarah.

"Yeah, and thanks for having me over. Thanks for the coffee." He let Emma take him by the hand and lead him to the truck.

"Heck, hate to see you go. And thanks for lunch. I owe you." She let his hand drop.

"Yeah, no problem." He hesitated. "See you."

"See you."

He climbed into the truck and shut the door.

Kristin met him at the door. "Hey stranger, where've you been? I thought maybe you'd been in an accident." She looked him in the eyes.

"It's a long drive back." He was hot from riding in the truck, and the AC felt good. He wanted to get out of his dress clothes. He followed her up the stairs and into the den. Edwin was in his recliner, and Gert was in a kitchen chair beside him.

"Guess what?" said Kristin. She noticed his swollen and discolored lip. "What the heck happened? Did she attack you?" She moved in for a closer look.

"I, uh, hit it on the steering wheel. Braked too fast, clutch caught. I'm okay, though." He felt like butter melting in a microwave.

"Really?" asked Kristin. "Here, have a seat. We're having a family meeting about this Emma."

Reece's gut clenched. "A family meeting?" He licked his lip and sat on the couch. He looked at Gert, and she looked at the carpet. "Where's Robyn?"

"She's not involved, and you're just joking. This is not a joking matter. This is an intervention." She sat beside him and crossed her legs. "Maybe I'll let Dad start."

Edwin wiggled his feet in his shoes and coughed. He glanced at Gert. "Reece, you have to understand that we have Kristin's best interest at heart. She's our youngest child, and we've always been protective of her." He paused to let that sink in. "Reece, Kristin is very worried about your behavior toward this other woman, Emma. I just have to ask, are you committed to being Kristin's life partner?"

Reece's lip throbbed with his heartbeat. "Of course. It's just circumstances. I mean, she saved my life over there, and now she's back. I owe her the courtesy of a visit, like going to church today. I had no idea how much her church knew about me. I kind of felt like Barney in a gun store."

"So, Mr. Barney, did you take her home and drop her off, or did you hang around and visit? You were supposed to drop her off, and I know you didn't. Am I right?" asked Kristin.

Reece gazed at her thin face framed in brown curls. She had put her mouth on his dick the night before. He was lost in thought.

"Reece?" She punched his arm.

Gert smirked and shook her head.

"What was the question? I'm sorry." He could hear Walter scratching at the back door.

"Oh brother," said Kristin. "Did you just drop her off today, or did you go inside too?"

"Her sister was there and wanted to meet me. I went inside. And then they were making coffee and showing photographs. I couldn't just run out."

"That's where you're wrong, Reece Myers. How hard would it have been to say that my fiancée is expecting me? I mean, you brought her to lunch before that. That was awkward. I couldn't believe it. And she was just so nonchalant about it. Like everything was okay. Pardon my language, but she's a hussy. She wants you for some reason, but you don't seem to be able to see that."

"She's just a bit shell-shocked at being home. Did you tell them what happened to her over there? The soldiers?"

He turned to Edwin. "She was raped right before she came back, two soldiers."

"Oh," said Gert. "I need to step outside." She did just that.

Reece felt that maybe the tide had turned his way.

Edwin spoke. "And what about this other woman, Sydni? You said she showed her breasts to you?"

"Dad, it's Cindy. It just all adds up to trouble."

"Yeah, Cindy. I had no control over that. She just did it out of the blue. Did I mention that she wanted to have sex in the boathouse, but I said no?"

That caught Kristin off guard. "It just gets worse and worse. What else haven't you told me? God knows, you have to be encouraging this. Nobody just pulls their top down."

Reece stifled a smile. "Cindy does."

Edwin cracked his knuckles. "Okay, so let's just try and work this out. I think Kristin needs a promise from you that you are committed to her in actions, thoughts, and deeds. Are you willing to provide her with that? As of this very minute." He was pulling something from his pocket.

Reece watched as he withdrew a small cord of purple rope with a knot on each end. Edwin passed the rope to Kristin.

"Dad, what's this?"

"Hold on, dear." He looked Reece in the eyes or maybe his eyebrows. "Reece, will you commit yourself to Kristin?"

Reece groaned. "I already have. I've done nothing wrong as far as I can tell. What else can I say?"

"Honey, you hold one end of the rope, and Reece, you

hold the other end." He was leaning forward with his hands in a steeple. "And Reece, I want you to ask God for the strength to be the fiancée that you need to be for my daughter, in the form of a prayer." He closed his eyes.

Reece looked at the rope and then at Kristin.

"Reece, it may seem silly, but let's do it. It's kind of like being baptized. Please?" She held the loose end of the rope out to him.

"Whatever, okay, I'll do it." He gripped the rope in his right hand. "Do we have to close our eyes?" He was thinking about Emma and Sally tickling him on the bed.

"Reece, quit stalling." Kristin's eyes were wide open. "Just say it. I'll feel a whole lot better."

Reece cleared his throat. He needed a shot of something substantial. "Dear Lord, please help Kristin know that I am committed to her. That we will be married in the spring. Amen." He let go of the rope.

"Amen," said Edwin. Gert came back in and walked into the kitchen.

"That wasn't very sincere," said Kristin.

"What?" said Reece. "What should I say then, word for word?"

"Honey," said Edwin. "Let's have faith that Reece is sincere. I believe that he is."

Kristin sighed. "Well, if you say so." She handed the rope back to him, and he put it in his pocket as if possessing a sacred relic.

"Kiss me."

Reece leaned over and gave her a quick kiss on the lips, hoping the ordeal was over.

"We're having chicken and dumplings," said Gert from

the kitchen.

"You're welcome to stay for dinner, Reece," said Edwin. "But there is one other, one other thing." He coughed, and the color drained from his face.

"Dad?" said Kristin.

Edwin sat back and folded his hands in his lap. "Gert told me about last night. About being on the couch, perhaps with your clothes off?"

"Oh boy," said Reece. He felt he would shoot through the roof and never come down.

"Dad, we're engaged. We didn't, you know, do anything. Plus, it was my fault. I led him on. I'm sorry." She snuggled close to Reece, and he put his arm around her.

"Okay, I understand," said Reece. He was exhausted and swallowed a yawn. "We just got carried away, that's all. It won't happen again. Right?" He nudged Kristin.

"Whatever," said Kristin. "Yeah. Chicken and dumplings. Reece, does that sound good to you? You didn't invite Emma, did you?" She punched him in the arm.

"No," said Reece. He didn't laugh. "Chicken and dumplings sound good. That's one of Dora's specialties, so I'll have high expectations." He managed a smile.

Gert peeked out from the kitchen. "It's my mother's recipe." She looked relieved that the trial was over.

Reece thought about Emma wanting him to help her with the slideshow. It was now or never. "Okay, and I promise not to be seeing Emma, but she asked me to do one thing, to help her with a slideshow at her church."

The air in the room went cold and lifeless.

"Reece! I say no way. And you better agree. You just got through saying you wouldn't see her again!" The front door opened, and Robyn jogged up the stairs in her uni-tard, the shoulder straps already down, supported only by her breasts.

"Hey guys. Like my sweaty body?" She did a twirl, and one boob slipped out. "Oops!" She turned and fixed herself.

"Robyn!" said Kristin. "Get out of here...you...slut! We were having a serious discussion."

Edwin looked exasperated. He hadn't seen her naked since she was two.

"It was just an accident," said Robyn. "Settle down. Reece is a nurse. He sees naked bodies all the time. Jeez. Let me get a shower, and I'll put my overcoat on." She left the room. "Smells good, Mom!" she said over her shoulder.

"See," said Reece. "Just like Cindy. I had nothing to do with it. Things just happen."

"They better not happen again, is all I'm saying," said Kristin. "I'll be right back. Maybe I'll put on my bikini, if I had one. And you're going to church with me tonight, buster. And forget that slideshow."

Reece gave Edwin a knowing look, and they smiled.

Reece had been wearing his dress clothes all day and felt sticky. His feet were sweating, and his shirt was wrinkled. He pulled into the parking lot of the Presbyterian mega-church, Kristin's church, which had its own interpretive ballet company. He'd been there a couple of times and had felt lost and small. The pastor was stocky and wore a buzz cut, reminding Reece of a drill sergeant.

They walked hand in hand and received a bulletin, which was eight pages and in full color. Reece felt like he needed a ticket and an usher to help them find a seat in the vast auditorium with curved pews of light oak and supple pew cushions affixed to the wood. It was like a vast aircraft, floating in the clouds. Classical music played. He followed Kristin halfway down to the front. No one seemed to know her, and he felt relieved at being anonymous.

"Look," said Kristin, pointing to the bulletin. "He's talking about love tonight, agape love, the love of God for us. That seems appropriate." She'd showered, leaving Reece to talk with Edwin about Israel, and changed into a tailored paisley dress that hit her knees. She looked fresh and smelled good.

"Interesting," said Reece. He tugged at his shirt. There was a small stain from the chicken and dumplings. Right away, his back began to hurt, and he rolled his shoulders, feeling stiff.

On stage, the choir was gathering, not wearing their robes. The pastor was walking up the aisle, greeting people and shaking hands. He seemed like a stewardess making her way down the aisle, asking about beverage choices. Reece was sitting nearest the aisle and braced himself for an encounter.

"They have an unmarried couples Sunday school class we should come to," said Kristin. "Would you?"

"Next week I need to go to my church. They've been expecting me. They want me to speak, maybe show some slides."

"You have slides?"

Reece had stepped in it. "No, but I could...borrow some of Emma's."

She gave him a cold, hard look. "You don't need slides. I

bet you're a great speaker." The pastor was two pews away. "You were shot. That's what people want to hear about. How you made the ultimate sacrifice."

The blocky pastor put his hand on the pew in front of them and loomed over Reece. "It's great to see you. God is in a blessing mood tonight. I can feel it." He held out his hand for Reece to shake, and he did, a firm handshake.

Kristin spoke. "I'm a member, and this is my fiancée, Reece. He was a missionary in Ethiopia. He sort of just got back after being shot." She beamed with pride.

"Jiminy Cricket, it's an honor to meet you. Let's have a quick prayer." He bowed his head and asked for blessings and continued healing. He patted Reece on the shoulder and moved to the woman behind them.

Reece felt disembodied. "Seems like a nice guy." He could still feel the handshake. "Do they baptize here?" He gazed at the array of organ pipes behind the choir, reaching to the ceiling.

"No, but they sprinkle the babies. They're so cute, and usually they cry. I can't wait to have babies." She took his arm and put it behind her. "Maybe I'm pregnant now."

"That would sit well with Edwin. He'd probably shoot me." He wanted to beg her to get a pregnancy test. "Plenty of time for babies."

The pastor was on his way to the stage along with the three associate pastors. The choir was in place, chatting and smiling. The choir director, a very tall man, flipped through sheet music. A thin woman with a violin was positioning herself.

"You know that's something we need to talk about. How many and what we'll name them," said Kristin. "You'll be a good father. I just know it." She looked around to see if she knew anyone.

"One would hope," said Reece. The choir stood, and the service was underway, preambled by the violin and then the massive organ. The room filled with sound, sending a chill down his spine. He put his elbow on the back of the pew and tried to relax.

The service ended with a rousing prayer, and they were dismissed back into the world. They walked to the truck arm in arm, Reece trying not to step on her feet. She wanted to go to Wendy's and get a Frosty, which they did. She paid, and Reece recognized the cashier, a young woman who had been in his nursing program, but she'd dropped out. Neither let on that they knew one another. Life seemed so short.

"Let's sit by the window," said Kristin. The dining room was crowded with churchgoers, gathered in large groups around small tables.

Reece dipped into his chocolate Frosty. "No ice cream in Ethiopia that I know of."

"That's depressing," said Kristin. "I thought we were talking about babies? What would you name a baby boy?" She leaned onto the table with her elbows.

Without thinking, Reece said, "Iggy. That's a great name. Like Iggy Pop."

"That's a horrible name. Other kids would make fun of him. I like Brian."

"Hmm, that's pretty plain. There's lots of Brians."

"Well, I like it." She ate a spoonful of vanilla Frosty. "What about a girl?"

"Gosh, I wouldn't know what to do with a girl. Maybe...I'm not sure. What, would you..."

"I like Ruth, a biblical name." She put her feet between his.

"That sounds kind of dry, don't you think?"

Kristin frowned. "Dry? It's a pretty name, especially for a little girl."

"Maybe Ruth is okay, but we have to get married first, right? How about Wendy?"

"No, everyone would just think of hamburgers, silly."

"Just kidding." He was thinking about Emma as a girl's name. "I know, Abebe. It means flower in Amharic."

"That sounds ugly, not for a girl over here. Reece?"

"Yeah."

"Will you ever stop thinking about Ethiopia?"

"I don't know. I mean, how could I?" Ethiopia had changed his life, had colored his being, even though he'd only been there for two months. "It's a strange place. It exists, right now. There, it's probably five in the morning. Little girls with clay pots are walking downhill for half an hour to get water. Then they have to trudge uphill. They do that two or three times a day."

"Reece, promise me you won't go back. It exists, but we exist here. This is our home."

"But the world is such a small place. I think of it differently now. Like it's just across the street. What if it's God's will that I go back? Would you go with me?"

Kristin sighed. "Of course, if that's what God wanted, but I'm not feeling it. Maybe in the future. Who knows? My Frosty is melting."

"Since you've already been there, it wouldn't be such a

shock. You were there under bad circumstances. Living in Godo was like living in the Grand Canyon. Not that I've been to the Grand Canyon."

"A family vacation to the Grand Canyon. That sounds like real fun. But we'll have to watch the kids, make sure they don't fall off. Little Ruthie and Brian." She reached over and put her hand on top of his.

"You're gonna wish yourself pregnant, if you're not careful. Right now, that would just be a real problem, I think." He pulled his hand away and dipped into his Frosty. She seemed so small sitting there, vulnerable. She was the type to give money to panhandlers with little cardboard signs or strangers who needed a bus ticket because their mom had just died in Montgomery.

"I do feel different somehow. If I am pregnant, you'd have to be nice to me." She pointed her plastic spoon at him and smiled a little smile.

"I am nice to you, though."

"I mean, really nice, like bringing me ice cream and never ever mentioning Emma. I'll bet she'd have sex with you if you wanted. Do you think?"

"No. That's just crazy talk. Let's talk about something else."

"What, you don't like babies?"

"Oh, babies make me nervous. If it was my baby, though..." He hung his head in a kind of defeat.

"But, they're so sweet. God, I'll bet it would look just like you. You'd make a good-looking girl, you know? Except for that receding hairline. Come on, smile. You know you want to."

Reece didn't want to. Then he froze. Cindy had walked in with an older guy, a guy with red hair and a goatee, and she was headed right for them.

After Reece left, Emma took a nap and then got ready for the evening service. One of her older sisters, Debbie, was going with her. Debbie was a branch manager at a savings and loan in Birmingham, but had never married and dated a plumber. Of the seven sisters, she was the plumpest and the most conservative.

Debbie, wearing new jeans and an embroidered blouse, didn't knock and found Sarah leaning against the counter smoking, a pot of chicken noodle soup on the stove. "Hey, Momma. I wish you wouldn't smoke in the house."

Sarah grunted. "I smoked outside when you kids were here."

"Where's Emma? Is she upstairs?"

"Getting ready. Go surprise her."

Debbie snuck into the living room and crept up the stairs. She edged along the wall and popped in the bathroom door. "Boo!"

Emma screamed, turned, and saw Debbie. "You son of a goat!" She threw herself at Debbie for a bear hug. "Made me pee myself."

Debbie was laughing and rubbing Emma's back. "Oh, baby, you look good. So skinny. Maybe I need to go to Africa." Her look changed. "But, you okay? Momma told me. I wanted to get over sooner..."

Emma frowned. "Let's not talk about that right now. You look great, Sis. I missed you." She gave her another hug.

"At least you're not pregnant. Mom told me about the

Seafood Box. That's just like Sally to pull a stunt like that."

Emma busied herself, combing her hair, talking to Debbie in the mirror. "She's a nut, but I'm glad she did it. I needed to know, but was afraid. I'm gonna do it again just to be sure."

"That's probably wise."

"The preacher called and said they were having a little reception for me tonight after church. You up for that?" Emma picked up her toothbrush, one she'd used in Ethiopia.

"Sure. Why not? Just don't let me eat a bunch of cookies." She patted her little belly.

Emma brushed and spat. They walked downstairs into the kitchen. Sarah was eating her soup. She was the thinnest of them all.

"Soup?" asked Emma. "You need a steak." She sat at the table.

"Mind your own business, Nurse Emma," said Sarah. She sipped her coffee.

Debbie laughed. "I'd give my eyeteeth to be as skinny as you two."

"Don't worry," said Emma. "I ate half a pecan pie yesterday, plus I had a big lunch today."

"Yeah, that's what Sally said. You saw the guy who was shot. What's his name?"

"Reece, yeah."

"And his fiancée was with him? Sally told me he's real cute."

"Jeez, there's no secrets around here." Emma toyed with a sugar packet.

"Nice young man," said Sarah. "I told Emma to be real

careful, but she won't listen."

"We're connected," said Emma. "That's all. And I think she was okay with it. It was just lunch, with the two of them."

"You can always get in a pickle more than anybody I know," said Debbie. She took a peppermint from her purse. "Remember that time you went with the black guy to prom? You nearly caused a riot."

Emma laughed. "Heck, we were just friends, that's all. But it didn't matter anyway. People are stupid sometimes."

"Stupid is right," said Sarah. "But you do get carried away. Just be careful is all I'm saying."

"I am. I will. I just can't seem to get him out of my head. I mean, we worked together, and then he was shot. I'd been there for months by myself and was glad for the company. If he'd been with me the day I was attacked, I don't think it would have happened."

"Emma, they had guns," said Sarah. "He'd probably be dead for sure."

"Nobody knows," said Emma. She checked her watch. "About that time."

They stood, and Sarah gave her a long hug. "Be careful, like Momma says, okay?"

Emma nodded, and they headed off for church in Debbie's red Mustang.

Once inside, Emma found herself surrounded by well-wishers, welcoming her back. She smiled and kept saying "thank you" over and over. In the short line that had formed beside her pew stood a young man named Nathan. He'd dated Emma over three years ago and had seen her off at the airport along with most of the family. He'd written her several times, but she'd never replied, and he was eager to find out why. Emma saw him and hoped the service would start before she had to speak to him.

Emma held onto the hands of a middle-aged man named Castor, who was mentally a child of ten or so. His adoptive parents stood on either side of him to keep him from getting carried away. Emma had always spoken to him and had volunteered one year to be his date at a church Valentine's banquet. It seemed to him that the date was only yesterday.

"You still so pretty," said Castor, a deep blush of red on his face. He went in for another hug, and Emma let him. He was a few inches shorter, and his head plowed into her bosom. His mother pulled him back, worried that he would rip her clothes off.

"Oh, Castor, thank you," said Emma. "And you know what you are?"

Castor let go of her and dropped his arms like lead weights. He grinned and said, "A handsome man!"

"That's right, a handsome man." Emma laughed and grabbed his hands again to keep him from squeezing her.

"I love you, Em-ma. You are my girlfriend." He laughed and snorted, trying to loosen his hands.

"I love you, too, Castor. Okay, you get three hugs. You've had two, so this is the last one, okay?"

Castor's eyes shone. "Okay, Em-ma." He turned to see if his mother approved, and she nodded. This time, he grabbed her and tried to lift her, his hands cupping her butt.

"Uh oh," said Emma.

"No, son," said Castor's dad. "Let go. You're gonna hurt

Miss Emma." He peeled him off of her. The piano began to play, and those standing began to find their seats.

Emma looked away from Nathan and sat on the other side of Debbie.

"I want to sit with Em-ma," said Castor. He was headed that way, about to crawl over Debbie.

It took both parents to retrieve him and escort him to the lobby so that he could calm down.

Nathan slid into the pew behind Emma and tapped her on the shoulder. "Hey, you're back." He worked at a tire dealership and was attending school to become an X-ray technician.

"Well, hey," said Emma. Pastor Tom had begun to speak, announcing the social for Emma after church. "Talk to you at the get-together, okay?"

Nathan looked blank and nodded okay. One thing that Emma had not found attractive about him was his belt buckle collection, which he wore with pride. With his bell-bottom jeans, he was wearing his mother-of-pearl buckle.

"Dear Lord, these people love you." Debbie whispered and poked Emma. "I bet Castor would marry you."

"He thinks he already has," said Emma.

Brother Samuel replaced the pastor at the podium and led the congregation in two songs. Next was a young woman Emma did not know who sang "Amazing Grace." It kind of sounded like she was singing bass. Soon, Pastor Tom was preaching on the laurels of being a Christian, referring to Emma and Reece several times. The service ended with the mournful "Come Home," but no one came forward, except for Nathan, who engaged the pastor standing at the front. Before ending in prayer, Pastor Tom announced that Nathan had come forward to rededicate his life to Christ and that he wanted to be baptized again. One Amen came from the audience.

"Stay close," said Emma. "I used to date that guy who went up front for about ten minutes. He wrote me a bunch of letters, but I never responded."

Debbie winked, and they made their way to the fellowship hall, which was decorated with a *Welcome Home Emma!* banner. A long table held a variety of sweets, small sandwiches of tuna fish and pimento cheese, potato chips, and several liters of soda. Emma surveyed the room for Castor, but his parents had taken him home. They worried that Emma upset his fragile life and preferred not to fight him in public.

Pastor Tom ushered Emma to the front of the line with Debbie and then set about shaking hands. By now, Emma was hungry, and she loaded her paper plate with food. She made a beeline for a table and sat on the end, holding the chair next to her for Debbie. The busy room was warm, bathed in bright fluorescent light, and smelled of pine cleaner. Emma bit into her sandwich and was glad when Brother Samuel and his wife Nancy sat across from her.

"This is quite a crowd," said Samuel. "The people here really missed you. You know that."

"We were worried sick about you, girl," said Nancy. "Is this your sister?"

Emma introduced Debbie. "It wasn't so bad. At the last place, I worked with a team of four guys, Ethiopians, and one was my translator."

"What about that poor young man who was shot?" asked Nancy. She was all ears. She held a small Bible study at her home on Tuesdays and wanted to have as many details as possible for the ladies.

"Yeah, Reece. You saw him this morning. He was a godsend, but then...Well, you know." She chewed a tuna salad sandwich and washed it down with some iced Sprite. "He'll be back. It'd be great if you guys would let him speak." She watched as Nathan, with his plate and drink, headed for her table.

"That would be a blessing," said Samuel. "Pastor Tom and I have already talked about it. But we want to hear more from you first. Well, hello there, Nathan."

Nathan was trying to keep his plate from bending. "Hey, y'all."

Nancy spoke up. "Nathan here said the most beautiful prayer for you a while back. I still remember it. Nathan, you pull up a chair."

"Thank you." He placed his plate on the end of the table and pulled up a folding chair.

"That was sweet," said Emma. "I appreciate all of the prayers." She moved her plate to keep it from touching Nathan's.

"This church loves you, Emma," said Samuel. He ate a potato chip, mindful of his diabetes.

"She's a special one for sure," said Debbie. She gave Emma a side hug. "She went through a lot over there, more than you'll ever know."

Nancy perked up. "I'd just love to hear about it. My Bible study group would love to have you. We meet on Tuesdays at ten in the morning." She laughed.

"That's sweet of you," said Emma. "I'd love to. Maybe in a couple weeks?"

Nancy looked a wee bit disappointed. "That would be just great. I'll let the ladies know. You promise, right?"

"I promise," said Emma. She glanced at Nathan, who was staring at her.

"I bet it was a real adventure," said Nathan. "I've only been to the Smoky Mountains...and Gatlinburg."

Emma nodded.

"So, Emma here is still exhausted. She'll need to get home and get some good rest tonight. Only been back less than a week," said Debbie.

"A whole week?" asked Nathan. "You should've called." He looked hurt.

Emma sighed. "I've barely had time to tie my shoes since I've been back."

"Did you get my letters?" asked Nathan.

Nancy and Samuel looked on with interest. Emma had written to the church at least once a week.

"Well, I got a couple, but the mail there is tricky. I had to send it out by helicopter. No way to even buy a stamp where I was." She bit into a peanut butter cookie. "Mmm, these are good."

"I made those," said Nancy. She beamed.

"I'll bet Mrs. Stubbs made the tuna salad," said Emma. "She always cuts off the crusts." She laughed, and Debbie laughed.

"You still staying with your mom?" asked Nathan. "She still works at the barbecue."

"Yeah, for now," said Emma. "Reece picked me up at the airport, the other missionary that I worked with, and you'll never guess what happened." She told the story of how they danced at the Waffle House. Debbie hadn't heard that one yet.

"It's just one thing and then another with you," said Debbie. "I can just see you doing something like that."

"It was the best welcome I could have had," said Emma. She drank more Sprite, chewing on the ice.

"I'm still in school, about to finish," said Nathan. "X-ray tech. I'll be glad to leave the tire shop. Only two more quarters to go." He tried to make eye contact with Emma. He'd pulled out a condom on their last date and held it between his teeth.

"That's swell," said Emma. She tried to look happy.

"You keep at it, son," said Samuel. "You didn't have an X-ray machine over there, did you?"

Emma laughed. "Well, no electricity. You had to go to Addis Ababa for that."

"No electricity," said Nancy. "That just sounds so exciting. I can't imagine it."

"Did you have a shower or anything like that?" asked Nathan. He held a chocolate chip cookie like an anvil.

"No shower," said Emma. She had lost her appetite and stared at her plate. She looked at Debbie.

"You tired, hon?" asked Debbie. "I think I better get this child home to her bed."

"Do you need a ride?" asked Nathan.

"Debbie brought me," said Emma. "Yeah, I hate to leave the party, but I'd better be getting home."

Nancy looked disappointed, but shook her head in agreement. "You go home and get rested. You deserve it."

A terrible racket, and in came Castor, held back by his

dad. He'd thrown such a fit at having to leave that they'd had to bring him back. His dad lost his grip, and Castor was upon them.

Cindy waltzed up to the table, leaving her man friend scratching his beard at the door. "Hey!" She wore a black miniskirt, a red short-sleeved shirt cut low, and high heels.

Kristin recoiled and bumped her elbow against the window. She gave Reece a what-the-hell look.

Reece started to stand but sat back down. "Hey, what are you doing here?"

"Been to a Leon Redbone concert. Somebody threw a cup at him, and he quit playing. Is this your girlfriend?"

"I'm his fiancée," said Kristin. "Reece?"

"Oh, this is…Cindy. The Sykes' granddaughter."

"Friends of the family," said Cindy. She pulled up a chair. Her man friend sidled up behind her. "And this is my good buddy, Clarence. He bought the tickets."

Clarence nodded and stroked his red goatee. "Hey now." He put his weight on his back leg.

"God, I need to hear some more of his stories. I can't believe he was shot and walking around like he is." Cindy touched Kristin's arm and smiled. Her teeth were very white against the bright red lipstick.

"You mean Cindy…from the lake?" asked Kristin.

"Well, I don't live there. My grandparents do."

"Oh," said Kristin. She kicked Reece under the table.

"Yeah, the nicest people in the world, the Sykes." He didn't know what to say next. "I used to play cards with her brother in the RV. We'd crank the tape player and make up games. How is he?" He folded his hands on the table as if about to sign a mortgage.

"Oh, he's good. I think I told you. Hates his job, though. Y'all should get together," said Cindy.

"Is this your boyfriend?" asked Kristin.

"We live together, if that's what you mean. He's my sugar daddy. He works on engines." She laughed. Clarence tried to laugh, but coughed instead.

"Nice to meet you, Clarence," said Reece. He reached out and shook his hand. "You didn't throw the cup, did you?"

"No way," said Cindy. "But I flashed him and made him stop playing for a second."

Reece could tell she wasn't wearing a bra. He tried to catch Kristin's eye, but she was looking out the window.

"Well, I won't keep you two," said Cindy. "Gonna get a burger and run. Nice to meet you, Kirsten."

"Kristin."

"Right," said Cindy. She stood, slapped Reece on the shoulder, and was gone with Clarence following in her wake.

Reece played with his spoon, waiting for Kristin to speak.

"She flashed at a concert?" asked Kristin. "Good Lord, what kind of people do you get tangled up with?"

"See, it wasn't just me. You want another Frosty?"

"No, I don't want another Frosty. What I want is for you to realize how this makes me feel. I mean, you've seen her breasts. Were you imagining them just now? I think you were. I could see her nipples through that shirt."

"No, hell no. I mean, heck no. She's just a friend, a crazy friend. I'll probably never see her again. Plus, she's living with that guy."

"Doesn't keep her from coming onto engaged men, though." Kristin pinched her cup in half.

Reece wasn't sure he should say it, but he did. "I like your boobs a lot better than hers."

"Boobs? I hate that word. Boobs." She folded her arms across her chest. "Well, I'm glad they're leaving at least. I was afraid they'd want to sit with us. You know, you are impossible. But you think my *boobs* are nicer?"

"I love them," said Reece, "along with everything else."

Kristin cracked a smile. "That's good to know. Nice recovery."

"You ready to go?"

Kristin nodded, and they left, getting into the truck. Soon, they were back at Kristin's.

Kristin walked ahead of Reece to the door. "Should I invite you in? You know we can't make out on the couch anymore. I think Dad was pretty upset when Mom told him."

"What? Of course, you should invite me in. We could get a blanket and go in the backyard, or maybe the basement."

Kristin laughed. "Oh, come on." She unlocked the door.

Edwin was already asleep, but Robyn and Gert were still up. Reece took his place on the couch, moving Walter to the middle, scratching his floppy ears.

"I'll be right back," said Kristin, and she excused herself to the bathroom.

Robyn was eating a red Popsicle, sitting in Edwin's recliner. "Been to church and then to Wendy's, right?"

Reece laughed. "Yep. And you?" He could see her panties up her blousy short-shorts and made a point to look at her face.

"I took a long nap. Working out makes me sleepy." She sprawled her legs, leaning back farther.

"How's work?" asked Reece.

"Just the same old same old. I'm going to the beach next week. Hey, Mom, you know I'm going to the beach on Tuesday?"

Gert appeared from the kitchen. "Yes, I know." She was drying her hands on a dish towel. "And you're going by yourself, which is crazy."

"I wouldn't say crazy. No one could go with me. Maybe Reece would go with me?"

"I start work on Tuesday," said Reece, as if it might even be a possibility. He tried to keep his focus on her face.

"Yeah, no vacation for you, bucko." She twirled her hair, which was a lot like Kristin's. "You excited about going back?"

"Not really. I mean, I need to, but not working is kind of fun. Plus, working in the clinic over there without doctors around was an eye-opener. Maybe I'll build a shack and open a clinic in the Walmart parking lot."

"Sounds like fun," said Robyn.

Kristin walked in. "Robyn? What are you doing? For God's sake, close your legs." She looked to Reece for support.

Reece looked at the ceiling. "I was looking at the ceiling. Here, sit down. You'll have to move the dog."

Kristin shook her head. "Gonna get a glass of water. You want one?"

"No," said Reece. "Thanks."

"Get me one," said Robyn.

"Get your own," said Kristin.

"She's a firecracker," said Robyn. "Hey, you can't go to the beach next week, can you?"

Kristin came back with her water. "No, I have to work. You know that. What beach are you going to?"

"Well, there's only one."

"Gulf Shores?" Kristin sat.

"Of course," said Robyn. "That's where we always go."

"I like Gulf Shores," said Reece. "When I get some vacation time, we'll go. Maybe camp at the State Park."

"And then I can go with you guys," said Robyn.

"You wish," said Kristin. "Just me and Reece."

"What do we get, two weeks a year?" Reece put his arm around her.

"I think that's for your second year. You may not have any vacation for the first year. You'll have to ask," said Kristin. "You going to bed soon, sister?" She raised her voice. "Because Reece and I want to make out on the couch."

Gert didn't respond. Reece put his finger to his lips and shook his head no, smiling.

"I need a boyfriend. Don't remind me," said Robyn.

"You dumped that last guy," said Kristin. "He was nice."

"All he ever wanted to do was go bowling. I hate bowling. He was a good kisser, though. Kristin says you're a good kisser."

"Here, let's try it." He turned and met Kristin's lips with his own. She pulled his head toward her and slid her tongue into his mouth. Reece kissed her and fell into her lap.

"Mmm, that was spicy," said Kristin.

"Mom, they're making out on the couch!"

Gert came in with her hands on her hips. "You guys

have to behave," but she laughed.

"So, you and Dad never made out when you were dating?" asked Robyn.

Gert looked annoyed. "I let him kiss me, but that was all. It wasn't like it is today. You don't even need to get married anymore." Gert had given them both the sex talk, saying that you just had to close your eyes and it would be over before you knew it. "I'm going to bed, y'all. Good night." She walked through the den.

"Night, Mom," said Kristin. "I'll do my best to make Reece behave."

"You do that," said Gert. "Night," and she was down the hallway.

Robin gazed at the two of them. "Don't let me stop you two lovebirds. I'll just watch."

"Go to bed, sister," said Kristin. "We need our privacy." She slid her hand beneath Reece's shirt and felt his stomach.

Reece flinched. "Ticklish." He put his hand on top of hers.

"Want me to scratch your back?"

"Yeah, would you?" He pulled up his shirt.

"Just take it off," said Robyn, getting a glare from Kristin.

"Watch this. He's like a dog." She raked her nails down his spine, and he arched over to tighten the skin there.

"Oh, man," he said. "Just go all over. Draw blood."

Kristin did nearly just that, raising long streaks of red on his back. "His back is his major sex organ."

Reece groaned little groans, stretching this way and that to guide her hand. "Gotta take my drug test tomorrow.

Yeah, right there. My itchy spot."

"Well, you better come up clean," said Kristin. "Just peeing in a cup?"

"Yeah, um, I think so. Don't stop."

She scratched for another few seconds and then gave him a finale of several grand rakes down his back. "Have to stop or you *will* start bleeding."

"Speaking of bleeding," said Robyn. "I need to borrow some tampons."

"Shut up," said Kristin. She then told Robyn about meeting Cindy at Wendy's, about Cindy pulling her top down at the lake, and flashing at the concert. "Can you believe that? Just walked right up like she owned the place."

"I wish I had a sugar daddy," said Robyn. "Sounds like she's a handful. Did you get a good look, Reece?"

Reece didn't want to talk about it. "Got an eyeful." He waited for Kristin to hit him, and she did. He knew the part about the boathouse was better left untouched.

"Okay, kiddos, I'm going to leave you to it. Gotta get up in the morning, unless you want to play naked Twister." She laughed and yawned.

"Leave," said Kristin, and she watched her go.

"You need to hit the hay?" asked Reece. "I should probably go. I've been wearing these clothes all day. About to go nuts."

"I'll take them off for you." Kristin looked to make sure no one was in the hall. "I want to give you another blowjob. Maybe you'll appreciate me more."

Reece raised his eyebrows. "I'm honored, but not in here. Plus, I'm super ticklish...down there. You'll make me...come." He kissed her on the forehead.

"Okay, you said the basement, so let's do that. It'll be creepy, though, with all that stuff down there. Come on." She kissed him and ran her hand back under his shirt.

"Okay," said Reece. A knot of expectation formed in his gut. He was already getting an erection and had to adjust himself. He tiptoed with Kristin down the steps to the landing and then down to the finished basement.

Kristin flipped a switch, and fluorescent light filled the room. It was the bed Reece had been on out of the hospital. Kristin made him sit on the bed and then stand. She closed the door and went to her knees. "You excited? I think you are." She undid his belt and button, slid down the zipper, and his pants followed. Kristin examined the lump caught inside his underwear. "You need new underwear. How long have you had these?"

"Yeah." He didn't want to say it. "I was wearing these... when I got shot. I'm pretty sure. They're my lucky underwear."

"Reece?" She stood and pushed him onto the bed. "Do you trust me? I mean, I could bite it off if you're not careful."

Reece put his hands behind his head, already feeling naked. "It's worth the risk."

Kristin stood there for a few seconds as if reconsidering, but then leaned forward and eased his underwear down. "God, it's just so big and red."

"He likes you, but is bashful," said Reece. His penis throbbed with his heart.

She took his underwear to his ankles. "Try not to get it on my face this time."

"Grab that pillowcase behind you, in the bag. But it

needs to be something you can toss."

Kristin fumbled in a bag of cloth scraps that Gert used for crafting. "Here." It was a square of bright green cotton.

Reece took the cloth and held his breath, watching her mouth come close. She kissed the tip and darted her tongue before taking him in halfway. He tried not to jerk away, and was breathing too shallow.

Kristin did her best at learning on the job and took in as much as she could without gagging, but gagged anyway. "God, it's so warm." She put her mouth on him again, trying to avoid the hair. She moved up and down with her hands planted on either side of him, drool sliding down. She stopped and slurped. "Sorry."

"Mm hm," said Reece. He was trying not to crane his neck and watch. "Oh, man."

Kristin got into it, sliding up and down, letting her teeth gently scrape him. But, before she could go any farther, Reece ejaculated onto the cloth.

"Sorry. I just get too excited. Can't help it." Fluid continued to run from him.

Kristin was on her knees. "Dang, that was fast. I guess I'm just too sexy. I always thought I would have to work harder than that."

"Hold on, we can keep going, if you don't mind." He sat on the bed, wanting to rip off the rest of his clothes, and hers too. "It's almost just too much. Such a powerful thing."

Reece stood. He couldn't decide what to do with his hands, but they went to the top of her head. "I'll make you work harder this time. I promise."

"You're still stiff. I thought you were supposed to go

flat." She looked up at him and slid her tongue around, taking him in again. She moved in and out, using a lighter touch this time, tasting him for the first time.

Reece closed his eyes, but nearly fell, and pulled her hair. She paused. "Sorry." He could hear footsteps coming down the stairs, but didn't want her to stop. She paused again, as if she had heard something, and then went back.

There was a tapping on the door, and it cracked open.

"Oops!" said Robyn.

"Robyn!" Kristin faced her through the crack in the door. "Go away and do not tell Mom or Dad. You hear? What is wrong with you?" She pushed the door closed and turned to see Reece completely dressed. "I mean really. You okay?"

"Just scared the living shit out of me is all. I guess maybe I should go. That was great, though, by the way. I seriously think we need to do this at the lake. The RV is perfect." He grabbed her and squeezed.

"I'm so mad. But I make you come. Never forget that, okay? I mean, we really should wait to have sex again when we're married. I feel like God is going to punish us."

"The enormous eyes of God," said Reece. He hugged her and kissed her and massaged her shoulders. "Take me to the beat-up truck," and she did.

On Monday, Reece had gone in for his drug screen and filled out some paperwork for human resources. He would work two weeks on day shift to get in a basic hiring requirement, but would begin night shift after that. Reece had popped up to the unit, said hey to the head nurse, Sheila, and then had lunch with Kristin in the cafeteria. He'd also received the results of his CT scan, which indicated all was well. He dreaded getting the bill and decided against any follow-up visits.

In the parking deck, his first day back at work, he spotted Kristin's Toyota and walked into the hospital, his stomach a jangle of nerves. He remembered his first days working as a nurse in CCU. He'd literally trembled from head to toe walking to the unit, thinking he would jump out of his skin. He walked up the stairs to two, trying to burn off some anxiety before entering the large double wooden doors into ICU. He pushed the wall plate, and the doors swung out.

Inside, nurses buzzed around, getting ready for shift change. He would work with another nurse for the first two weeks, so wouldn't have patients of his own, of which he reminded himself. He looked around for Shelia and found her in the supply room, checking out a chest tube drainage system.

"Hey there," said Sheila. "Boy, you'll be helping us out today. Karen called in sick a few minutes ago. Said she has the flu." She smirked. "So that means you get your own patients today, if you feel up for it."

"Uh, okay," said Reece. "Do you know who I'll have?"

"Yep, two and six. We do report at the rooms instead of the lounge, so go ahead and clock in. You'll do great. Two of the easier patients, although Jones in two will talk your ears off. Got it?" And she was out the door.

Reece examined the supply cart, seeing all the familiar items there: IV kits, IV fluids, catheters, and plastic urinals. He knew some nurses in ICU, but some he had never met. He went to the rack for the charts of two and six. He saw six, grabbed it, and sat at the high desk facing the rooms. Elbert Jones. A 62-year-old white male with chest trauma from a riding lawnmower accident. Looked like he would be discharged soon. He checked room six to see if the nurse named Ingrid was ready to give report. She was sitting in front of the room, charting on a bedside table.

"Ingrid? I'm Reece, the new guy taking over."

Ingrid looked exhausted, her long blonde hair a mess. She kept scribbling before looking up. "Hey, you want report? I'm ready if you are. You're a lot younger than I thought you'd be." She was looking at the scars on his head.

Andrew, another night nurse whom Reece knew, walked by, tapping him on the shoulder. Reece turned and waved. "Yeah, if you're ready." The curtain to the room was partially pulled, and he could only see the patient's feet sticking out from under the sheet. The TV was on.

"So, this is a nice older guy with chest trauma, irregular ECG. His pericarditis has mostly resolved." She told him that Mr. Jones was a farmer from Cullman County. He grew tomatoes, and the lawnmower that had flipped him was a small tractor with a bush hog, and he was lucky to be alive. He was tethered to a cardiac telemetry unit and had orders to wear TED hose. He had slept well through the night and could get up and go to the bathroom by himself. His Lidocaine drip had been discontinued the day before, but he had a maintenance IV of normal saline at 60 ccs an hour. "Any questions?"

"Does he have a chest wound? Anything to dress?" Reece scratched his thighs and realized he'd forgotten to change into scrubs.

"No, just some nasty bruising. He's easy and could go onto the floor today. You gonna get changed?" asked Ingrid. Her tired eyes looked slightly bruised.

"Yeah, I was thinking about that. Okay, great, sounds good. I guess he'll need a bath today, or maybe a shower."

"I'd let him shower. Just wrap his IV. Oh, he likes to watch *The People's Court,* so make sure you remind him." She laughed. "I think it comes on at two or three."

"Super," said Reece. He shivered and went to get dressed in the break room, putting on white scrubs stamped with the Carraway logo. Back on the unit, number two's chart was in front of the unit secretary, who was taking an order for a new med and putting it into the system. Reece sort of knew her. She was a rich brown with stylish hair. She looked snappy in a fitted blue jacket.

"Hey, Laronda?" Her badge was turned backward. "I'm the new guy, Reece, and I've got two today. I used to work in CCU."

"Hey there. Yeah, I recognize you. Heard about you, too." She gazed at his head. "Number two, Mrs. Laramore. Just got a new order for Lasix on her. First dose as soon as possible." She handed him the chart and gazed back at the green letters on her CRT screen.

"Thanks." He checked the eraser board for Laramore's nurse, and it was Andrew, but he was in another patient's room. He read the admission note. Janese Laramore was a thirty-eight-year-old black female from Bessemer who had been in a single-car accident. She had a broken shoulder and kneecap, a deep facial laceration, and a history of chronic renal disease. She'd been to a birthday party and was driving back in the rain when she lost control and hit a bridge abutment. Her urine output had been dropping, and edema was building in her legs, thus the Lasix.

"Hi," said Andrew. He touched Reece on the shoulder. "You have Mrs. Laramore?" Andrew was effeminate and had long fingers. He was light in his loafers, as Reece's grandfather would say. "I'm so glad you'll be working with us on nights."

"Yep. And you've always worked nights?" He watched a pack of doctors making the rounds.

"I would never work day shift. Too many people around," said Andrew.

"That's true."

"So, you had quite an experience, I hear, over there. Where was it?"

"Oh, that," said Reece. He pointed to his head and made a gun with his fingers. "Yeah, Ethiopia."

"Gracious. I'm so glad you're okay. You'll have to tell me all about it one night when it's quiet." He toyed with his short, blond hair and adjusted his black-framed glasses.

"Yeah, maybe I'll bring some photos one night. Well, anyway, got a new order on Laramore. Lasix, but I'll get it to her."

"Yes, she needs it, poor thing. Let me tell you about her. Did you read about the accident?" Reece nodded. "Well, she's a kidney patient as well, and her urine output has been dropping. She only had about 150 ccs last night, even though her IV is at 120 per hour, plus she's drinking water and juice. Anyway, that's the primary problem. She's in a shoulder harness for her broken clavicle. Her knee is swollen and purple, but otherwise she's fine."

"Does she get up to the chair?"

"Not at night, but she has orders to be up t.i.d. She's a big woman, poor thing. Her breasts are as big as I am."

Reece laughed, still jittery but calming. "Do they have names?"

"Yes. Thing One and Thing Two." He grinned and put his hand on Reece's shoulder for a second. "What else? Hmm, that's about it. Just needs a bed bath sometime. I did change her sheets last night because she sweats."

"Sounds good." Reece imagined big, sweaty breasts. He wondered if he'd be able to hear her heart sounds with his trusty Littmann. "Thanks," and Andrew left him to tidy up his rooms.

Reece was thinking about Kristin next door when she walked onto the unit. He smiled. She smiled.

"Hey, buster. You getting settled in? You look good in your tidy whities."

"Thanks a million," said Reece. "Yeah, I've got two patients. I thought I'd be shadowing, but a nurse called in sick. You look nice, as usual."

"This is fun, having you here. I hate that you'll have to go to nights." She made a frowny face. "Hey, I've still got Mr. Odo, the garbage man I was telling you about. You'll have to come meet him. He's off the ventilator, but his jaw and neck are still a mess."

"Yeah, I'd like to meet him. Never met a garbage man before. He's a driver, right?"

"Yep, and the nicest guy in the world." She asked him about his patients, and he described Jones and Laramore. "Sounds like fun. Let me know if you need any help. If I get Mr. Odo up, I may come over and get you to help. Well, gotta go."

"Okay, sounds good. I'm gonna go and meet Mrs. Laramore. Have to give her a bolus of Lasix." He watched her leave and walked to number two. "Knock knock," he said.

Mrs. Laramore lay in bed with her head up, breathing noisily with an oxygen cannula in her nose. Her eyes were big and round, and her face looked moist. Reece introduced himself and asked her if she needed anything.

"Your name Rice?" She paused for a breath. "That's a funny name." She was trying to shift her hips but couldn't.

"No, Reece. Like the peanut butter cups. You want to turn?"

"If...you don't mind. I'm so uncomfortable."

Reece examined her IV fluids, checked the heart monitor, and looked at his watch, counting her respirations. Thirty per minute. He retrieved a blue wedge from the chair and put it on the bed. "Okay, gonna turn you." He bent her right leg, grabbed the draw sheet beneath her, and with a mighty push, got her onto her side, wedging the cushion behind her. He took an extra pillow and stuffed it between her knees. "There, how's that?" A young doctor, an intern, was peering into the room.

"She get her Lasix yet?" asked the doctor.

"Just waiting on pharmacy to bring it up. I can run get it if you want."

"Well, I wanted her to have it asap."

The doctor smelled of cologne or aftershave. Reece couldn't tell, and he wanted to say that the doctor should have put stat on the order.

"Yeah, that would be great." The doctor left.

"Gonna run and get you some medicine for that swelling and to help you breathe a bit easier," said Reece.

"Thank...you," said Mrs. Laramore. "My name... Janese."

Reece nodded and stepped back onto the busy unit. He decided to pop in and introduce himself to Mr. Jones before going to the pharmacy, but Laronda was standing there with the Lasix that had arrived in the vacuum tube system. He said thanks and went to the medicine cart for a syringe. After pushing the Lasix, he headed over to six, saying hey to a couple of nurses he knew.

Mr. Jones was sitting up in bed, twirling his thumbs. "Hey there, fella. My breakfast on the way? And turn off this damn light. Doctors left it on." He pointed to the ceiling.

Reece flipped off the light and stood beside him, visually assessing him. "Should be here soon. You must be hungry. My name is Reece, and I'll be taking care of you today."

"You not a doctor? I thought you was a doctor. Not many men nurses is they?"

"Nope, a nurse." Reece noted that his skin looked healthy, although his nose looked like it had been permanently sunburned.

"I never met a guy with a name like that. Reece, you say? I'm J.D. What's your last name? Maybe I know your people."

"It's Myers. Gonna check your blood pressure." He took down the cuff from the wall.

"Well, hot dog. You got kin up in Cullman County? I know me some Myers." He coughed and spat into the plastic emesis tray.

"I do. Most of my folks live in Birmingham. Got some relatives in West Point and Hanceville. My parents are from there. Born there." He pumped the cuff and put his stethoscope on his arm. "One thirty over eighty-eight. Pretty good." He decided to do the physical.

"Well, hot dog. I can't wait to get out of this place. They tell you what happened?"

"The tractor?"

"That's right, turned over on me." He then went into the details of that day, how he'd been cutting a bank.

Reece nodded and then listened to his chest, moving down to his big belly. He checked his carotid pulses and then moved down to his feet. "Can I look at your chest?"

"Well, sure. That's your job, ain't it? Got a hell of a bruise there." He pulled down his untied gown.

Reece examined the long, deep bruise there, touching it. "Still hurt?"

"Not hurt, but kind of aches."

Reece glanced at the cardiac monitor, noting a stray PVC here and there. He checked the ECG leads, then took the emesis tray to the sink and rinsed it, feeling that all was well. He had a recurrent nightmare about coming to work and having a tiny baby for a patient that somehow came up missing during the shift.

"Can I go home? You know my wife has to have our

daughter drive her down, and it's rough on her. My daughter works at the A&P. She's a single gal. They'll be in some time." He coughed and spit. "Damn, I need me some Red Man bad."

Reece laughed. A young lady came in with a breakfast tray and put it on the overbed table.

"There she is," said J.D.

Reece adjusted the height and pushed the tray over the bed. J.D. lifted the lid and looked disgusted.

"One damn egg. I told that doctor I needed more food. I think they're trying to starve me." He fumbled for the fork.

"Need anything else for now?" asked Reece. "I'll let you eat and check back. I can get you a sandwich or something if you're still hungry. Maybe a can of Ensure?"

"No, you go on. I'll let you know."

Reece nodded and headed back to Mrs. Laramore's room to do her physical and see about a nursing assistant to help him give her a bath. It occurred to him he could call Emma and maybe discuss the slideshow at her church, and he did just that when things slowed down.

Emma slept late again. The day before, her sister Amanda and her husband had visited. Emma had gone through the story of her attack and Reece getting shot. She was getting a little tired of having to repeat the story, but was looking forward to the whole family, except for her brother Randy, getting together on Friday. Sarah was at the barbecue, and Emma had the house to herself, which felt strange.

She walked downstairs in her underwear and surveyed the empty living room, so quiet she could hear the clock ticking on the wall. She walked to the window and pulled back the curtains halfway, wincing at the bright sunshine. She looked out at the big yard that Sammy mowed for her mom and felt a twinge of happiness mixed with longing. Her thoughts went back to the shelter, the ladies and their rambunctious children, and hoped they would somehow be taken care of. She sat on the couch for a few minutes and then headed into the kitchen. She didn't have a car to drive over to the barbecue and surprise her mom.

In the fridge, she found some slices of American cheese and set about to make herself a sandwich, dropping two slices of white bread into the toaster. She made a cup of instant coffee from a jar that was over a year old and sat down, eating her lunch. She finished the sandwich and rummaged through the fridge again, finding a jar of green olives. She ate a few and popped open a can of 7 Up, taking in the quiet. She was thinking about how she would get Afewerki over to the States when she heard a car in the driveway. From the sound, she knew right away who it was. She first glanced at the phone on the wall and then opened the door, peering out.

"Dammit." She realized she was in her underwear, locked the door, and ran upstairs to pull on some clothes. From her window, she could see the beat-up VW in the driveway. She watched, and the door opened. It was Daryl for sure. "Dammit to hell," and she walked back downstairs, reminding herself of where the pistol was. She sat on the couch, waiting, hoping he would leave if she didn't answer the door.

A minute passed, and it seemed like an hour to Emma. She imagined him creeping around the house, looking for an open window, and stood, suddenly cold. What the hell was he doing? She glanced through the door into the kitchen and listened. The window there was too high for him to see into, and she tiptoed in, pulling back a chair and sitting. Another long minute passed, and she heard it, the screen door opening. She watched the doorknob, and sure enough, he was trying it. She felt sick and angry, but stopped herself and sat there waiting for something to happen.

He didn't knock, and she finally made herself stand and go to the counter for a butcher knife, which she placed on the table. And then there was a knock, a light knock, followed by a harder, longer knock. She decided he was a pitiful fool and went to the door, ready to yank it open and give him hell. Instead, she said, "Who is it?"

"It's me, Daryl, your daddy. I want to...apologize...for the other night."

"Why are you coming when Momma's not home?" Her voice seemed small and distant as if she were in another room.

"You know why. Open the door. I won't come inside."

Emma could tell he was sober or trying hard to be. "Why are you here? You know you're not supposed to come here."

"Just open the door. I'm not the boogieman. I was drunk...the other night."

"Yeah, you were," said Emma. "And scared the living daylights out of us. That was a good way to welcome me home." She grabbed the knife from the table and put it in the waistband of her shorts behind her back.

"Well, I wanted to apologize, but not through the damn door."

"Step away from the door and close the screen door." Her heart pounded in her chest, and she wished that Reece was there or maybe Sammy.

The screen door whooshed and closed. "It's closed!"

Emma unlocked the door and cracked it. He stood on the carport, wearing a camo shirt and jungle boots. "Move back."

"What am I, a criminal?" He stepped back and then sat in a folding chair. "How's that?"

"According to the law, you are, and you're breaking the restraining order." She opened the door halfway.

Daryl shifted in the chair, putting his elbows on his knees and hanging his rough head of jet-black hair. He looked up. "I won't hurt you."

"No, you won't." Emma touched the knife and opened the door. She pushed out through the screen door, waiting for him to leap at her. She would just let him run into the knife.

"There's my little girl," said Daryl. He grinned, showing his missing teeth.

"My name's Emma, in case you forgot." She stepped down onto the cool carport in her bare feet and walked onto the driveway, feeling the hot sun.

"You make me feel bad," said Daryl. He started to stand but didn't.

"Well, how do you make me feel?" She felt she could outrun him if she needed to. The phone was ringing inside the house. She wanted to answer it, but stayed put.

"I guess I don't know. But about the other night. Like I said. I'm sorry about that. But you know you didn't have to shove me like that. That wasn't very respectful." He spit on the cement.

"You're lucky Momma didn't shoot you."

"She'd never do that. She still loves me." He laughed.

Emma felt a rush of adrenaline. "I doubt that, Daryl." His name left a bad taste in her mouth. Something moved in the bushes, and a scraggly old man emerged with a blank look on his face. "What the hell? You dirty bastards." The man was stepping toward her, trying to drive her onto the carport.

Daryl stood and laughed. "Well, lookie here. My old buddy come to the rescue."

Emma panicked and froze halfway between them, but focused her attention on the strange man. He looked like he'd been digging a ditch, and it had caved in on him, and he was drunk, red in the face.

The man wobbled and took a few more steps.

"I'm warning you," said Emma. A car was pulling into the driveway, Sally's car, and it slowed to a stop. Emma felt tears coming on, but held them back.

Sally was running down the driveway, cursing. The man wavered and turned, a dumbfounded look on his face. He swiveled back to Emma, but she had darted off to the side and was making her way around the VW, meeting Sally.

"What the hell's going on here?" asked Sally. She saw Daryl. "You want to get yourselves killed? I've got a thirty-eight, and I'll damn well use it."

Emma took a deep breath. "Said he was here to say he was sorry, but then his friend here jumped out of the bushes."

"I'll give you thirty seconds to clear out, you bastards," said Sally. Her pistol was under the seat.

Daryl laughed. "Yeah, we'd best go," and he walked toward the VW. "Come on, Cotton."

The drunk man spat and got in, looking over his shoulder. Daryl fell in and cranked the noisy engine. Just like the last time, he backed over a flowerbed, then gunned it, headed back to the road, nearly hitting Sally's open door.

Sally put her arm around her. "We're calling the police this time, dear sister. You okay?"

A few tears streamed down Emma's face. "That bastard. I can't believe it. My own dad..." She could feel the knife digging into her back.

Sally led her into the house and locked the door, then headed to the phone to dial 911. Emma sat at the table, looking at the crusts of her sandwich, listening to Sally give the details of what had just happened.

"There," said Sally. "I hope they arrest his ass and throw him in jail along with that bum that was with him."

"God, you came at the right time," said Emma. "I was

about to pull that knife."

"Looks like we all just need to strap a gun on with him running around. You know he never came by once while you were gone. There's something about you. I think he's afraid of you. The way you used to stand up to him."

"Jesus, why does he have to be such a...damn fool?" She spun the knife on the table.

"God made him that way, I guess," said Sally. "Look, I came by to take you over to the barbecue. Did you forget?"

"Yeah, I guess I did. Slept late. What time is it?"

"It's twelve-thirty. Let's get something to eat, but don't tell Momma while she's working. Tell her when she gets home." Sally rubbed the top of Emma's head. "Okay? And then I'll hang around till it's time to get Heather from school. You can go with me. Okay?"

Emma nodded. "Let me brush my teeth and comb my hair first." She went upstairs to the bathroom.

Soon, Sally pulled into Duck's, the barbecue joint where Sarah worked. The parking lot was full as usual. "Let's get us some ribs."

Inside, they spotted Sarah working a table. She saw them and smiled, headed their way with her little notepad in her apron pocket and a pen behind her ear.

"Hey, girls, come on and sit down. Got a table for you over here. Just gotta wipe it down. We're as busy as Chinese rice." Ceiling fans whirred in the open room, stirring smells of smoke and meat. There was a glass-cased counter full of candy bars where the cashier stood. On the walls were framed NASCAR posters and photos. Two other waitresses bustled back and forth.

They sat down while she tidied up the table. Emma was

still rattled and looked it. She slumped in her chair and stared at the menu.

"What's wrong, baby girl?" asked Sarah. She coughed and put a hand on one hip. She was wearing pantyhose with her brown skirt and a pair of white sneakers.

Emma looked at Sally, tired. "Oh, nothing, just hot outside is all."

"A real scorcher," said Sally. "This'll be her first barbecue back in the States. You still got some brisket?"

"Well, don't look so puny," said Sarah. "I guess you'll have to adjust to the weather. You sure you're okay?"

Emma tried to look chipper. "Fine, just having some bad memories is all."

"It's nothing to do with Reece, is it?" Sarah pulled out her notepad. A customer was waving her down for more sweet tea. Sarah nodded. "Okay, let me grab your orders real quick. I got folks with ants in their pants."

They both ordered the brisket with fries and coleslaw. Sally took a Bud Light and Emma sweet tea. Sarah whisked off to take care of her tables, burning for a smoke break.

"Momma knows something's up," said Sally. "She's like a detective sometimes."

Behind Emma was a big-boned farmer in his overalls, devouring a rack of ribs. To their left was a table of four young professionals in business attire. The room crackled with conversation and noise from the kitchen, the big lids on the pit grills opening and closing.

Sarah put their drinks on the table and smiled and was gone.

"I wonder if he's on probation for anything?" asked Emma.

"Gosh, I don't think so, but who knows? Anyway, he's violated the restraining order, plus he brought that drunk-ass bum with him. He's always fought dirty like that."

"Momma says his dad used to beat him and that his mother ran off with a preacher. I guess that's all true." Emma sipped her tea.

"Well, it's probably true. I've never met them or seen them as far as I know." Sally drank some water and winced. "Gettin' a sore throat, I think."

"Maybe that's why he's so mean."

"It's no excuse, Emma. Momma's daddy whipped her when she was a kid with a belt and a board, but she's as nice as cake, right?"

"He whipped none of us as far as I can remember, except for Randy. Dad caught him drinking beer in the garage."

"Yeah," said Sally. "What he did to us girls was worse than any beating."

"I know, I know," said Emma. "There's just always a story, a reason. Like that administrator in Godo who was so mean, the Hyena. He was awful, but I'm sure somewhere down the line, he was abused. Like they can't help it. You know?"

"Emma, don't wear your heart on your sleeve. Daryl is a dangerous man. He was planning on hurting you today, or that thug who was with him. Maybe you should come over to my place during the day for a while."

"I was thinking about that. Maybe for a couple of days, unless he gets locked up. Look, here comes Charley."

Charley, the owner, brought their orders to the table. "Emma! I thought we lost you to the world." He put the plates on the table and stood back. "This is on the house, dear. We're just glad to have you back." Charley was wearing jeans and a white T-shirt with a duck on it.

Emma blushed. "Thanks, Charley. I missed coming here. I ate a lot of meat over there, but no barbecue." She looked at her plate of glistening brisket on a piece of garlic bread.

"You didn't have to do that, Charley," said Sally.

"My pleasure," said Charley. His voice was a bit high for a man. "Well, y'all enjoy."

"God bless you, Charley," said Sally. "Ain't he the nicest?"

"Yep." Emma cut her brisket with her fork and took a bite. She rolled her eyes. "Man, that's good." She dipped a fry in the sauce.

They ate in silence for a few minutes, watching people come and go. Emma saw Castor's dad from church and waved.

"So, what about Reece?" asked Sally.

"What about him?"

"You talk to him since Sunday? I can't believe he busted his lip like that on Heather's hard head." She laughed.

"Not since Sunday. I expect he'll call, though. He wants to help me out with the slideshow at church." She seemed to perk up. "You liked him, though?"

"Yeah, he'd be a lot of fun. I bet he and Sammy would get along. Does he seem a little crazy to you, or is that just me? I mean getting shot in the head..."

"Not crazy, but maybe a little shy. It's hard to tell if he's happy or sad, kind of has a blank look sometimes. He doesn't seem that different to me."

Sarah came over and refilled Emma's glass. "Only one beer for you, though."

"It's all I ever get," said Sally. "But you need to slow down, Momma. You're making me dizzy running back and forth." Sarah laughed and hurried off. "Yeah, a real nice young man, and I can tell he likes you. You're not trying to wrangle him away from his fiancée, are you? Not that I would blame you, if you like him so much." She pushed with her tongue at some meat caught between her teeth.

Emma smiled. "I hate to think of myself doing something like that. He just doesn't seem committed to getting married. I mean, when we're together, it feels like we're on a date. I told you about kissing him on the carport, and he kissed me back. And it wasn't just a friendly peck. Heck, I wonder if he's tried to call me today. I have his grandparents' number too. I mean..."

"Emma, just don't get hurt, is all. If it's meant to be, then it will be, but he's officially engaged. I don't think I'd be kissing him like that. Who knows? She might be crazy."

"If she knew he kissed me, she'd probably cut him off. That's my impression. I kind of wish she'd find out." She poked at the soggy toast on her plate, thinking. "I haven't told anybody this yet. Can I tell you without you telling anyone else, especially Momma?"

Sally was all ears. "What? You didn't sleep with him, did you? My goodness."

"No, no. Well, the night he was shot, he was standing behind me. I was sitting in a chair. I'd asked him to rub my neck, and well, his hands kind of dipped down inside my scrub top, and I wasn't wearing a bra. I thought I'd about die. If he hadn't been shot right then, who knows what we would have done? I was just desperate for some physical contact. God, I wanted him so bad."

"The plot thickens," said Sally. "My, my. You are the adventurous girl. You asked him to rub your neck? You know what that's gonna lead to." She laughed.

"Don't laugh. This is serious. But there's one more thing I haven't told you. And maybe I'm the crazy one." She crunched some ice from her glass.

Sally scooted forward. "What? Now you're making me nervous. You're not planning on killing his fiancée?" She looked just a little grim.

Emma rolled her eyes. "Heck no. That's just wild. It was something I did after Reece was shot. I was feeling desperate, like the whole world had ended. I guess you would call it depression. I missed him so much, Sally. You just can't imagine how lonely I was."

Sally tried to imagine it. "Oh, my goodness, what did you do? Tell me or I'll choke you."

"Well," said Emma. "I guess I tried to kill myself." She ate a fry while looking at her plate. There was no response from Sally, and Emma looked up. Sally was shaking her head and looking at her plate.

Sarah walked up. "Meals are on the house. Charley tell you?" She paused. "Now what in the devil are you girls talking about. You better not have any secrets from your momma." She folded her arms across her chest.

"No, Momma," said Sally. "Emma was talking about some of the suffering she saw over there. It breaks your heart."

"You two look like you're up to something. Anyway, welcome home again, baby girl. I'm glad y'all dropped by."

She scooted off to seat a tall man and his fat daughter.

"Emma, dear, I can't believe it. You tried to kill yourself? I don't think I even want to know how. Oh, Emma." She reached across the table and touched her cheek.

"I jumped out of the helicopter." Emma looked at Sally with apology on her face.

Sally leaned back. "You what? Well, how are you still here if you did that?"

"Terry, the pilot, saw what I was doing and dropped the helicopter. I was only about ten or fifteen feet off the ground. I landed on my shoulder in some dirt and little rocks. It still hurts, but..."

"But why would you do that? Because you were lonely, because of Reece? I'm not blaming you, honey."

"Sally, I think I love him, and that's all I can come up with. He just came along at the right time, and then boom, he was gone. It made me sick. Maybe I wasn't in my right mind. I don't know." She fought back tears and swallowed hard.

"Emma, I wish you'd told me sooner. I'm the one you always tell things to. Gosh, when you mix love up in it, that's just a big mess. Does he know you did that?"

Emma nodded. "Yeah, I told him. He took it pretty well. I mean, would his fiancée be willing to die for him?" Her eyes flashed.

"Now maybe that's crazy talk. You can't judge her that way, Emma. I guess she loves him, seems to care about him from what I can gather."

"But he understood. She'll never be able to understand him after his time there and what happened. He even said as much, said that he'd changed."

"Well, gosh, this is just getting so complicated, but I'm glad you told me, little sister. Don't ever do anything like that again. You hear?"

"It just happened. I hadn't planned on doing it."

"And then those two soldiers attacked you. My, you've been through a lot. You need some time to digest it. If you love Reece, then that can't be helped, I suppose."

"I've never felt this way before, Sally. I just know he feels the same way about me, but he's trapped."

"Promise me that you'll just take this slow and let things happen as they may. Don't do anything desperate. I think you should move in with me so I can keep an eye on you. Would you do that?"

Emma thought. "No. I've got my room there. I love it there. Once I get a job, things'll be better. I was kind of hoping we'd wind up at the same hospital, but he's back at Carraway. What if I got a job there?"

"They both work there, right? I don't think that's a good idea. Just slow down and let time take care of this, okay?"

Emma said, "Okay," and sighed.

Reece finished his first shift without any calamities. He felt alive and glad to be back at work. He'd called Emma, but no one had answered. Kristin had finished up a few minutes early and walked over to ICU, waiting for him to complete his charting, and then they walked out to the parking deck together.

"God, I'm bushed," said Reece. The parking deck was dim and warm, the ceiling very low.

"Yeah, the hardest job in the world," said Kristin.

"It really is," said Reece. "You headed home?"

"I thought I could come out to the lake with you. We could sit on the pier. Maybe I'll pull my top down." She laughed.

"Well, that would be a surprise for sure. Yeah, sure, come on out. You gonna go home first?"

"Nope, I can just follow you out there. Wait, no, follow me to my house, and then you can drive me out and bring me back. Give us more time to talk. I like it when you drive."

Reece nodded.

Within an hour, Reece turned toward the lake. He passed the closed pool and the public pier. "Wonder what Granny has for dinner?" He threw it into low, pulled into the driveway, and hit the parking brake.

"As long as it's not fried green tomatoes. Yuck. She's a great cook, though."

"We cleaned out the corn patch and made a ton of cut corn. I'm sure that's on the menu. Maybe she'll have fried okra too. Those go good together." He ran around and opened Kristin's door for her.

Inside, Reece could smell something frying. "Hey. What kind of victuals you got going?" He walked past Dora at the stove, and she swatted him on the behind.

"Hi, Mrs. Myers," said Kristin. She gave her a side hug.

"I hope you're joining us for dinner, sweetie. We got creamed corn, okra, and pork chops."

Reece moved into the den.

"How'd your day go, son? First day on the job." Horace smiled like he was congratulating Reece on getting a PhD. "I see you brought the young lady."

"Hey, Mr. Myers." Kristin walked that way. He was fiddling with his hearing aid. The AC was on and noisy.

"This is right about ready," said Dora. "If y'all want to wash your hands." She turned the pork chops, simmering in cream of mushroom soup.

"Oh, baby," said Reece. "I'm ready."

Everyone washed their hands and gathered at the table. The phone rang just as Horace reached for a pork chop. Kristin was closest, and Reece leaned over to answer. It was Mrs. Sykes from next door. She said to hurry, that Elbert was acting funny. Reece hung up.

"Come on, something's wrong with Mr. Sykes."

"Dear Lord," said Dora. "Go see about him."

Kristin followed him, jogging next door on the pine straw to the back door. Reece just went in. Elbert was sitting at the table, slumped a bit with a wild look in his eyes. "Damn, he's having a stroke," said Reece. "Call 911. Kristin, run back and get Granny's blood pressure kit." Reece pulled up a chair beside him. "Mr. Sykes? It's me, Reece."

Elbert tried to speak, but couldn't. The left side of his body was giving way. "When did this start?" asked Reece.

Maybell was standing there, wringing her hands. "Elbert, Elbert, you okay, hon?"

"Did this just start?" Reece said again.

"Well, come to think of it, he was acting peculiar when he come in from the garden, said he had a headache. Is he having a stroke?"

"I think so," said Reece. "You need to call 911, okay? Right now."

Maybell just stood there in shock.

"Here, hold him up. I'll call." He stepped to the phone and dialed. He gave the address and said to hurry. He ran back to Elbert. Kristin was back with the kit.

"Let's get him to the recliner. Mr. Sykes, can you stand?" asked Reece. "Here, help me."

Reece took the left side, which was giving way, and Kristin the right. His left foot dragged as they manhandled him to the first recliner and let him down easy. Reece noticed a creeping stain on his crotch. In a flash, he had the battery-powered cuff on him. The cuff inflated and then began to deflate. Reece was checking his brachial pulse, which was bounding like a swollen creek. The cuff beeped.

"Damn, two-twenty over one-sixty." He looked into Elbert's eyes and could see fear. "It was awful hot today. Has he been staying hydrated?"

Maybell looked dumbfounded. "No, he won't drink like I tell him. Elbert! You okay?"

Elbert's eyes just rolled.

"Shit," said Reece. "Somebody go outside and flag

down the ambulance when it gets here." The nearest fire department was in Palmerdale, about a ten-minute drive.

Dora and Horace came inside, whispering.

"He's having a stroke," said Reece. He kneeled beside Elbert, watching his respirations, which were a bit ragged.

Dora stood back, about to cry. Horace didn't know what to do and sat at the kitchen table.

Soon, the sirens, and Kristin waved the ambulance into the gravel driveway. A fire truck followed the ambulance, and three paramedics piled out with a supply box and ran into the house through the carport door. Another was getting the stretcher from the back. The lights swirled, keeping time with the cicadas roaring in the trees.

Glen, the lead paramedic, ripped off the cuff and applied his own. "Two-thirty over one-forty. Give me forty of Procardia and a needle."

Reece watched the paramedic poke holes in the liquid capsules and squirt the liquid under Elbert's tongue. Another was starting an IV. Maybell had taken the recliner beside him, her face pale, her brow wrinkled. She pushed her upper dentures in and out with her tongue. The stretcher was at the sliding glass door, and Reece slid the door open.

"What hospital should we take him to?" asked Glen.

"What hospital?" asked Reece to Maybell.

"Carraway. We always go there."

"What meds does he take?" asked Glen.

Again, Reece repeated the question to Maybell.

"Well, he takes his blood pressure medicine, and he's got some nitroglycerin. He won't take that, though. Says it gives him a headache..."

Working together, the paramedics lifted Elbert and dropped him onto the stretcher, raising his head and strapping him down. His eyes fluttered, and he was silent.

"We'll get him on the ECG in the truck," said Glen. "Somebody needs to follow us to Carraway."

Soon, they loaded Elbert into the ambulance and, with siren blaring, sped away.

"I'll drive," said Reece. "Mrs. Sykes, do you have your insurance card in your purse? You'll need that. Kristin and I will drive you, okay?" He realized the TV was on and glanced at the big screen, *Wheel of Fortune.*

Maybell stood and stumbled her way to the bedroom to get her purse, her breath now in little sobs.

"I'm proud of you, son," said Horace. "Anything we can do?"

"No, maybe just save us some dinner." He glanced at Kristin, and they were out the back door to get the truck, driving around to pick up Maybell.

"I'll be right back," said Reece, but Kristin followed him inside to help with Maybell.

Together, they got her in the cab. Reece relaxed a bit and jumped in. "Here we go. He's gonna be okay. I promise," said Reece.

Maybell sat like a Kewpie doll, squeezed between them. She was a short but large woman, wearing her worn-out house shoes. Tears streamed down her cheeks, and they rode in near silence as Reece gunned it.

At Carraway, Reece made a parking space outside the emergency room. Inside, he and Kristin walked Maybell up to the intake window, waiting behind an elderly black man. Two TVs played to the waiting room without sound.

Reece had to repeat everything the secretary said to Maybell, and then walked her to a chair. "They'll let us know when we can go back, okay? You just relax."

Kristin put her arm around her. "Do we need to call anybody?"

Maybell pondered the question, playing with her dentures. "I hate to do it, but we need to call Ricky, and Cindy too." Ricky was Cindy's dad, but they hadn't spoken in years.

Kristin glanced at Reece. "Okay, what are their numbers? Reece, get a pen and paper."

Reece took an empty form and a pen from the secretary, but then Maybell couldn't remember Ricky's number. She knew Cindy's by heart, and Kristin wrote that down. They watched as Maybell struggled through her purse, looking for Ricky's number, but she couldn't find it.

"Don't worry, Mrs. Sykes, we'll look it up in the phone book. You want to call?" asked Reece.

Kristin hesitated. "No, you call. It's okay."

Reece found a phone on the wall, but had to wait for a few minutes as a young white lady in shorts and a bathing suit top relayed bad news. Then he dialed. A man answered.

"I need to speak with Cindy."

"Who is this?" asked the voice. It was Cindy's sugar daddy, Clarence.

"I'm the Sykes' neighbor out on the lake. Her granddad's had a stroke."

"Well, fuck. Hold on."

Reece waited.

"Hello?" said Cindy. She'd been drinking vodka tonics

and had just finished a bowl of pot.

"Hey, Cindy. It's Reece, from the lake."

"What's wrong?"

Reece told her the story and waited.

"Oh, my poor granddaddy. I'll be over in a flash. Is Granny okay? She there?"

"Yeah, she's okay. We're in the emergency room."

She hung up, and Reece walked back and sat down. Beside him was a little girl, swinging her feet, looking bored.

"She's coming, Mrs. Sykes." He glanced at Kristin, who had a stony look on her face. "I need to call your son, Ricky." He went back to the receptionist and took a phone book. He turned the thin pages, looking for a Ricky Sykes. There were a Richard and a Ricky. He had to wait again for the phone, but then dialed and got an answering machine. The voice sounded haggard and lifeless. He left a detailed message, but the machine cut him off. He figured he'd left enough information and went back to his seat, but a large black woman was sitting there. She was sweating and wore a large red bandanna. He just stood, but soon paced, waiting for Cindy to arrive.

Within twenty minutes, Cindy burst into the ER with Clarence on her heels. She ran right past them toward the secretary behind her shield of glass.

Reece caught Clarence's eye, and Clarence took Cindy and guided her toward Maybell.

"Granny, is he okay?" She was slurring her words and looked like hell, wearing a short, thin skirt with a Birmingham Barons t-shirt and no bra.

"Well, we ain't seen him yet. He's had a stroke." Maybell looked forlorn and lost.

Kristin stood. "Here, take my chair." She rolled her eyes at Reece.

"Thank you," said Cindy. She plopped down, staring at the wall. "Where's Reece?"

"I'm right here," said Reece.

Cindy looked up. "Oh, hey. Thank you so much for bringing Granny." She burst into tears, and Clarence stepped closer, putting his hand on her shoulder.

A nurse in blue scrubs pushed through a double door. "Sykes' family?"

No one moved, so Reece raised his hand.

"Two family members at a time," said the nurse.

"You two go," said Reece. "We'll wait."

Clarence helped Cindy to stand, and Reece did the same for Maybell. They passed beyond the doors, and no one spoke.

Reece wanted to say something to Clarence, but he seemed to be in his own world, leaning against the wall. He turned to Kristin. "Thanks for coming with me."

Kristin nodded. "It's a crazy world you live in, Reece Myers." She managed a smile.

A disheveled man with unruly blond hair entered, looking around the open room as if searching for a friend. From across the room, Reece could see that he had enormous hands, just like Elbert's. The guy sauntered to the secretary's window, and she was pointing toward Reece. Reece figured it was Ricky and waited for him to come over, but he didn't, looking somewhat sullen. Reece waved at him and stood. He knew that he'd molested Cindy and wondered what she'd do when she saw him.

"Hey, I'm the one who called. You looking for the

Sykes?"

Ricky put his hands in his pockets and winced. "Yeah, my dad. You said he had a stroke? Can I see him?" He smelled of cigarettes.

"Well," said Reece. "Your mom is back there right now... with Cindy." He noticed that Clarence was taking interest and watching them.

Ricky frowned. "Oh." He looked behind him and glanced around the room as if hunting a place to hide.

Clarence walked up, putting two and two together. He looked cool and calm. "What's up?"

Reece wavered. He waited for Ricky to speak, and it took a while.

"I'm Ricky, his son. You a friend of the family?"

"You could say that," said Clarence. "Heard about you but never thought I'd meet you." He was clenching his fists and had lifted his chin just a bit.

"What you've heard and what you know might be two different things," said Ricky. He was meatier than Clarence, but shorter.

Reece had a bad feeling. "Hey, we're here because of Mr. Sykes."

"I know why we're here," said Ricky. "What are you staring at?"

"I'm staring at a child molester," said Clarence. "Cindy is my girl."

"You're as old as I am," said Ricky. He pulled his hands from his pockets. "So, who's the child molester?"

"Guys, this is not the place." Reece glanced back at Kristin, who was holding Maybell's purse.

Clarence relaxed his jaw. "Just you don't get near Cindy

is all I'm saying."

"Gladly," said Ricky. He turned and walked away.

"Motherfucker," said Clarence.

Cindy emerged from the back. She ran into an orderly, then made her way to Reece. She seemed to be out of breath, and then she saw Ricky. "What the hell?" She pushed between Reece and the wall. "What the goddamn fuck are you doing here? He don't want to see you, and neither do I." She stumbled.

Clarence braced himself. "Cindy, don't."

By now, the entire emergency room was focused on them, waiting to see what happened next.

"Well, hell," said Ricky. "Then why'd you call and tell me to run down here?" He was about a body length away from her.

"I didn't call you, you fool." She looked back at Reece.

"Mrs. Sykes told me to call him. Just relax. I'm sure he'll get away as quick as he can." Reece was in the spotlight, like a referee at a boxing match.

"Don't put words in my mouth, whoever you are," said Ricky. "Let her make a fool of her own self." He snickered.

"Get...out of here!" Cindy took two steps forward, but was being pulled back by Clarence.

"Simmer down, babydoll. I'll take care of him. Why don't you just go, fella? You can come back and see him later."

"Fella?" asked Ricky. "Who you calling fella?"

Clarence laughed.

"Kick his ass," said Cindy. "He's not going back there as long as I'm here." She lunged at him, and her nails caught his face, but then Clarence had her again.

"I said, let me take care of this. You been drinking. They'll come in here and arrest us. Don't do it," said Clarence.

A security guard burst through the double doors, stopping to assess the situation. He moved in. "What's the trouble here? This is an emergency room, not a playground."

Reece stood back.

"This asshole needs to leave. He's a goddamn rapist," said Cindy. She pulled away from Clarence. "My granddaddy's had a stroke!"

The security guard put himself to the side of Cindy. "You been drinking, ma'am?"

"Don't get on me! It's him! He's no right to be here."

Clarence spoke. "We were doing okay till he showed up. It's best that he leave. Family matters. She'll settle down if he leaves." He held Cindy in his arms, loosely restraining her.

"Sir, to make this easy, I'm gonna ask you to leave for now." The security guard moved toward Ricky.

"He's my dad. I've every right to be here. He's the one that raised me." He smirked at Cindy.

"I'll give you one chance," said the security guard. "Y'all can work this out somewhere else." He took Ricky's elbow with a firm grip.

Ricky jerked away. "Yeah, I'll leave. But if he dies before I see him, you'll have hell to pay. I'm leaving." With his shoulders slumped, he went around the backside of the room and exited through the automatic doors. Before they closed, he turned and gave them the finger.

The next day, Reece was bushed. He and Kristin had stayed for another hour or so, but never got to see Mr. Sykes, who was admitted to CCU, where Kristin worked. Clarence had volunteered to stick around and take Maybell home.

During report, Reece learned that Mrs. Laramore wasn't doing well. The Lasix hadn't jumped her urine output, and her lungs were getting crackly. Mr. Jones was still there but would be transferred out, meaning that Reece would probably get a new patient. He popped over to CCU to say hey to Kristin and asked if he could see Mr. Sykes. He'd had an intracranial hemorrhage, the cause of his stroke, and was on an experimental drug, IV Nicardipine, to manage his blood pressure.

"He's still obtunded," said Kristin. "But he may recognize you." She pulled back the curtain.

Elbert lay on his back, an oxygen cannula in his nose. He worked to turn his head, and Reece could tell that he knew him.

"Hey, Mr. Myers. It's me, Reece. You've had a rough time, but you're in a good place."

Elbert cracked a half smile and mumbled. He reached up his right hand, and Reece shook it. He stood there for a minute and left to find Kristin.

"He looks good, but I hope he's not paralyzed on his side like that. Maybe it'll resolve."

"Is his wife coming to visit?" asked Kristin.

"Yeah, Horace's going to drive her in today. Well, I better get going on the other side." He saw Brad and kissed

Kristin on the cheek.

"Okay, see you. But that was plain crazy last night. What'll happen next, I wonder?"

Reece laughed and left. He needed to get his physical on Mrs. Laramore as soon as possible. He checked her chart for new orders and then went into two.

Janese's head was raised to 45 degrees, oxygen at 3 liters per minute, her face glistening. She watched Reece but said nothing, breathing noisily.

"Hey, Mrs. Laramore. It's me, Reece. I'm taking care of you again today."

Janese managed a labored "Thank you."

Reece went through the motions, heart, lungs, belly. She was on continuous blood pressure monitoring, and the few ounces of urine in her catheter bag were dark yellow.

"Are you in any pain?" He checked the edema on her feet, and it was three-plus, even with the TED hose.

She shook her head no. "Having...trouble...with my breath." She coughed, and a gob of mucus filled her mouth.

Reece took the suction wand and cleared the mess. "Let me take a look at your backside. Make sure your skin is doing okay." He lowered her head a bit and turned her with the drawsheet. Her giant breasts held her on her side. He pulled her gown open and saw the skin broken over her sacrum, a redness. "Hold on." He popped on a glove, took some lotion, and massaged her tailbone. "Gonna leave you on your side for now, give your backside a rest." He raised her head again. He'd get the intern to order some Duoderm for her.

Her breakfast tray came, a low-calorie, low-salt diet. "Can you feed yourself, or do you need some help?" She didn't respond, just looked at him with vacant eyes. "Tell you what, let me run and check on another patient, and I'll be back to help you eat. Okay?"

She seemed to nod okay, huffing for air.

Reece headed into six, and Mr. Jones was eating his breakfast. "Got me two boiled eggs today." He held one and took a bite. "Mmm, mmm."

"How you feeling? Ready to get out of here?"

"Damn straight," said J.D. He ate a bite of grits. "I been thinking."

"Yeah? What about?" Reece glanced at the bedside monitor, normal sinus rhythm, seventy-two beats per minute. He took off his stethoscope, ready to listen to lung, heart, and bowel sounds.

"You ain't one of them homo-sex-uals, are you? You don't seem like it. I mean, you're not very ladylike, but you are a nurse. Nurses are women. There's that other man nurse who works nights. I'm pretty sure he's one."

Reece laughed. "I don't think I am. I'm engaged to a woman. But you never know." He winked at J.D.

"Well, that's good to know. Some are and some aren't. I don't believe I've ever met one until now." He sipped his coffee, as serious as a heart attack.

"There's not a dime's worth of difference if you get to know them," said Reece. He felt J.D.'s pedal pulses.

J.D. just grunted. "I'd say I'm far from it. Got me three kids and a wife." He smoothed back his thinning hair.

"Okay," said Reece. "You don't have discharge orders yet, but looks like you're going to the floor today. I'll call your wife if you want me to, or will she be in today?" Visiting hours were at ten, two, and six.

"She'll be in." He bit into his second egg, covered in salt and pepper.

The room intercom came on. It was Selena, the monitor tech. "Hey, you need to check on two. I think a lead's off."

"I'll be back in a few minutes," said Reece. He pulled the sheet back over J.D.'s socked feet.

He walked in and rushed to Janese's side. Mucus hung out of her mouth. Her eyes looked fixed. He looked at the monitor, which showed a flat line. "Holy shit." He grabbed the suction wand and cleared her mouth. She wasn't breathing. He shouted, "Code Blue!" and felt for a carotid pulse. Nothing. The monitor sent out a piercing tone.

An intern stepped in. Laronda called in the code, and "Code Blue ICU" rang out over the intercom. A nurse, Glenda, pushed the crash cart toward the room. Soon, the room held six people. A resident named Dr. Jersey took control, but Reece had already lowered her bed and was doing chest compressions. He grabbed the Ambu bag and gave her two quick breaths. Andrew from night shift took over the Ambu bag, and Reece resumed compressions on her massive chest.

"Paddles!" said Jersey. He ripped up her gown and slapped two gel pads on her chest and side. "Two hundred...Clear!" He pressed the paddles onto the pads.

Mrs. Laramore's chest jumped with the shock. Still flat line.

"Epi one milligram," said Jersey. He grabbed the syringe and pushed the drug.

Reece put his might into the compressions, praying that she would respond.

"Clear!" said Jersey.

Her torso jumped, and the current arced to the bed rail, shocking Reece.

"Shit," said Reece. He resumed compressions, but felt dizzy.

A crazy rhythm appeared on the monitor, then settled into a slow rhythm of exaggerated complexes. Reece stopped the compressions.

"Atropine zero point five," said Jersey. He took the syringe from Glenda and pushed it into the IV.

Thirty seconds passed, and a rough normal rhythm appeared, punctuated with PVCs. She was breathing as well. Jersey stood with arms folded and pushed his glasses up on his nose. Everyone milled around as if waiting for coffee. Jersey took his penlight and checked her pupils, which were sluggish but reactive.

Reece could smell that Janese had soiled herself, but she seemed to be back in the world of the living. His heart was racing, and he took a deep breath. "Mrs. Laramore, hold on. You're doing good."

The attending physician, Dr. Christie, walked into the room and was briefed by Jersey. "Let's get a BP."

Reece took the cuff. "Ninety over sixty."

Everyone stood back to let Dr. Christie listen to her heart and lungs. "Put the O2 on a face mask and start a dopamine drip. What's her weight?"

Reece said, "Three hundred and twenty at last check."

"Thirty per minute," said Christie. He patted Jersey on the shoulder and went out to write the orders.

Reece surveyed the room, which looked like a wreck. He caught the eye of the nursing assistant and asked her to help clean up Mrs. Laramore, while he grabbed an oxygen mask. Glenda pushed the crash cart out. Reece placed the mask and cranked the oxygen. "Hang in there. We got you covered, Mrs. Laramore." He then picked up trash from the floor and removed the gooey gel pads from her chest, keeping an eye on the monitor. Out of habit, he trotted over to check on Mr. Jones. Anything could happen.

"Doing okay? Had a little emergency."

"Just waiting to get out of here," said J.D. He started to tell Reece about his tomato farm, but Reece said he'd be back in a few minutes and apologized.

Reece checked the new orders and made the dopamine drip. He found an IV pump in the clean laundry room, lugged it into the room, and set up the drip. Christie had ordered a jugular IV, but a doctor would have to put that in. He watched Janese's eyes roll in her head and said thanks to the nursing assistant, Rochelle, who was drawing up a pan of warm bath water, and reminded himself that he would have to restock the crash cart.

He raised the bed, then the head of the bed to 30 degrees. "Mrs. Laramore? You've had a rough day. Squeeze my hand if you hear me. She squeezed his hand. "Good, good. We're gonna get you cleaned up and comfortable, okay?"

Rochelle was ready with the bath cloth, and Reece pulled Janese onto her side. Liquid stool pooled on the blue pad. Rochelle put a towel in the mess and rolled it, containing the liquid. As Reece held Janese, she cleaned her.

"Let's put some lotion on her backside and her back too," said Reece.

Rochelle nodded and rubbed in the lotion.

"Gonna turn you," said Reece. He grabbed the drawsheet and lifted, pushing her over. He grabbed the dirty rolled sheet, pad, and towel and pulled them out. Rochelle handed him a new drawsheet, already rolled with a clean blue pad, and he stuffed it under Janese. "Gonna roll one more time." Rochelle had hurried back to her side and pushed, pulling the clean linens beneath Janese's massive bottom.

"All good. You comfortable?" asked Reece. Janese seemed to nod, but he wasn't sure. "Thanks," said Reece. "Rochelle, right?"

"That's me," said Rochelle. "You need anything else?"

"I'd like to give her a bath. But let's wait a while." He pushed the IV pole closer to the bed, turned off the bright overhead light, and glanced at the monitor.

"Not a problem," said Rochelle, and she left the room, followed by Reece.

"Hey." It was Kristin. "Was that your patient?"

Reece sat down on a rolling stool. "Yep. Scared the bejesus out of me. Holy cow."

"She stable?" She looked cute in her white scrubs with a tiny red bow in her hair.

"Yeah, for now. Damn, that was close." He felt like a flower beneath the heel of a cow.

"Okay, just wanted to check on you. You look a little pale."

"I swear I almost had a seizure while I was doing compressions. Got shocked." He looked around for a pen.

"Are you serious?"

"Yeah, but I'm okay. Just the adrenaline."

"Okay, but don't overdo it, cowboy. I think you need to come and say hey to Mr. Odo, the garbage man. He's off the vent."

"Sure, let me do my charting. I've got a patient that's transferring out."

Kristin tousled his short hair, stood, and left, Reece looking for his pen.

The day before, the cops had come by and filled out a report of what had happened. Sarah wasn't home by then, but soon Emma had told her about the encounter with Daryl and his drunk buddy. The cops had left, headed to Daryl's trailer, and had arrested him for violating his restraining order. Just to be safe, Sally came the next day and brought her to her place. Emma sat on the couch, recounting the ambush by her flesh and blood.

"He's just a dead man walking," said Sally. She sipped chamomile tea. She was wearing ripped tight jeans and a t-shirt. She'd already dropped Heather at school.

"God, he's such a loser, over and over. You'd think he'd wise up and behave." Emma put her legs on the floral-print couch and shielded her eyes from the sun coming through the window.

"He'll never learn," said Sally. "He's never been a daddy and never will. You want to do something today? Maybe go to the zoo or the botanical gardens? What about the Galleria?"

"Oh my God, the Galleria," said Emma. "That just seems so foreign to me now." She paused. "What I'd like to do is talk with Reece. I thought he would call yesterday." She grabbed a cushion and hugged it.

"There's that Reece again. If he hadn't busted his lip that night, I think we could have got him naked." She laughed.

"That would take the cake," said Emma. "Maybe with you and Heather not around."

"You've got your sights set on him, but it could be one

big disappointment. Don't get your hopes too high. Wanna go grocery shopping with me?" She finished her tea. "It's not so crowded right now."

"Yeah, sure." Emma thought about a grocery store, the aisles of food, the vegetables, the fruits, the meats. It would be surreal after attending the markets in Ethiopia.

"Okay, let me spruce up." Sally hopped up and headed to the bathroom.

Emma put her feet on the floor, suddenly craving fresh pineapple. She gazed around the small living room. Overhead was a loft, Heather's bedroom. The floor plan was open, and she could see through the dining room to the kitchen and the black appliances there. Maybe Reece had called her and left a message.

"Let's do it." Sally held her keys and stylish purse with a horse embroidered on it.

They drove in near silence to the Food Saver, and Sally parked. Inside, it was cool, and it was double-coupon day. Emma took in the six registers and the specials that lined the way to the produce department. Clorox was only sixty-nine cents a gallon. She thought about the dingy clothes of the people of Godo who never had the luxury of washing them.

"Good Lord," said Emma. "So many colors." She picked up a cantaloupe and thumped it. "This'd be good."

"Put in the basket. I'm gonna get you fat."

"Ooh, what I want is some pineapple." She put the cantaloupe back and looked around. "You know what? They don't have apples in Ethiopia."

"You want some apples? Get some apples," said Sally. "I've got Sammy's charge card."

Emma picked out two large Fuji apples and put them in the cart. "I feel like I'm in some kind of toy land." She saw the pineapples and headed that way. There was a man with a very large bottom there, and she waited. The man turned to her and spoke.

"Looking at the pineapples?"

Emma laughed. "Yeah."

The man had a twinkle in his eye. "Do you need a church home? Are you a Christian?"

"Not really. I already go, a Baptist church."

"Well, bless your heart. That's mighty good news. Young people these days have lost their way." He held out his hand. "I'm Eugene Standifer. I attend the Gospel Apostolic. I don't much hold an opinion about the Baptist churches, not being the true way."

Sally pushed the buggy up behind them. She'd seen the man before, handing out pamphlets in front of the store. She bumped the cart into Emma.

Emma searched for words. "But we both like pineapple, right?"

Eugene made a sour and funny face. "Well...I guess we do." He pulled a bright orange pamphlet from his pocket and handed it to her. "This here will set you on the right path, God's path." He looked like Napoleon presiding over a triumphant victory.

Emma glanced at the pamphlet and put it in her pocket. "Nice to meet you, sir." He looked like a bowling pin.

Sally nodded for Emma to move on, and they did, leaving Eugene to ponder his encounter. "He's a nut," said Sally, and Emma smiled, still holding her pineapple. Sally gathered red potatoes, onions, and a head of lettuce before moving on to encounter the long line of meats.

"You wanna have dinner with us tonight? Maybe some grilled chicken?" asked Sally. "Heather would love it."

"No. Well, maybe another time. I want to be home when Momma gets there." She surveyed an array of steaks and hamburger meat. A man wearing a hair net was putting out rib eyes.

"I get you," said Sally, turning into the aisle with coffee and oatmeal. A loudspeaker came on, announcing a special on toilet paper. "We all need that. Say, did you have toilet paper over there? You never told me."

Emma fingered a bag of Eight O'Clock coffee. "You can buy it in Addis, which is what I did. But the villagers all just used smooth stones or just went with a no-wiper."

"Gross," said Sally. "Stones? My word, that sounds just awful." She put some granola bars in the basket and a box of chamomile tea.

"They have the best coffee in the world, though. They grow it. Originated there." She gazed at the packets of sauce mix.

"Sammy don't drink coffee."

A woman passed by them. In the seat of her cart was a Living Bible, which she was reading as she shopped. Emma looked, and the pages were marked, almost to the point of being unreadable.

They passed up and down the aisles, Emma stupefied at the selection of food. Sally didn't have any coupons, and the cashier, taken aback, gave them one for the canned biscuits. Emma tossed in a pack of Dentyne, not having had gum for two years. As they left, she popped in a piece, wondering at the texture and flavor in such a small object.

Outside, a lanky man had taken up shop, selling ballcaps to benefit veterans.

Soon they were home, unloading the groceries in the kitchen. Emma checked her watch, and it wasn't even noon. She was desperate to talk with Reece, but knew he was at work. Maybe she could call him there? Kristin wouldn't be around, or so she hoped.

Reece kept vigil outside of Mrs. Laramore's room. Mr. Jones had transferred to the floor, and six was empty for now. Janese's breathing had him worried, and her urine output had increased only a tiny bit, most likely due to the dopamine, but her lungs were increasingly congested. He had the sliding door open all the way and the curtain pulled open so he could see her. Every time she coughed, he went in and suctioned the mucus from her mouth, and it seemed to get thicker and thicker. He'd talked with Janese's brother, and he was on the way to the hospital.

The phone rang, and Glenda answered. She called for Reece.

Reece took the phone. "Hello."

It was human resources. They needed him to fill out a W-9. He walked around the unit, thinking about lunch, whether or not he should go, and sat back in the chair outside of two. He could hear Janese's rumbling chest from there, decided to let the intern know, and had Laronda page him. He called back and said he would be by as soon as possible. Reece's thoughts turned to Godo and Emma. Janese was coughing again, but nothing was coming up, just churning in her lungs. Her breaths were labored, and she looked afraid.

The intern, whom everyone called Scottie, arrived and listened to Janese's lungs. He ordered an arterial oxygen level stat but was pretty sure she needed to be intubated before she went into respiratory failure.

"Yeah, just don't want her to code twice in one day." Reece gathered the syringe, needle, and cup of ice for the blood gas. Hitting the radial artery hurt like hell, and Reece apologized to Janese beforehand. He slid the needle in, and the blood pumped into the syringe. He watched the monitor, which showed an increase in PVCs. One PVC falling on a t-wave could send her into fibrillation. He filled out a lab slip and ran the blood down, then hurried back to her room.

"Reece!" Laronda was holding the phone.

Reece jogged to the phone. "Hello." It was the lab with the blood gas. Oxygen saturation was 60%. She was doing poorly. He had Laronda page Scottie. He was next door in CCU and trotted in.

"Let's go ahead and tube her. I've talked with Dr. Christie, and he's good with it. Get me the scope and a four point five."

Reece explained to Janese what they were about to do. She didn't respond. He took the headboard off the bed, lowered it, and then turned on the overhead light. Mucus filled her mouth and throat, and he suctioned as fast as he could. He moved aside for Scotty to take his place behind her with the scope.

"Tube's going in, Mrs. Laramore. Squeeze my hand," said Reece. He held her flaccid, wet hand.

Scottie backed the curved scope into her mouth and slid it down. He was in his crisp white intern coat. Janese gagged and raised up, reaching her hands out in a vague fight. Scottie took the tube and passed it through the scope into her windpipe. Right away, a gush of thick mucus shot out as she coughed. Reece had notified respiratory, and just as he was taping down the tube and attaching the Ambu bag, the ventilator arrived.

"Lots of PVCs in two!" said the monitor tech.

"Got it!" said Reece. He squeezed oxygen into Janese's lungs with the Ambu bag.

Janese was struggling, moving her head from side to side. He hit the call button. "Need a suction catheter in two, please."

Laronda hurried to the supply room. She laid the open package on the bed. Reece donned sterile gloves and hooked the tube up to the suction, released the Ambu bag, squirted in some sterile saline, and suctioned her deep through the tube. Nearly 100 ccs of yellowish phlegm came out. He resumed the Ambu bag, waiting for the vent to start up.

Scotty stepped back inside. "Good work. Let's put her on fifty percent and twelve per minute, okay? Also, we need a chest film to verify placement and another blood gas in half an hour. I'll write the orders."

"Want to culture the mucus?"

"Yeah, let's do that."

Soon, Janese was attached to the vent, which breathed for her twelve times a minute. She continued to cough, setting off the alarm. The mucus was super thick, and Reece needed to squirt more saline down the tube to break it up. He put the headboard back on, decided his tape job wasn't secure, and redid it. He stepped back, glad that he could see Janese stabilized.

"Hey, Reece, phone. It's on hold at the desk," said Glenda at the curtain.

Reece needed a drink, and he ran to the clean utility room and grabbed a cup of cranberry juice. He ran back to the phone.

"Hello?"

"Hey, Reece!"

"Oh, hey!" He imagined her.

"You working hard?"

"Well, just intubated a patient." He noticed Laronda waving at him. "Hold on. Something's up." He pulled the phone from his ear.

"Got a new patient coming in from CT scan via the ER. Just a heads up," said Laronda.

Reece gave an OK sign. "I'm first admit and got a new patient coming in, so can't talk for long."

"That sucks," said Emma.

"Yeah. So, what's up?"

"I don't know. Just bored, I guess. You'll never guess what happened. Daryl came by the house and threatened me again. He had his drunk buddy with him."

"That sucks, too. You okay?"

"Kind of rattled me, but he's in jail. So, all's good for now. You still want to help me with the slideshow?"

"Kristin doesn't want me to see you again, so I don't know. I'd like to."

"Oh," said Emma. "Well, it's for a good cause, right? Kind of like a Bible study."

Reece laughed at that. "Let me check, and I'll get back with you. Okay?"

"The folks at church would love to see you again. You know they want you to speak as well. Getting shot makes a body mighty popular."

"I guess so." Reece wanted to commit and say yes.

"Anyway, just call me when you can. Maybe tonight? It's already Wednesday."

"Dang, it is, isn't it? Well, heck, yeah, I'll give you a ring tonight. But I better get going before this patient arrives."

"Okay," said Emma. "Talk to you then."

"Right, bye." He hung up the phone, and it rang again. He figured it was CT scan calling report, and it was. "ICU, Reece." He listened to the details, a sixty-five-year-old white male who had fallen off a ladder. He was responsive only to pain.

Reece hung up and prepped the room, putting fresh blue pads on top of the drawsheet. He raised the bed to stretcher height and rigged an IV pole with a pump. Within minutes, the new patient with his papers on his chest had arrived. His eyes looked like wet stones, and there were family members in the hallway.

Reece let the intern and resident do their thing while he untangled IV lines and went to review the chart for orders. The patient's name was Eddie Riggins, and he'd been changing light bulbs at church on a tall ladder when he fell and hit the back of his head. There were questions about whether he'd blacked out and fell or just fell. He was on a mannitol drip to draw off fluid and reduce the pressure inside his skull, plus a slow drip of normal saline.

Reece popped in to check on Mrs. Laramore and scooted into six as soon as the doctors left. He talked to Eddie, letting him know everything would be okay while he did his assessment. He hooked him up to the ECG monitor and transferred the mannitol drip to the pump. The catheter bag was full of pale, yellow urine. Reece washed his hands and wondered what Emma was doing all day. He would ask Kristin about the slideshow, as if it were a Bible study like Emma said. He remembered the little rope game of Edwin's and sighed. He also decided to buy a six-pack of beer and bring it home. Dora would pitch a fit, but Horace would understand. He remembered the family in the hall.

"Riggins' family?" In the hall stood six people. Three sons, a daughter, a wife, and the man who'd been working with Eddie when he fell. Everyone was crying except for the friend who stared at his shoes.

The wife stepped forward, her entire face wet with tears. "Are you his nurse? Can we see him?"

"Sure," said Reece. "I'm Reece. He seems to be stable, but he's still not responding. We can let in two at a time." He could feel the tidal wave they were riding on.

"You go first, Momma," said the oldest son. He wiped at his tears. "And take Cynthia. We'll go next."

"There's a waiting room just around the corner here," said Reece. He waved his hand as if guiding a battleship through a narrow channel.

Reece led the way to six, where Eddie lay on his back. His temp had spiked in the ER, and Reece needed to check it again. He pulled back the curtain, and the two rushed to Eddie's side.

"Oh, Daddy," said the daughter. She grabbed his hand and squeezed it.

The wife was more composed now, and she walked

around to the other side, taking his other hand. Reece stepped out to check the chart for orders.

"Got you hopping," said Laronda. "Give me a second with this chart."

"Yeah, for sure," said Reece. "I'm gonna get some water. Be right back." He passed Brad, who was so hot for Kristin, and nodded. Brad had two patients in the ICU. Looking down at him, Reece could almost see the hairline on top of his head. He walked back and took the chart from Laronda. There was an order for a cooling blanket if Eddie's temp remained elevated. He stepped into six. "Maybe a few more minutes, okay?"

"What was your name again?" asked the wife. She was in an old pair of brown knit pants with a blue short-sleeve button-up.

"It's Reece."

"Well, thank you, Reece." She went back to holding her husband's hand.

Meanwhile, Janese's brother had arrived and was peeking into the unit. Glenda guided him to Reece, and Reece took him into Janese's room. He explained what had happened, but the brother was upset.

"How long she gonna stay like this?"

"Hopefully not long. She couldn't breathe. That's why they put the tube in."

"Ain't you supposed to get the permission of the family?" Janese's brother George was barrel-chested with muscular arms and wearing a ballcap.

"Well," said Reece. "Does she have a living will?"

"A what?"

Reece explained what a living will was. Otherwise, the

doctors would do whatever was needed to get her well.

"I just hate to see her like this." He took off his cap and spoke to Janese. "Hey, Sis. It's me, George."

Janese raised her eyebrows and coughed, filling the tube with phlegm and causing the ventilator to alarm. Reece unfastened the vent tube and suctioned her. He explained she needed the tube to keep her lungs clear.

"She know me," said George. "We all prayin' for you, Sis."

"I'll be back in a few minutes," said Reece. "We're gonna give her a bath soon."

"Thank you, sir. We just don't want her sufferin' is all." He looked around the room as if in a gymnasium.

"I understand," said Reece, and he hurried back to six. "You guys about ready to let the others come in?" He watched Eddie's deep and slow respirations.

The wife and daughter nodded and walked out, hugging each other.

Reece found a place to chart at the desk and began writing, wondering at how fast time passed on day shift. He dreaded the slow plodding of night shift, watching the clock hands turn as if in syrup.

After standing by his parents' bodies for what seemed like hours, Reece was ushered outside. Ambulances, patrol cars, and a fire truck filled the parking lot. News crews had descended and were interviewing the people, some just onlookers. For the first time, he noticed a splash of blood and what could be brains on his yellow t-shirt and jeans. Why hadn't he been shot? How did the guy with pistols blazing miss him? He looked at the mess of glass and could see the pickup truck inside, as if it belonged there. A cop had said something about giving him a ride home, but he had the key to the Mercury Bobcat parked in the lot near a low hedge.

Not knowing what to do next, he drove home and pulled into the driveway. He supposed he should call his grandparents. Inside was cool and dim. His mom always kept the curtains pulled tight. He opened them and walked into the kitchen. Dishes sat on the drying rack. There was leftover oatmeal in a pot. Usually, his dad would come along and eat it. He walked into their bedroom, and the bed was neat as a pin. Where would their bodies wind up? Would there be a funeral in Texas or back in Alabama? The black-and-white TV called to him, and he turned it on. There was live coverage of the shooting on two channels, but he went to PBS. It was *Mister Rogers' Neighborhood*.

Reece sat on the hard yellow couch that had followed them for ten years. There was xylophone music. Mr. Rogers was singing and putting his coat in the closet. He was going to a dinosaur museum. Reece stood and turned up the volume. He thought about the high school he hated with a passion and wondered if he'd already spent his last day there. He took solace in that. He'd go to the high school near his grandparents, finish out his junior year there. The aquarium. He looked at his twenty-nine-gallon aquarium, the mollies, the neon tetras, the little catfish that scuttled along the bottom. The phone was in the kitchen, and it was ringing. No one ever called.

Reece picked up the green handset. "Hello?" It was his grandfather.

"Reece, we saw you on the news. What happened? What happened?" asked Horace.

The line was scratchy, and Reece adjusted the cord where it went into the phone. *What to say?*

"A guy just shot up the place. We were there." He looked out the sliding glass door. The dog sat on the tiny cement landing. He'd forgotten about the dog.

"Reece, where are your parents? Where are Larry and Macy?"

Reece choked up. "They...got shot."

"Oh my God, Reece, are you sure? Are they alive?"

"Yeah, I mean no. The paramedics checked. I couldn't look. I'm at home." Reece could hear his grandmother crying in the background.

"Well damn, son, what're we gonna do? We need to get out there. You hang on, okay? Oh, dear Jesus. You give everybody our phone number, okay?"

"Okay." Reece felt strangely peaceful. His wish, now dark, was coming true. His grandparents were coming to get him and take him back to Alabama. "I'll just wait here."

"Reece, this is Granny." She sobbed as she talked. "Are

you sure? Are you sure they're not alive? Oh, dear Jesus."

"Yeah, pretty sure." He pulled the cord and sat at the tiny dining room table.

"Pretty...sure! Reece, you have to know. Tell me the truth."

"He crashed through the restaurant glass in his truck and started shooting. He shot a lot of people. He shot Mom and Dad." His mind drifted back to the scene, the smell of fried chicken and gunpowder.

Horace was back on the line. "Reece? You there? Reece?"

"I'm here." He pushed the light-blue, plastic saltshaker around. He imagined sleeping in the house alone, how creepy that would be.

"Look, we'll fly out there, okay? We'll do it today if we can. Oh God, I can't believe it." He choked up. "You're gonna be okay, boy, you hear me?"

"Yeah," said Reece. He had this insight that his life was forever changed, that a switch had been hit. "I'll stay here."

"Reece, you'll need to pick us up from the airport. Can you do that? I'm not sure where we'll land. Well, maybe not. Look, we'll figure it out, okay, son? I'm just watching this on the news. I can't believe it. Had you ever seen this guy before?"

Reece pushed the saltshaker next to the peppershaker. "Never. He just drove right through the windows. He yelled something about women and just kept shooting. People were under the tables. He just shot them. I kept my eyes closed. I was afraid to move." It was the first time he'd ever been truly afraid, and the feeling gnawed at him, like the danger had yet to pass.

"Reece, I'm gonna hang up. Just stay put. Oh, what is your address? Never mind, we have it in the address book. What will become of this world? Reece? I'm gonna hang up. You've got our number?"

"Yeah." He had it memorized. He said the number. "Two oh five, six eight one, seven three one four."

"That's it. Good. Good. Okay, I'm going now. We'll be there as soon as possible. Probably tomorrow. Okay? You call if you need anything. If you can't reach us, then call Randy. I'm gonna call him right now. Okay?" Reece could hear his grandmother talking in the background. "And Granny says for you to call your pastor at the church. Call him, okay?"

"Okay," said Reece. "I will. I'll see you tomorrow, I hope." He thought about not having any money, but there was food in the house.

It was Dora. "Reece, you take care. Okay?"

"Yeah, Granny. I will."

"Okay, goodbye, son."

"Goodbye."

Reece put the phone on the table, and the cord scooted it onto the floor with a cracking sound. He opened the sliding glass door. Floppy wagged his stubby tail, and Reece walked out and sat on the stoop, rubbing his long ears. When it rained, his mom would put sandwich bags on his feet with rubber bands. He could hear Mr. Rogers chatting in the background, and he cried.

Kristin wanted Reece to come and visit Mr. Odo. Mr. Sykes had stabilized and was desperately trying to talk, but all that came out was a growl. Mrs. Sykes had visited at ten and then again at two, brought there by Cindy, who had taken the day off. Kristin was pretty sure that Cindy hadn't spoken to Reece, but couldn't be sure. It seemed as if she was destined to have Cindy and Emma in her life. And then there was Brad. He came into Mr. Odo's room while she was packing the open wounds under his jaw with iodoform gauze.

"Your fiancée in ICU is trying to kill them off one by one." He put his hands on the bed rail and winked at Mr. Odo, who didn't speak, looking askance at Kristin.

"Hush. Don't say things like that. He probably saved her life, for all you know. What do you need?"

"How's Mr. Odo doing? He is my patient, right?" He gazed at the cardiac monitor as if gazing at a rare cheese. "Good job with the packing, by the way."

"He's doing great. But you could ask him yourself. He's right there in front of you. Right, Mr. Odo?" She took a comb and pushed back his thick black hair. "Looking good."

Mr. Odo smiled, showing his missing front teeth. "Can I...sit on the side of the bed?"

"Well, of course you can," said Brad. "I'll write an order for him to be up in the chair three times a day. You feel like getting in a chair? We're pleased with your progress." He held out his hand for Mr. Odo to shake, but Mr. Odo just looked through him as if it were a joke.

"That's super," said Kristin. "We'll get you up in the chair here. Just let me put a sheet and a pad down. Okay, Dr. Phillips, here's where you can be of great assistance. You get on one side after I sit him up." She raised the head of the bed all the way, then lowered the whole bed, and pulled Mr. Odo's giant legs over one at a time.

"Sure we don't need more help?" asked Brad.

"Nope. Mr. Odo, I'm gonna lean in and you put your arm around my neck."

Mr. Odo blushed but did as he was told and was soon teetering on the edge of the bed, his tiptoes on the floor. "Don't let me fall."

"Don't worry, we won't. Okay, Dr. Phillips, you get that arm, and I've got this one. On three. One, two, three," and up came Mr. Odo, wobbling in their grip. "Pivot him over."

"Jeez!" said Brad. He grunted and held onto Mr. Odo for dear life as he sank like a ten-ton anchor backwards into the chair.

"Shit on a biscuit!" said Mr. Odo. He took a few deep breaths. "Made me dizzy." His IV line was straining, blood backing into it, and Kristin reached behind him for the slack.

"There," said Kristin. "Good work, Brad. I mean, Dr. Phillips."

Reece stood outside the room, watching. "Knock, knock, fellow healthcare professionals." Brad looked like a frog standing next to Mr. Odo.

"Hey!" said Kristin. She wiped the hair from her eyes. "Let me get him situated." She took a towel, folded it, and laid it across his lap. "Do you want your feet up? Want to recline?"

Mr. Odo nodded no. "Thank y'all."

"You're welcome," said Brad. "Need to get out and check on another patient," and he left.

Reece smiled at Kristin, but didn't say it. "Well, introduce me."

"Oh," said Kristin. "This is Mr. Odo. And his name is Reece."

"Nice to meet you, sir." Reece wanted to ask him if he drove a garbage truck. Somehow, that sounded like the most interesting job in the world.

Mr. Odo blinked and nodded, wheezed, then sneezed. "Excuse me."

"Bless you," said Kristin. She pushed the overbed table closer to him with the water pitcher and a plastic cup.

"I'll pop over and say hey to Mr. Sykes again." Reece straightened his name badge.

"Go see him. I'll be here. His family was in the waiting room, but I think they've gone."

"His son show up?"

"No, not as long as that Cindy is around. She's hell on wheels."

Reece laughed. "She must have brought Mrs. Sykes."

"Don't get any ideas. Go see him."

Reece said bye to Mr. Odo, left, and went two doors down to ten. Mr. Sykes was on his side, holding the bed rail. Winston was his nurse.

"Knock knock," said Reece. "It's me again. Reece."

Mr. Sykes managed half of a drooly grin.

"You've had a heck of a time," said Reece. "Got everybody worried, but you're looking good. We'll have you out of here in no time." He put his hand on his shoulder and squeezed. "What's that?" Mr. Sykes was trying to speak. Reece strained to hear through the garble. "You need the bedpan?" Mr. Sykes grimaced and nodded. "Hold on." Reece stepped out and asked Winston if it was okay to put him on the bedpan.

"Let me help," said Winston. "You doing okay over there with all them train wrecks?" He grabbed the bedpan and squirted baby powder on the rim.

"Rough day today. A code and then first admit." He pulled the foam wedge out and rolled Mr. Sykes onto his back. He bent one leg, while Winston bent the other.

"Push up," said Winston.

Mr. Sykes groaned and pushed with his good leg. Reece reached under and helped lift, and Winston pushed the bedpan in place.

"I'll give you a few minutes," said Winston. "Okay? Just do what you gotta do." He raised the head of the bed a bit more, and Reece followed him out of the room. "Thanks, man. There was a good-looking blonde asking for you earlier." He winked. "This man's granddaughter. You know her?"

"Yeah. I better head back before something happens." He looked around the unit, a mirror image of ICU, and saw Brad on the phone. Kristin was still in twelve with Mr. Odo.

He walked off the unit and turned the corner to the tiny waiting room, where he saw Maybell, Mrs. Sykes. She was sitting ramrod straight with her belly in her lap, wearing an old-fashioned dress with violets on it. She was squinching her eyes trying to make her glasses go up on her nose.

"Hey there," said Reece. He sat next to her in the maroon upholstered chair. Two others, a man and a woman, were there. A phone hung on the wall.

"Hey, buddy!" said Maybell. Her face broke into a smile. "We been hunting you. Did you see Elbert? We can't go back in until six o'clock, of all the blasted rules."

"Yeah, but maybe Kristin can sneak you in. Did you see her?"

"Sure did. I didn't realize she was a proper nurse and all. Cindy's around here somewhere, off to get coffee, I think. She drinks more coffee than a Turk." She laughed, and her top denture poked out. "But Lord, don't he look pitiful? I wonder if he'll ever be able to walk again?"

"I'd be surprised if he didn't. He's pretty hard-headed. The good news is he's stable." He patted her hand.

"Well, lookie what the horse drug up," and it was Cindy, wearing a short dress with short sleeves and a pair of heels. "I was afraid to come in and bother you. Did you see Pawpaw?"

"Here, take my seat. Yeah, I went in and said hey. He looks good, considering what could have happened."

"Yeah, you saved his life. That's what I told him."

Reece stood, and she moved closer. "No, the paramedics did. Not me. But anyway, he's okay for now, but he has a rough road ahead of him, learning to walk and talk again."

"Well, son, we sure appreciate what you did," said Maybell. She caught a tear with a Kleenex. "We surely do. You know we been married fifty years come next year? Lord, he's gonna miss that garden."

"He's a good guy," said Reece. "He'll pull through."

"You're so sweet," said Cindy. She looked as if she might

like to slow dance.

Kristin appeared in the doorway. "Oh, you found them. I thought maybe they'd left." She held a bag of normal saline, kneading it like dough.

"Oh, hey. Yep, found them." He just stood there, wondering why he'd even come out.

"That's a pretty dress," said Kristin. She meant the compliment for Maybell.

"Thank you, ma'am," said Cindy. She did a little twirl. The phone rang, and she answered it. "Hays family?" A man stood and took the phone.

They chatted a bit more, focusing on how Elbert would miss his trophy tomatoes and rows of silver queen corn. Reece excused himself to get back to the unit, and Kristin did the same, stopping outside the door to CCU.

"Well, you had to go looking for her, didn't you?" She rolled her eyes.

"They're like family. You know that." He held his hand over the bright steel door button.

"That's a good one. Okay, no fighting. I'm just tired, is all. At least she wasn't wearing a tube top."

Reece looked defeated. "Yeah, no fighting. Okay, I better go. He looked at his watch. Only another half hour." He pushed the button, realizing too late that she wanted him to kiss her. "Hey, I'll come over tonight? What about that?"

"If that's in your busy schedule." She made a feeble smile.

"Stop, really?" he said, deciding that now wasn't the best time to ask about the slideshow with Emma.

Exhausted, Reece showered and headed back to Kristin's house. He'd called Emma, but no one had answered. He just wanted to go to bed and sleep. A few times that day at work, he'd had a creeping sensation, as if he was about to have a seizure, kind of like trying to sneeze. He drove down Old Springville Road past a housing development where several homes were being rebuilt following the tornado. His head nodded, and he yawned, wondering if they would make out, which seemed to be becoming routine. He got a little thrill, thinking about how aggressive Kristin could be. He would have never suggested she give him a blowjob. That had been her idea. There was a flower shop along the way, and he stopped.

He crossed the road and pulled in. A woman was at the door, turning the sign from open to closed, but she opened up for him.

"Sorry," said Reece. He walked into the cool room filled with decorative pots and stands of flowers.

"Not a problem. What are you looking for?" She was in her forties with long brown hair and dimples.

"Yellow daisies, if you have them. Just a bunch. How much are they?"

"Yeah, we got lots of daisies. I can give you a bunch for $8.99. How's that?"

Reece had a ten. "Sounds perfect." He followed her to a refrigerated locker.

She wrapped them in green paper with a red bow around the middle. Reece took his flowers and was on his way, feeling that he had done a good thing. Soon, he was pulling into the steep driveway.

He jumped out with his flowers and knocked on the

door. Gert answered.

"Did you bring her daisies? She loves daisies. That's so nice." She gave him a rare smile. Reece followed her up the stairs. "Kristin! Reece is here," and she disappeared.

Reece made eye contact with Edwin in the den and had to go in. "Hey."

"Hello, young man. How are you?" He turned down the TV volume. "Got you some flowers, I see. Are they for me?" He looked dead serious.

Reece laughed. "Yeah, and I want a big kiss." He waited for Edwin to laugh, but he didn't. He kept standing, waiting for Kristin.

Robyn came into the den. "Yes, a smart man. Are they for me?" She laughed.

Reece grinned. "I guess they're for everybody." He took out one and gave it to her.

"Hey!" said Kristin. "Those are for me. Put it back, sister." She wore a clay facial and looked like she might audition for a play. "You're supposed to be gone, anyway."

"Nope. He gave it to me." Robyn took her flower and hurried to the kitchen.

"Sorry," said Reece. "She just seemed so sad."

"Well, she is sad," said Kristin. She took the flowers and gave him a long kiss, making Edwin squirm in his recliner.

"Maybe y'all can move or sit down," said Edwin. He was watching the news.

Reece took a seat on the couch, while Kristin put her flowers in a vase. He wanted to say, "What's up, old man?" Instead, he turned his attention to the news, a piece about a Crimson Tide defensive back hurt in practice. He wondered at the luxury of being able to be concerned about an injured football player versus being worried that your whole family might have malaria or typhus.

There was no coffee table in the den, and Kristin put the vase on top of the TV. Reece and Edwin made eye contact and nearly spoke at once.

"That's a bad idea, honey," said Edwin. "Water on the TV."

"I knew you would say that." Kristin was in soft jeans and a pink scrub top that was too big.

"Put them on the table," said Gert from the kitchen. She was making stir-fried broccoli with beef strips and rice. In the oven, a peach cobbler bubbled.

Kristin did as told. Walter was scratching and whining at the back door, and she let him in. Walter ran to Reece and jumped on his legs.

"Hey, buddy," and he rubbed his head.

Kristin fell onto the couch beside him with a big smile. "Reece had a tough day." She snuggled against him, and he put his arm around her. "Didn't you?"

"Sort of." He could tell that Edwin wasn't listening, but knew that Gert was. "Busy for sure. I'm so sleepy. Nearly fell asleep coming over."

"Poor baby," said Kristin.

Robyn waltzed in, wearing a blue one-piece bathing suit. Reece raised his eyebrows. "What do y'all think? My new suit. I'm going to Gulf Shores in the morning."

"Robyn, can you give it a rest?" asked Kristin. "Good Lord, just go."

"Robyn?" asked Edwin.

Reece could see where she'd shaved. "Looks good."

Kristin smacked him on the leg as Robyn did a slow

turn. "Not as good as me, though." She stood, but Robyn zipped into the hall, laughing.

"Hey, I brought *you* flowers. You look cute in that pink top."

"That's better," said Kristin. "I'd take it off, but Daddy's here."

Reece held a straight face. "Yeah, a tough day." A breaking story about an armed robbery was on, and everyone turned their attention to the TV.

Soon, supper was ready, and everyone gathered at the table with Robyn back in shorts and a long white t-shirt. Reece knew Edwin would ask him to say the blessing, and he did. Reece made it short and sweet as usual. He wasn't too sure about the broccoli, but took some. It was crunchy, which surprised him.

"Real good sauce," said Reece. "I guess in Ethiopia, you'd call this a wot, except we would have enjera with it instead of rice."

No one commented.

"Tastes delicious, honey," said Edwin. He paused and smiled at her.

"Did you tell Reece about the hope chest?" asked Gert. She fluttered her eyelashes.

"A hope chest?" asked Reece.

"For when we get married, silly," said Kristin. "To put blankets and linens in. Mom bought me one."

"Every girl needs a hope chest," said Gert. "I had one. It's still in the bedroom. Ordered it from Sears." She balanced a piece of broccoli on her fork.

Reece nodded his approval. "I guess that makes sense."

Robyn laughed. "Feel the pressure?"

"Of course it makes sense," said Kristin. "You know we

have to talk about the details, the invitations, the caterer, what church we want it to be at. I'd like for us to do it at my church, but Mom has her own ideas."

Reece listened, wondering if he would have any say in the matter.

"Well," said Gert. "There is this lovely lady at church, Mrs. Gillespie, and she's volunteered to let us use her house. She lives in Mountain Brook in a pretty old house. She's practically told me she won't have it any other way."

"Oh," said Reece. "Do you know her?" He looked at Kristin.

"I've met her. She's nice," said Kristin. "It would be cheaper to do it that way."

"Huh," said Reece. He hadn't thought about who would pay for everything. "I think Horace and Dora were thinking about their church. But it's good to have options." He glanced at Kristin with a blank look.

"That's just a little country church," said Kristin. "The house is in Mountain Brook. Mom says it's perfect."

"She's a very nice lady," said Edwin.

Reece thought. "I guess that sounds fine about the house. But then maybe we could get my pastor to do the service there. The church was very supportive of me. They were like my sponsor for Ethiopia."

Gert tapped her plate with her fork and looked at Edwin for guidance.

"Well," said Edwin. "Let's think about it. I guess we should let you two make that decision."

"Perfect," said Kristin. "We'll decide. Maybe my pastor would do it, but I think the church charges. I'd have to check."

"Well, you always pay the preacher," said Gert. "No

matter who it is. Our pastor will do it, and we'd give him a hundred dollars."

"Huh." Reece let the scene of the excommunication at their church play through his head and kept quiet. He and Kristin could work it out. "This beef is tasty. Did you use soy sauce?"

Gert seemed annoyed. "Yes, and some garlic salt."

"I'm getting excited talking about this," said Kristin. "Are we going to write our vows? I think we should. And I want a violin player at the house."

"A violin?" asked Reece.

"Well, you'll need music," said Gert. "Mrs. Gillespie's nephew plays violin."

Reece could see how it was going to be and nodded. "Looks like it's in the bag."

Robyn laughed. "You're in the bag."

Kristin gave her a sharp look. "Oh, shut up, jealous. No-body'll ever marry you. You hussy." She slapped her with a cloth napkin.

Robyn took it in stride. "I'm just saying." She winked at Reece, but he didn't catch it.

After the peach cobbler, everyone scattered. Edwin went back to the TV, and Gert cleaned up the dining room and kitchen. Kristin took Reece into the living room and onto the plastic-covered couch. It made a crinkle noise when he sat, and soon made his back sweat.

"You know you're lucky that Mom is so involved. She'll do a great job."

"Are we hiring her?"

"No, silly. She just wants to help. I'm the first one getting married, and she wants it to be special, and so do I.

You'd marry me in a barn if I let you. Here, let me scratch your back, big boy."

Reece could never pass on a back scratch and leaned forward. The feel of Kristin's nails on his skin felt great. "I suppose. If you say so. I'd just imagined my family, Horace and Dora, being more involved." He arched his back as she ran her fingers down his spine. "Mmm."

"Well, what have you done so far? Not much. Somebody has to get this thing going."

"I suppose," said Reece. He was lost in the back scratch. "I'm fine with it, but not their preacher."

"What about the marriage counselor we went to before you left?"

"Heck no. He was so creepy in his dark blue suit. Reminded me of the KGB." He tilted his shoulder.

"Well, your preacher is so old."

"No, he's not. He might be sixty," said Reece.

"No, he has to be seventy."

"What does it matter?"

"I don't know. I want Mom to be happy."

Reece relaxed his neck. "We don't have to decide tonight, right?"

"When will we decide? I'll keep scratching your back."

Reece felt like Esau selling his birthright to Jacob for a pot of stew. "Whatever. I mean, okay. Let Gert decide. But we have to have some part in this, right?"

"Of course. We'll be the highlight of the wedding. We'll write our own vows. Nobody can do that but us, right?"

"What if my parents were still alive? How would we work that out?"

Kristin stopped scratching. "Of course, we would have

included them. But...they're not here. I'm sorry."

"Yeah, I guess. So, I'll write my vows. Do you have to see them ahead of time? Do I see yours?"

"No, that'll be part of the magic. The preacher will see them, but that's all. Oh, Reece, I'm getting excited." She lowered her voice. "I just wish we hadn't had sex..."

Reece gave her a sly look. "I don't. It was great."

"You're a bad boy," and they cuddled on the couch.

At nine, Reece was ready to go. He'd not had the nerve to ask Kristin about the slideshow, and said he needed to get home and get in bed. He felt like a slimeball just thinking about asking her, but he was compelled and confused. He drove home with the windows down, the warm air whipping through the cab, cicadas roaring in the trees. Reece felt he was in a box, being opened by different people. One of his headlights went out, and he worried about being pulled over, so he put on his high beams.

"Lord, look what the cat drug in," said Dora. She was sitting in her recliner next to Chester in his. The small table with the lone lamp separated them.

"You need to get some rest, boy," said Horace, looking up from his *National Geographic*. "You look mighty tired."

"That's for sure." Reece sat on the love seat in front of the AC unit, blowing cold air on the back of his head.

"How's Kristin?" Dora combed her thin hair with a pick, already dressed for bed in a light-blue satin gown.

"She's good. Getting the wedding planned." He sighed.

"You don't seem too happy about it," said Dora.

"It's just that her mom wants to handle everything. Wants us to get married in her friend's house." He ran his fingers through his hair, feeling the oil.

"What? Not a church? Well, that beats all," said Dora.

"I guess it's gonna be her private little party with her friends."

"Oh, that can't be true," said Horace. He fiddled with his hearing aid, making it squeal.

"True enough," said Reece. "But that takes some of the pressure off of me, I suppose."

"Don't just let her run over you, boy," said Dora. She laid down her pick and took up a pair of tweezers, going for some hairs on her upper lip.

"I'm not. I guess I'm just overwhelmed with work and everything. I do need to make a phone call. And I know you're gonna say not to."

"You want to call that Emma, don't you?" Dora looked at Horace over the little table. "You're playing with fire, son."

"She wants me to help her with a slideshow at her church. Plus, I can borrow some of her slides for my talk, too." He waited, but no one spoke. He stood and went to the phone, took it, and reached up to dial.

Emma, wearing pajamas, was curled up with Sarah on the couch when the phone rang. Her heart slipped into her throat, and she spilled a bowl of popcorn.

"Lord, girl. It's just the phone." Sarah turned down the volume on the TV movie.

Emma bypassed the nearest phone, ran into the kitchen, and answered. "Hello?" She adjusted her bra.

"Hey! It's me."

"Hey there! I was worried you wouldn't be able to call."

"Just a long day. Had a code and was first admit on day shift."

"Yeah, that's rough. Did the patient make it?" She sat at the table.

Reece told her about Mrs. Laramore, the code, and the intubation, then about Mr. Riggins, who'd fallen from the ladder. Then he told her about the neighbor, Mr. Sykes, who'd had a stroke. He left out the parts about Cindy.

"Lord, that's a lot. Maybe tomorrow will be a better day, less stressful. But I can tell I'm already missing it." She laughed. She wondered if he'd seen Kristin, if they ate lunch together at the hospital.

"What do you think you'll do about work?" asked Reece.

"I'm thinking about home health care. Maybe something different. I think it would remind me most of the clinic. Being autonomous and all." She pushed a full ashtray back and forth.

"I hadn't thought about that," said Reece.

"There's a bunch of agencies in Birmingham."

"Huh, let me know how it goes. So, I'm calling about the slideshow. I'd like to see what you have."

"And I'd like to show you what I have." She smiled. "I mean, I have about fifty slides and then a bunch of photos, some with you in them. Yeah, I'd like to show them to you. When's a good time? Did you ask Kristin about it?"

"I saw her today, but the time wasn't right. She'll understand, I'm pretty sure."

"Do you think I should show the slide of me leaving from the airport, or should I just dive right into the slides from over there?" She felt a little breathless.

"I think you should just start over there. Maybe start with the clinic in Gundo Meskel and then work your way up to when you left Godo."

"Yeah, that's pretty straightforward. I'm so glad you can do it. I'm staying at Sally's during the day for a while, but I'm back here by four." How about tomorrow, Thursday? Or maybe Friday? We're having the family over that day, which you're invited to."

"Oh," said Reece. "I'll have to check, you know, with Kristin. Maybe let's shoot for Friday, around six?"

"Yeah, that sounds super." Emma picked up a half-smoked cigarette and put it to her lips. "So, do you guys eat lunch together? I mean, you get to see her on the unit."

Reece paused. "I had to skip lunch today, but we did yesterday."

Emma nodded to her mom and put her hand over the receiver. "It's Reece." Sarah nodded and went for the last cup of coffee in the pot. "After we eat, we can look at slides. Some of them are kind of gross, pictures of leg sores, you know."

Reece laughed. "Yeah, they'll get a kick out of those. I'd

show them. Makes it more real."

"Yeah, it was real for sure." Emma felt she was running out of words. "So, how's the grandparents. I'd love to meet them."

"They're fine, just eavesdropping is all."

"Yeah, Mom's in here too, trying to act busy." She waved Sarah away and laughed. "Drinking her coffee. I don't know how she sleeps."

"I don't know if I'll be able to come to your talk, though. I'm sure Kristin wants me to go to church with her. That morning, I'm going to church with my grandparents."

"Really? I'd just assumed that maybe both of you would come. She'd do that, right?"

Sarah went onto the carport to smoke. The screen door whooshed behind her and slammed.

"Huh," said Reece. "Maybe, but I'm not sure. She's pretty touchy these days."

Emma held her tongue. "It's just church, though. Mission work." Emma heard Reece cough.

"True. I'll work on her. I promise. I'd love to hear what you have to say."

"Do you think I should wear my scrubs or just dress like regular?" Emma stood and leaned against the Formica counter.

"I think regular clothes would be fine. You might have someone want you to check their blood pressure otherwise."

"That's what I was thinking." Emma swung the long phone cord like a jump rope.

And they talked for another hour, reminiscing about Godo, wondering how the team was doing, what would become of the clinic and its store of medicines, the classy bottles of Icelandic IV fluid with the red stoppers. Reece said he had to go, that he couldn't keep his eyes open, and Emma understood.

"Goodbye, Reece."

"Night, Emma."

Emma dropped the phone onto the hook, grabbed a glass of ice water, and pushed outside to the carport. A dozen moths were swarming the light fixture.

"Lord, Lord, Emma. You and this Reece," said Sarah.

"It's all good." She pulled up a folding chair and slapped a mosquito. "He's coming over Friday to help me with the slideshow."

"We got the family coming over that day, remember?" White smoke trailed from her cigarette.

"Yeah, maybe some of them will be around when he comes. He said six. I think I'll take him to the Seafood Box." She thrummed her fingers on the aluminum armrest.

"Emma, we'll have barbecue galore left over. Just let him eat here."

"Maybe you're right," said Emma. "We always get too much."

"What all do you need help with for this slideshow? I'd like to see it, so I'll come."

"I don't know, Momma, just helping to pick the slides, plus I want to show him. He's in some of them. Kristin won't let him come over just to visit, so this is more legitimate, more practical." She swatted another mosquito. "If we were in Ethiopia at this elevation, we'd get malaria."

"Didn't you have malaria over there, when they put you

in the hospital?"

"No, they thought it was dengue fever. I thought I was going to die. Hurt like hell. They call it break-bone fever for a reason. Other folks got malaria. But they're both spread by mosquitoes. I had this red rash all over my body."

"Oh, baby girl, you are so lucky."

"The worst, though, was the amoebiasis. God, that put me down fast. I couldn't eat or drink for days. Makes me want to vomit thinking about it. Plus, I had it twice. I lost about fifteen pounds the first time."

"No wonder you're so skinny. But we'll get you fat." Sarah laughed and coughed, phlegm roiling in her chest.

"Well, not fat. Just back to maybe one-twenty. That seems to be a good weight." She was wearing her half smile in the dim light. "Anyway, I'd love for you to come on Sunday night. Reece might make it. Not sure just yet."

"So, you'll see him Friday and Sunday? That fiancée of his will have a fit, and can't say that I blame her." She ground out her butt and tapped out another cigarette.

"But you like him, right?"

"Well, of course I like him. Seems real nice, plus he helped you out over there. I'll sing the praises of anyone who helped get you back home in one piece."

"I just have this nagging feeling that he's not ready to get married, like maybe he's made a mistake. I mean, Kristin is pretty and nice and all, but he's too young to get married."

"I got married when I was seventeen, baby girl. How old is he, about your age?"

"Yep, twenty-two, I think. Sometimes I doubt if I'll ever get married." She caught a mosquito mid-flight and then let it go.

"There's plenty of time," said Sarah. "What about that boy at church you was dating before you left? He seemed nice."

Emma sort of frowned. "Oh, Nathan? He collects belt buckles, if that means anything. And wears them. He's a bit of an odd duck."

"There's a million fish in the sea. No need to get fixated on just one, especially now. You need to be free to get your life back on track."

"What are you, a counselor?" Emma laughed and waved away smoke from her eyes.

"I'm your wise old mother. Mosquitoes biting my ankles. Let's get back inside. Maybe that movie is still on."

"Let me show you some more pictures," said Emma. She followed her mom into the house and walked upstairs to her room for the box of photos. Back downstairs, she took her place on the couch.

"Now, don't show me anything that'll make me sick." The TV volume was turned down, and Sarah left it that way.

"Here's an old woman. I just love her look, like she's survived a thousand disasters. Look at that tooth sticking out." The frail woman looked to be eighty, even though she was fifty. She had eleven children, four of whom had died, one during the famine.

"That dress she's wearing looks so rough, and that rag on her head." Sarah held the photo toward the overhead light. "She does look patient."

"Here's one. Check out his straw hat. He had tapeworms. I took this one at the clinic in Gundo Meskel."

"He's a young one. Skin looks smooth and healthy. How'd you know he had tapeworms?" Sarah frowned.

"It was always the same, headache and stomachache. Plus, he saw them in his stool. We gave them a drug, niclosamide, but sometimes they'd sell it."

"I guess they needed the money to buy food."

"Probably," said Emma. "Here's one with the grain stacked in the warehouse. The two guys in the picture worked with me."

Sarah nodded and looked at each photo as Emma handed them to her. Most of the images were of men and women dressed in rags. When Emma showed her one of a baby's prolapsed rectum, she said that was enough, that she needed to get to bed.

"Okay. Night, Momma." She hugged her and resumed looking at the photos, wondering if Reece was asleep, wondering if he'd ever dreamed about her. She'd dreamed about him, but only about the night he was shot. In one dream, they had been having sex on her cot when a bullet somehow found him. He'd collapsed on top of her, blood soaking her pillow. She shuddered and opened a box of slides, holding them up to the light.

By Friday, Reece still hadn't broached the topic of the slide-show with Kristin. Mr. Riggins was on a cooling blanket, his core temp hovering at 105 degrees. A doctor had placed a central line for all of his IVs. Mrs. Laramore was still on the ventilator, but the antibiotics seemed to be helping with her secretions. Her lungs were still noisy, but Reece was getting less and less when he suctioned the tube.

It was ten, and he'd promised Emma that he'd be over around six. He adjusted the sheet over Mr. Riggins and then pushed a bolus of Decadron to help with the brain swelling. Things were calm, and it was now or never.

Reece took a deep breath and entered CCU through the adjoining door. Kristin was in Mr. Odo's room, and Reece peeked around the curtain. "Hey."

"Hey, what's up? Doesn't he look good?" She had just shaved Mr. Odo and was about to re-pack his jaw wounds.

"Hey there, Mr. Odo," said Reece. "You look ten years younger."

"Got me...a good nurse. Shaved me up real good." Mr. Odo managed a crooked smile."

Kristin patted Mr. Odo on the back. "I'm going back out, but push the button if you need anything? Okay?"

Mr. Odo nodded.

Reece followed her to the long black desk and sat beside her. "How's Mr. Myers doing? I'm gonna say hey before I head back. Just had some downtime."

Kristin smiled and charted. "You look nervous. Everything okay? My other patient is on a bedpan, so need to check on her soon."

"I don't mean to interrupt if you need to go." His throat felt dry, and he licked his lips. "I did need to ask you something, though."

Kristin nodded, still writing in her swirling cursive. "What about?"

"Well," said Reece. "Emma...needs me to come over tonight and help her with the presentation she's giving at church on Sunday."

She dropped her pen. "Reece, no! We've talked about this. If you go over there one more time, my parents will disown you, and maybe me too."

"Think of it like...Bible study. Just looking at slides is all." He watched her stand and leave. "Damn." He followed her to four and peered around the curtain. A tiny elderly lady sat on a bedpan. "Can we talk when you're through?" But Kristin was talking to her patient. She didn't even glance at him.

Reece felt a poke, and Winston had just passed by. Reece waved, wondering what to do, and walked over to say hey to Mr. Sykes.

Kristin had left without saying anything to him. Reece jumped out of the truck, seeing Dora and Chester in the yard cleaning corn. He walked that way, avoiding the spray of the hose on dull yellow ears.

"What a mess!" said Dora. "We could buy corn, but he has to have it this way."

"Hey, son," said Horace. He was hosing the corn, and then Clara was going over it with a vegetable brush.

Reece sat in the swing beside her. He needed to leave in

an hour to make it to Emma's by six. "Can I help?"

"Yes, pick up those corn shucks if you don't mind. Looks like a bomb went off."

Reece took a white plastic bucket and picked up the bright green shucks, getting his tennis shoes wet.

"Thank you," said Dora. "You staying for dinner?"

Reece leaned against a pine tree and looked up. "Actually, no."

"Having dinner with Kristin's folks?"

"No, I'm gonna drive down and help Emma with a slideshow for her church. Probably eat there."

"Reece, you're not. Does Kristin know?" Horace couldn't hear over the sound of the spray.

"Well, she knows, sort of. She's not happy about it."

"Reece, you're gonna lose her if you're not careful."

"Gonna lose who?" asked Horace.

"Oh, nothing," said Reece.

"He's going down to see that Emma."

"Uh oh." Horace grimaced and hosed more corn.

"I need to leave at five, maybe before then. Rush hour traffic." He wiggled off a chunk of pine bark and looked at it.

"You do the right thing by her, now. You hear me?" said Dora, scrubbing the corn. Next, they would cut it off the ear and bag it for freezing.

"I just wish everyone wouldn't get so excited about Emma. We're just good friends. I deserve to have a good friend."

"Maybe, but she's competition regardless," said Clara. "I don't blame Kristin for getting on your case."

"Okay, but I'm gonna get a shower. I'll call Kristin

before I go." He dreaded doing it and went inside. Green beans cooked in the pressure cooker, whistling steam. He looked at the phone, and it looked back at him. He should go ahead and call before he showered. *Get it over with.* He sighed and dialed each number, pausing between them.

"Hello?" It was Gert.

"It's Reece. Is Kristin there?"

"Um, yeah, but...well, just hold on."

Reece sat at the table and waited. He was hungry and went to the cabinet for an oatmeal cream pie. There was only one left, and he took it. He could hear talking in the background.

"Reece?" It was Kristin.

"Hey. I just—"

"If you called to say you're going down there, then I'm hanging up."

"No, wait, don't do that. Look, I just need your okay, is all. This is a unique situation. Yeah, we're friends, but that's all."

"So, are you going? You're not getting my approval, by the way."

Reece sighed. "I guess I am. I just wanted to be honest with you." And then there was the dial tone. "Dammit." He hung up the phone and went to get a shower.

Dressed in jeans and a green pullover, Reece backed out of the driveway. Every foot he traveled seemed like a foot away from Kristin. He felt he was doing irreparable damage to their relationship, but was compelled to see Emma. He hit the steering wheel and shook his head. Why was he being such a dumb ass? But why couldn't Emma be his friend? They had a powerful connection that couldn't be ignored. He hoped that time would take care of every-thing, then realized he was doing fifty in a thirty-five and slowed. He would just focus on the next hour as it came, and then the next.

Nearly deaf from the wind whipping through the open windows, he exited and soon passed the Waffle House where they had danced. Turning into her driveway, there were several cars and a truck. People on the carport. He figured everyone would be gone by now and prepared to meet more of Emma's family. She was walking out to meet him, wearing cut-off jeans and a t-shirt tied in a knot at her side. She was barefoot.

"Hey! Come meet the family!"

Reece stepped out and let her hug him. "Wow, the whole world is here."

Takeout from Duck's Barbecue covered a table on the carport. All eyes were watching as they approached. Sally came toward him with open arms. Reece let her squeeze him.

"Wow."

"Hey, boy, glad you could make it! Come meet the gang. Mostly the ladies, but you'll meet the men soon enough."

And then Emma was holding his hand, leading him forward. She stopped at the edge of the carport with ev-eryone watching as she went down the list of names. "Sit-ting in the chairs, that's Mindy and Debbie." They waved at Reece. "Over here is Amanda, and she works at the zoo, and Greta and Rhonda." They all smiled and waved. A man with red hair approached with his hand out. "And this here is Sammy, Sally's husband."

"Hey, Reece," said Sammy. "Heard a lot about you." He

gripped Reece's hand.

Reece just nodded. "You work at the quarry?"

"That's me."

"Strong hands," said Reece.

Sammy swatted him on the back.

A woman larger than the rest came through the screen door. She had short hair, kind of like a man's. "Reece, I'm Debbie. Heard so much about you." She glanced at the scars on his head. "I'm the sensible one, by the way. The rest are crazy as bats." She laughed.

Emma then led him around to meet the others, all standing and hugging him. He felt like the star of a big birthday party. Sarah pushed through the screen door. "Hey, boy. Glad you could make it." She gave Reece a side hug.

"Yeah, thanks for having me." Reece waved at Heather, who was curled up in a chair. "Nice to meet everyone."

"Randy's not here. He's in Austin, too good for us Alabama crackers." Emma squeezed his hand and let go. "You eat yet?"

"No, not yet. Looks great. Is this from your mom's place?"

"Yep, best barbecue in town. Fix a plate. The tea and soft drinks are there. I'll fix your drink. What do you want?"

"Sweet tea is fine," said Reece. He picked up a stiff paper plate and gazed at the food: ribs, potato salad, vinegar slaw, a coconut cream pie, and what looked to be a key lime pie with one slice left.

Mindy joined them at the table. She had long black hair and a deep tan. "I work at the State Park in Gulf Shores. You like the beach?" She took a half slice of coconut cream pie.

He wanted to say that was where his honeymoon would be, but didn't. "That's cool. What do you do there?" He took two ribs.

"I'm the restaurant manager. Been there for five years. Emma loves coming down. You should come sometime." She left him there before he could respond.

"Yeah, Mindy's at the park," said Emma. "Debbie works at a savings and loan. Sally, well, she's lazy and doesn't work. I told you that Amanda works at the zoo. Rhonda over there works at Red Lobster, and Greta is a beautician, got her own place."

"Hey," said Sally, "I have to keep up with Sammy and Heather. That's a full-time job, sister." She jabbed Emma in the side, and Emma poked her back.

"Here, sit a spell," said Emma. She led him to an empty chair beside Amanda. "Watch her, though. She works in the snake house."

Reece sat with his full plate and glass of tea, trying to balance everything. Sammy pulled around a small bench made of redwood-stained pine for Emma and sat with her.

"It's good to have another guy around," said Sammy. He looked mischievous in general, kind of like Emma.

Reece nodded, tearing off some rib meat with his fork.

"Look, Reece is eating ribs with a fork!" said Emma. "He's a dandy."

Everyone laughed.

"Use your fingers, boy," said Sammy. "You're in Hueytown, not New York City."

Reece laughed. "In Ethiopia, we always ate with our hands." He picked up the rib and took a bite.

"Hey, Emma's got a slideshow for us. You gonna stay, right?" asked Amanda.

"Of course he is," said Sally.

"Yeah," said Reece. "I was gonna help her with it." He glanced at Emma.

"Well, there's the home version and the church version. I've got one of Teresa breastfeeding her baby. Remember her?" asked Kristin. "The administrator Ben's wife."

"How could I forget? It seemed every time I went over, she was breastfeeding. Just seemed kind of weird, but that's neither here nor there," said Reece. "Maybe I'd do the same thing."

Sally laughed. "Emma said you could do most anything. I guess she's right."

Reece smiled. He felt so damn welcome. Why couldn't it be that way with Gert and Edwin? He wondered if they'd excommunicate him from the family. He leaned back in his chair and tried to relax.

"Hey, y'all leave that last piece of key lime pie for Reece, you hear?" asked Sarah. "It's our specialty at the barbecue."

"Uh oh, he's got Sarah on his side," said Sammy. "That's saying something. Took me years."

"He's a nice young man," said Sarah. "I appreciate all he did for Emma over there." Her voice cracked just a bit, and she pulled out her cigarettes.

"A real lifesaver," said Emma. She reached over and rubbed his shoulder.

"How's your fiancée?" asked Sarah.

The carport got quiet. Just the sound of cicadas and crickets, a few mosquitoes.

"Well, Kristin. She's okay. Just working day shift at Carraway." Reece waited for the next question.

"You should have brought her," said Mindy, her voice inflected with just a bit of sarcasm.

"She might come to Emma's church on Sunday night," said Reece. "She couldn't make it tonight."

"She kind of hates me," said Emma.

"I wouldn't say that," said Reece.

"All's fair in love and war," said Sally.

Reece felt entwined and insulated, like the core of a golf ball. "Don't tell Kristin that. She might buy a gun." He tried to laugh. He wanted to put his arm around Emma and pull her close.

"See, I told you," said Emma. "Oh, we're just buds, is all, fresh from the battlefield."

Everyone chatted back and forth, picking over the disappearing food. Sammy had brought a bottle of blackberry brandy and was passing it around, campfire style. Most just kept passing it, but Reece had a few swigs and was feeling buzzed. Sammy had whispered a few things in his ear that caught him off guard. The light began to dim before Reece realized it was eight o'clock, his target time to leave, but Emma had the slideshow, and inside they went, everybody squeezing onto the sofa and chairs, some sitting on the floor. Reece sat at the end next to Sally, who put her arm around him. He could smell a faintness of underarm odor.

The off-white wall opposite them was blank and would serve as the screen. Emma snapped the carousel of slides onto the projector that sat on a wooden TV tray and turned it on. Someone turned off the lamp, and a new bottle of brandy began making the rounds. Sally took a sip and handed it to Reece. He didn't need more but took a swallow anyway and passed it over to Emma, who was sitting in a table chair. She took a small sip, coughed, and on it went.

A bright square of light hit the wall at a slight angle. "All right, here we go," said Emma, and the first slide was of her at the airport, wearing a red power suit and a white ruffled blouse with family gathered around her. Her sisters murmured like roosting hens, commenting on what a sad day that had been.

The next slide was of Emma standing outside the guest house at the Baptist Mission compound in Addis Ababa. "That's Tesfaw beside me. He was the office manager. He had polio as a child and walked with crutches."

"Guest house looks nice," said Sarah. "Did you have electricity?"

"Most of the time," said Emma, "although it would go off in the afternoon." She cycled through a few more slides, including one of Teresa breastfeeding, which got some remarks. "This is the helicopter we rode in upcountry. The pilot's name is Terry."

"Oh, he's good-looking," said Mindy.

Emma laughed. "Yeah, but so is his wife."

"Shucks," said Mindy.

"Now, we're in Gundo Meskel. This was before we built the clinic, and we slept in tents. There were three of us nurses: me, Jill, and Dot. That's Jill there, her fiancée killed himself, and that's a team of six English-speaking guys from Addis Ababa." The next few slides were of the team and of stony-looking men in tattered clothes carrying hundred-pound sacks of grain from a German C160. "Look at the veins popping on their calves."

"That's a lot of food," said Debbie. "Amazing. Was it just the Germans?"

"No," said Emma. "We had deliveries from the British and Polish as well. By December, we were getting food in trucks from Assab up on the Red Sea. Here was our first clinic."

A slide of a white tent with the front open, Jill and Dot inside. A slide of a Polish soldier. A slide of an old priest with a fly swatter and a heavy Orthodox cross around his neck. A slide of worried-looking children, standing, shading their eyes with their hands.

"What did you treat mainly?" asked Amanda. "Besides giving out food."

Emma spoke like an old pro. "Oh, mainly diarrhea and worms. Reece can tell you about that. Right?"

Reece nodded and said, "Yeah." He gripped the edge of the couch with one hand and held the brandy with the other, just an arm's length from Emma. Each slide amazed him, wondering at how much more Emma had seen than he had, and he felt bad for having left so soon.

"It didn't take the people long to build us a clinic with poles and tin roofing." A slide of the structure, and then one where it was daubed and painted white. "That was a blessing, but not as much as the house they built for us." A slide of a rectangular house, about twice the size of the one in Godo.

"Why does everyone have a gun?" asked Debbie.

"For protection," said Emma. "You had to pretty much take care of yourself against thieves and hyenas."

Emma progressed through the slides, coming to Godo after about an hour. "Here's my sweet little house in Godo. Tell them about the shintabet, Reece." Emma reached back and patted him on the leg.

Reece thought for a moment. "Yeah, the toilet seat was cemented into the floor." He laughed. "They just didn't know what to do with it, I suppose." He felt he was becoming one with the couch and with the room.

Emma ended the slideshow with an image of Reece, the one where he was stooped over a small boy irrigating his ear with peroxide. Everyone wanted to know what he was doing, and he told the story about the boy who had gone deaf. Everyone groaned at the part about the flies, pus, and wax. And then there was the bright square of light, the projector humming to keep the bulb cool.

"Dang, that was something," said Mindy. "I can't believe that was you over there."

Emma smiled, thrilled at being able to share her trials and tribulations with her family and Reece.

"You didn't get any pictures of me after I was shot, did you?" asked Reece.

Emma paused. "No slides, but I do have a couple of photos of you on a makeshift stretcher. You don't want to see it."

Reece just nodded, even though he wanted to see them.

"How long were you there before you were shot?" asked Debbie. "That must have been just awful."

"About two months, I think," said Reece. He wondered if his words were slurred. Just as he realized that it must be ten o'clock, the phone rang on the lamp table beside him. Emma turned and answered it.

"Hello..." She put the phone to her chest. "Oh Lord, Reece, it's Kristin." She handed him the phone. He'd given her Emma's number as a show of faith.

Reece looked around at the faces watching him. No one spoke, as if waiting for the lions to be released.

Kristin had been crying on the couch for over an hour when she called Reece, holding the piece of torn church bulletin with Emma's number on it. Edwin had gone to bed, and Robyn was in Gulf Shores.

"Reece, what are you doing? It's after ten and you're still there. And don't tell me you're working on a slideshow." She wiped her nose with a tissue.

"Hey, I'm sorry. Her family is here. We were looking at slides. I swear."

"Reece," and she hiccupped, "if you don't leave right now, we're through. My parents are ready to kill you." She glanced at Gert, who was nodding, a frown on her face.

"Okay, okay, I will. Just hold on. We just finished...with the slides. I think you'd like to see them."

"No, I don't! Don't you get it? I want to forget that place exists. We were just fine until you went over there and got hurt."

"Yeah, but I'm back, a better person for it. A miracle, right?"

"You sound funny. Have you been drinking? Do not tell me that you've been drinking." She locked eyes with Gert.

"Not much, just a little. Sammy brought some brandy. It's made from wine. I'm not drunk, if that's what you mean."

"I knew it. How are you going to drive back? You can't spend the night there, although I'm sure you'd like to. Reece, we have to get back in counseling asap to make this thing work."

"I'm fine, and I'm leaving right now. Do you want me to come by? I don't have to work tomorrow, although they asked me to."

Kristin pulled her hair. "Yes, of course I do. This should have been a date night for us, but you're down there whooping it up with a bunch of strangers."

"Okay, look, you'll have to let me go so I can leave. I'll stop by, maybe in fifty minutes or so. Okay?"

Kristin took a deep breath. "And tell Emma no more visits. Got it? I'm dead serious this time." She tugged at the lapel of her oversized flannel shirt. "Reece?"

"Fine, fine. Look, I'm going now. Okay? The longer we talk—" but the line went dead.

Kristin stormed into the kitchen, looking for food. She found a biscuit from that morning and got out the butter and syrup, and then popped the whole thing into the microwave for twenty seconds.

"Honey, just calm down," said Gert. "At least he's honest with you."

"But can you believe he was drinking with her? Some missionary. He'd never even had alcohol before he went over there, and now he's buying it, drinking it, getting drunk. God, what's happened to him, Mom?" She checked her watch, counting the minutes.

"It's a mystery to me. I guess you're lucky that he's alive, but he can't be seeing her anymore. I totally agree. She just sounds like trouble."

"Maybe she'll go back over there. God, that would be a relief." She wolfed down the warm, gooey biscuit and went to the fridge for some iced tea. "Do we have any ice cream?"

"Honey, just slow down. Don't eat so much. It's late." Gert busied herself in the fridge, moving things around. "Why don't you watch TV till he gets here? Just keep the volume down."

"I don't want to watch the damn TV." She went to the sink, washed her sticky fingers, and then opened the fridge. She grabbed the vanilla ice cream and then a spoon.

"Get a bowl at least," said Gert. She fished a bowl from the drying rack, and Kristin took it.

Kristin went into the den and shooed Walter from Edwin's recliner. He dropped onto the floor, puzzled and yawning. "Sorry, buddy." She checked her watch.

Gert tidied up a bit more and headed to bed. "Good night, honey. Don't give up on him just yet. Maybe he's just having a hard time adjusting. I'm sure he'll come around."

"Well, he'd better, and we are going back to counseling like Dad said. If that doesn't help, nothing will. Good night, Mom."

Kristin pulled a thin blanket over her legs and waited, thumbing through Edwin's Sunday School book. Her eyes felt heavy, and she was soon drowsing, and then came the knock at the door, almost a tapping. It took her a second to gather her bearings, and she went to the door.

"Hey," said Reece. His hair was a mess from the wind, and he looked like he'd been in a hurricane. A thrum of cicadas followed him into the house.

"You sure look guilty." Kristin let him follow her up the stairs. She wore blue running shorts.

Reece followed her into the den and waited for something to happen. He tugged at his shirt and said that he was sorry for being so late, for going to Emma's even though she didn't want him to. He reached down and scratched Walter on the head, wondering if he should sit.

Kristin sat on the couch, silent, twirling the hair over her ear. She locked her gaze to his and said nothing.

"Can I sit down?"

"Yeah, sure." She pulled her legs beneath her, adjusting her shorts. "Are her legs as pretty as mine? You always said you liked my legs."

Reece sat beside her, giving her plenty of room. "Yours are the best. Trust me. My breath probably smells like barbecue. They had a bunch of ribs." There was a plastic bag of ribs in the truck that Sarah had given him.

"That was nice of them. Liquor and ribs. You don't look drunk."

Reece laughed a bit too hard. "It was Sammy, her sister's husband, who brought the brandy. He's kind of rowdy like that, I think." He reached and squeezed Kristin's ankle. He could see the bottom of her butt and underwear.

"Did you touch her while you were there?"

"Touch her? Well, maybe in passing. She has six sisters and a brother. They're a hugging bunch, if that's what you mean."

"That's good to hear, that there's more of them. You make it sound like they're family."

"I didn't mean that. They're certainly friendly, likable. One works at the zoo, in the snake house."

"Huh," said Kristin. "Well, how was the all-important slideshow? Did you two get that worked out?"

"Emma showed us one, maybe not the same one she'll show at church. There were a couple with me in them."

"So, you'll be wanting to see that one naturally, right?

And you're gonna say that I'm welcome to tag along if I like. Right?"

Reece stuttered and smiled, though he knew he shouldn't. "That would be the last thing, if you're okay with it. And we'll go together."

Kristin sighed. "I just can't believe that you're that hard-headed. You, what's the word, obfuscate me. I just don't believe that you said that. And, by the way, we're going back to premarital counseling, and you're paying for it, bucko."

"Not a problem," said Reece, although there was nothing more that he'd rather avoid. "The same guy? Maybe we can find someone else? He was kind of creepy."

"There you go, changing things. Yes, the same guy. He already knows us, knew you before you went over there." She uncurled her legs and moved closer. "You promise, right? I can make an appointment for next week. Okay? It's fifty dollars for an hour."

"I only make twelve an hour. I didn't know it was so expensive."

"Wrong answer," said Kristin. "What's the right answer?"

Reece said, "Okay, I'll do it. Starting next week. But..."

"But what?"

"Will you go with me on Sunday night? To see her talk?"

"What if I can't go? I may be coming down with a cold. I'm all sniffly."

Reece considered his options. "It's the last thing. I promise."

"So, you would go without me?"

"Maybe not if the counselor said not to, but that's next

week."

"If I scratch your back, will you go?" She gave him a wicked smile.

"Oh Lord, don't do that. That's blackmail."

"It sure is."

Reece scooted closer and put his hand on her bare leg. "Look, I'm sure you'll be able to go. We can't play at worst-case scenarios."

"Right now, the worst-case scenario for you is that I don't scratch your back." She made a feeble scratching motion on his shirt. "Make your choice."

"Okay, okay, I won't go if you can't go."

Kristin ran her hand up his back and dug in her nails. "You like that?" She raked them down his spine.

"I do." Reece felt disconnected from the universe, as if floating in a giant jar of pool water.

Kristin moved closer and told him to lean over. She pulled up his shirt and went at him with both hands, scratching deep, long, and hard. Reece arched his back and moaned, massaging her soft thigh. One thing led to another, and soon they were stretched out on the couch, hands exploring, kissing, and playful biting.

Reece had left Kristin's at two in the morning and slept in until ten. He knew Horace wanted him to burn the cornstalks in the garden and mow the grass, which grew until November. He and Kristin were supposed to go to Oak Mountain for a hike. His expensive hiking boots hadn't made it back from Ethiopia, and he would just have to wear running shoes.

The house was quiet except for the AC, which would blow as long as the grass was still growing. An oily baking tin of biscuits sat on the stove beneath a dishtowel. He peeled one off and ate it cold, feeling the grease on the roof of his mouth. No one was around, so he took out the pitcher of orange juice, made from concentrate, and drank in big gulps. He belched and went outside, suddenly wondering if it was Friday or Saturday. He took a deep breath.

Clara sat in the swing, shearing corn into a large stainless-steel pan. She was wearing her sleeveless shirt with the bold purple stripes, a towel in her lap.

"Hey." He reached to the tops of the pines and stretched. He'd promised Emma that she could visit him at the lake. Kristin had said nothing about Emma visiting him. He wondered how that would work out or if he should bring it up in counseling.

"Hey, boy. You were out awfully late last night. You know I don't like it." She sliced off a side of corn, milky juice flooding the knife.

"I was at Kristin's."

"I wondered if you was at Emma's the whole time.

Makes me feel some better."

"No, just had some barbecue with her family and watched a slideshow that Emma made. It was really interesting. She went through a lot more than I did."

Dora cocked her head. "Well, she didn't get shot, did she?"

Reece hadn't told them about the rape. "No, but maybe something even worse." He flexed his bare toes on the pine straw.

"Mercy, then I don't want to know. You gonna get that grass mowed before it gets too hot?"

"Can't get too hot for me." He loved sweating in a noonday sun.

"Well, go on now and hurt yourself. You're as contrary as can be sometimes."

"Horace in the garden?"

"What do you think? He's going to visit with Elbert soon, though. He's gonna take Maybell with him. I reckon I'll go too. Poor thing, your granddaddy doesn't know what to do without him. That's his buddy."

"I'll take him a glass of ice water," said Reece. "Mr. Myers was looking pretty good when I saw him yesterday. Trying to talk, though, but not so good."

"Okay, you go on, but don't forget the grass."

Reece fetched a glass of ice water and walked down to the garden. Horace was pulling corn stalks into a pile with a hoe. Horace stopped, leaned on his hoe with one hand, and smiled.

"Hey," said Reece. He held up the glass. "Come and get it."

Horace walked down the row toward the chairs beneath

the shade tree. "I was needing that. Sit a spell."

They sat in the webbed folding chairs. Horace took the water and sipped. "You can burn the dry corn stalks when you get a minute."

"Yeah," said Reece. "I'll do that while I mow down here."

"Where's your shirt? You didn't leave it at that girl's house, did you?" He smiled.

"I wasn't there the whole time. I was at Kristin's pretty late, though. I met all of Emma's sisters. Six of them."

"They all from Hueytown?" Chester sipped his water and set it on his narrow armrest.

"As far as I know. I think they have some kin in Cullman County."

Chester adjusted his sweaty hearing aid. "You don't say? There's a pile of Smiths up there. What part?"

"Not exactly sure, I think around Holly Pond."

"Holly Pond," said Chester, as if announcing a train stop. "I used to date a girl lived in Holly Pond. A Suggs."

"Was she pretty?"

Horace eyed him. "What do you think?" He laughed.

Reece nodded his appreciation. "Granny says you're going to visit Mr. Sykes."

At that, Chester looked stymied. "Well, brother, I nearly forgot. I better go and get cleaned up. Thanks for reminding me." He used the hoe to stand.

"I'll take care of those corn stalks." Reece sat for a minute, admiring the placid lake, the pale blue sky. He walked down to the bottom of Mr. Sykes' garden where the blackberries grew in a long bushy row filled with chest-high brambles. He saw a few fat ones and popped them into his mouth, a spot of blood rising on his hand. He saw the little Honda on the road and knew that it was Cindy. He suddenly felt naked in his cotton shorts and walked toward the house.

At the road, he watched her get out of the car. He waved. She waved and, with a beach bag and a small cooler, trotted down to meet him.

"Hey, big boy!" She was wearing her glasses and had her hair in two tight pigtails like a little German girl.

"Well, hey." Reece folded his arms across his chest. "What's up?"

"Just gonna tan on the pier. Wanna join me?" She wore a Budweiser cover-up over her bathing suit with flip-flops.

"Uh, maybe. But I have to mow the grass and do some stuff." He could see Maybell standing in front of the sliding glass door, waiting on Horace. "Your grandpa seems to be doing well."

"But he's so sad with his paralysis and all. You think he'll be able to walk again?" She put the cooler on the grass, sprinkled with pine straw.

"He's a tough one. I think so."

Cindy moved in and hugged him. "I wish you were his nurse. That Winston is nice and all, but you'd be better. You know him."

"Wish I could, but he's on the other unit." He felt a stirring in his shorts. "Hey, let me get going on the grass, and I'll check on you. Going on a hike with Kristin in the afternoon."

Cindy looked disappointed. "Sure, do that. Got some brews. You go on and mow that damn grass." She smirked and laughed.

Reece said bye and went inside to put some sunscreen

on his shoulders and find a ballcap. He grabbed some matches and newspaper and headed to the garden, saying goodbye to Dora and Horace. It took a few minutes, but soon the stalks were crisping and burning in the hot sun, a pale white smoke winding upward in the calm air. There was still a danger that a burning shuck would drift into some dry grass, and he hurried back to get the riding mower.

He pushed it backward out of the garage, hoping the battery was charged. The starter was broken, and he had to bypass it with a thick piece of insulated wire. He put the parking brake on, turned the ignition, and applied the wire. The engine exploded with life, and Reece throttled it down. He'd forgotten to check the gas and cut the engine. "Dammit." He went for the gas can, then filled up the tank and started over, but soon was out of the driveway and headed to the garden at a brisk pace. Crossing the road at the same time was Cindy in a yellow bikini. He turned just in time to miss a telephone pole and waved. She waved back.

The fire seemed to be going nicely, and he went below the garden to start cutting. He had a method, moving from the lake toward the road, and he engaged the blade, sending the mower from a loud roar to more of a loud whine. He first edged the cattails along the bank, glimpsing Cindy on the Sykes' pier. He turned sharp right, then right again, and soon edged the garden, then reversed his path to throw the grass outward. And the long oblong circles began, the engine vibrating his body, the sun heating his shoulders, thighs, and arms.

Within thirty minutes, he moved to the sides of the

garden and then between the road and the garden. The fire had died to vaguely smoking. There was a short, steep slope he had to be careful on, and he leaned uphill to keep from flipping over. The row of irises always got in his way, and he cut them close, mowing down a few. He wondered what time it was and imagined it was approaching noon with the sun nearly overhead. He decided to take a break before mowing around the house and drove down to the Sykes' pier, cutting the engine. He stepped off the mower, still feeling that he was moving. On the pier, he could see Cindy on the end beyond the small boathouse.

She lay on a Disney towel with her top untied, on her stomach. She could hear and feel his steps. "Hey, down here. Get yourself a beer." She raised up on her elbows, barely covering herself, a beer in a coozie in front of her.

"Hey." Reece tried not to stare at her backside and sat on the hard wooden bench. "What kind you got?" He opened the cooler.

"Nothing fancy, Colonel...just some Miller High Life. Take it or leave it." She was facing away from him. "Can you turn the radio on? I turned it off while you were mowing. I can't reach it, unless you want me to." She laughed.

"Sure." He popped open the cold beer, sipped the foam, tasted it, and pushed the play switch. It was ARS with "Spooky," and he imagined Cindy as being just a little spooky.

"I'm glad you're here," said Cindy. "I need some oil on my back. Can you do me?"

Reece looked out over the lake and then back at Cindy. "Sure. In the bag here?"

"Yep, don't do the sunscreen, do the oil. I wanna look

like toast when I leave."

Reece imagined he was just taking care of a patient at work, just applying some lotion. He put his beer down and put some oil on his hands. "Okay, here it comes." He knelt beside her and could see her breasts resting on the towel. He rubbed the oil in circles, careful not to go too far into what he deemed forbidden territory.

"Oh, that feels good," said Cindy. "Go down to my butt." She wiggled her butt for emphasis.

"Okay," and he did it, wondering if he should stop or keep rubbing.

"Up on my neck and shoulders too." She lay flat, with her arms at her side. "You are one crazy dude, you know?"

That caught Reece off guard. He was oiling her shoulders, a full erection in plain sight if she looked. "Crazy? How's that?" The smell of coconut and hot skin.

"You're just so damn nice, a missionary, for God's sake. But you'll rub me with oil like I'm your sister." She laughed a little laugh, a mischievous laugh.

"Kristin would kill me if she saw this. Sister? Is that good enough?" He moved back to the safety of the bench.

"Yeah, perfect. I appreciate you. Really. I'm so glad you got Pawpaw to the hospital. Close your eyes. I'm gonna raise up."

Reece looked out over the lake. Cindy sat up, losing her top, but soon had it back on. "Tie me up, if you will." She sat cross-legged, facing him.

He went to his knees, crawled behind her, and tied the string. He stood, bent over, and kind of lunged for the bench.

"Got yourself a woody, I see," said Cindy. "I don't mind.

Hell, I'll take care of that for you if you want."

"What about your friend, Clarence? What would he say?"

"Ha, he's cool. He just loves me, is all. I do what I want to do. But the better question is what would Kristin think, right?"

ZZ Top's "Cheap Sunglasses" came on.

"Yep, right on the money." He sipped his beer. "I'll have to get back to mowing after this beer."

"The boathouse is right there." She chased a fly from her face.

Reece thought about kissing Emma in the driveway, how that had become a terrible secret to keep from Kristin. "Better not. I don't think I could stop, well, you know." He felt totally out of his league with Cindy.

"I know, and maybe you're right. You're a credit to the human race, Colonel." She lay back on her towel, knees propped up.

"I guess," said Reece. "Don't get me wrong. I think you're...gorgeous, but I am engaged." He swallowed a lump in his throat. He took a big drink and then another until the can was empty.

"Thank you, kind sir. That means a lot." She extended her legs, highlighting what Reece thought of as her mound of Venus.

"Okay, off to mow some damn grass. After that, I have to get ready." He wanted to ask if she'd like to go hiking.

"Okay, see you, Colonel." She shaded her eyes and winked at him.

Reece tried to crank the mower and then remembered he needed the wire, which was wrapped around the deck lifter. Soon, he was bouncing back toward the house, wondering if life had always been so rich and that he'd just now noticed it.

The front and back yards took longer than below the road, due to the numerous trees. It took about forty-five minutes, and then he went straight to trimming around the bushes with the push mower, working up a mighty sweat. When he was through, dirt and clippings clung to his legs and ankles. Back inside, he wolfed two cold biscuits and drank two glasses of ice water, then showered as fast as he could, worried that he would be late for the hike.

It was just after two-thirty when Reece pulled up, his hair still wet in the back. Kristin wasn't quite ready, and he decided to wait outside and watch Harvey scoot around his baby pool, shaded by a big beach umbrella.

"Hey, buddy," said Reece. There were a few acorns and dry dog food scattered around a weighted bowl.

Harvey flicked his tail and made chewing motions, watching Reece, maybe waiting for a carrot, which he loved. Reece thought that Kristin should let Harvey go, that he'd do just fine with three legs. He pulled a plastic chair beneath the shade and waited, thinking about Emma and her sisters. He wondered how long Daryl would stay in jail and worried he would be after Emma again. The back door opened.

Kristin emerged wearing bona fide hiking shorts and hiking boots. She'd been drying her brown curly hair, which hid her ears. "Are you bonding with Harvey? That's so sweet."

"He's a strong little booger," said Reece. He stood. "You ready, Freddy?"

"Ready as I'll ever be. Let's take my car for the AC." She let him hug her.

"You look great in your hiking duds."

"Thanks! These are Robyn's boots, though. Don't you ever tell her. She'd kill me. Come on!"

They walked through the house, said bye, and Kristin headed to I-59 toward Oak Mountain, which was about halfway to Emma's house. Kristin paid the two-dollar fee and soon parked in a crowded lot. It was the hottest part of the day, but the tall pines and mixed hardwood forest made the trail seem relatively cool. The leaves were just getting ready to turn.

"Where we headed?" asked Reece.

"Up to Peavine Falls. This is the Green Trail." She had brought a small backpack with water and snacks. "Here, why am I carrying this?" She handed it to Reece.

The trail was worn and rocky with some roots and bits of limestone and gold-flecked mica.

"It's pretty much all uphill, about two miles. You think you can handle it?" Kristin looked back for a reaction, but Reece was staring at the trail.

"Oh yeah, four miles should be fine. I've done plenty of longer hikes, mostly on the Appalachian Trail in Georgia. I've never been here, though. Seems pretty popular." Up ahead, he could see an older couple wearing bright green daypacks.

"Is this as steep as Ethiopia?" asked Kristin. She let Reece catch up with her.

"No, it gets a lot steeper over there." He noticed how the trail wound its way over little hillocks that stretched upward. "No trees like this, though."

They hiked in silence, passing the older couple, and saying hey to a group coming down. Reece liked to hike, but often found that it was too tame, even dull. He felt just a bit out of breath, but chalked it up to his injury and recovery. How long had he been out of the hospital, a month, two months?

"Did I tell you about the CT scan?" asked Reece.

"Yeah, you said that it looked good, that the hematomas

were about gone."

"It also showed some kind of shadow. They thought it was just an anomaly of some sort, but it seemed to cover my entire head."

"That's weird. You didn't tell me that."

"Yeah, I just remembered it. I don't think it was related to the gunshot." He stopped and took a deep breath.

"You okay?"

"Oh yeah, just out of shape still, I guess." He wiped sweat from his forehead.

The higher they hiked, the more oaks and hickory they saw. Reece saw a toad and played with it for a minute.

"You ever do a beeline hike?" asked Reece. He was thinking of adding some spice to the hike. He reached and took her hand on a wider section of trail.

"No, what's that?"

"It's when you hike in on a trail and then, on the way back, you shoot straight for the parking lot, off trail. Wanna try it?"

"For Pete's sake, this is just a hike, not an adventure. You always want to ramp it up." She squeezed his hand.

"It's fun. You have to do some scrambling."

"And you could get us lost."

The trail got steeper.

"I doubt if we could get lost, as long as we're going downhill." He wiped more sweat, wishing he had a bandanna.

"Ugh, I say no to that." She let go of his hand and moved forward.

"Let's give it a try." He felt a little wobbly.

"Looks like you're having a tough enough time without

getting off the trail. Can't you just take no for an answer?"

Reece held his tongue, following her. Short flat stretches broke the long uphill stretches, then down a steep hill, and soon they reached an intersection with the Yellow Trail.

"You okay?" asked Kristin. "Let's take a water break."

"Sounds lovely," said Reece. He took off the backpack. Just off trail was a downed pine good to sit on. Brown pebbles and sand littered the ground.

"You want a snack?" Kristin dug in the pack and pulled out two cinnamon Pop-Tarts. "One for you and one for me. I'll save the apples for when we get to the falls."

"Thanks." He took his pastry and drank his water. A group of robins hopped through an empty patch of woods, keeping low to the ground. "This is a lot steeper than I thought it would be. Pretty, though."

"That's my man," said Kristin. She patted him on the back. "You don't want to go back, do you?"

"I'm fine. This is good, to rest a bit. How's your cold? You said you were coming down with a cold."

Kristin frowned. "I think it was because of the crying, because of you, bucko. I feel fine now. Is this headed where I think it is? Because I would like to have an Emma-free day."

"Sorry about the crying. That was my fault...You said yesterday that you couldn't go to her church tomorrow night if you had a cold, and that meant I couldn't go. See, I didn't even say her name." He finished his Pop Tart.

"Yikes," said Kristin. "We're going to counseling, remember that. If it's so important that I go with you, then I'll go, since it's church." She screwed the lid back on her water. "Okay?" She stood.

"Yeah, sounds good."

He stood and fell in behind her, heading southwest up the mountain, and they soon passed a family of four with a slobbering Labrador on a leash. Kristin said it was cute and scratched its head. In about half a mile, the trail tilted up, and they stepped onto the wide Red Trail, a mountain bike trail, and then reconnected with the Green Trail, headed northwest. Sweat soaked Reece's shirt, his eyes beginning to sting. He thought a beeline hike back to the car would take less time, and then they could get some Gatorade at a gas station. Mowing the grass, and now this, gave him a headache.

Kristin had stopped to look at a carpet of green lichen. "It looks like a tiny little kingdom." Water seeped from the ground just there.

"Like a little Ireland," said Reece. "Getting just a bit of a headache."

"Sorry," said Kristin. "I have some acetaminophen in the car. Can you wait?"

"Sure, just need some Gatorade." He plodded along behind her.

The trail had flattened into a meandering ridge walk with wiry trees surrounding them.

"Haven't seen any squirrels," said Reece.

"They live in the suburbs." The back of her gray t-shirt showed a small spot of sweat. Through the trees, a pair of mountain bikers sped down the Red Trail, to which they were roughly parallel.

Even on the flatter ground, Reece felt a bit winded. "What about the beeline hike? Any thoughts?"

Kristin stopped. "What? I thought we had settled that. I don't want to get lost."

"Right." Reece thought Emma would be all for it. A meadow opened up, and then they were heading down a long section through pines. "Just thought you might have... changed your mind." He coughed and spat. His running shoes were taking a beating on the rocks underfoot.

"Nope," said Kristin. She made a growly sound. "You are just about the most stubborn human being."

Reece laughed, perhaps too loud. He needed to pee. "Need to pee." There was a large slab of rock just ahead, and he darted behind it, looking both ways. He soon rejoined her.

"Did you wash your hands?"

"I did. There was a sink with Hibiclens back there, but no paper towels."

"I hate that stuff. Makes my hands itch thinking about it. I wonder how Mr. Myers is doing?"

"Well, Horace was driving Mrs. Myers to see him today." He wondered if he should mention seeing Cindy.

"I guess that Cindy girl had to work today."

"Probably," said Reece, thinking about her lying on the pier.

They hiked on for another half mile and emptied into the crowded Peavine Falls parking lot. Most people drove up and walked down to the falls from there. They headed left onto the Peavine Falls Trail proper, onto a rooted path slick in places, passing a young couple. The tall man was carrying a poodle and looked sullen. Soon they crossed Peavine Branch, and the sound of the falls was just ahead, where the water coursed through a chute and to the bottom about a hundred feet below.

"We did it." Kristin looked fresh as a daisy.

"Can't see the falls. Want to climb down?"

"Are you kidding, you'd kill us both." She found a rock to sit on, and Reece joined her. "Just the sound of the water is nice."

"So, do we just go back the way we came? I mean, we've already seen it."

"Duh," said Kristin. "And don't say beeline hike."

"Why won't you just try it? Maybe just to the bike trail. It'll be fun and probably quicker." He braced himself.

"Reece. No! How can I say it so that you'll understand? I don't want to."

And then it just blurted out. "I'll bet Emma would do it."

Kristin gave him a sidelong glance. "Did you just say what I think you said? You're not with Emma. You're with me." She stood. "Let's just go. You're impossible. Now I wish we hadn't come. For real?"

"Okay, that was bad of me." He stood and followed her, mentally flogging himself.

"I don't think I should give you a ride home." She was talking over her shoulder. "Maybe Emma can come and get you."

"Alright, I apologize. Just forget I said that."

Kristin kept walking, and a sprinkling of rain hit the leaves above them, followed by thunder.

The day dawned with roosters crowing, pipettes of smoke curling through steep thatched roofs. Afewerki's white hen pecked this way and that on the dirt floor. He drowsed for another half hour and then emerged from the sleeping bag that Emma had left him. He rubbed his head, which he had shaved, and shouted for his brother to bring him breakfast. Right away, his thoughts turned to Emma and her promise to him.

His youngest brother hustled in, wearing his ragged green sweater, carrying a platter with bits of leftover enjera stirred with eggs and peppers. Afewerki said thanks and reached for his IV bottle filled with water from the stream so far away. Tiny ants had gathered at the red stopper, and he brushed them away. He ate and thought, not having much to do during the day. He was going to help his father buy a donkey with what was probably his last paycheck from the Mission. Afewerki finished his breakfast and carried the platter next door to his parents' tukul. Inside the dim hut, his mother tended the fire, preparing spicy kiyawot with boiled eggs and plenty of soybean oil from the Mission. She knew of his plans to go to the United States, but could not imagine it. The ferenj had promised him, but that seemed about as likely to happen as snow, which she had never seen, not even in a picture.

Afewerki chatted with her, almost a mumble, asking her if she needed firewood, and she smiled and nodded no, squatting there by the fire, the pot beginning to bubble. He walked outside, and his younger brothers, one six and the other eight, were gathering the goats to herd them to the pasture. "Bataam taruno," he told them and looked at the sky filled with billowing clouds that he could reach out and touch.

Mariam and Barra had already left, leaving Isaac to close down the warehouse and distribute the food inside until it was finished. Afewerki walked around to the back of the compound and saw his older sister there. She had just arrived from Gojjam, leaving her husband, probably for good. On the other side of the fence, prisoners were taking small nut-brown loaves of bread, giving her pennies in return. The jail did not feed them, and they had to rely on family for most of their meals.

The ground was muddy from the rains, and he stopped to smear away the black goo from his hiking boots with a stick. They were Reece's boots, a size or two too large, but they were his prized possession for now. He'd written two letters to him so far, but had not received a reply. He worried that his letters, sent out by jeep, were being opened and discarded by the drivers. He had yet to write Emma, nervous about her reply, but he had an aerogram with her address on it. He tried to imagine the big house she no doubt lived in, with electricity and hot water, and only shook his head. He felt that a great game had been played, but that no one had won.

The goats in hand and whacked with long switches, he followed his brothers into the muddy lane, every pothole filled with water. It was the time of the long rains, and he knew it would rain again that day. It was a short walk to the old compound, and he dreaded not seeing Misrak and Zenebek in the cook house. Misrak would be home soon, or so Dr. Guthrie had said, minus one breast. He made a face and tried to think of more pleasant things, nodding at men and women hurrying along the path.

Afewerki knocked on the gate out of habit and heard Irigit whistle. He was no longer being paid by the Mission, but couldn't seem to let his job go. They spoke for a moment, and he could see that Isaac was still in his room. He looked at Emma's tiny house with its whitewashed walls and felt a fever in his stomach. She had hugged him more than once and even said that she loved him, but she had said that to the others as well.

"Isaac! Sleepyhead!" Afewerki leaned against a pole, waiting.

"Abet! You wake me!"

Afewerki spat on the ground and chased flies from his face. The grass was getting high.

Soon, Isaac appeared, wearing his mechanic's jumpsuit and glasses. He stretched and yawned.

"What is it, my brother?" asked Isaac. "You are working so early?"

"Shall we get tea?"

"Yes, yes, beautiful tea. The girl there is very pretty." Isaac smiled. He was buying all of his meals since Zenebek no longer cooked, although the Mission was still paying him, along with Mariam and Barra. "I must wash my hands," and he called for Irigit.

With a broad smile and wearing his tattered hat, Irigit fetched a can with water and a ragged bar of white soap. He poured as Isaac washed his right hand and splashed his face. Irigit said his wife needed money to buy some sugarcane for the children as a treat, and Afewerki gave him three birr.

"Shall we go?" Isaac smiled and patted his thighs. He grabbed Afewerki and put him in a loose headlock, laughing.

Afewerki's bald head slipped out, and he pushed Isaac away. "Not like the child today." Irigit was laughing at them. "Let us go, big child."

"Oh, I am the big child. What is it?" Isaac shadowboxed Afewerki to the gate.

They took a right and then a left, headed past Afewerki's house toward the teahouse off the village square. They walked from stone to stone, careful to avoid the slippery and sticky mud, passing farmers with clods of mud stuck to their feet. The teahouse was a traditional tukul with seating on a low structure of flat stones that ran around the interior. Over the stones, planks had been fashioned.

Isaac greeted the young lady tending the charcoal fire and kettles, and three other men. Afewerki mumbled his greetings. Isaac rubbed his hands together against the morning chill and eyed a pile of kita smeared with buttery niter kibbeh.

They both ordered hot sugary tea with cloves and ginger. The girl serving them was fourteen but not yet married. She was gorgeous with high cheekbones and a lithe figure, but her right leg was withered and bent, and she walked with a limp.

Inside the hut, everyone whispered. One man asked Isaac when the grain would run out, and Isaac replied that it would be perhaps one week, possibly three, depending on how many people showed. They still had to have the yellow ration card, but they were no longer weighing the children or sending the sick ones to the clinic, which was closed, although Afewerki had opened it numerous times to treat worms and trachoma of those who came and begged.

"The white woman is not coming back?" asked another. He seemed sad. Everyone in the village knew that soldiers had raped her, just as everyone knew that the Hyena had shot the white man.

"Yes," said Isaac. "She has left us." He made the hand motion of a jet flying.

Afewerki wanted to say that he would be going there, too, to go to school and maybe live with Emma, but he didn't, fearing they would laugh at him. They drank their tea, had a refill, and Isaac munched on half a round of kita, getting his hand greasy. Afewerki paid two birr, and they stood, stretched, and headed out into the morning.

Just near the administrative compound, they saw a little girl carrying her little sister on her back. Her face was a mess of snot and flies, her eyes moving with them like a cartoon. Afewerki said, "Tsk, tsk, tsk," and called to the little girl, who stopped and stared at the ground. He asked where she was going, and the little girl whispered so that he couldn't hear a thing she was saying. "Come with me," he said, calling her mamoosh, little one. It was things like this that he wanted to leave behind. In his heart, he suspected there were no flies in America, and maybe no snot either. The little girl followed, trembling and breathing deeply as if about to cry. Isaac just followed, amused.

"Innat!" he called to his mother, pushing in the door to the compound. She came to the hut's door, surrounded by swirls of smoke. Afewerki told her to bring some water, and he went to his little square room to fetch a four-by-four. His mother calmed the little girl, her eyes and nose teeming with the tenacious flies. The little girl unwrapped the cloth holding her sister to her back and let her to the ground on wobbly two-year-old legs. She, herself, was only five.

Afewerki took the pan of water and splashed the little one's face, then dipped the bandage in the water and removed the snot and crusts from her eyes, sending the flies away, but back they came, and he repeated the measure until her face was clean.

"Good work, my brother," said Isaac.

Afewerki examined the little one's red eyes, but the lashes had not yet begun to turn inward. He said that they had to come to the clinic for eye medicine. He caught a few flies in his hand, shook them, threw them to the ground, and stepped on them. His sister appeared, and he told her to bring a bun for the little girls, which she did. Bundled again, the young sisters were on their way, buns in hand, headed to an aunt's house as their mother was too sick to care for them.

"What a hell," said Afewerki, and drops of heavy rain began to fall.

They rode mostly in silence on the way back to Kristin's house. Reece's headache was full-blown, but he let the idea of Gatorade go, his hands folded in his lap. She pulled into the steep driveway, opened the door without a word, and headed to the house.

"My keys," called Reece. "They're in the house." He felt like a little plastic soldier missing its head. "And I'm sorry!" Kristin looked back and left the door open, disappearing inside. With a heavy chain around his neck and his head pounding, there was nothing to do but get his keys, and he walked inside, wondering where he had left them. Kristin was gone, but Gert was in the living room, wringing her hands with a worried look on her face.

"What's wrong?" asked Gert.

"Uh, need to find my keys."

"They're in Kristin's room, on her dresser."

"Oh." He just wanted to run screaming. He walked to her closed door and knocked, but there was no answer. He tried the doorknob, but it was locked. "Kristin?" He could feel Gert's eyes boring into him. "Kristin? My keys are in there."

The door opened, and Kristin tossed his keys onto the carpet, and then she slammed it. Reece picked up the keys and, without looking at Gert, made his way to the truck. He wanted beer and focused on that, and some Gatorade for his headache. The little gas station on his way home in Clay didn't sell beer, so he wound his way into Trussville and stopped at the first gas station there. He tried something new, picking out a six-pack of St. Pauli Dark and a quart of orange Gatorade.

In the truck, he slammed the Gatorade and then made his way back to the lake. The Buick was gone, and he guessed that Dora and Horace were still at the hospital, but Cindy's little Honda was still in the driveway next door. He went inside the cool house, washed his face, took three Tylenol, unloaded his keys and wallet, and holding the beer, went back outside. He walked into the front yard and looked over to see Cindy in the hammock, her radio on the ground, playing rock. He walked that way.

"Hey!" said Reece, but there was no response. He walked over pinecones and pine straw toward her. She was asleep and snoring, wearing her cover-up.

He approached the hammock and gently swung it. "Hello?"

Cindy opened her eyes wide and gazed at him. "What the hell? Where did you come from?" She sat up, tipsy from the beer and sun. "Your hike over with? Where's Kristin?"

"It's over with for today, anyway. I got some beer."

She threw her legs over the side, yawning. "Lord, I was dreaming about another planet."

Reece laughed. "Sorry to wake you from that."

"It's fine. Yeah, I'll have one. Here, sit on the hammock."

Reece realized he didn't have a bottle opener. "No opener."

Cindy leaned over and pulled one from her bag. "Here you go, Colonel."

Reece sat down slow, but his weight pushed him next to her.

"Well, hey there, buddy," said Cindy. "Pop that fancy brew."

Reece opened two bottles. "Get enough sun? Looks like it."

"Yeah, too much. Need to drink some water and eat something." She undid her pigtails. "So, how was the hike?" Robert Plant was singing about big-legged women.

Reece looked up into the pines, swaying just ever so much. "Not so good. I said something I shouldn't have. She's pissed." He told her about the beeline hike, the Emma comment.

"Uh oh, in deep shit. But a beeline hike sounds pretty interesting." Her shoulder touched his, their thighs mashed together. "So, who's this Emma again?"

Reece explained that she was a nurse, that they had worked together, that she had been with him when he was shot. "Just a good friend is all."

"Wow," said Cindy. She drank some beer and burped. "Sorry about that."

They sat there and drank and talked for half an hour, the occasional car passing by. And then there was a minute of silence.

"You know what you need?" asked Cindy.

"What?"

"A good old-fashioned back rub."

"What?" asked Reece. "I need one?" He felt her hand on the back of his neck. He arched and swiveled his head back and forth. His headache was better, and he took a big drink of beer.

"Feels good, don't it?" asked Cindy.

"Well, yeah." He made a little groan and wondered if he

should be on the phone to Kristin.

"Okay, don't stand up or I'll flip over." She maneuvered behind him and, on her knees, massaged his shoulders. "You've got broad shoulders, but you're so skinny."

"I guess so," said Reece.

With her fist, she pushed into his back around the spine. "You know this would be a lot easier if we were inside. That good with you?"

"Okay." Reece felt as if tethered to an invisible rope that was tugging him. He waited as she hopped off the hammock and stood.

"Come on, Colonel," she said, grabbing his hand and then the radio. "You bring the beer."

Inside, the Sykes' kitchen was a wreck, a skillet with grease on the stove, an open bottle of maple syrup, the table cluttered with dishes. "When Pawpaw comes home, they're gonna make him a room in there." She pointed into the dim den, the radio doing a double shot of Led Zeppelin.

Cindy led him into the spare back bedroom, paneled just like his grandparents'. A twin bed was against the wall, an old dresser against another wall. A braided rug on the floor. He put the six-pack on the floor and took a swig from his bottle, emptying it.

"Okay, here we are. Take your shirt off, so I can get some skin." She laughed and took off her cover-up, wearing only her bikini.

"I have to say that you're...really something." Reece stood there like a plane stopped mid-flight, then pulled off his shirt and tossed it on the bed. "Just lay down?"

"Yeah, on your stomach. You'll remember this for a long

time. But take your shoes off, silly."

Reece worried that his feet smelled, but took off his tennis shoes and left on his socks. He lay on the thin brown bedspread, his arms by his side, and felt her crawl on top of him, sitting on his legs, and she began to massage his back, going from his neck down to his butt and repeating.

"God, that feels good."

"Got some nice muscles on you, but I can't see all of them." She began to tug his shorts and underwear down, and he let her, feeling that he was in a movie, that this was the script. She got them down to his knees and rubbed his butt. "Just relax. You're so damn tight."

Reece tried to relax, but it was tickling him, and he squirmed. She had stopped, and he could tell that she was taking off her top, and then she was pressing her chest to his back, her breasts warm and soft.

"Okay, flip over." She slapped his butt.

Wanting to cover himself, he turned over, his manhood standing there in all its glory, her white breasts with tan lines and large maroon nipples.

"Oh my God," said Reece. She was truly beautiful, and she was telling him to sit up, and she was touching him there, grabbing him there, and soon he was standing, and she was bearing down on him in a mild frenzy of mouth on cock. Reece couldn't hold back and out it came, all over her chest and breasts, and he let out a deep sigh, as if he had just found water in the desert. "Jesus, I'm sorry." He couldn't get over the sight of her perfect breasts.

Cindy laughed. "It's one hundred percent natural, Colonel," holding him by the butt cheeks. She stood, and soon they were kissing, holding tight, stumbling around the room, hitting the walls. She pulled him onto the bed, and he fell on top of her, and soon he was kissing her stomach and breasts. With one hand, she shed her bikini bottom and arched into him, grinding and moaning.

Reece had never given oral sex but kissed his way down and stared at the shaved bush of blonde hair in all its glory, and began to lick, receiving moans of pleasure in return. She arched and shuddered, asking him for more, and he obliged until his jaw muscles ached. She pushed him away and turned to her knees.

"Hurry," she said.

And Reece hurried, penetrating her from behind into a great warmth and wetness that had his heart racing. With each thrust, he trembled, the howl of "Cashmere," gripping her thighs. And then the screen door to the carport banged. It was Mrs. Sykes.

"Don't stop!" said Cindy.

"Cindy?" said Maybell.

"Oh shit." Reece panicked and pulled out, closing the bedroom door, grabbing his underwear, which were tangled in his shorts. Cindy was laughing, lying on the bed with her legs spread. "Should I go out the window?" He walked to the window and lifted it. There was a screen.

"Cindy?"

"Hey, just settle down." She was putting her bikini back on." Just play it cool. She's a grown woman. Maybe she thinks I'm at the lake."

Reece was fully dressed, but his shirt was on backward. He forced his feet into his shoes. A knock on the door. "Cindy?" The door opened a crack.

"Hey, Mawmaw, Reece and I were having a beer, listening to some music." A car dealership commercial was on. She turned up the volume for effect.

"Reece is here. Well, that's fine. Just come on out, and I'll tell you all about Pawpaw."

"Okay, Mawmaw." She giggled and put on her cover-up. "God, you had me so hot." She pulled a stunned Reece close and kissed him, going deep.

"Wow," said Reece. He was dazed and confused, unsure of what to do next.

"Going to the bathroom. Be right back."

"Okay." Reece sat on the bed, looking at the braided rug. He practiced what he would say to Mrs. Sykes and tried to put on an innocent face. There was a faded mirror over the dresser, and he peered into it, wondering if it was him. He heard the toilet flush.

"Come on, Colonel." She grabbed him by the hand and led him into the tiny living room. Maybell sat in her recliner, eating a Snickers.

"Hey, y'all." She grinned and then told them how Elbert was doing, that he was sitting on the side of the bed, and that he could once again say goddamn and hell, but that he still slurred.

Reece stood in front of the fireplace, laughing his approval, while Cindy had taken the other recliner. He felt caught between two worlds, maybe three, and could only think of Cindy bent over in front of him. His next thought was of Kristin. It took Maybell half an hour to recount her visit with Elbert, and then Cindy said that she'd better be moving along, seconded by Reece.

"Let's just walk around the garden," said Cindy.

"Sure, but then I need to get back to the house."

"You need to call Kristin, don't you?" She looked a little sad.

"No, well maybe." They walked side by side through the grass and to the road.

"Hey, there's this great French restaurant in Mountain Brook. Would you take me sometime?"

"Uh, sure, but..." They were beside the first row of pole beans, picked dry for the season.

"Yeah, I know, but look, we're just buddies. We can do stuff like that. Don't let her get such a stranglehold on you."

"It's not that. Oh, hell, I'm so confused. But God, you're..."

They ambled to the row of blackberries and kissed.

"You're a good man, Charlie Brown. I mean, Colonel." She laughed, slapped him on the behind, and ran toward the house, daring him to catch her.

Thoroughly exhausted with Reece, Kristin called her friend Amber for consolation. Amber suffered from scleroderma, a painful and rare skin condition, but she was as patient as Moses and a good ear to have in times of trouble. She was employed as an adjuster at a large insurance firm. They agreed to meet in the food court at Eastwood Mall. Gert had wanted to know what the devil had happened, but Kristin was too tired to explain it at the moment.

Kristin parked and walked into the out-of-date mall anchored by a Service Merchandise. The air was cool, the walkways overly wide and carpeted. Only three food vendors had survived the mall's downturn, and half of the retail spaces were shuttered. The bright and open dining area seemed a spot of privilege, as if no harm could ever befall it. She took a table in the middle and waited.

Within a few minutes, Amber walked in, her gait slightly affected, her neck drawn tight, pulling her head to one side. She was all smiles and greeted Kristin with a hug. "Hey, girl!"

"Hey!" Kristin felt a wave of empathy for her friend, grateful to have her. "You need a drink or anything? Thanks for coming."

"No problem, I'm fine. Amber to the rescue." She giggled and sat on a hard chair. She got right down to business. "So tell me again what happened. To be honest, I'm not surprised. He's just so out there." She had met him once at church.

Kristin revisited who Emma was and what a thorn in her flesh she had become, and then the incident on the trail. "If I didn't know better, I'd say he was in love with her. She's got her hooks in and doesn't want to let go. Maybe I'm just crazy."

"No, no," said Amber, "he should never have said that about the beeline hike. Plus, he shouldn't be visiting her, regardless of the circumstances."

"I've made it known, and then the next thing he says is that he wants to help her with a slideshow, and then he wants to go to her church to see the slideshow. This whole engagement seems like a bad slideshow sometimes."

"Well, you're doing the right thing. He has to know where you stand. But you do have to remember what you have versus what you could lose. He's just lucky to be alive on one level and being a jerk on another."

Kristin sighed. "That's the trouble. I love him, and he says he loves me. I mean, we're engaged, for goodness' sake."

"I'd just kill for a date," said Amber, without emotion.

"Amber, don't guilt me. I hate to even bother you with this, but you're such a good friend. I mean, I didn't say a word to him after he brought me home. He left, and that was that. I thought he would call, but he hasn't, which worries me that I went too far. To be honest, I'm dying to call and make up."

Amber smiled. "You know, I'd say you do call him, but don't agree to see him anytime soon. He has to know you're serious. So, he wants to see her at church tomorrow?'"

"He wants to go to this slideshow she's doing about Ethiopia." She said Ethiopia like she was referencing a dirty dishrag.

"Well, he is a Christian, right?" asked Amber.

"He was before he left, before he was shot. I don't know what he is anymore. It's like he's changed. Did I tell you he was drinking alcohol: hard liquor and beer?"

"That's not good," said Amber, frowning. "That's a warning sign for sure."

"Warning sign for what?"

"That maybe he's lost his faith. But it could be temporary, maybe just because of the trauma of it all."

"Yeah, I've thought about that. Something happened over there, maybe something he's not telling me."

"You don't think he had sex with her, do you? That would be the end."

"No...And I didn't tell you this either. Just between you and me, okay?" Kristin's mouth was dry, and she fought off a yawn.

"What?" Amber looked breathless.

"Well..."

"Uh oh, you didn't do it, did you?" She was on the edge of her chair.

"Yep, we did, and he said it was his first time, and it was mine too. But it was so...great. I felt that we were one. And then he starts talking about Emma."

"Right after?"

"No, not right after, but it might as well have been." Kristin slumped a bit. "Maybe I'm to blame. Something I'm doing wrong. I don't know."

"No, honey, it's not your fault. But maybe you shouldn't have had sex. I mean, that's why people, Christians at least, get married. It's a holy bond."

"You're still a virgin? Right? Except for that creepy guy you told me about. But you didn't do it?"

Amber blushed. "Yeah, I can't have sex. I have to have some minor surgery first. I guess I found out the hard way."

"I'm sorry. I have it so easy."

"So, where did you do it? Not at your house?"

"Well, we almost did one night, but Mom walked in on us. It was in his grandparents' RV at the lake, the second time."

"Second time, gee whiz."

"Well, yeah, but I mean I felt that night like I was...made to have sex. If you know what I mean. I'd always thought it would be this painful ordeal, but it wasn't, although I was sore the next day." Kristin gazed around the empty food court. The woman at the information booth was reading a magazine.

"Gosh, I'd kill for that, but that's neither here nor there. So, are you going to let him see her tomorrow? Maybe if he sees her a few times, he'll forget about her."

"I've thought about that. Mom even kind of said that. What do you think I should do?" She propped her chin on her hands as if having her fortune told.

"Do you want to go to the slideshow? Because if you do, I'd make him take you."

Kristin shook her head no. "To be honest, the last thing I want to see is her giving a slideshow about you know what. I mean, get over it. You were there, and you came back. Get over it. There's plenty of good to do right here."

"Yes, but mission work is a calling. He almost gave his life for it. You have to consider that."

"Maybe. So, should I let him go? What if they go to

Wendy's afterward and then back to her house?"

"Do you trust him?"

Kristin had to think. "I used to, but now I'm not so sure. That's one reason we're going back to counseling." A large woman pushing a baby in a stroller meandered through the tables, passing them.

"I'd see what the counselor says, but you know what? I say let him go to church with her tomorrow and bring that up at your next session. Maybe he can talk some sense into Reece. He's a he, right?"

"Yeah, but I kind of wish it was a she. So, let him go? Let him see the slideshow and get that out of his system?" Kristin looked thoughtful, as if unlocking a room filled with gold. "That's not my inclination, but maybe you're right. Sometimes I feel like his mother."

"Yeah, that's a good way to put it, but don't act like his mother, unless...well, you know," said Amber.

"And then there's his parents getting killed in Texas. That has to have some bearing on his actions, but I don't know how." Kristin adjusted her bra strap.

"Yeah, you told me about that. What are the odds, all three being shot?"

"It's just so, so evil. Let's not talk about that. But I'll take your advice, I think, and let him go, and I won't go with him. I'll trust him to do the right thing."

And they talked for another hour or so, getting sundaes at the Dairy Queen there, and then Kristin was ready to leave, ready to go home and call Reece, eager to see him as soon as possible.

After Cindy left, Reece went back to the house, filled with wonder and horror at what he had done. He sat through a supper of cornbread and collard greens relatively silent, making some small talk about his hike with Kristin, listening to Horace and Dora's account of visiting Mr. Sykes at the hospital. As soon as he finished eating, he planned to call Kristin, hoping she wouldn't want him to come over, fearful of what he had done with Cindy. The phone rang, and he reached for it without thinking.

"Myers' residence."

"Reece? Myers' residence?" asked Kristin.

"Hey, let me get on the other phone." He ran to pick up the phone beside the recliner. "Hey."

"Are you eating?"

"Yeah. I'm glad you called. I was just about to call you." Reece played with the phone cord. He could see his spunk globbed onto Cindy's breasts and chest. "What a day, huh?"

"Are you really, truly sorry for what you said today?"

"Yeah, that was uncalled for. I was just frustrated." He hadn't told Dora or Horace about his Emma comment.

"Okay. I had a long talk with my friend Amber today, and she said that I should let you go to Emma's church tomorrow, but we have to talk about it and your comment today with the counselor, hopefully next week."

Reece groaned inside at the mention of the counselor. "That's cool, sure, we'll discuss it, and thanks for letting me go."

"I guess you need to thank Amber," said Kristin.

"Yeah, her too, for sure." He cleared his throat.

"You okay? You sound a little funny."

"Yeah, yeah, okay. Mr. Sykes seems to be doing well, according to Dora and Horace. That's good."

"Yeah, that's good to hear. He could be my patient next week if Winston has a day off. I'll take care of him regardless of his crazy granddaughter. She didn't show up today, did she?"

Reece thought quick. Better to just say yes. "Well, she came out. I was mowing the grass and saw her."

"Were you going to tell me that on your own? Not that I care." Her voice was more matter-of-fact now.

"Well, I wasn't thinking about her." He pinched himself.

"Gosh, she probably came out there to see you, knowing that her grandmother was going to be gone."

"I doubt that. She was asleep in the hammock. I saw her, and she was asleep." He rolled his eyes at himself—too much information. Now she would ask more questions. Horace and Dora sat very quiet at the table.

"Sleeping Beauty?"

"She kind of had a sunburn, so maybe Snow White." He didn't know if that was a good or bad answer.

"Reece, I want to come out and see you. Is that okay?"

"Tonight? Well, sure, of course. You haven't been out in a few days." But how could he face her?

"Swell, old buddy. I'll be out in an hour. That good? I don't want Cindy to be the last pretty girl you see today." Her voice had gone childlike.

"Hey, you know what? Maybe bring Walter. Let him see

the lake."

"Maybe some other time. He would have to be watched, and I want to spend quality time with you."

"Yeah, you're probably right. Some other time. Say, do you want to go to church with me in the morning, at my church? I think they're gonna give me a plaque or something."

"Oh, that's sweet. Maybe they should give you a Purple Heart. Will you pick me up? I know it's out of your way to do that."

Reece nodded his head. "Of course, I'd love to. Then we can go eat, maybe with Horace and Dora." He'd spent the last of his money on beer and wouldn't be paid for another two weeks.

"Okay, well, let me go. See you soon."

Reece said bye and hung up the phone. A plan was developing in his head, but he didn't know if he could pull it off. He stood, stretched, and then stood in front of the AC.

"You want an oatmeal pie, son, for dessert?" asked Dora. "Kristin's coming over?"

"Yeah, maybe I should get a shower."

"I thought you already showered?" asked Dora. She bit into an oatmeal pie, Little Debbie.

"Got kind of sweaty on the hike." He felt he was just a pipeline of lies and half-truths.

"I thought you showered after the hike. There was a wet towel in the bathroom."

"Probably from this morning. But let me get in there quick. Did you check the grass?" Dora usually checked after he mowed, to see if he had missed anything, an old habit from when her boys used to mow.

"Looked real nice, son," said Horace. He nibbled his oatmeal pie. A meal wasn't a meal unless you had something sweet.

"Yes, it looks very nice," said Dora. "Did you mow around the yellow bells?"

Reece laughed. "Yes, always the yellow bells. I know, they came from your momma's place in Hanceville." He slipped into his bedroom for some underwear and headed to the shower. He hadn't used a condom with Cindy, but he was sure she was on birth control. He hoped she didn't have herpes, but he'd been right in there and hadn't seen anything malignant.

There was a rap at the back door, and Kristin let herself in. "Knock, knock." She wore tights and a sleeveless workout shirt that she'd scooped from Robyn's room.

"Come in, come in," said Dora. She gave Kristin a side hug. "Don't you look pretty?"

Kristin grinned and said hey to Horace. "Where's Reece?"

"Hey!" Reece emerged from his tiny bedroom. He was in blue shorts and a lumberyard t-shirt, his hair still wet in the back. "Look at you." He whistled.

"Aw, shucks." Kristin rolled her eyes and let Reece kiss her on the head.

"Smell good too." He felt a tiny bit breathless. "Wanna go to the pier? Maybe do some fishing?"

Kristin said, "Yes," and they were out the door.

Reece took his pole from the garage, the one with the Jitterbug. "You want a pole?"

"Not a pole, but maybe your pole, buster." Cicadas

hummed in the trees, and clouds hurried overhead.

"Whoa," said Reece. "My pole is your pole." He took her hand, and they walked past the garden to the lake, stepping onto the pier that he'd helped Horace build when he was fifteen. In the water were swirls and bloops of startled fish, tangled moss undulating. Reece cast out to the side close to the cattails and reeled in the Jitterbug, which made bubbles and *blub blubs* as he jerked it in and reeled. He had a hit, but the fish swam away.

"You look like you know what you're doing," said Kristin.

"Hey, I'm pretty good with the Jitterbug. I guarantee I'll catch one." He tossed the lure and reeled. *Blub blub blub.* "I like your outfit, if I didn't already say so. Nice curves."

"Thanks. I could tell you were turned on." She bent over and palmed the deck. "Geez, I need to exercise. You run around the lake, right?"

"About twice a week. It's the best, but it's really best at high noon when the humidity is two hundred percent. Your skin is just one big kidney, right? My hat turns yellow after three runs." He cast again.

"Gross," said Kristin. "I mean, exercise at a gym, like Robyn. You think she's hot, don't you?"

"Well, she is your sister." He dodged her slap and reeled, jerked, reeled. A near hit.

"What if you were really in love with Robyn, and only using me to get to her?" She did a few jumping jacks.

"You'll scare the fish. And actually, I'm in love with Edwin." This time her slap hit his butt.

"How do you like that, bucko?" She waved her hand at a cloud of gnats.

Reece laughed. "More?"

She slapped his ass again and did a little groping.

"Ooh." He reached and pulled her to him and kissed her, nearly dropping his pole.

The sky was dimming in notches, lower, lower, the sun even with the ridge across the lake. A warm breeze of lake essence—fish slime, mud, and moss. The lake empty of humanity and showing spots of calm.

Reece tried to cast while kissing and threw the lure into the cattails. "Oops." He dropped the rod and grabbed her to him, kissing her deep. She groaned a bit and grabbed his butt.

"Better than fishing," said Reece. He held her at arm's length, pretending to dance.

Kristin giggled. "Stop, you'll make us fall in."

Reece picked up the rod. "I have a promise to keep," and he cast extra-long almost to the Sykes' pier. He jerked and reeled, and a tremendous pop and splash hit the lure. He pulled back, and the fish was on, zigzagging. He winked at Kristin and pulled and reeled, pulled and reeled until the foot-long bass was in sight, nearly the same color as the greeny water. He reeled and then pulled the fish from the lake, its gills flaring, its mouth gaping. Kristin moved back, and Reece grabbed the lower jaw with his thumb and forefinger and then pulled the hook free. "You want him for breakfast?"

"Wow, manly man, no, I don't. Please let him go."

"I always do," said Reece, and he let the fish drop into the water, and off it shot. "That was special, just for you."

"Well, thank you," said Kristin. She looked pleased as punch. "Let's sit." She walked to the end of the T-shaped pier and sat on the bench nailed to the weathered dark-gray deck. Reece joined her and cast straight out, not expecting any bites there. He just let the Jitterbug sit on the water, its treble hooks dangling.

"This is my favorite view," said Reece. He scanned the lake, its water a dark green overall.

"And I'm your favorite girl, right?" She scooted into the crook of his arm.

Reece felt electric. "You bet," and he kissed her hair. "Turning me on, for sure."

"I like to hear that. We can stay up late and do what we want. No work tomorrow. Right?" She turned and looked into his eyes.

"Yeah, we should take a stroll, maybe play cards in the RV?" He squeezed her, feeling devilish and guilty.

"Oh, the RV. I know what you're thinking, you bad boy. You know we can't have sex again, though, until we're married. Sorry. Is your little man getting excited?"

"Probably," said Reece. "But you can't blame him." He pulled his arm away and reeled in the lure, just letting it burble. It caught on the end of the pier, and he had to stand. He felt alone for a moment beneath the wide-open sky, a few bright stars already showing.

They agreed to walk and went toward the public pier and the swimming pool and then to the road. His arm around her made it difficult to walk, but they moved along without care, talking about Mr. Odo, the garbage man, and other patients. They walked around the circle in the increasing darkness, passing houses and yards until they were back at his place at 8487.

"Maybe we should go and talk to Dora and Horace,"

said Kristin.

"What? And not listen to John Denver on the tape player?" When he went camping with his grandparents, they always listened to the tape over and over. He sang a snatch from "Grandma's Feather Bed."

"Come here." She leaned against her Toyota and drew him close. He obliged and pressed his body to hers.

"So warm," and he kissed her, and they stood there kissing in the increasing twilight for the next ten minutes, soon moving to the RV, and to the sounds of John Denver singing about sunshine on his shoulders, had sex.

Kristin awoke early and couldn't go back to sleep. She'd started her period the day before but hadn't told Reece. Her mother had warned her that having sex with a man would decrease his interest in her. She threw back her lavender blanket and stood, sore from the sex, but somehow feeling satisfied and rather adult. She stood in front of the mirror and practiced the face she would wear in front of Gert. Edwin was easier to deceive, or so it seemed to her.

She stepped into the hallway and glimpsed Edwin in his recliner. She knew that Gert was in the kitchen cooking bacon. "Hey, Daddy!" She sat on the couch and hugged a pillow to her chest.

"Hey, honey. Got in a bit late last night, didn't you?" He peered over the top of his reading glasses, the bulky Sunday paper on his lap. Gert appeared around the corner, fork in hand.

"Yeah, after midnight," said Gert, and then she was gone.

"Oh, that's not late," said Kristin. "Reece caught a fish on the pier."

"I always wondered if he fished. He never talks about it," said Edwin.

Gert reappeared. "He's fishy alright," and she laughed and disappeared again, back to the stove.

"What did he catch?"

"I think it was a bass. He let it go."

"Why did he let it go?"

"He's just kind, I guess." Kristin lay back on the couch,

her head resting on the armrest, facing away. "I'm going to church with him today, at his church."

"Just don't go Baptist on us." Edwin chuckled and resumed his paper. "Alabama routed Notre Dame yesterday."

"I like it that Reece doesn't care about football." Kristin stared at the ceiling—the night before, the lake, the walk, the sex. She felt a chill and trembled.

Breakfast was soon ready, and they gathered at the table, eating their toast, eggs, and bacon. Kristin avoided eye contact with her mom as well as she could. She then showered and was ready at ten-thirty, ready for Reece to pick her up, worried he had changed his mind. At the last minute, she called, but he was on the way. She heard him drive up and went out to meet him, Bible in hand, and let him hug her.

"You okay?" he asked. He opened the truck door for her. "You look nice." She wore a white dress with a wide collar and a gold necklace with a tiny pendant.

"Just a little confused is all."

He closed the door. "Buckle up. It's going to be a lesson in Baptist 101." He laughed, but she didn't, and they rode in silence for a minute.

"I don't think we should have done that last night," said Kristin. "I feel guilty." The wind blew her curls, the smell of a dank fall in the air. "I feel like you seduced me."

Reece coughed, steering with one hand. "But it was great. Don't feel bad." He felt uncomfortable and pulled his pants down from his crotch, braking for the slow car in front of them.

"What does God think?"

Reece had a variety of answers for that question. "We love each other, so that's all that matters, right?" He knew they shouldn't have done it as well, especially after having unprotected sex with Cindy. An alarm bell was ringing in his head. There was HIV that he'd been reading about in the paper, and it appeared to be fatal and wrought with a bucket list of unpleasant consequences. The words Kaposi's sarcoma came to his lips, a type of deadly cancer. He slowed for a light, and a yellow jacket flew into the cab.

Kristin squealed, and Reece picked up a paper sack and waved it at the insect. It took a minute, but he managed to swat it out the window.

It took another fifteen minutes, and they pulled up to the crowded parking lot. Reece had to park across the street. On the marquee was "Welcome Home Reece Myers!" He groaned, and Kristin squeezed his arm. By the time they were able to walk up the ramp and enter the front door, no fewer than five people had stopped him, congratulating him and gazing at the scars on his temples. In the foyer, he had to greet all of the deacons before taking his bulletin and escorting Kristin inside. He spotted Horace. Dora was in the choir. They scooted past Horace into the packed pew. Reece wanted to crawl into a hole.

"It's good you came," said Kristin. "Gosh."

Smiling, Horace offered him a peppermint, and Reece took it like communion. Reece put his arm behind Kristin and began to feel antsy, crossing and uncrossing his legs. The organ played "The Old Rugged Cross" and chatter was high. The two women behind him were discussing lemon bars. Reece looked around and waved at friends he'd known for many years from his summers at the lake and his last year and a half of high school there. Horace fiddled with his hearing aid, making it squeal.

The preacher, Pastor Scoggins, entered from behind the organ, followed by the choir director and then the robed choir members, wearing maroon and gold, also the colors of the high school. The choir robes matched the maroon pew cushions. The piano player, whom Reece had dated briefly, moved into position and joined the organ as the service got underway.

Pastor Scoggins stood and brought the service to order. He was mid-sixties and balding with thick glasses. He wore one of his stock Sunday suits, this one a shiny black. He welcomed everyone, gave Sunday School attendance, and asked if there were any visitors in the audience. He instructed visitors to fill out the little card in the pew backs with the tiny pencils provided for such.

"Raise your hand," said Reece.

"No, I've been here once before," said Kristin.

A young man with pimples raised his hand, and everyone turned to take a closer look at him. Next, everyone stood, while the piano played, and shook hands with their neighbors, many making their way to say hey to the lonesome pimply visitor. There was a rousing chorus of "To God Be the Glory." Next came the offertory with prayer by Deacon Busby and the passing of the plate as the organ hummed a pleasant tune. Reece dropped in a dollar.

Pastor Scoggins then took the pulpit with his large-print preaching Bible and tugged at the collar of his starched white shirt. A coolness drifted from the vents across the congregation, light chasing away shadows through the simple stained glass windows.

Pastor Scoggins tugged at his collar again and recognized Reece in the audience. "Raise your hand, son, and is that pretty lady with you your fiancée?"

Reece glanced at Kristin to make sure she was still there. "Yes sir," he said.

Kristin blushed.

"Now we often have missionaries in our midst, but now we have one that we can call our own. We thought he'd be gone for longer than he was, but God saw fit to bring him home early, alive and in one piece, although bruised and battered." He then went on to compare the spear in the side of Christ to the bullet hole in Reece's head. Reece crossed his legs and shrugged his shoulders.

Pastor Scoggins then had them turn to the Book of Job to see why God visited calamity on the seemingly righteous. Reece discerned a pattern in the wood of the back of the pew in front of him. The stained wood swirled into the image of a sad man with unruly hair, and he focused on that, his shoulders aching from sitting still.

"So, Satan answered the Lord and said, 'Skin for skin! Yes, all that a man has he will give for his life. But stretch out Your hand now, and touch his bone and his flesh, and he will surely curse You to Your face!' And the Lord said to Satan, 'Behold, he is in your hand, but spare his life.'" He went on to describe the disgusting sores that Job had to endure at the hand of Satan, who was determined to make Job curse God.

Reece thought of the people of Godo, of the deep and weeping tropical ulcers he often saw, usually on the legs.

Pastor Scoggins nagged his collar and continued: hunger, fever, depression, nightmares, putrid breath, and rotting teeth, not to mention the loss of his wealth and his children. Job was a royal mess, but still his faith held steadfast. Reece leaned over to Kristin and whispered, "What, no tornado?"

But Pastor Scoggins had him covered, and that was the next miracle, Reece being spared from the F-5 tornado that destroyed parts of University Hospitals. But like Job, Reece had endured. Reece felt a little hot and embarrassed as the story of Job's life unfolded as his own.

With noon approaching and bellies growling in the audience, Pastor Scoggins finagled his collar one last time and called the service to an end, leading into the invitation.

"And I want Reece to come and stand beside me today," said Pastor Scoggins. "There may be someone here today who is hurting like Job, who needs an encouraging word, and perhaps there is someone here today who needs to dedicate their life to Christ." Beads of sweat had gathered on his pale, hairless brow.

Kristin poked Reece and nodded for him to stand by Pastor Scoggins, who had left the pulpit for the carpet in front of the altar. Reece squeezed beside Horace, who patted him on the hip, and stood beside Pastor Scoggins. Reece folded his hands, gazing at the clock on the back wall. He knew the invitational would be accompanied by that saddest of songs "Come Home," and soon everyone was standing, singing that mournful tune, the perfect ending to a tragic story.

One stanza went by, and no one came. But during the second stanza, the visitor with pimples scattered across his forehead came forward. Reece kind of froze as he watched him approach. He was Reece's age, named Randy, and he took Reece's hand in his own, leaning in to whisper in his ear.

"I, I've turned my back on God. I lost my girlfriend to a truck driver."

Reece pondered the words. "Do you need prayer?"

"Yeah sure," said Randy. He seemed ready to accept any morsel of hope.

Reece said a quick prayer, asking God to let Randy back into the fold, to forgive him, and to work out the situation with his girlfriend and the truck driver. By now, they were into the third stanza, and Randy just stood there holding Reece's hand as if waiting for a confirming rumble of thunder. Reece leaned over to Pastor Scoggins and told him that Randy would like to rededicate his life to God, and moved Randy his way, nodding in affirmation, and Pastor Scoggins took over. The song ended, and Pastor Scoggins announced Randy's intent to several amens from the congregation, and then asked Horace to stand and lead in a final prayer, which he did, while toying with his noisy hearing aid.

Over with, it took Reece and Kristin forever and a day to extricate themselves from the crowd of well-wishers and curiosity seekers. Reece felt exhausted, eager to be gone and have a nice lunch with Kristin, thinking about the slideshow that night at Emma's church, which he had permission to attend.

After church, Reece had gone with Kristin and his grandparents to Costa's for lunch, eating a big barbecue sandwich and onion rings. He had taken Kristin home, eager to take a nap, which he did, dreaming of a little boy who had lost his parents in a tornado. The service at Emma's church started at six, and he had promised Kristin that he would come by her house no later than eight.

He wondered what he should wear, hoping that he wouldn't be asked to speak, and decided on jeans and a short-sleeve plaid shirt. The closer he got to Emma's house, the more excited he became, eager to see her after a week. He pulled into the long driveway and parked. The sky was a gentle purple with a few looming clouds towering. She met him at the door.

"Hey! Come in. We need to get there early to set up the projector. That's a cute shirt." She wore faded brown corduroy slacks and a designer top that outlined her curves. "You eat? Got some baked beans with sausage."

"No, but thanks. I've eaten enough for three people today." He followed her into the kitchen. "Hey, Mrs. Smith." Sarah was smoking and drinking coffee.

"Call me Sarah. I'm going with y'all, you know that?" She tapped her ash.

"Yes, Momma," said Emma. "Debbie and Sally are coming too. Well, let me see, got my slide reel here. I think I'm ready to go. Want to go in Mom's car?" She clapped her hands and gave Reece a spontaneous hug.

Reece let the hug linger. She smelled like yellow Dial.

"Sure." But he knew that could delay his getting back to Kristin, and worried.

"This'll be great," said Emma. "I'm so excited you could come."

"Yeah, me too." Reece couldn't take his eyes off her. Her short brown hair parted down the middle, her bright eyes hitting him at chest level. "You look cute."

"Well, thanks," said Emma. She seemed to soften just a bit. "So, guys, let's go. What do you say?"

Sarah had to fetch her keys and purse, and soon they were on their way. Inside, the church was brightly lit, a screen set up in front of the altar, a slide projector on a rolling cart between the two rows of pews. Pastor Tom stood ready, not wearing a jacket.

"Emma! Our little hero." Pastor Tom gave her a big side hug, his jet-black hair in place. The pews were lightly scattered with early comers, eager to see the slideshow. There was a rumor that she was going to show a slide of Reece after he was shot. "And Mr. Reece. Glad to see you back." He shook Reece's hand as if meeting the president of a large corporation, and then he made over Sarah, telling her to visit more often.

Debbie, Emma's sister, had arrived and joined them, but Sally probably was going to be late as usual, said Emma. She saddled up her reel of thirty slides with the projector and turned it on. A bright square of light hit the screen, bleeding off the edges to the back wall. With Reece's help, she adjusted the light to fit the screen with a few minutes to spare, and then Castor came loping in and made a bee-line for Emma, his mother running after him.

"Castor!" She let him hug and squeeze her as Reece

stepped back. Castor smelled of shampoo and maybe something fried.

"Em-ma, I love you." Castor looked into her eyes, being the same height.

"I love you, too, buddy. Hey, Mrs. Dobbs." Emma untangled herself from Castor and let his mom take over, dragging him to a pew, as he whimpered.

"He likes you," said Reece.

"Yeah, he's a handful," said Emma.

More people filtered in, spacing themselves in the pews as if measured. Sally and Heather walked in and joined the party in the middle of the pews. It was time to begin, and Pastor Tom brought the wireless microphone from the pulpit, getting the show on the road. He announced a brotherhood breakfast for the following Saturday and then introduced Emma and her slideshow.

Emma's sisters, then Heather, Sarah, and Reece, were sitting on pews halfway down to the front, just even with Emma behind the projector. Brother Samuel dimmed the lights. Emma started by thanking everyone for coming, including her family, and gave a special thanks to Reece for being a solid partner in his time with her in Godo. The projector clicked, and the bright square of light switched to a barren scene of rocky ground with green cloth tents, provided by the Polish Army, and a few thatched huts in the background, the scene in Gundo Meskel when she first arrived.

The images flowed. A pretty young girl with braided hair. An amputee. A pallet of grain. A helicopter. A young boy clinging to his mother's back. A young boy tending two goats. Another nurse, the one whose fiancée had killed himself. The rudiments of a clinic being built by skinny men in tattered shorts. A rough table with a platter of enjera and wots. Emma, with her stethoscope, listening to the heart of an old woman.

Each image fascinated Reece, burning a desire to return and perhaps finish what he had started. He listened as Emma spoke matter-of-factly about diarrhea and trachoma. A young boy with a knot of hair on his head, his eye sockets filled with flies. A few moans from the congregation. And before he knew it, there was Emma's little house in Godo. Irigit with his rifle. Afewerki and the team arrayed in front of their living quarters. Misrak and Zenebek in the cook house door, smoke swirling. And then three slides of him working in the clinic. Sally squeezed his leg. The monk who had been carving the church into the rock, his neck covered with pustules. Irrigating a little boy's ears. A woman with a large goiter. He found it hard to believe that it was him in the photos, that Emma had been behind the camera, that Ethiopia existed. He looked over at Emma and felt a longing like he had never felt before, and swallowed hard.

The last slide was of Emma at the guest house in Addis, standing between Dr. Guthrie and the administrator Ben. She looked small and wasn't smiling. It took a minute for the lights to rise, and Emma was standing, as if waiting on a plane to whisk her away to the next exotic location. A man in the back clapped, and then everyone clapped, perhaps hoping for more.

Pastor Tom stood and motioned Emma to the front. "That was about the most interesting thing I've ever seen," he said. He looked humbled and meant what he said. "I think now, Emma," and he gave her a side hug, "that the congregation might like to ask a few questions. Is that alright?"

Emma nodded and folded her hands in front of her, gazing out over the sprinkled pews. A man in back stood. "Is Ethiopia a communist country? I read where it was." He sat down.

Emma looked puzzled but gave a half smile. "Well, technically, it's a Marxist military government, although it's referred to as a dictatorship." There was the whole story of the deposing of the emperor Haile Selassie, but she just let it go at that.

"So, you weren't free the whole time?" The man didn't stand this time. "Like here?"

Emma thought. "I was as free as I wanted to be. They were pretty strict with travel documents, but that's all. In the countryside, there was no law of any kind, and people got along as best they could."

The elderly Mrs. Stubbs raised her hand. "Did they let you pray?"

Emma smiled and looked at Reece, who looked as puzzled as she was by the questions. "Of course, I prayed every day. Just like here, there was a church or churches in every village. The government didn't seem to care. The Mission in Addis Ababa printed Bibles."

Mrs. Stubbs smacked her lips and looked around.

Castor had been unusually quiet during the slideshow. He whispered to his mother now, and his mother raised her hand.

"Yes?" asked Emma.

"Well, Castor wants to know why all the children were

black."

Emma laughed and caught Reece's smile. "Well, Castor, the people are Ethiopian. Most of them are black, just like black people here. Does that answer your question?"

Castor whispered into his mother's ear again, and she tried to hush him. There didn't seem to be any more questions, and a silence ensued until Pastor Tom stood and dismissed the service with prayer. He thanked God for Emma and asked His blessings on her and on Reece as well. "Amen" and the slideshow was officially over.

After a long hug with Castor and a lengthy conversation with Mrs. Stubbs, Emma was free to go. She suggested that they all go to Wendy's, and Reece agreed.

"That was surreal," said Reece. He and Emma sat in the backseat of Sarah's Chrysler.

"I guess I know what you mean," said Emma. "What do you mean?" She was strapped in on the far side against the open window.

"I mean, even I can't believe you did what you did, and that I was there."

"Yeah, I kind of felt like a doll standing up there and that someone was moving my lips." She laughed.

"It was so good, honey," said Sarah. She turned down the radio, playing country and western.

"You did great, Emma. It was fascinating. You'll have to help me do my slideshow at my church. I mean, I'll need to borrow some of your slides. I only have photos, which I can make into slides, I think."

"That would be great. Yeah, as long as you have the negatives, I think you can." Her short brown-blondish hair rippled in the window breeze.

From the side, she looked like a little girl, and Reece kept glancing, remembering that she'd jumped out of the helicopter. He worried about her, wondering if she was acclimating to home, wondering if she was still in danger. He wanted to reach over and hold her hand, pull her closer.

"You doing okay these days? Thinking about a job?" asked Reece. Wendy's was up ahead.

"As good as can be, I suppose. It's hard to sleep, just thinking and thinking about everything that's happened." She looked sad in the twilight. "I'm gonna do home health care, got an interview next week at BamaCare."

"That's cool. Well, if you ever need anything, you can call, right? I mean...well, you know."

Sarah pulled in and parked. The others were right behind them. "Now y'all can't keep me up too late," she said. "I'll come in just a minute. Gotta smoke."

"I know. You gotta work tomorrow," said Emma.

Debbie, Sally, and Heather joined them in the parking lot, and they all sauntered inside and ordered Frostys plus one for Sarah. Sally paid, much to Reece's relief, as he was broke. They crowded around the only empty table, everyone congratulating Emma on a job well done.

Reece checked his watch. It was seven-fifteen, and he had to be at Kristin's no later than eight. Surrounded by her family, Emma seemed as solid as stone. They lingered until eight, and then said their goodbyes and parted ways, and soon Sarah pulled into the long driveway.

"Can you stay awhile?" asked Emma. She brushed her bangs from her eyes.

Reece rechecked his watch. "Need to leave in about forty-five minutes."

"Well, heck, we can write a book in that amount of time. Let's sit outside. Gotta pee first."

"Yeah, me too," said Reece, and he followed her inside.

Sarah was outside smoking, but she went back in, leaving them to themselves. Reece and Emma took chairs and positioned them to face out toward the front yard. The air was cool, and the cicadas called as if screaming for milk.

"I did miss that sound," said Emma.

"Yeah, me too, and thunder. It never thundered over there."

Emma thought. "You know, I hadn't realized that. You're right."

"Didn't mean to steal your thunder." Reece laughed.

"Well, maybe you did when you got shot. Oh, I shouldn't make jokes about that."

"Might as well," said Reece. "Laughter's the best medicine."

"I reckon." They sat in silence for a minute, listening to the bugs drone. "Did you see that?"

"Yeah, heat lightning...You know, you said you prayed over there every day. Is that true? I know I did at first, but then I just couldn't anymore. Still can't." Reece was slumped in his chair, and he sat upright, putting his elbows on his knees.

"I guess I didn't pray every day. I had a devotional that I tried to do at night, but I did kind of lose interest, especially after you left, although I did pray for you."

"I appreciate it," said Reece. "I guess I did pray in the hospital. I kept trying to get everybody to notice that I was moving. It was that nursing assistant, Debbie Dee, who first saw me move. She was a piece of work."

"Ha, Debbie Dee. Sounds like a cartoon character."

"After I could sit up, she'd drag me into the shower and give me a good one. I thought she was going to drown me."

More heat lightning played in the distance, roiling orange.

"Well, that's what nurses do, baths and mealtime."

"Yep." He watched a sowbug hit the cement and buzz around like a maniac on fire.

"Move a little closer," said Emma.

Reece moved closer.

"Lean over like you were. I feel the spirit leading me."

"What?" He caught her gaze and looked away.

"Just do it."

Reece leaned forward, and Emma's hand was on his shoulder, kneading the muscle there. A mosquito landed on his arm.

"Skinny as a rail, boy. Here." She stood and moved behind him, putting both hands on his shoulders. "That feel okay?"

"Yeah." Reece closed his eyes, remembering that he'd been behind her when he was shot.

"Need to put some meat on your bones."

"I guess we both do." He rolled his head forward and backward, avoiding looking at his watch.

"You think the slideshow went well?" She put muscle into her massage.

"Oh, yeah. It...was great." He felt himself melting into a puddle.

"So, do you think God exists?" She moved her hands down his sides. "Ticklish?"

"Yeah, I mean, I don't know anymore. If he's real, then

what sort of God is He? Not very fair if you ask me." He made a little groan.

"Yeah, me too," said Emma. "Kind of leaves a big blank spot, though." She swatted a mosquito.

"Yeah, and I wonder how long it'll take to fill that back in?" Reece wondered what he should do next. But he knew he should jump and run screaming through the night.

Emma massaged his neck and spine, running her hands to his waistband. "It'd be better if you'd take your shirt off."

Reece felt a thrill run through his body. "Oh…I can't. I mean, Kristin and all. Look, maybe I should go. I just don't know if this is right."

"Feels right to me," said Emma.

"It certainly feels good, but I'm engaged." He felt like a loser and a saint all at once.

Emma looked hurt. "Okay, I understand. I think."

Reece took her hands and pulled her to him. "You are very special, I'll admit that. But I have to work things out with Kristin." Emma came in close, and they stood there embracing beneath the single bulb.

"You're solid as a rock." She tilted her head back for a kiss, and Reece brushed his lips against her cheek.

"I should go, but you still have to help me with my slideshow, right?"

"But be sure and ask Kristin." Emma sighed and stood back, inspecting him from head to foot. "What do you think would've happened if you hadn't been shot and taken away?"

Reece thought he knew. "I can't say for sure. I mean I'm very drawn to you, if that's what you mean."

Emma smiled that half smile. "Yeah, me too. Life is so damn weird."

"Hard and only gets harder." Reece leaned in and gave her a proper kiss on the lips.

Reece had made it back to Kristin's, albeit two hours late, and they'd talked late into the night, but he hadn't mentioned Emma, other than a few words about her slideshow. Monday morning, and Reece was exhausted. Mrs. Laramore seemed to be doing better, her lungs clearing, but she was still on the ventilator, her eyes talking to him in panicked blinks. Mr. Riggins had not fared so well. Doctors had inserted an ICP line into his spine, and then he'd bled out somewhere deep within his brain, filling the fluid collection bag with blood. His family was a wreck, his EEG was flat, and they had a painful choice to make, which they did in the best interest of easing his suffering.

Wednesday came, and Kristin had arranged an after-hours appointment at five with the counselor that Reece didn't care for, Calvin Dobbs, PhD. His office was in a glassy building, inhabited mainly by a bank. Kristin drove, and in the elevator, Reece punched the button for the fourteenth floor, riding up in silence, except for the music.

"Here we go." He followed Kristin to the end of the hall and into the small waiting area that smelled of paper. Cindy was weighing on his mind, and he wondered if he should just spill his guts.

The receptionist, overly bubbly, was just leaving, but assured them that Dr. Dobbs would be out to fetch them, and so they sat side by side in matching chairs.

"This will be great, Reece. Thanks for doing this. It means a lot."

Reece nodded, crossed his legs, and checked his patellar reflex. His leg jumped off his knee. "Hyperreflexia," he said.

"What? You made your leg jump," said Kristin.

He tapped just below his knee again, and his leg jumped. "See?"

"Now you're being weird, like your displaced radial artery," said Kristin.

"Yep, that's real too." He held out his wrist for Kristin to check, but she'd already done that before.

The door opened, and it was Calvin. He wore a shiny blue, three-piece suit and had a serious receding hairline, but smooth tan skin. "Hello! Come on back." He held the door for them as if to a fancy restaurant. "Would you like some tea? I think I would like some tea."

"Oh, no, thank you," said Kristin. Reece just nodded no, and they sat on the leather love seat.

Calvin drew off a cup of hot water from a tall electric pot and dropped in a teabag. Reece inspected his eyes and could tell that he wore contacts. He looked for earlobe creases, which were correlated with heart attacks. Calvin was probably fifty or so with just a slight chicken neck poking out of his collar, and he reminded Reece of the news guy Tom Snyder. Calvin took his seat, an overstuffed leather chair on wheels that reclined. He crossed his legs, revealing thin nylon socks.

"Well," and he looked at a sheet of paper on his desk, "Kristin and...Reece, let's get this show on the road." He rubbed his hands together as if they were cold, maintaining a steady smile. "Where shall we begin? Well, where did we leave off all those months ago?" He suddenly remembered that Reece had been shot, that he had gone to a foreign country to work.

"We're engaged, of course," said Kristin. "Reece and I. We're both nurses, and Reece was away in Ethiopia doing mission work when he was shot. Needless to say, he survived and is back home."

"Amen," said Calvin. "I'm sure there were lots of prayers in the making. But not everyone can cut that mustard, I'm sure. Am I right?" His head was oily beneath the fluorescent light that hummed.

"And then the tornado nearly got me." Reece kept a straight face. There was a floor-to-ceiling tinted window in the lobby. If he confessed about Cindy, would Kristin try to jump? Would she push him through it?

"Nearly got us all," said Calvin. He wrapped the teabag around a spoon and squeezed out the goodness into his light purple cup that said "Awesome God!" "So, how has it been, the two of you back together?"

"Good," said Reece.

"Maybe not so good," said Kristin. "Reece, that's why we're here." She scolded him with a frown. "There's this big problem that we're having."

Calvin raised his bushy eyebrows. "Oh, a big problem. Let's just let the cat out of the bag, shall we? No need to beat around the bush, right?" He sipped his tea, made a little ouch face, and then blew on the cup.

Reece waited to hear what the big problem would be. He noticed Calvin's PhD certificate on the wall from a college he'd never heard of. The certificate was very small and printed in red ink.

"Well," said Kristin. "There's another woman in the

picture. Her name is Emma, and she was a nurse with Reece over there."

"In Nigeria," said Calvin.

"Ethiopia," said Reece. "We worked in a clinic together for a couple of months."

"Did she get shot as well?" asked Calvin. He put his chin in his open hand.

All Reece could think of was how the little man Castor had asked why all of the children were black.

Kristin glanced at Reece. "No, that's not the issue. I mean, he's lucky to be here at all. I thought I had lost him, and well...I don't want that to happen again."

"What do you mean by that, his being shot?"

Reece stifled a grin and imagined a herd of donkeys walking around in a big whooshy circle. Maybe if he hadn't been shot, he would have died from malaria.

"No," said Kristin. "Just that I don't want to lose him again."

"And, so, this other woman, Nettie."

"Emma," said Reece.

"Yeah, Emma. I think she has a crush on Reece, and he's...well, I think he's leading her on...without really knowing it." She looked to Reece for support.

"I helped her with a slideshow for her church," said Reece.

"Yeah, but then you went to the slideshow, and you talk about how great she is...what a great nurse, what a great person. I keep telling him he can't see her, and then he finds an excuse to see her."

"Kind of like the cat and the mouse," said Calvin. "So, who's the cat here?"

Kristin raised her voice. "Well, she is, of course."

"But the mouse is smart, right. He knows that he's engaged to another mouse. Right?" He looked at his sheet of paper. "Reece?"

"Well, we're not exactly both mice," said Reece.

"Reece, you know what he means." Kristin adjusted herself on the cushy cushion.

"Let's see here," said Reece. "I've told Emma, I mean Kristin, that I won't see her, Emma, again."

"But you've said that before," said Kristin. "When do I start believing you?"

"I mean, now," said Reece. "Unless there was a good reason, right? What if she wants to come to my church and hear me speak, my slideshow? Compared to going out to dinner with her, which I would never do."

Calvin looked like he was watching a game of Pong, but broke the silence. "Reece, when God makes you a rooster, you can't suddenly become the hen. You can see why Kristin is concerned, even angry with you. You have dedicated your lives to one another in the eyes of God. That counts for something." His bushy eyebrows moved when he spoke.

"My words exactly," said Kristin. "We're like soul mates, and there can't be another woman in the middle. It just won't work."

"But I can have friends, right? And friends occasionally see each other," said Reece. He watched Calvin reach and scribble on paper.

"When two lines cross, they share a point, right? The key is to continue the line and not get stuck there. Kristin thinks you are stuck there."

"At the intersection of two lines?" asked Reece.

"Reece, you're being difficult. Do you see why I'm so frustrated?"

"Reece, do you find this other woman attractive? If she were a flower, what kind of flower would she be?" Calvin tippled his tea and smacked his lips.

"Lots of people are attractive. You can't just have ugly friends, right? Maybe she's like a dogwood blossom, but Kristin is like a white daisy."

"And what kind of flower are you?" asked Calvin.

"Me? I'm more like a pine tree." Reece could tell that Calvin had shaved early that morning, that Calvin's five o'clock shadow was showing.

"Solid and swaying but with lots of pinecones for other people to step on," said Calvin. "Right?"

Reece imagined himself as a pine tree. The hammock that Cindy had been in was held up by two massive pines. He looked to Kristin for help.

"Well, trees and flowers," she said. "A dogwood blossom? I mean, they're really pretty."

"Yeah, but they only come out around Easter," said Reece. "Daisies grow year-round."

"That's a good point," said Calvin. He uncrossed his legs and put down his cup of tea. "So, this Emma is a god-like figure to you, something sacred, whereas Kristin... Well, you know where I'm going with this, and you have to understand how Kristin feels, like a lone daisy in a glass vase." He was getting warmed up. "Have you ever seen someone whose face looked like a brown balloon? That's what I'm seeing here."

"Am I the brown balloon?" asked Reece.

Calvin nodded, waiting.

"Regardless, what can we do to make Emma stay out of the way? I don't think she realizes all the trouble she's causing." Kristin adjusted herself to keep from sinking.

Reece drifted to Cindy in the back room of the Sykes. She was on all fours, naked.

"Well," said Calvin. "Reece needs to make it clear that his driveway is occupied. That the house is for you and not for her. Is there something Reece could do to facilitate that? Reece? You seem to be drifting away."

He was inside Cindy, and the screen door had opened and slammed shut. "Okay...I'm the problem. Emma's not the problem as far as I can tell. We went through some hard times together, that's all. It's up to me, I suppose. I'm the plunger that won't break the clog. There." Cindy had said to keep going, but he had panicked.

"Now the ball is rolling," said Calvin. "Kristin, are you hearing what Reece is saying. You know I totally forgot to start with prayer, but we'll end with prayer." He looked at his silver watch.

"I hear him," said Kristin. "Do you promise to let her know what a stumbling block she has become and promise not to see her again? You have to say that. I can't take this anymore."

Reece felt like he was about to explode, and then he just said it. "I had sex with Cindy. I'm sorry." He hung his head, waiting for the room to collapse.

On Tuesday, Emma interviewed with BamaCare and by the next day had her first assignment, shadowing a nurse and a private patient who lived in Mountain Brook in a brick mansion. He was sixty-two and divorced, a retired bank executive who had been in charge of fourteen savings and loans, and who was an alcoholic and a womanizer, according to the nurse Darlene. The man, Charles Rickers, not only had hepatitis C, but he was also infected with HIV. That had happened a year ago.

Darlene pulled into the half-moon driveway paved with red brick, followed by Emma. The three-story house loomed over them. Ornamental pears lined the drive with extensive landscaping in the front and on the sides. A towering water oak centered the yard. An older Hispanic man with a ballcap was raking beneath a shrub.

"Mr. Rickers likes his yard," said Darlene. Her cheeks seemed pasted to her face, her body like a pillowcase stuffed with cloth. Like Emma, she wore blue scrubs stamped with the BamaCare logo. "He's got three nurses right now. We stay three days and two nights, and rotate. We're going to relieve Sally."

"So, does Mr. Rickers like to be called Mr. Rickers or Charles?" asked Emma.

"I don't know. We just call him Mr. Rickers. He can have a temper, but he's usually too sick to make much of a scene. Whatever you do, don't deny him his bourbon when he asks for it. That'll get you fired right off."

"Wow," said Emma. She'd read about all the meds Rickers was taking and wondered about the interaction with alcohol. "Who buys it for him?"

"He has a girlfriend, Trish, a young thing with a credit card. I don't think they have sex, but I could be wrong." Two arched oak doors fronted the entrance. "I have a key if no one comes." She jingled her key ring and opened her trunk, taking out a small suitcase and a cooler with deli meat, cheese, bread, grapes, and diet root beer. "He has food you can eat, but I bring most of my own." Darlene waddled to the front door and rapped with a giant iron knocker.

Sally answered the door. "Hey, y'all. He's in bed eating some toast." She was thin and tall with a plain face and wiry arms. She surveyed Emma in her youth. "I'm Sally. He's gonna like you," and she laughed.

"Hey," said Emma. Inside, the entrance was grand, with a curved staircase and three chandeliers. The rug looked expensive, and there was a half-circle designer couch. Rooms branched off at every turn. "Do you have to clean the house?"

"No, maids come once a week. You have to empty the trash can by his bed and keep the bathroom picked up, but that's about all. Well, I'll get my things and go. He's got his meds for another week or so. Suppositories for nausea and for fever, and then his vitamins. Nothing new to report except that he runs a fever most of the time and gets pretty bad headaches. Not eating much, so he's just skin and bones. Keep on him about drinking water or his Gatorade. You might have to bolus him with a liter or two of normal saline if he won't drink. That's about it."

"Any blood draws or appointments scheduled?" asked Darlene.

"No, his last T-cell was about fifty, which was up a little.

So that's good." Sally picked up her bag and purse, ready to hit the road, and left.

"So, how did he get HIV?" asked Emma.

Darlene pondered the question. "What I've heard is that he got it from a prostitute in Atlanta. He swears, though, that he got it from a blood transfusion. So, who knows? He's lucky he's lasted this long. A few weeks ago, he went into the hospital for a lung infection. He was on a slew of antibiotics."

"Wow," said Emma. "This is all new to me. I'll probably ask a lot of questions." She gave her lopsided smile.

"Well," said Darlene. "Let's go meet the master of his domain. Follow me and don't get lost." She laughed and led the way up the stairs.

"Does he get outside?"

"Not really. He's got a stunning garden out back with a pond and some fish. Mostly, he's in bed. It's hard for him to get up and down the stairs. Need an elevator in this hotel."

Darlene reached the second floor and went left, passing two bedrooms, each with their own bathroom. At the end of the ornately paneled hall was an open door. From ten feet away, a smell of sweat and body odor hit Emma.

"Knock, knock!" said Darlene.

Emma followed her into the large bedroom with a vaulted ceiling. The room curved on the outside with four huge windows and fifteen-foot drapes. Then she saw him, sitting in the bed, propped against a leather headboard. He looked like hell, haggard and unshaven, his cheeks sunken. Even sitting, she could tell he was a tall man. He turned his pale head toward them.

"Hey, Mr. Rickers. You look good," said Darlene. She

went to his bedside with Emma.

"Who's this?" Rickers' voice was deep and gravelly. His eyes dark and bloodshot. He coughed and then took a few deep breaths.

"Yeah, it's me, Darlene, and this is Emma. In a couple of days, she'll be staying with you. I'm getting her trained."

"Hey," said Emma, smiling. He was too far away for her to shake his hand, but he was holding it out. She put one knee on the bed and leaned in and shook it, feeling clammy bones. She wondered if she could get HIV through sweat.

"Hello, good to meet you," said Rickers. "I'm Rickers. I live here, and I'll probably die here." He tried to laugh.

"Not while we're here, buddy," said Darlene. "Can I get started and listen to your lungs, check your blood pressure and temp?"

"Well, if that's what they're paying you to do, then by all means."

"How about getting in the chair there? Make it easier, plus you need to be moving around." Darlene gathered the cuff, her stethoscope, and a thermometer.

Charles clawed his way to the side of the bed, pulling on the fitted sheet, taking deep breaths. Emma noted that his lips were taking on a bluish tinge. "Mr. Rickers, pull up on me, and we'll step over to the chair." Emma readied herself.

"If you say so," said Charles. He let Emma drag his legs over the side of the bed. "Need a damn bath and some clean clothes." He was wearing sweats.

"Charles, put your arms around my neck, and I'll help you stand." Emma squatted a bit. "Good, here we go." She lifted him and moved back a step. "Need to take two steps, and then we'll pivot into the chair."

"Very...efficient," said Charles. He put a foot forward and then brought the other forward. "You like bourbon, Emma? What's your last name?"

"First, one more step forward." He did that, and Emma swiveled him into a high-backed padded chair. "Good work. It's Smith. And I'll drink with you anytime, as long as I'm not working."

He tried to laugh and coughed.

"Good work," said Darlene. "She's gonna do real nice, Mr. Rickers."

He sat in the chair with a surprised look on his face, as if he had ridden a magic carpet. "Well, that's good news."

Glenda checked his vitals. "BP's a little low, heart rate is one hundred." She waited for the thermometer, holding it beneath his tongue.

Emma watched, imagining the thermometer in her mouth, and swallowed.

"Hundred-one point six," said Glenda. "You feel like swallowing some Tylenol?"

"God no," said Charles. "Give me the suppository."

"Will do," said Darlene. She popped on a glove and took one of the foil-wrapped suppositories on the bedside table, lubing it with a bit of K-Y jelly. "Emma, you help him stand."

Emma reached under his armpits. "One, two, three, and stand."

Darlene pulled his sweatpants and underwear down. "In she goes."

"Just another excuse to see my ass," said Charles. He

sat back heavy into the chair. "But you're not the first. Oh brother."

Emma laughed. "Next time we'll take a picture. Lasts longer."

"She's good," said Charles. He made an effort to smile and then began gagging.

Glenda grabbed the bedpan just in time as he vomited his toast and what looked to be orange juice. "Oh dear."

"Well fuck," said Charles. He smacked his wet lips.

Emma looked around for the restroom. "I'll get a wet rag. You want to rinse your mouth?"

"That would be dandy," said Charles. He gagged again and coughed.

Soon, he was spitting mouthwash into an emesis tray, and Emma wiped his mouth. "Didn't lose the Tylenol, did you?"

"No," said Charles. "But thanks for asking. It's the thought that counts, right?"

"You're a pistol," said Emma.

"You said it," said Darlene. "Let him rest a minute, and then we can get him into the shower."

They let him rest in the chair, and Glenda gave Emma a tour of the second floor and then the third floor, which housed a library with puffy leather chairs, a billiards room, plus two more huge bedrooms and a large bathroom with a bidet and a phone. Thick rugs lined the halls, and portraits and paintings hung on the walls.

"Okay, let's get the master into the shower," said Darlene, and she led the way back to his bedroom.

Charles was where they'd left him, his shoulders and head sagging. He looked like an old eggplant wilting on the vine. "You're back, that's good."

Emma scoped out the large walk-in shower lined with brown marble. There was a shower chair there, but no rails. She turned on the water and let it run through the hand-held unit until it was nice and warm. Soap and shampoo sat on a ledge.

"Here's the fun part," said Darlene. "Think you can let us walk you in? Or do we need the wheelchair?"

"That's what I'm paying you for," said Charles. "What does Emma think?"

"Yeah, let's walk. Do you good."

They each took an arm, and he stood, putting most of his weight on them. He took little steps, and they led him to the shower.

"Drawers coming down," said Emma. She pulled his sweatpants and underwear down. "Top coming off."

"Good Lord, such precision," said Charles, standing there buck naked. Then, sitting on the shower chair, he took deep breaths and shivered.

"You lucky devil," said Emma. She sprayed him with the warm water while Darlene lathered a washcloth.

He sat there gripping the arms of the chair as Darlene washed him from head to toe and Emma rinsed. Then they washed his thinning hair as he spluttered.

"Whoo, look brand new," said Emma. "Just about soaked me, though."

"We'll get his teeth brushed, and he'll be good to go," said Darlene.

"Yeah, then you can watch TV like that other nurse," said Charles. "Get me dried. I'm freezing...my ass off."

They went at him from both sides with thick towels.

"Too bad I'm still a virgin," said Charles. He wobbled

back and forth between them, still naked. "Can you get me some more sweats? God, I'm cold."

"Yeah, she's gonna work out real nice, Mr. Rickers," said Darlene.

"I think we'll get along," said Emma.

"Let's not call it so fast," said Charles. He took a deep breath and grinned. "Now the two of you...be quiet and get me...some clothes."

They dressed him in a green Nike tracksuit with a long-sleeve t-shirt and walked him to the high-backed chair where Darlene combed his hair and Emma brushed his teeth. He spat in the tray.

"You feel like drinking some ice water?" asked Darlene. "With your fever and the vomiting, you need fluid."

"No, I do not," said Charles. "Just thinking about it..." He gagged. "And don't punish me with an IV."

"Is there a standing order for IV fluids?" asked Emma.

"Yep. He has to take in at least 1,500 ccs a day, at the very least, one way or the other. As long as he's peeing, though. He should have a hep lock to plug into. What happened to your hep lock, Mr. Rickers?"

"My what?"

"Your IV. The one we keep in. Did you pull it out?"

"Hell, I don't know."

"We'll wait until you need some fluids. Give you a break," said Darlene.

"Well, thank you so much," said Charles. "Get me back in the bed."

Emma glanced at Darlene. "Oh, no way, buddy. You can't get better lying in bed. Want to go outside after you rest?"

"It's a chore getting him down the stairs," said Darlene.

She puffed out her chest and adjusted her plastic-looking cheeks. "We do have to take it slow with him."

"Yeah, no need to kill me...on your first day."

Emma laughed. "You'll feel better if you move around."

"No, you'll feel better if I move around," said Charles.

"Well, Charles, we'll both feel better. How's that?" asked Emma.

"It's Rickers...Mr. Rickers," said Charles. "You're a fresh one all right."

Darlene was frowning. "Okay, Mr. Rickers. You just sit tight in the chair, and let us look over paperwork. She'll learn."

Emma put her hands on her hips, but nodded her head.

"At least recline me," said Charles.

"This chair reclines?"

"Yep," said Darlene. She pulled out the foot and leaned the chair back. "Now, we're going downstairs, unless you want to join us."

Charles just grunted.

"You can't push him too hard," said Darlene, going down the staircase.

"Yeah, sorry," said Emma. "He's cantankerous, but I think I've got his number."

"That would be new. Let's look over his chart." Darlene led the way to the oversized kitchen with two islands. All of Rickers' paperwork lay out on a large farmhouse table. "You see those purple spots on his nose? Those just came up about two weeks ago."

"I was reading about that," said Emma. "What's it called?"

"Kaposi's sarcoma. Not a good sign." Darlene sat at the

table and patted the seat beside her.

"So, this is all new to me. As I understand it, there's no specific medicine to fight the virus, just treat his symptoms like the nausea and fever."

"Pretty much. They have some meds in the works, though. I just hope he lasts long enough to get them." She reviewed his chart with her and entered her morning assessment while Emma gazed out the windows.

"Need some breakfast?" asked Darlene. "You're welcome to whatever is here. Just have to cook it. His ex-wife keeps the fridge pretty full. She usually comes on the weekends. Never says a word to him. Kind of strange."

"Yeah, and I've eaten. Maybe have a snack later."

They heard a faint yell from upstairs and looked at each other.

In an instant, Kristin was off the love seat. "What did you say? You had sex with Cindy?" She stood over Reece as Calvin fumbled his pen. "When? Why?" Tears dampened her eyes.

Reece put his face in his hands.

"Now hold on," said Calvin. "Who is Cindy? Did you mean Emma?" He glanced at the paper on his desk.

"No, Cindy is different," said Kristin. "I knew it. I could see it in her eyes. So, was it the day she pulled her top down? Reece, talk to me!"

"It was last week. She...seduced me. She was on the hammock—"

"Last week? We had sex last week! Are you just having sex with everybody you meet? Did you use protection? God, you better say yes."

"Wait, wait," said Calvin. "Let's stop for a minute. Kristin, will you sit over here in this chair?" He pointed to a desk chair. "We have to sort this out. Reece, who is Cindy? You had sex with her? Last week?"

Kristin sat on the edge of the chair, shaking her head. "Oh, this is great. I can't believe it."

"Cindy is the neighbor's granddaughter, an old friend. She asked me to come into the house, and then we were having sex. I'm sorry. It just happened." Reece considered jumping through the window.

"Reece, how could you?" asked Kristin.

"So, Reece is confessing," said Calvin. "This could be a breakthrough moment. Kristin, does this surprise you?"

"Well, yeah! He's engaged to me and having sex with other women!"

"We were talking about Emma, as I recall," said Calvin. "Reece, now that the can of worms has been opened, have you had sex with Emma as well? Has Pandora's box entered the equation?"

"Dear God," said Reece. "I love you, Kristin. It just happened. She...got naked. We were alone."

"Did you or did you not use a condom?" asked Kristin. She folded her arms across her chest.

Reece stared at the floor. "No. It was so fast. It wasn't planned. I've never even bought condoms. I don't even know how much they cost."

"Okay, Reece is confessing, spilling the beans as it were," said Calvin. "Let's not get lost in the details. A hen lays an egg, usually in the nest. Right? Let's go from there. Let's get this under control before the rooster starts crowing."

"Egg in the nest," said Reece. He stifled a laugh.

"You think this is funny, huh, mister?" asked Kristin. "This is the worst day of my entire life. I can't believe it. We were talking about a slideshow and now this. Reece, say something."

"I'm blank," said Reece. "I promised not to see Emma again, unless there was a good reason, right?"

"We have that," said Calvin. "Let's hold onto that. Things are coming together, kind of like making a complicated dinner. Let's just keep talking." He wiped sweat from his forehead.

"Maybe we should just go," said Reece. "I've screwed up everything."

"Yeah, you have," said Kristin. "As far as I'm concerned, the engagement's off. Do you hear that?" Fresh tears appeared.

"I'm sorry," said Reece.

"Let's hold on tight," said Calvin. "The ship hasn't sunk just yet. It's just leaking. I've never lost a couple yet, and you can't be the first. Okay?" He scribbled in a flurry on the piece of paper.

"Forgive me this once and last time?" asked Reece. "Normally, I don't do things like that. Since I was shot, I'm just different somehow."

"Yeah, real different," said Kristin. "But I'm not marrying you as of right now. Got it. There's nothing you can say right now that will change my mind."

Reece felt relieved somehow. Maybe this was what needed to happen. But what did that mean? Was he supposed to propose to Cindy? And where was Emma in all of this?

"Now," said Calvin, "I think ultimatums are natural in a situation like this. But let's keep the big picture in mind. Kristin, what does Reece need to do now?"

Kristin scowled. "Nothing, he's done enough." She wept into her hands, wetting her fingers.

"Reece?" asked Calvin. He motioned for Reece to join Kristin to comfort her.

Reece couldn't move. He watched Kristin weeping and hung his head. He started to stand.

"Don't...come near me," said Kristin.

Reece sank back into the soft love seat and sighed. He tried to gauge his feelings. He felt blank and at his wits' end. He let the sex scene between him and Cindy play through his head. It had been so natural, like sharing a meal, but more exciting. "Kristin…" He imagined Emma and her half-smile. Somehow, he knew she would understand. Maybe there would be an earthquake, a fire. A brief silence ensued.

Calvin wiped his brow with a tissue. He held out the box to Kristin, and she took one, blowing her nose.

"This is just unbelievable. My parents warned me. Reece, how can you say that you love me and then have sex with a floozy? I just don't understand."

"She seduced me, but I'm still guilty. I could have left. I don't know what I was thinking. I wasn't thinking anything. And then it happened." The words *I love you* failed him. What good would it do?

"And when you said, 'I love you,' I guess that was a lie," said Kristin. Her arms were still folded.

"Reece?" asked Calvin. "Make it good. We're on pins and needles here." He checked his silver watch.

"Kristin, I care deeply about you. When I said I love you, I meant it. It's just…that things have changed. I'm not me anymore. Ethiopia and getting shot changed me."

Kristin looked like she wanted to vomit. "God, Ethiopia. I wish I had never heard of that place. It's over. It's over." She sobbed and hiccupped.

Reece felt like he weighed six hundred pounds. He rallied and stood and walked toward Kristin. He put his hand on her shoulder, but she pulled away. "I'm sorry. I really am."

"What? That it's over? Well, it is, bucko. I mean it. And don't bother taking me home. I'm calling Dad."

Calvin fidgeted. He seemed at a loss for words. "Was

Cindy wearing provocative clothing?"

"What does it matter?" Reece looked away. He went and stood by the floor-to-ceiling window and fingered the curtain. "I mean, I'm not to be trusted, I suppose. Maybe we give it a week and get back together."

"Now we're talking," said Calvin. He rubbed his hands together. "We have to work on a solution to this jigsaw puzzle. What do you say...Kristin?"

"I'm calling Dad. Can I use your phone?" She didn't wait for a reply. She dialed.

Calvin made eye contact with Reece across the room and nodded toward Kristin.

"Dad?" Kristin's voice quavered. "Can you...pick me up? I'm at the counselor's office. Reece can't bring me home...I'll explain later." She held the phone to her chest. "What is this place? What's the address?" She sniffled and grabbed a tissue.

Calvin started to explain.

"Oh, never mind, it's the tall building near the Piggly Wiggly in Homewood. The bank building. I'll be out front, or maybe in back. You'll find me...No, I'm not okay, and that's why I need you to come get me..." She hung up the phone.

Reece held out his hands in a what-can-I-do gesture.

Calvin stood between them. "Are we on for next week? Kristin?"

"No way," said Kristin. She walked through the open door and disappeared.

"Brother," said Calvin, "you may have broken the camel's back." He looked exhausted.

"Yeah," said Reece. "Maybe we'll call.

Reece drove back to the lake, reliving every word in between thoughts of Mrs. Laramore and Mr. Riggins. He comforted himself that he could be in their situation, but it didn't seem much worse than his own.

He pulled into the driveway, noting how clean it was. He swept it at least three times a week, and so did Dora. He felt that he had swum the English Channel wearing a lead belt and had to sit in the truck for a minute. He gathered his marbles and walked into the house. Dora and Horace had finished dinner, but the food was still warm on the stove. He nodded, lifted the tin foil from the skillet, and saw the fried cube steak.

"Thought you'd be out later than this," said Dora. "Fix a plate and eat."

Horace grinned at him and went back to reading the newspaper.

The phone rang, and Reece grabbed it. "Hello?" It was Kristin.

"Reece, I want to talk to your grandmother and now. My parents are furious, and your grandparents need to know what you did."

"Wait, hold on. That's not necessary. I'll tell them in good time."

"I'll just come out there and tell them myself. How's that? And the engagement is off. So, what do you think about that?"

Reece could picture Gert hanging onto every word from the kitchen, Edwin trying to watch TV. He could tell that Dora was listening with a keen ear as well.

"No, don't do that either. Please, Kristin? I admitted

what I did. I was forthcoming, and I'm sorry. I won't ask Emma to help me with the slideshow. I'll, I'll...lock myself in a box."

"Reece, how could you do that? That's the worst thing you could have done. So, she seduced you? Tell me how she did it. Did she throw you on the bed? Did she have handcuffs?"

"No, it was my fault. Yes, she seduced me, but well, I can't talk about it right now." He lowered his voice. "Please don't punish me." He glanced at Dora. She was whispering to Horace, who couldn't hear her.

"I'll punish you if I want to. God will punish you, Reece. You broke one of the Ten Commandments."

"Hasn't he already punished me? Maybe someone will tie me up and burn me alive." Reece felt heated, ready to lash out.

"Oh, you're impossible," said Kristin. "But I am going to tell your grandmother. She needs to know what kind of person you are."

The AC kicked on, vibrating the window. "Please, don't. What if you had done something with that guy Brad at that party you got wasted at? Would you want me to punish you?"

"Don't bring that up. Nothing happened, and I told you that. At least I was faithful. What were you drinking when she supposedly seduced you?"

Reece sat at the table. "Well, truth be told, I'd had a beer or two. I was just so frustrated after the hike, and then she just happened to be out there, and one thing led to another. Look, I don't want to talk about this right now. Okay?"

"I'm sure you're inconvenienced. What about me...my

whole life is ruined. But better to find out now than later. If we were married, I'd divorce you in a heartbeat. Oh, and Robyn will be back soon. I'm going to tell her. I suppose she tried to seduce you when she came out in her bathing suit."

"Okay. Just do whatever you want. I'm willing to get together and talk, or meet you again at the counselor. Maybe we can work this out. Can we try?" Reece somehow felt that he'd passed through a door and that he was trying to fight his way back into a room where he possibly didn't belong.

"Well, you give up pretty easy. So put on your grandmother if you're serious."

"You can call back. But I'll have already explained it to them. They're not going to turn on me."

"So, now you're the victim? That's just dandy. And don't come over to my unit tomorrow and try to talk to me. Got it? God, I'm a wreck as it is. I can't believe you did that!" The phone went dead.

Reece stood there, holding the phone to his ear, wondering what to do. He decided to eat and hung up the phone.

"Boy, what have you done this time?" asked Dora. She was gripping the arms of her recliner. "Is it about that Emma?"

"Well, not really." He picked out a square of cube steak, some cut corn, some green beans shiny with oil. "I made a mistake." He sat back at the table, no longer hungry, but cut his steak with a fork and chewed a piece.

"What did you do?" Dora used her stern voice.

Reece chewed and swallowed. He was behind Cindy,

his shorts on the floor, her beautiful ass reared toward him. "It's about Cindy. While y'all were at the hospital visiting Mr. Sykes. She was in the hammock."

"Uh oh," said Dora. She glanced at Horace, who was fiddling with his hearing aid. "She has a reputation. You know she lives with a man."

"Yeah, I know." He mixed some corn and beans. He wondered if he would tell Emma.

"What happened, son? You might as well talk. Is the wedding off? Oh, Reece, what have you done?"

Reece chewed and swallowed, and then told them in as few words as possible.

Dora put her hand over her mouth, and Horace grunted.

Reece had the nursing assistant Janice help him give Mrs. Laramore a bath. A towel covered her giant breasts. He removed her TED hose and washed her legs and feet, noting the pitting edema. He took lotion and rubbed them. She was still on the ventilator, was better, but she would need dialysis soon if her kidneys didn't kick in. To wash her back, he had Janice pull Mrs. Laramore onto her side. He rinsed the washcloth and worked through all the folds of fat and rubbed her tailbone, which was still reddened.

"Janice, can you finish up?" He felt sad and heavy, working in a haze.

"Okay," said Janice. "You want a gown on her?"

"Yeah," said Reece. He pulled off his gloves and washed his hands. He stepped through the curtain and headed toward Mr. Riggins' room. They were letting his wife stay in the room, as things looked bad. He said a silent prayer for him. He passed Laronda at her station and went in six. The sight of the still body on the cooling blanket depressed him. He smiled at Mrs. Riggins, who stood over her husband, rubbing his silvering head. "Hey. I'm back."

"Anything new?" she said. "He just looks so peaceful this morning." She was a short woman with a pudgy face.

"His blood pressure is a bit low. His temp is still high, and we're still giving the Decadron for the brain swelling. We just have to keep him comfortable." The ventilator breathed, and Mr. Riggins' chest rose. Reece glanced at the IV pump and the heart monitor. He put his hand under Mr. Riggins' back, and it was so cold. If he coded, they were to do nothing.

His wife just kept smoothing back his hair, looking lost. "Should we give him a bath? Make him feel better? I'll help."

"Sure," said Reece. He felt he was putting square pegs into round holes. He wondered if Kristin was chatting it up with Brad next door. He supposed he couldn't blame her. "You guys live in Center Point?"

"Yes."

"It's really growing." Reece washed his hands again and put on gloves.

"Yes."

Reece filled the bath pan with warm water and squirted in some liquid soap. He positioned the pan on the bedside table and gave her a washcloth. He felt he could crawl into the pan and drown. He let her take the upper body, and he took the rest, taking his time, rinsing the washcloth.

She washed his right arm where there was a faded tattoo of an anchor with a floral dash in green ink. "He got this in Hawaii, during the war," she said.

Reece smiled. "Nice. Did you guys meet before or after the war?"

Her eyes brightened. "Oh, we were sweethearts before. I met him at a horse farm. I still have his letters." She washed his face like it was a fine piece of porcelain.

"I know this is hard on you," said Reece. He put the white socks back on Mr. Riggins' feet.

"It's just a dream right now. You know you only find true love once."

That startled Reece, and he felt a deep pain in his gut. "Yeah."

"You're so good with him. We appreciate everything that y'all have done."

"Not a problem," said Reece. "You want to swab his mouth?" He handed her a pack of lemon-flavored glycerin swabs and watched her rub his teeth and gums.

"You like that, honey?" asked his wife.

"Let me do some eye drops," said Reece. Mr. Riggins had lost his blink reflex. He pulled back the lid, dripped in a few drops, and massaged the bloodshot eye, then did the other one.

"Can my daughter come in? She's in the waiting room. The boys are at work. She loves her daddy." A tear gathered and fell.

"Sure," said Reece. "Let me get a clean sheet for him and pull him up. He's slid down." He walked to the linen cart and returned. "Mr. Riggins, gonna pull you up in bed." He bent Mr. Riggins' legs and had his wife hold them. He reached under his shoulder, pulled him up a foot or so, and put on the clean sheet. "You want me to get her?"

"Would you?"

"Sure," and Reece walked through the busy unit. X-ray was there with the portable machine. Residents and nurses sat charting and chatting. He left the unit and went to the waiting room, which was full. "Amanda?"

"Yes?" A short blonde woman with a pretty face about his age stood. She held a huge purse on her shoulder.

"Your mom wants you to come back."

"Is everything okay?" She gripped her purse as if it held gold.

"Yes, he's just had a bath." Reece turned and knew that she was following him. "Here she is, Mrs. Riggins."

Amanda walked in as if it were an autopsy, her eyes wide, and Reece left them to check on Mrs. Laramore and then do some charting. He wanted to talk with Kristin, but knew that it would go badly.

The day progressed one task at a time, the clock slowly spinning to three. He thought he might see Kristin at lunch, but didn't. The news was out, though. Sheila, the head nurse, had cornered him and said that she heard the engagement was off. She was worried that he might quit. Reece clocked out and waded to his truck, feeling as low as he ever had. He supposed, for the time being, that he could call Emma and talk to her. He even had thoughts of driving out to visit, but would call first. He didn't know that she was already working as a private-duty nurse in Mountain Brook. The old white Ford F-150 was there in the parking lot, and he took some comfort when the engine turned over. He backed out of his narrow space and headed to the lake, thinking and thinking, thoroughly exhausted. He made one stop at a liquor store and bought his first bottle of golden tequila. Chester had given him a hundred dollars until his first check came in. He even considered buying a pack of Camels, but held off.

He pulled into the spotless driveway and stashed the tequila under his seat. The truck's engine popped and groaned. Dora was in the backyard trimming the yellow bells, and Horace was in the garden. She shielded her eyes and waved at him.

"Hey," and he felt some better, being back in his element, the lake he had craved as a youngster, his solace from moving from one Army base to the next. He liked to imagine his summers there had kept him alive all those years. He felt old.

"Hey," said Dora. "Get out here and take over. I have to cook dinner." She gave him a sly look. "You talk to Kristin?"

"No. Let me get some shorts on. It's hot." He took the hand shears from her and laid them on the hood of the truck.

"You're in a real pickle, son. But...Oh well." She wiped sweat from her forehead.

"I guess I like pickles," and he went inside to change, passing the phone.

Dora came back inside, rummaging in the fridge. She gave him a look as he passed.

"Glass of water?"

"Yeah," said Reece. He took the amber glass and carried it outside, taking sips and belching. He put the empty glass on the truck toolbox and gathered the old shears. For a better cut, he went into the garage and found some motor oil, which he smeared on the blades. He gave the air a few quick slices and then wiped his hands on pine straw. He imagined that Kristin was going to pull into the driveway and shoot him, and he surmised that he'd deserve it, but hoped that he would survive.

Along the ditch in the back, there were three sprawling yellow bell bushes, each one pushing out dozens of thin, straight limbs with tiny bright yellow flowers. The bushes were about as wide as they were tall, six feet, and Reece aimed to get them to shoulder height and give them a round look. He leaned over the top and snipped and snipped. Right away, he began to sweat, and his arms felt tired, but he kept at it, going around the bush. He locked into a rhythm and soon was clipping in robot mode, his mind a complete blank slate. He wiped the sweat from his eyes with his shirt and, within ten minutes, had the first bush trimmed.

He stood back to assess his work and made some minor adjustments here and there. Like a brick to his head, the memory of Kristin's reaction jarred him. He tried to shake it off, but her angry voice persisted. He pulled off his shirt and went back to work, soon regaining his trance mode, thinking about Emma and her lopsided smile. He would call her and told himself that he would not feel guilty about it. How was she? Had she found a job? Maybe they could have dinner somewhere and just talk. He clipped and clipped, his shoulders getting a good workout, sweat running down his back and gathering in his waistband.

Soon, he was finishing the third bush, the ground littered with trimmings. He had to make himself keep going, to finish the job before he called Emma. He looked up, and it was Dora.

"Well, look at that. You did a good job, boy. Just came out to check on you. Don't want you to have a seizure or anything."

Reece wiped sweat and laughed. "Thanks." His upper body and arms felt fully pumped.

"Don't forget to clean up and put the shears away. They'll rust if you leave them out." She wore long knit shorts and a sleeveless pullover.

"I know," said Reece. "I'll make a burn pile and let it dry for a couple days."

"Okay. Let me get back to dinner. We're having fried chicken thighs and more corn. Lord, we got corn." She shook her head, as if corn was problematic in her life.

"Sounds good," said Reece. He put the shears away, grabbed a gravel rake, and began to make piles of trimmings, then he made one big pile next to the burn can, a rusted fifty-five-gallon steel drum. His shirt was too wet to put back on, and he sat in the swing to cool down. He thought about Mr. Riggins with the flat EEG and hoped that he was comfortable, that he would pass quickly and easily when the time came, which seemed to be soon. He thought about Mrs. Laramore and her giant bosom, which needed a nurse of its own. But soon he was thinking about Emma, the night he was shot. He winced. Then he thought about the day they'd gone to visit the monk building the church into the rock, how she'd gone back later by herself and been accosted by the Hyena and his cronies. She was a fireball for sure and braver than most men he knew, even braver than he was. He remembered the tequila in the truck.

He walked back and retrieved the bottle in a paper sack. He stepped into the RV and sat on the narrow couch there. It was doubly hot inside, and he started to sweat again. What did tequila taste like? *Only one way to find out.* He unscrewed the lid and took a whiff. It had a strange smell, unlike anything he'd smelled before, kind of like maple syrup and alcohol. He lifted the bottle and let the liquid touch and burn his tongue. It tasted like a marshmallow dipped in hard cider. He tilted the bottle and took a small swig. He swallowed and coughed. "Damn." He waited a minute and then took a larger swallow, bringing out notes of hot pepper.

Reece sat holding the bottle, as if he were an expert

drinker, waiting for some sort of effect. He didn't feel anything and took another swallow, coughing again. It was too hot in the RV, and he stood, and then he felt a slight surge in his head. That was enough, and he stashed the bottle in an overhead cabinet filled with placemats and dish towels. Right away, he started to think about liquors—bourbon, vodka, Scotch. He wondered what they tasted like and made a promise to himself that he would find out in due time. Something had melted inside him, and he felt a strange peace as he stepped out of the RV onto the grass covered with pine straw. He wondered if Dora would be able to smell it on him, and decided to take a walk around the garden and say hey to Horace.

He crossed the road, pausing to wave at a car, and went around the garden the long way to Chester, who was picking green beans into a wicker bushel basket. "Hey!"

Chester looked the opposite way and then found him. "Hey, boy."

Reece walked over. "Mostly shell beans?"

"Yeah, but they sure taste good." Horace's overall legs were dusted with red dirt, his gardening shoes falling apart. "Makes good soup."

"Need any help?"

"Naw, about got 'em." He leaned down to get some bulging beans at the bottom of the wire the beans climbed on. "You get things worked out with Kristin?"

Reece followed a group of swallows swooping in the sky. "Didn't talk to her today. I don't know..."

"Well, here's some advice I never gave you." Horace stood erect. He looked so country with his greasy straw hat.

Reece folded his arms and smiled. "What's that?"

"Think with your big head, and not your little head." Horace coughed and grinned.

Reece laughed. "Never heard that one before."

"Big head, little wit. Little head not a damn bit." Horace looked over at Mr. Sykes' garden. "We got to help Maybell clean that garden out. Tomatoes rotting on the vine."

"I hear you," said Reece. "But it may be too late, if you know what I mean."

"Yeah, I been watching you, and you seem to be trying to wiggle out of this engagement. Could be for the best, but don't tell your granny I said that." Horace pushed up his glasses onto his reddened and peeling nose.

"I've been wondering about that myself. I mean, I made a real connection with Emma over there, and I've been confused ever since."

"I wish you'd never gone, son. But that's water over the dam. Just glad we got you back. Maybe we need to meet this Emma."

Reece felt the alcohol. "Yeah, she would like that. I'll talk to her. I'm gonna call her tonight."

"What about Cindy?" Horace made a face.

"I don't know. Things happen. She just seems to appear and then disappear." Reece widened his stance.

"She's a pretty girl, for sure. I wish I was your age."

Reece didn't know what to say. "Maybe I'll just go ahead and call Emma. I'd like for you guys to meet her regardless."

Chester snapped some beans from the vine. "It's your life, son."

"Thanks." Reece walked away, feeling that something

grand had been accomplished. He could see Mrs. Sykes standing behind the glass patio door and waved. He imagined she was lonely without her husband there. He walked to the back door, kicking off his dirty tennis shoes and peeling off his wet socks, which were ringed with dirt.

Dora stood at the stove, cut corn bubbling in butter. "Hey, the phone rang, but I didn't answer it. It might've been Kristin." Chicken thighs sat in a green plastic bowl.

"I doubt it," said Reece. "I think maybe I've tanked that relationship."

"You gonna give up that easy? I think that girl loves you."

That hit hard. "I'll talk with her when she's ready." Reece felt his head entering a cloud, and he remembered the alcohol on his breath. He went and put on a clean t-shirt, the one he usually ran in, and then sat in her recliner. He had Emma's number memorized and picked up the phone. He dialed and let it ring a dozen times, his heart pounding, but no one answered.

"She not home?" asked Dora. "You were calling Kristin, right?" She put her hands on her hips.

"No one home. I was calling...Emma. I think you guys would get a kick out of meeting her."

"Lord, Lord," said Dora. "You just can't keep your mind on anything else. Well, except for maybe Cindy. I don't know, son. I would like to meet her, though. She saved your life."

"There's that," said Reece. "She's just so...interesting, is all."

"Is she pretty?"

"Well, yeah. Pretty and smart."

"But so is Kristin." She slapped at a fly that Reece had let in. "I just don't want you hurting her. She's such a sweet girl, and a nurse too."

Reece picked up the phone but then put it down. "Maybe Emma can come out this weekend. I'll grill something."

"If you say so. Gee whiz, boy, life has gotten exciting since you went over there. I don't know what to expect next." She took aim at the fly with a dishtowel and zapped it on the edge of the sink. She took a paper towel to the wiggling carcass and tossed it in the garbage. "Don't be letting flies in here."

Reece laughed. "Yeah, you're murder with the dishtowel." He pushed back in the recliner and sat that way for a minute. The fake pendulum clock was going over the TV. It made a slight grinding noise when it was quiet.

The phone rang, and it was Emma.

Emma had managed with Darlene to get Charles down the stairs to sit on the huge half-circle couch. He'd fallen out of a chair that morning and had cursed them as if it were their fault. He cursed them even more on the slow journey down the stairs. Darlene was spending the night, but Emma was leaving at five and coming back the next day. She would begin staying overnight the next week, if all went well.

Emma sat at the farmhouse table, using the wireless phone. It was four-thirty, and she was bored. Charles was back in bed, watching TV or pretending to.

"Hey!" said Emma.

"Hey!" said Reece. "I just called your house, and no one answered."

"I'm on the job. Got a private duty job with BamaCare. I'm here till five."

"Where at?" asked Reece.

"At a mansion in Mountain Brook." She laughed. "The guy is a real character named Charles."

"That's great. What's his diagnosis, or is that confidential?"

"I guess it's confidential, but he has AIDS and a slew of complications. Real nice when he wants to be, but he's really sick and needs help with just about everything. How are you?"

"Pretty good. Work was busy. One patient on a vent, and the other comatose. Just got through doing some yard work. Hot as blue blazes."

Emma adjusted the paperwork on the table. "So, how's Kristin?" There was a huge bird feeder outside the large window over the double sink.

Reece paused. "Not so good. We had a huge fight, and she said that we're through. But, I don't know."

"Wow, that's news. It didn't involve me, did it?"

"Not at first. I guess I did something I shouldn't have," said Reece. "It's a long story."

"Can you talk about it? Other folks in the room?" Emma stood and walked around the table. He seemed to have trouble talking.

"Yeah, I'll tell you later."

"Sure, I understand." Emma paused at the gas range, a Viking model. She turned a knob, clicking, and a flame whooshed. She turned it off.

"So, what's this guy's name?"

"Charles Rickers. The other nurses call him Mr. Rickers, but I'm calling him Charles. I'll be spending two days and three nights with him every week. Pretty good schedule. How's your grandparents?" She moved on to the paneled fridge and opened the door.

"They're good. We were talking, and they said they'd like to meet you. Maybe this weekend?" He coughed.

"You sure, Reece? That might upset Kristin." Emma examined the expiration date on a half-gallon of orange juice, a few days to go.

"At this point, it doesn't matter, I think. She can't dictate who my friends are, right?"

"That's what I've thought all along, but I guess she has the right, so to speak." She stood at the large sink and watched nuthatches on the feeder. She wondered who would refill it and guessed that she would.

"Anyway. Can you come out? I mean, I'd be glad to come and get you."

"Yeah, I'd love to meet them. You don't mind driving me?"

"Are you kidding? I'd be glad to."

"Is it because I saved your life?" She laughed and sat at the table.

"Ha, I guess so. You and the nursing assistant, Debbie Dee. She saved me from the tornado."

"You should visit her, maybe buy her some flowers." Darlene walked in and sat down to chart. "Look, I need to go. Wrap things up here. Yeah, so Saturday is good, right? What time?"

"How about I pick you up at four?"

"Okay, sounds good. Four it is. Maybe call me before then just to make sure."

"Will do," said Reece. "Talk to you soon."

"Okay, bye, Reece." She hung up the phone, a little thrill in her chest.

"That your boyfriend?" asked Darlene.

"Well, not exactly. He worked with me in Ethiopia. He was shot...in the head and had to be evacuated back here. He's a nurse."

"Wow," said Darlene. "And he's up and talking?" She scratched at a wart on her middle finger.

"Heck, he's working already, back on the unit at Carraway. ICU. He's lucky, is all I can say. I really like him." She smiled. "I can't put my finger on it, though."

"Yeah, you looked entranced on the phone. Maybe he'll drop by. I'd like to meet him. Was there something in the paper about him?" She mentally totaled up Mr. Ricker's urine output for the day.

"Could have been. I'm not sure. I haven't been back long. Do you fill the bird feeder?"

Darlene chuckled. "No way. You have to get on a ladder. The other nurse, Sally, I think she fools with it because she likes birds."

"It's about five, so I'll go say bye to Charles. He might be glad to see me go." Emma laughed.

"Okay, go on," said Darlene. "I'll heat some of that ravioli in the fridge that his ex-wife brought. Looks good."

Emma wound her way into the grand entryway and went up the stairs. Mr. Rickers was in bed, leaning against the headboard with his eyes closed. Emma had shaved him, and he looked like a little boy. She walked to the edge of the bed. His urinal was there with some dark yellow pee in it. She emptied it into the toilet and wrote "50 ccs" on the clipboard in the bathroom. She washed her hands.

"Hey, Charles," said Emma.

His head rolled, and he opened his eyes. "It's Rickers, I told you."

Emma put her hands on her hips. "How can we be friends if I call you mister? You get to call me Emma. Right?" She smiled.

Charles coughed and glared at her. "Oh, whatever, just get me...some ice water."

"Got it," said Emma. "Be right back." She trotted down the hall and stairs back to the kitchen and fixed a big cup of ice water. "He wants ice water."

"Good for him. Hope he doesn't vomit." Darlene stood at the stove.

Back in the bedroom, Emma crawled onto the bed and presented the water to Charles. "Here you go, mister." She sat on her knees, waiting for him to drink.

Charles took the big plastic cup with both hands. "Are the glasses dirty?" He gave Emma a sly look. "I said glass. Just seems more civilized."

Emma rolled her eyes. "Oh, go on, it's water just the same. Next time, I'll get you a real glass. Drink. I want to make sure you don't get sick. I'll get a towel just in case." She went to the bathroom. "You know, we do a load of laundry every day? To keep you in towels and washrags."

"That's beautiful," said Charles. He sipped and stared at her. "You ever been to Jamaica? You remind me of a girl down there I got acquainted with."

Emma laid a plush maroon towel on the bed, along with the emesis tray. "Nope. So, I guess this other girl was good-looking, right?" She laughed.

"Yeah, I guess you could say that." He took a deep breath and then a drink of water, and sighed and coughed. "Here, that's enough."

"Drink it while you got it," said Emma. "You feel okay?"

"I said, take it." Charles held it out like a chalice. He examined it. "This damn thing came from a gas station. It's not even mine."

"It doesn't have any holes in it, right?" She took the cup from him. "There. Well, it's time for me to head out, okay? I'll be back at eight tomorrow."

"Where do you live?"

"I live in Hueytown."

"You like NASCAR?"

"Not really," said Emma. "I don't keep up with it. I

told you I just got back from Ethiopia. No NASCAR over there, except for the taxi drivers. It was nice to meet you, Charles." She held her hand out to him, but he didn't take it.

"Well, goodbye," said Charles, and he closed his eyes.

"Tomorrow I'm gonna get you out in that garden out back. I promise. You need some sunshine."

"To hell with the garden," said Charles with his eyes closed.

Emma laughed and said goodbye. She trotted downstairs, said bye to Darlene, and opened the front door to see if Sally was there to pick her up, and she was. She waved and closed the door.

Sally sat in the Corolla, engine running and AC on. She took one of Heather's magazines and tossed it into the back seat. "How was it?"

Emma closed the door. "Whoo, he's a pistol, is all I can say. Real interesting, though. Frail, but his head is still sharp."

"Damn, this house. He must be filthy rich," said Sally. She pulled around and onto the oak-lined street.

"Yeah, he was a banker. He's been all over."

"How old is he?"

"Sixty-two, but he looks older. Divorced."

"Oh, money bags." She punched Emma's thigh.

"Ha. Not in a million years. His ex-wife still comes around, buys groceries and bourbon for him."

"Bourbon?"

"Yeah, he likes to take just a sip now and then, which is fine with me. As long as he can keep it on his stomach." She admired the large homes on the street.

"You do need a man. Right? You heard from Reece?"

Emma smiled. "As a matter of fact, I talked to him today. He had a big fight with his fiancée. He wants me to come out and meet his grandparents."

"Uh oh," said Sally. She took a right onto Shades Creek Parkway, which was packed with rush-hour traffic. "What does that mean?"

"I don't know. But I'm kind of excited about it. When we first met, I had this instant attraction to him. I couldn't believe that he was there. And then, boom, he was gone. But here he is again."

"I really like him. Mom kept going on about him. Sammy and Heather like him, too." They passed the road to the mall and headed for I-65.

"I wonder if I should get a new outfit? What do you think?" asked Emma. She put her small purse on the floorboard.

"Honey, you deserve a new outfit. Whatever floats your boat. Maybe we could go to the Galleria, do some shopping?"

"That sounds good. I'd like that. Maybe Saturday morning. He's picking me up at four."

"Sounds like a plan, sister. He's a little quirky, though. Kind of shy."

"Yeah," said Emma. "I just wish he wasn't engaged, dammit."

"Well, it could be worse. He could be married."

"Yeah, that might be creepy." They passed Samford University. "This traffic beats all."

"Folks getting off work, headed home like zombies. You know he'll have to bring you back home. Maybe I could be there when you get back. Just to say hi."

"Sure," said Emma. "Be my sidekick." She laughed. "But don't stay too long."

"I'll know when to leave." Sally laughed. "You feel like getting a drink? I know you don't drink much. Maybe the Mexican place. Margaritas. Ooh, that sounds good." She waited at the intersection with Greensprings.

"Maybe not today. You could make some margaritas when Reece comes over. How about that?"

"Look at this freak next to us," said Sally.

The man looked to be thirty, blowing kisses at them from his heavy-duty truck filled with Hispanic workers. The truck pulled a trailer filled with lawn-care equipment.

Emma glanced and looked away. "Jerk."

Sally looked at him and gave him the finger. The man's jaw dropped, and he threw up his finger, mouthing something.

"Bastard," said Sally. She moved ahead, blinker on, and pulled onto 65, which was at a near crawl at first. "Damn if they haven't pulled behind us."

Emma looked back. "Oh, they'll go away. Anyway, come over and make us some drinks. Maybe Sammy can come."

"Sounds like a plan. We'll loosen Reece up and see if he'll talk about his fight with his fiancée. Sammy can teach him to drink. He hates mixed drinks, but loves tequila. He'll be off the next day." She kept glancing in the rearview.

"Sounds like a party," said Emma. "God, what if he kisses me again?"

"Yeah, when you told me that, I knew something was up. I think you've got a crush on him, and I think maybe he has the hots for you. This could get pretty interesting. I wish that damn truck would pass us and go away. I told you about that guy who was jacking off beside me."

"No, when was that?"

"A couple of weeks ago. I was just minding my own business, and this car kept right beside me. Anyway, he made it pretty clear what he was doing. I'd like to have wrung his neck or his pecker. I didn't tell Sammy. He would've tried to track him down."

"Ugh," said Emma. "Men can be real creeps."

As they approached the interchange, traffic slowed again. The truck was right on their bumper. Off to their right, the city of Birmingham abruptly pooched skyward, with tall buildings. The sun glared in their eyes. They soon made the shift to I-59 South and picked up speed. Sally looked back and cut into the next lane. A horn blared.

"Careful, sis," said Emma. "Need to get out of these scrubs and take a bath. I'm not in any danger of getting HIV from him, but I still need to be careful."

"You mean your patient?"

"Yeah, Charles. We had to give him a liter of fluid today, and I was really careful with the needle. That's how I would get it, a dirty needle."

"That's fatal, from what I know. I think we're losing them." She gunned into the lane to her right.

"Yep, he'll most likely die. He's got full-blown AIDS."

"So, HIV causes AIDS?" asked Sally.

"Yeah, the white cells that fight off infections die off, and then there's a whole slew of complications from that. He was in the hospital a couple weeks back with pneumonia, I think."

"That's scary stuff. You be careful, sister."
"Don't worry, I will."
The truck eased up beside them.

Friday came, and Reece was ready for the weekend, maybe for the New Year. His first week back at work had given him a workout, and he couldn't wait to sleep in on Saturday. When he walked onto the unit, he was sad to hear that Mr. Riggins had passed away during the night, but going peacefully. He still had Mrs. Laramore and another patient, a mid-twenties man who had undergone a double amputation after being found lying beneath a house not far from the hospital. Reece wanted to go next door to CCU and visit Mr. Sykes, but was afraid of meeting Kristin. At the moment, she seemed so far away.

He took report from night shift and set about his day of unending tasks with the five other nurses, first checking in with Mrs. Laramore. She had an order to take her off the ventilator that morning. Reece assessed her, taking her vitals, making sure she was comfortable. Her urine output was up, which was a bonus. He hoped she wouldn't have to begin dialysis. He turned her on her left side and raised the head of the bed to 30 degrees. He suctioned her ET tube, squirting in a few ccs of sterile saline to break up the mucus that was running clear. He apologized as she coughed and strained against the vent.

"We're getting that tube out of your throat this morning for sure, okay?" He squeezed her hand, and she nodded, though breathless, with a look of hope. Before he washed his hands, he adjusted the wick on the room air freshener that smelled like citrus candy. "You need anything? Some ice chips?" Mrs. Laramore nodded her head no, and he stepped through the open sliding glass door onto the unit.

Glenda sat charting at the desk, and the head nurse Sheila, who had two patients herself, was on the phone with pharmacy. Reece took a rolling stool and sat down to read more about his new patient, who was schizophrenic. He liked the crazy ones. They seemed to make the most sense. Rodney Lasseter was a twenty-eight-year-old black male from Orlando. It looked like he'd hopped a bus out of fear that he was being followed and rode all the way to Birmingham. Panicked that someone was out to kill him, he'd fled the bus station, run ten blocks, and crawled under a small turquoise two-bedroom house on Thirteenth Street North. He'd curled into a ball and hid in a hole in the dirt, gnawing on a root for three days, terrified out of his mind. The renters in the house heard groaning and called the police, who found him there. He'd stayed in one position so long that he'd occluded blood flow to his legs, basically killing them, resulting in the double amputation. His family had been notified, but no one had yet to show up.

Reece went to six and walked in, announcing his entry. "Hello, coming in."

Rodney lay in bed, his head raised all the way. Liberally dosed with antipsychotics and anxiety meds, he sat there, looking at Reece with a blank look.

"Rodney? I'm Reece, your nurse. You okay?" He moved toward him with his hands above his waist.

"I am doing okay," said Rodney. He was a large man with a heavy stomach and a scraggly beard. "You are my nurse." He looked placid and somewhat peaceful with a hint of alarm.

Reece moved toward him and touched the bed rail. "You've had quite a journey. You're from Florida, right?"

"Yes." Rodney put his hands across the sheet and into his lap. "I am Rodney. I have schizophrenia."

"Nice to meet you, Rodney." Reece surveyed the IV pump and the heart monitor. "Do you mind if I check your blood pressure and your temperature? You look pretty good, considering everything. I just want you to feel comfortable."

"Okay," said Rodney. "Is this a hospital?"

"Yep. It's called Carraway. You're in Birmingham, Alabama. You took the bus here."

Rodney's eyes flared a bit. "Is my momma here?"

"No, not yet. We've contacted your family. Hopefully, someone will be here soon."

"I want to see my momma, if you please."

"She's not here right now. Hopefully, she's on her way." Reece took off his stethoscope and retrieved the blood pressure cuff from behind the bed. Rodney watched his every move. "Gonna check your blood pressure, okay?"

"Okay."

Reece finished and reached for a thermometer on the bedside table. "I need you to hold this thermometer under your tongue, okay, Rodney?" He shook down the mercury and watched Rodney's reaction. "Gonna put this under your tongue," and Rodney let him. Reece glanced at his watch and held the thermometer there for two minutes. "Good job. Thanks."

"Thank you," said Rodney. He licked his lips.

"You need some water or juice?"

"I need me some apple juice," said Rodney.

"Not a problem," said Reece. "I'll get you some after I listen to your chest and have a look at your bandages. You know what they had to do to your legs, right?"

"What's that?" asked Rodney.

"Well, the doctors had to amputate them, remove them from about here down." He pointed to his own legs.

"They did?" Rodney looked alarmed and peered down at the sheet covering his stumps.

"It's okay, but the blood flow was cut off. You have bandages where the legs used to be. I know that's hard to believe, but it's true. Gonna listen to your heart now." Reece listened and then moved to the pressure bandages, lifting the sheet. The tan bandages looked neat and unrumpled with no drainage. "I need to check the pulse in your thighs. Might tickle just a bit."

"Okay."

Reece pressed his fingers and felt the bounding pulses. "Looks good," and he replaced the clean sheet. "Here's breakfast." A young woman wearing a hair net slid a tray onto the overbed table and smiled. After she left, Rodney craned his neck to watch her leave, a slight look of fear on his face. Reece uncovered the tray. "You like eggs and sausage?"

"Yes sir," said Rodney. He made chewing motions.

"Great," said Reece. He pulled the table over the bed and poked a straw into the orange juice. "I'll get you some apple juice too, okay? You like coffee? Got coffee here too."

"No sir." Rodney took the silverware out of the plastic and ate, keeping an eye on Reece.

"You want me to open up this curtain so you can see, or should I leave it closed?" asked Reece.

"I, I don't know," said Rodney. He made exaggerated chewing motions.

"Okay, halfway then. How's that?" Reece pulled the curtain back a bit.

"Thank you," said Rodney, and he seemed preoccupied with his breakfast.

"Alright, Rodney. You can call me anytime. You just press this white button if you need anything." He put the large button beside Rodney. "I'll be back to check on you," and he stepped back onto the unit, bumping into Clarisse, another nurse. "Oh, hey."

Clarisse held a bag of IV fluid. She was tiny and in full makeup. "Got you a good one there," she said and walked away.

Reece saw the intern Scottie standing outside of Mrs. Laramore's room and walked that way. "Taking the tube out?"

"Yeah, you her nurse? Just stay with me. Standby with the suction." He threw back the curtain and entered the room. "Hey there, we're gonna get that tube out of your lungs. How's that? Good?"

Mrs. Laramore stirred, and she lifted her eyebrows.

"I'll be here with you, Mrs. Laramore. Hold my hand." Reece took her hand and squeezed, watching Scottie undo the tape and unhook the tube from the ventilator, which alarmed with sharp beeps. Reece hit the silence button. Mrs. Laramore's grip tightened. Before Reece was ready, Scottie had the tube out, and Mrs. Laramore was coughing, rearing up in bed. "Hold on, deep breaths. Deep breaths. There you go." He watched her heart rate jump from ninety to one-twenty. He took a suction wand and cleared her mouth.

"All done," said Scottie. He was already washing his hands, the extracted tube lying on her chest. "Stay with her for ten minutes and keep an eye on her after that, okay? And let's do a blood gas in half an hour."

"Sure thing," said Reece. He watched Mrs. Laramore as she took spasmodic breaths, her eyes watering. "Hang in there. Doing good. Let's wash your face and get that tape glue off." He returned with a hot washcloth and wiped her face as she coughed and swallowed. "Doing good, real good. Looking much better." He counted her respirations at thirty per minute. He went out and pulled in a rolling chair and sat beside her as she settled down, breathing on her own.

At eleven, all seemed well, and Reece was chatting with Sheila. She wore braces on her teeth and had a plain face, but was quite curvy. He learned from her that Kristin had taken the day off, and he wondered why, hoping that it wasn't because of him. He helped her get an elderly woman with a hip replacement onto the bedside commode and then, after she was back in bed, they went to the cafeteria for a quick lunch.

It was crowded as usual, but the line to the steam tables went fast with three cashiers moving the people along. They sat.

"So, is she sick?" asked Reece. He surveyed his plate of mashed potatoes and macaroni and cheese with a bowl of collard greens.

"Don't tell her this, but she called me and talked to me this morning. Said she was nauseated." Sheila watched for Reece's reaction.

"Oh," said Reece. He poked at his potatoes. "Did she talk about me?"

"She's still pretty angry with you. She told me what happened." She paused. "Sounds like a sticky situation."

"Oh Lord," said Reece.

"Sounds like you have your work cut out for you. If you know what I mean."

"I wish that maybe she wouldn't spread everything around like that. I don't know what to do." Reece took a bite of greens.

"Here's what you have to do. You with me? It's just my idea. I mean, I'm a girl, right? Not that she said this is what you have to do." She had the fried catfish and cole slaw.

"So, what's that?"

"First, send her a dozen roses today. Order them on the phone. Then, go by her house and see if she'll see you." She spoke like an accountant doing taxes.

Reece thought. *What would Kristin do if she found out Emma was coming to the lake?* Did he want to end the relationship? Now was a good time, if he did. Otherwise, he would be back in the same boat, not able to see Emma and forever paying the price of having sex with Cindy.

"You know she's gonna talk me to again. It's like I'm the go-between. You have to do something."

"Yeah," said Reece. "It's complicated. Did she mention Emma, the nurse from Ethiopia, or just the other thing?"

"Geez, she said something about her, but mostly it was about this other girl. The one, well, you know."

"Her name is Cindy, and that was a one-time thing. Emma is different. She's like a good friend, and Kristin won't let me see her. That's the real problem, for me anyway." He mixed some macaroni and cheese with mashed potatoes. Visitors, doctors, and nurses buzzed around them. The cafeteria was loud.

"I guess you thought getting shot was difficult, huh?" Sheila took a big bite of catfish, wiping her mouth with a napkin.

How much were a dozen roses? He'd have to borrow the money from Horace. Would Gert even let him in the house? He swallowed his food and frowned.

Kristin felt sick the minute she woke up, nauseated, nothing like she'd ever experienced before. She'd called work, letting them know she wouldn't be in, which she rarely did. Plus, she was depressed and bewildered from the counseling session on Wednesday when Reece had dropped the bomb on her about Cindy. She felt lifeless and slept in, curled up in a ball. Gert was worried about her and peeked in every now and then. She worried that Kristin might be pregnant and was dying to know if they'd had sex. She would just have to ask.

Kristin dreamed short dreams in fits, waking and falling asleep between each one, sleeping until ten, and then feeling a little bit crazy.

"You want something to eat, honey?" asked Gert. She wore a short-sleeved plaid shirt. "Or are you still nauseated?"

In the den, Kristin lounged in a pair of white scrubs and bare feet. "Yeah, a little bit. Maybe some chicken noodle soup?"

"Okay. I'll make it." Gert found a can and opened it. "You needed a day off, honey. You've been just a wreck."

"I'm sorry. But why is life so difficult? I mean, really, what's next?" She glanced at the phone, wishing it would ring, hoping that Reece would squeeze through the line into the room. "I want to hate him, but I can't."

"He's not to be trusted, honey. I hope you've learned that. As far as your dad and I are concerned, it's over. You know that."

Kristin frowned and shook the curls from her face. "It's easier for you to say. I mean, you're just trying to protect me, but I still love him. I don't know why, but I do."

Gert coughed and left the pot on the stove with the timer on. "You know, honey, that when a man has...sex with a girl, he loses interest. I'm just saying, if you know what I mean. So...did you? I won't tell your dad."

Kristin walked to the table and sat. She put her arms on the table, and then her head. "Yes, but not here, at the lake." She blushed thinking about it.

"I thought maybe you had. Oh, baby, you don't think you're pregnant, do you?"

Kristin sighed. "I mean, I had my period the next day. I was a day late."

"That's a relief. But still. You might want to get one of those tests." Gert lifted the lid on the pot and looked at the soup, the heat moving the liquid. "He didn't force himself on you, did he?"

"Oh no. I was a willing partner." She feigned a laugh. "And it's nothing like you said it would be, by the way. I mean, I didn't want to close my eyes and get it over with."

Gert turned a little red around her neckline. "Well, some women like it and some don't. Anyway, what's done is done. Just don't expect to hear from him, okay?"

"But I do expect to hear from him. That's the problem. I guess he could rob a bank, and I'd still want to see him. I mean, we'll definitely go back to the counselor."

"Promise me that you won't call him. Let him call. I don't want him here, though. I'm getting mad thinking about it. Your dad is mad too, but he's so easy going."

Kristin let Gert serve her the bowl of soup. "Thanks.

Gosh, I don't know what to do with myself. I feel like I should go in and work evening shift. I hate calling in." She stirred the hot soup, testing it with a finger, and then waited a minute. She ate in silence and then went to the deck and sat in the sun, talking to Harvey in his baby pool. The day was warm, and a very light breeze stirred. She began to sweat and went back inside, and decided to read a magazine, soon falling asleep on the couch.

The doorbell rang at three, waking her. She heard Gert going to the door. Maybe it was Reece, but he'd just be getting off from work. She listened as Gert walked back up the stairs.

"Oh my gosh," said Kristin.

"Yep," said Gert. She held a vase with a dozen red roses and a small card. "For you."

Kristin brightened and took the flowers, smelling them. "Wow, they're gorgeous. Is the card from him? Let me see." The card read "I'm sorry. I love you, Reece." She wondered if he'd talked with Sheila and decided to call her.

"Well, I guess he's trying," said Gert. She sighed and tousled her graying hair.

Kristin dialed and spoke with Laronda, but Sheila was in report. She asked Laronda to have Sheila call her, then she placed the roses on the dining room table.

"Shift change," said Kristin.

Reece spent extra time with Rodney, introducing him to the evening shift nurse. He'd gone into great detail with her about Rodney's crazy journey. He peeked in one last time at Mrs. Laramore, saying goodbye for the weekend, and went to his tiny locker to change into street shoes.

He'd called Dora, and she had ordered the flowers, congratulating him on doing the right thing.

On the way to the parking deck, he was filled with a combination of joy and dread. He was going to take Sheila's advice and drop by Kristin's house to see if she would talk to him. Driving there, he practiced a range of facial expressions that expressed remorse and tried to think of what he would say when, hopefully, Kristin would answer the door. He imagined the roses in a pile in the driveway.

Before he knew it, he was exiting I-59 and headed toward her street, a quiet but busy street lined with split-level ranchers. He wondered what other people were doing, if other people were as confused as he was. And then there was the steep driveway. Edwin wasn't home yet.

Reece slammed the squeaky door and walked up the steps to the landing. He stood there a moment, clearing his throat, and then knocked and then knocked again, each knock like the beat of a far-away drum. The door was opening. Kristin peered at him through the storm door, a quirky smile on her face. She pushed the door open, and he opened it the rest of the way.

"Hey," said Reece. He looked at his feet and wiped them on the doormat, and then stood there.

"Hey," said Kristin. "Come in, okay? I got the flowers."

Reece walked in, waiting for the appearance of Gert. His stomach hurt, and he felt a little shaky. He followed her up the stairs and into the familiar den. He'd imagined that he would never see it again. Everything was in its place. Walter lay on the floor, half asleep and wagging his stubby tail. Where was Gert? He imagined her coming out with a small pistol and aiming it at him. He saw the roses on the table in the dining room.

"Aren't they pretty?" asked Kristin. "Want to go on the deck?"

"Uh, sure," said Reece. At the back door, he glanced into the kitchen and saw Gert. He waved, and she waved. They sat in the folding chairs, the sun filtering through the trees.

"How was work?"

"Fine, I guess." He wanted to tell her about Rodney and his amputated legs.

"You're brave to come here, bucko. You know that?" She looked thin and somewhat helpless, but full of life.

"You feeling better? Sheila told me you called in."

"Oh, so the flowers are because I'm sick?" She stared at him.

"No, no. She just told me is all. There was a note with the flowers, right? I'm officially apologizing." He leaned forward and clasped his hands.

"Yeah, I know. I was just kidding. That was sweet of you, but I haven't forgiven you just yet. I mean, how could I? I just hate that Cindy."

"Maybe hate me instead," said Reece.

"I don't hate you. I'm just so ready for us to do the right thing, but you're not helping. You know?" She touched his leg.

"I appreciate it. I've got this cool new patient, schizo-phrenic, like your other patient. Remember her? Mrs. Dunlop." He gave her the whole story. "He's so paranoid. He kept looking at the TV and asking me if there was a camera."

"That is crazy. Is he upset about his legs?" Kristin moved

her chair so that she was facing him.

Reece laughed. "Not really. It's kind of like he doesn't know they're gone. He wanted to get up and walk to the bathroom, even though I told him about the amputations."

"How's Mr. Sykes?"

"I didn't see him. Totally forgot. I was just thinking about you all day."

"Aw," said Kristin. "I imagine they'll discharge him to the floor soon. So, you're really sorry? And you'll never do anything like that again?"

Reece thought about Emma, his pending date with her at the lake with his grandparents. "Promise." He heard a door slam and figured that Edwin was home and tensed.

"So, did you enjoy it with her, Cindy?"

"What?"

"You heard me. Was it as good with her as it was with me? But she wasn't a virgin, of course. Maybe she's more experienced and exciting than I am."

Reece cringed. "No, no. It was so fast, over and done. Her grandmother came home."

"I hope you felt terrible, right?"

"Well, yeah. I didn't want to tell you, but I did."

"We have to go back to the counselor, to see Calvin, Dr. Dobbs. We forgot to pay him. Will you go next week?"

"I don't like him. I mean, I understand why. Maybe someone else?" The whole idea of the counselor poked a hole in him, made him feel empty.

"Who's behind the eight ball? Not me, right?" Kristin frowned. "I think maybe we can move beyond Cindy, but we still need to talk about Emma. Have you talked with her? You better say no."

Gert opened the back door, and Walter sauntered onto the porch.

"Big sigh," said Reece. He sighed.

"Reece?"

"Yes, I talked with her. I was desperate to talk to somebody." He waited for the fusillade.

"Reece, no. How could you?"

"I'm sorry. I just did, okay?"

"So, you told her that we were breaking up?"

"Well, that's what you made pretty clear."

"Now she thinks you're a free man? Do you have a date with her?" She pushed Walter away from her legs.

"I surrender," said Reece. "She's coming out to meet Horace and Dora tomorrow night. She's my friend."

"Reece Myers!" Kristin stood, wrapping her arms. "Are you going to leave and send me some more roses? I cannot believe you." Her voice shook. "Leave, right now, and don't ever come back." In tears, she pushed into the house.

Reece looked directly toward the sun, hoping that a chariot would sweep down and carry him away. The last thing he wanted to do was enter the house, and he went down the stairs and around to the fence gate. The air conditioner there whummed. He put his hand over the warm air and paused. He didn't know what to do and just went to his truck and got in. He sat there for a minute, waiting for the roses to come flying out the door. He put the key in the ignition, turned it, and there was a clicking noise. He hit the steering wheel and cursed, thinking he would need a jump from Edwin. A surge of adrenaline went through him, and he popped the hood. In record time, he twisted the battery cables, hoping for the best, feeling the eyes of the world on his every move.

Saturday morning, Sally and Emma went to the Galleria with Heather in tow. They rode the merry-go-round and ate lunch at the Greek place. Just having fun, they shopped for an outfit for Emma to wear to the lake and wound up in the dress department of Parisians. They settled on a little black dress with short sleeves that fit her like a charm. They looked at shoes, too, but Emma decided to wear a pair of black pumps from home.

At three on the dot, Reece began the drive to Hueytown. He hadn't talked to Kristin and tried to convince himself that he was doing the right thing by having Emma over. He just wanted some peace in his life and tried to clear his mind, intent on enjoying the drive and seeing Emma. Traffic was light, and he pulled into the driveway a few minutes early. He checked his teeth in the rearview and hoped he wasn't underdressed.

Sarah met him at the carport door, cigarette in hand. "Hey, boy! Come on in. Emma's upstairs getting ready."

"Hey. Good to see you." Reece stepped into the kitchen, wondering if he should hug her. He followed Sarah into the living room and sat on the couch that was backed up to the stairs.

In the bathroom, Emma checked her lipstick and adjusted a small gold chain. She didn't like how her hair was flat, and turned on the blow dryer. After another five minutes of fussing with her look, she slipped on her shoes and headed down the stairs.

"Surprise!" She did a little twirl and grinned. Her

expression said that she was elated, that she'd been visiting this very moment all day long.

Reece was stunned. "Wow." He stood, embarrassed by his jeans and t-shirt. "I didn't know we were going out on the town."

"Special outfit," said Emma.

"Looks real good," said Sarah, grinning. "Y'all don't stay gone too long, though. I think Sally's coming over."

"Well, we have to visit," said Emma. "But tell Sally we'll be back by nine. Does that sound good, Reece?" She patted her thighs and snapped her fingers.

"Um, sure. You ready or do you need a few minutes?"

"What? Don't I look ready?" She laughed. "I got my hair fixed like I wanted, but the wind in your truck's gonna give me a new hairdo."

"Sorry about that," said Reece. He stood and stretched, and Emma moved in for a quick hug.

"So glad to see you." She squealed and let him go.

"Oh boy." Reece felt a little dizzy. He felt like a part of something larger, that he somehow belonged, that each minute was passing with purpose. He caught Sarah's eyes, pleased at what she was seeing, her arms wrapped around herself, the cigarette dangling from her thin hand perilously close to her knit sweater.

"Y'all git," said Sarah.

"Yeah, let's git," said Emma.

"While the gittin's good. Bye, Sarah," said Reece, following Emma outside with a silly grin on his face, like a little boy getting a whole stick of gum when he was used to half.

In the truck, Reece made small talk, watching Emma's

bouncy hair flail in the window breeze. He wished she'd sat in the middle. She mentioned Kristin, and he told about the afternoon at the counselor, leaving out the salient details, about the roses, and then about her storming off after he'd said that Emma was coming to the lake. The truck hadn't cranked, and he'd had to let it roll out of the driveway, and then he'd popped the clutch as he coasted downhill, cranking it.

"You never told me what the first big fight was all about? It wasn't just about me, right?" The roar of the wind diminished her words.

Reece didn't answer at first. He had the look of an organ grinder whose monkey had bitten a passerby. He sighed and said that it was about Cindy, the Sykes' granddaughter.

"Speak up!" said Emma. "This is getting interesting. Cindy's a real looker, I gather. Nothing wrong with that. So, what happened? Tell me. Or let me guess."

"Okay," said Reece. "Guess." He was tired of confessing.

"You had sex with her!"

Reece cringed and nodded his head. He assumed a look of guilt.

"Oh boy," said Emma. "Now you've done it. And you told her? Wow, that's heavy."

"Yeah, at the counselor's office. This guy named Calvin. I can tell he thinks I'm a loose cannon. I think we overwhelmed him. He forgot to ask us to pay and never did get around to asking us to pray." Reece tried to laugh.

"Did she seduce you? It wasn't planned, was it?" She reached and squeezed his thigh. "But you're a guy, right?"

"I would say she seduced me. She was in a bikini when

I saw her that morning, and then later she asked me to come into the house, and she got naked pretty fast. I shouldn't have done it, but it was after another fight that afternoon, and I was feeling a little angry."

"Is that all you do? Fight? Doesn't sound healthy to me. What was that fight about?"

Reece told her about hiking and wanting to do a beeline hike, and then what he'd blurted out, that Emma would do it with him.

"Holy cow. Yeah, I'd do the beeline hike with you. God, she just sounds so controlling." She rolled her window up halfway.

"Well, she deserves someone better than me. I just keep running into these dead ends with her. I'm losing my mind." They passed through the 59/65 interchange with downtown to their right. The sky was a cloudy white, the sun large and yellow. "Do you hate me for having sex with Cindy?"

"I'm surprised, but we're not dating, right? But, hey. Let's forget about the trouble and have a good time. I'm looking forward to meeting your grandparents. I can almost see them. I think they must care about you."

"They're more like my parents than my parents were. I hate to say it, but it's true. So, tell me some more about your patient. What's his name?"

"Charles Rickers. Filthy rich, but I like him. I think I've got his ticket. He likes to play tough, but he's a softie inside. So weak, though. The virus is doing a number on him." She put her hand out the window, the wind splaying her fingers. She told him about the other nurse, Darlene, how she was dumpy and unhealthy looking, but that she was an excellent nurse.

"So how did he get HIV?"

"Womanizing is what Darlene said. You can tell he used to be good-looking. There are pictures of him with his wife and kids, and he has this dark black hair. Now it's just about white. He only weighs ninety pounds. Just skin and bones."

"That's too bad," said Reece. It occurred to him that he needed to buy some condoms. He would have never predicted that he would have sex with two women in the same week, and both times had been unprotected. He imagined what it was like to weigh ninety pounds.

"Yeah, life just caught up with him. HIV is scary. Did you use a condom with Cindy?" She looked away and out the window.

Reece didn't want to talk about it but said, "No. It was the heat of the moment, but she's as healthy as a horse. I guess I should be worried." He took the exit for Tarrant City.

"You can get tested at the public health clinic downtown. I'm thinking maybe I should get tested. Maybe we should both go and get tested." She bit her lip, thinking about the two soldiers, her bruised shoulders, the rocks in her back, the dirt in her clothes. How she had been helpless against them.

"Hmm," said Reece. "I guess Kristin should go too. I guess everybody should go." A weight settled on his shoulders, and he stretched his neck. Tarrant City was dingy and run down—a boarded-up gas station, a motorcycle dealership, a coke processing plant spewing white smoke.

"Yeah, it could kind of be like a date, but not with Kristin. That would be too weird. You think she'll talk to you again?"

"Ha, maybe." Reece couldn't believe he was thinking about Kristin, as if she were in the past. "If we got back together, she'd make me get tested."

"Let's do it, okay? Maybe next week?"

"I work day shift for another week. Maybe when I go to nights, I could go during the day. So, the next week. Heck, we could go to Shoney's afterward."

Emma laughed. "Hey, that sounds like a plan."

Reece drove and talked. They took the right in Pinson and headed toward Palmerdale, and then turned to the lake. "Here it is."

"Wow, this is pretty. I never knew this lake was here." Emma pulled her dress down to her knees.

"They were one of the first to live out here. It used to be vacation cabins. Horace added a big living room and a garage." He turned and then pulled into the driveway. Dora sat in the swing, shelling green beans. "That's Dora. I call her Granny."

Reece jumped out and hustled around to open the door for Emma.

"Thanks, kind sir," said Emma.

"Hey, boy," said Dora. "Is that Emma?" She took the newspaper and beans from her lap.

Emma went straight to her. "Hey, Mrs. Myers. It's me, Emma."

"Well, let me hug you, girl. You sure are pretty." They hugged.

"It's so good to meet you," said Emma.

"I'm glad to finally meet you, too. I sure do appreciate

everything you did for Reece over there. He might not be here if it hadn't been for you. I can't ever forget that." A tear came to each eye. "Go on down and get Horace. I'll get in the kitchen. Reece, you got to grill those pork chops."

"Yeah, I know. Come on." He led the way through the tall pines to the road. Emma took his arm. He felt like a king about to open a new box of treasure. "He's in the garden, making more work for Granny. She fusses at him for it."

"Look at that lake. I can smell it." She followed Reece's lead through the grass and could see Horace sitting in his chair beneath the black walnut tree, his hoe between his legs like a staff. He was wearing his dirty straw hat and turned toward them.

"Hey!" said Reece. "Got someone for you to meet."

Horace struggled to stand using the hoe. "Well, come on over."

Emma took the lead. "Hey there, Mr. Myers, I'm Emma." She held out her hand, and he shook it.

"I'd give you a hug, but I'm filthy." He squinted and assessed her. "That's a pretty dress."

Emma laughed. "Thank you."

"Yep, heard all about you and how you helped Reece. Sure do appreciate it." His eyes were watering, and he blinked, and he took a handkerchief and wiped his brow. They chatted for a minute, Horace wanting to know where her people were from.

"Hey, I've got to get up there and start grilling." Reece tried to assess his well-being and found it to be surprisingly good. He hadn't grilled in a while and wanted to get the coals going.

"Alright, y'all go on. I'll be up directly," said Horace, wandering toward the garden. "Oh, I'll bag you up some late tomatoes. Give 'em to your momma. Reece said you live with your momma. The neighbor here has a boatload."

Emma said thanks, and they walked up to the house together. Reece rolled the rusty grill out of the garage and found half a bag of charcoal and some lighter fluid.

"Real men grill," said Emma, watching him work.

Reece laughed. "Let me get a match. Real men use matches. You want to go inside or stay out here?"

"Let me go inside for a while and cool off. I'll talk with Granny."

Reece led the way, found the matches, and went back outside. Dora was frying okra on the small four-burner electric stove.

"You need any help?" asked Emma.

"No, no, you just sit there at the table," and Emma sat down.

She told Dora all about the clinic she'd started in Gundo Meskel and about the little village of Godo where she and Reece had worked together.

"Things are sure different for a lady these days. I can't imagine doing what you did." She stirred the sizzling okra breaded with cornmeal. Emma noticed the purple varicose veins on the backs of her legs.

Reece came in with black on his hands. "Coals are roaring. Y'all talking about me?"

Dora pointed the warped and partially melted spatula at him like a knife and jabbed. "What's so interesting about you?" She laughed as Reece parried the spatula.

"I was shot in the head." He went to the sink to wash his hands.

"Not in my clean sink! Go to the bathroom," said Dora.

"She means business," and he did as he was told.

"So, where were we?" asked Dora. "They eat okra over there?"

"I saw it in the markets. Not sure how they cook it, probably in a wot or stew."

Reece dried his hands and looked at himself in the mirror. He brushed at his hair. Kristin had never held a conversation longer than ten minutes with either of his grandparents. She wasn't shy but was reserved in the company of others. He joined Emma at the table.

"They've got okra in Africa, says Emma."

"Really? She might be pulling your leg."

Emma laughed. "You saw it. I only saw it a couple of times." Her legs were crossed, and Reece kept looking.

"You should've brought your slides," said Reece. "Dang it."

"Hmm, you can get them when we go back. You want to borrow the projector from the church, too?" She uncrossed her legs and adjusted her gold necklace.

"Sure," said Reece. "I won't keep it long. Maybe they'll let me do a slideshow at my church on a Wednesday night. Won't be so crowded."

Dora stirred the okra and checked the bubbling creamed corn. "I don't have any bread. Y'all want some cornbread?"

"Don't go to the trouble," said Emma.

"What she said," said Reece. "Although those pork chops you bought are pretty thin. Were they on sale?"

"Oh, shut up," said Dora. She gave Reece the stink eye. "Thin is more tender. I don't like those fat ones. How long before those coals are ready? We need to get Horace up here so he can get cleaned up. Been in that dang garden all day."

"I'd say twenty minutes or so," said Reece. "Need to burn off the lighter fluid real good. Wanna go outside?" He was thinking about the tequila in the RV.

"Wait," said Emma. "Can I set the table for you, Mrs. Myers?"

"Oh no, I know where everything is. Y'all go on outside. Making me nervous." She winked at Emma.

Reece stood and waited for Emma, watching her stand in her black dress. "I still can't believe you wore a dress."

"Women wear dresses," said Dora. "You should've put on some nicer clothes." She talked with her back to them.

"I'll put on a suit," said Reece. He laughed, and Emma followed him outside.

He checked the grill. There were still small flames on the coals. Cicadas were oohing and aahing in the pines, two groups taking turns with their song.

"Want a drink? Got some tequila in the RV."

"Oh Lord," said Emma. "You drink tequila? I thought you were a Baptist."

"Come on." He stepped into the RV, the step creaking under his weight. Inside was dim and stuffy.

Emma followed. "This is cute. But the tequila's gonna be warm. I think Sally is going to make us some drinks when we go back, so just a sip."

Unaccustomed to having his own liquor, Reece felt amateurish. He pulled down the bottle of Cuervo Gold. "No glasses, just a sip like you said. Here."

Emma took the bottle and pursed her lips. "Here goes." She swallowed and coughed. "Oh, that's enough."

Reece took a swig and made a face. "Yeah, it is warm." He felt the alcohol in his stomach. "Bad idea." He screwed the lid back on and replaced the bottle in the cabinet.

"Does Dora know you have that out here?"

"Not yet."

They were standing very close to one another, doing a little dance to keep from touching. Reece could feel her body heat and admired how her dress fit her breasts perfectly. His hand brushed hers, and he wanted to hold it, but led the way back outside into the cooler air.

"Let's go get Horace and take a peek at the lake."

They walked side by side, soon reaching the garden.

"Hey, Granny wants you to come up. I'm gonna start grilling in a few minutes."

Horace paused with his hoe, digging out little clumps of Bermuda grass around the pole beans. He smiled and squinted, his face sweaty. "Okay. Take her down to the lake."

"Yeah, we were headed down." His hand was so close to hers, and they walked through the grass to the pier.

"You cut all this grass?" asked Emma.

"Yep. Every week during the summer, up until November, it seems." He stepped onto the pier and looked to see if she would offer him her hand, but she didn't. A large bass swooned in the shallows, gulping in mouthfuls of water, then turned and shot away, leaving behind a swirl of mud and moss. The sun was just even with the ridge across the lake, and a gentle breeze blew that didn't mark the water.

They sat on the narrow bench at the end of the pier.

"Is this where Cindy pulled her top down?"

"Oh," said Reece. "That. Well, over there on the Sykes' pier. Just as pretty as you please."

"She sounds like a character. You sure you don't have a thing for her?" Their thighs touched.

"Oh no. If things were different, I might. But she's a free spirit. Can I put my arm behind you?"

"Sure. But I'm not gonna pull my dress down." She laughed.

Reece blushed. "Well, sure. Of course not." He swallowed and put his arm behind her. The back was high and not exactly comfortable for his arm, but he kept it there and adjusted his hips.

"Can you believe I was in Ethiopia not more than three weeks ago?" said Emma. She stared at the lake and moved closer. "I mean, that's eight thousand miles away, but it seems like another planet."

Reece's heart was pounding. "Yeah, hard to believe. But you've got the slides to prove it. It kind of hurts my head that we exist while they exist. I lay awake thinking about it."

"And you've got the scars to prove it." She looked up at him and traced the scar on the side of his head.

"Yeah. Inside and outside. Look, there's Mr. Turtle." He pointed to a dark green head poking out of the water, and it went under, leaving little circles.

"You don't like to talk about yourself, do you?" She let her hand rest on his thigh.

Reece thought. He didn't really know. "I guess not. Not that interesting. You're the most interesting." He wondered if that sounded corny, and it did.

"We're just both nurses who had an adventure."

Reece felt a deep longing in his bones and sighed. "What an adventure. It'll take me years to make heads or tails of it. To be honest, I feel lost. Like I've gone down a road and can't find my way back."

"Maybe you're just supposed to keep going."

"I keep thinking that way. But what will I lose?"

Emma bit her lip. "But what will you gain?"

Reece laughed. "You're better than that damn counselor."

"Nurses are kind of like counselors, right?"

"Yeah, and we have to change diapers and make a lot less." He let his arm slide down to rest on her shoulder. "I...just feel so comfortable with you. I'm not being too forward, am I?"

Emma smiled. "Far from it. Why don't you just give up and kiss me?" She looked away as if she hadn't spoken.

Reece felt that ache and thrill. "Well, maybe I will."

She turned toward him. "I'm waiting."

Reece leaned in and felt her lips on his, and they kissed long and slow.

"Reece!" It was Dora calling them.

"Oh heck, the pork chops. I forgot." He waited for Emma to stand.

Emma pulled him in for one more kiss. "That's real nice, Mr. Pork Chop." She stood and helped him stand. Their eyes met, and Reece felt like he might fall into the lake. She laughed. "This way, wounded nurse. This way."

Reece took her hand, and they walked that way as far as the garden, and then, as if by mutual consent, their hands fell apart.

Dinner went well. Reece's pork chops, prepared with just salt and pepper, were a hit, and after another hour, it was time to head back to Emma's. Horace had grilled her on her kinfolks, conjuring up his kinfolks all the way back to North Carolina.

"You come back anytime," said Horace. Emma hugged him and kissed him on the cheek.

"Don't give an old man ideas," said Dora. "Give me a hug."

Emma hugged her. "Thanks again for dinner. I love fried okra. You'll have to meet my momma sometime. She's the one who knows about family."

Reece beamed, feeling that he'd won the lottery, wondering what kind of drinks Sally was making for them. "Okay, we're outta here. Probably be late, so don't wait up." He touched the small of Emma's back.

"Let me visit the ladies' room first," said Emma, and she did.

Reece stood there jingling his two keys on the key ring from Six Flags. He felt as light as a summer mushroom.

"She's a real doll," said Dora. "No wonder you like her so much. But you still have Kristin to think about. Don't go doing the wrong thing, boy." She patted his waist.

"She sure can hold a conversation," said Horace. He winked at Reece and went to take his place in the recliner.

"Ready, Freddy," said Emma. She had washed her face and looked fresh.

"Ready, Betty," said Reece, and they went out to the truck. "I hate there's no air conditioning."

"Save your money and get a convertible. Although this is like riding in a convertible." She buckled and rolled her window up halfway.

It was dim out but just dark enough for headlights. They talked about Godo, about what people would be doing there, probably getting up with the roosters to herd the goats and fetch water from the stream that was so far away. Before he knew it, they exited I-59 and were soon at Emma's house, which was lit up like a Christmas tree.

"Oh, good, a party!" said Emma. She was out before Reece could open her door, but she stopped him and gave him a wraparound hug. "Come on!"

Reece sped up his walk and caught the door as she disappeared inside. Everyone sat around the kitchen table: Sammy, Sally, Heather, and Sarah, with her cigarette.

"Hey," said Reece to a chorus of return heys. Sally was hugging Emma as she whispered into her ear. There was a large pitcher of margaritas on the table, and extra glasses.

"Here you go, sport," said Sally. She dipped a glass rim in salt and poured. "Need extra lime?"

"Uh, well, sure," said Reece.

"Lime's on the table," said Sammy. He stood. "Good to see you, man." He squeezed Reece's bicep.

"How was dinner?" asked Sarah. "Y'all sit. I'm gonna stand over here with my cancer stick."

"Great," said Emma. "Reece grilled pork chops. His granny made corn and fried okra. They're good people." She was all smiles. "They want to meet you."

"I'd like to meet them," said Sarah. "Bring 'em down to the barbecue one day."

Reece nodded and sipped his drink. It was sweet and

sour, but there was something strong, and he wasn't sure what it was. He just pretended that he'd had a million margaritas and watched Sally pour one for Emma.

"Reece, sit down," said Sally. She'd had a couple already and was a little giddy.

They talked about this and that, and soon moved the party out to the carport, with a host of mosquitoes that everyone slapped at. Reece was on his second margarita and feeling boisterous. Sally wanted to know what he'd thought when he first met Emma.

Reece thought. His folding chair sat between Emma and Sally. "First of all, she was a legend before I got there. Everybody talked about how great she was, how tough she was. I thought maybe she'd have a beard."

Everyone laughed at that.

"Aunt Emma is the best," said Heather. She was sitting with her legs folded on a chaise lounge beside Sammy. Sarah paced back and forth.

"No, I said, what did *you* think of *her?*" asked Sally. She twisted her hair, sipping her drink. The pitcher was empty, but she was going to make another.

"Right," said Reece. "No beard, that's for sure. I guess I was kind of stunned." He wiggled his fingers around his glass and glanced at Emma.

There was a collective "Oh" and then an "Mmmhmm."

"We just clicked," said Reece. He felt uncomfortable, realizing he still had to work things out with Kristin.

"You look good together," said Sally. "Real good."

"Reece is gonna do a talk at his church, but I thought he should do one at mine too," said Emma. "Y'all would have to come." She was on her second drink as well. She slapped a mosquito on her ankle, leaving a spot of blood.

"Of course we would come," said Sarah. She coughed long and hard.

"Momma, you okay?" asked Sally. She rubbed Reece's knee, and he flinched. "Ticklish, huh?" She grabbed his knee, and Reece spilled his drink. She laughed, and Emma was laughing too.

"Sally," said Sammy. "Don't torture the boy." He was solid with his red hair and muscular forearms, and always with a mischievous look in his eyes.

"Yeah, I'll let Emma torture him. We need some more drinks. Sammy, make us some drinks, por favor." Her eyes glistened in the porch light.

"Momma's on the way," said Heather.

Sally swatted in her direction. "I'll be on your way. To-morrow's a day of rest, and I'll rest. So there."

Sammy slipped into the house.

They talked for another hour, everyone but Sarah and Heather getting just a little drunker. Reece felt it and nursed his fourth drink, thinking his bladder would rup-ture.

"Men's room," he said.

"Just go on in," said Sarah. "You know where it's at."

"Emma, give us some dirt, while he's gone," said Sally. "He has so got the hots for you it's pitiful. You should see the way he looks at you. Engaged my foot."

"Just hush. We're getting acquainted, is all. We never really had a chance over there, so busy all the time. And then, well, you know." Emma sipped her drink. "This is my last one, y'all."

"Did he kiss you? At the lake?" asked Sally.

Emma blushed, wanting to change into something more comfortable. Her shoes were off, and she rubbed her calf with her toe over a bite. She twiddled her thumbs and looked to Sarah for help.

"Don't badger the poor girl," said Sarah. "She'll tell what she wants to tell."

The screen door pushed open, and Reece was back.

"Reece, you like to watch football?" asked Sammy.

"Sometimes," said Reece. His legs felt a little unsteady.

"Yeah, you'll have to come over. You an Alabama fan or an Auburn fan?"

"I bet he's a nasty Auburn fan," said Sally. She cackled and slapped Reece on the thigh.

"Well, let him talk," said Sarah.

"I used to watch Alabama play in high school. I guess I'm an Alabama fan. But I root for Auburn when they play."

"You can't do that. No way," said Sally. "It's all or nothing, boy."

Emma looked at Reece, and he looked at her.

"That would make for an interesting Iron Bowl. We could go for Alabama, and he could go for Auburn. Put a little money on it, right?" Sammy downed his drink and reached for more.

"Hey, we're just poor missionaries," said Emma.

"What? Make more than I do at the quarry," said Sammy. He turned and hocked a big one off the porch. "What do you make an hour?"

"Sammy, that's personal," said Sally. "My word. But I know. She told me. About ten bucks an hour, right?"

Emma nodded. "To start."

Sammy whistled. "See, I told you so."

"Let's not talk about money," said Sarah. She paced with her cigarette.

"Yeah, money sucks," said Reece. "I know I don't have any." He clapped a mosquito mid-flight.

"We need some music," said Sally. "Sammy, get the radio. We'll show Reece how to dance."

"Uh oh," said Heather.

Sammy came back out with a small radio, plugged it in, and turned it on. It was set to a country station, and he turned the knob to the rock station playing "Fly Like an Eagle."

"Hey," said Sarah. "I like my country."

"Mom, we don't want to cry and fall asleep for God's sake," said Sally. She sat on the edge of her chair, took a drink, and put the glass on the cement. She sang along with the refrain, then stood and wavered, kicking her glass over. "Ooops!" She moved toward Sammy and grooved in front of him, but then she made for Reece. "Come on, boy. Let's dance!"

"Go on," said Emma. "Show us some moves." She stood and did a slow dance, holding her drink, soon joined by Sammy.

Sally grabbed Reece's hands and put them on her bare shoulders. She was wearing a tank top and cut-off jeans and no shoes. Her nipples were rock hard and showing. Reece moved like a robot back and forth, trying not to look too deeply into her eyes. She pulled him closer, and he almost fell over.

"Dang, boy," she said. "Don't kill me." She turned her back to him and ground on him.

Reece just let her have her way with him, trying to keep up with the changing moves. She drew his arms around her waist and held them there, swaying back and forth. Black Sabbath's "Hole in the Sky" came on, and she did a Rebel yell and pumped her head back and forth. Reece did his best to nod along with her. He watched Sammy and Emma dancing, wanting to switch partners with him. Heather just watched with her hand over her mouth.

Sally was up against him and pushing his hands up higher on her stomach beneath her tank top. He could feel the bottom of her bra. Sammy and Emma were watching them. "Hey, y'all let's get nekkid," said Sally. She pulled away from Reece, stumbled to the wall switch, and turned off the porch light. Only the light from the kitchen illuminated the scene, and she pulled off her tank top, revealing her bra. Reece was stunned.

"Sally, settle down," said Sammy, but he was grinning and pulling off his t-shirt. He had a black heart tattooed on his bicep.

"Oh, Lord," said Emma. "I'm wearing a dress."

"Y'all are crazy," said Heather, but she joined in anyway and danced by herself.

Sally was back to grooving with Reece. Her breasts were much larger than Emma's, he imagined. "C'mon, boy, shirt off," she said. Reece hesitated, and she did it for him, and he let her. She whooped and threw his shirt onto a chair. "Look at this skinny kid!" She ran her hands up his chest and then pulled him close. Reece was mesmerized and dizzy, and looked around to see Sammy unzipping Emma's dress, and it slid to the carport. She stepped out in her bra and panties. Reece stumbled.

"Okay, change partners," said Sally. She tweaked Reece's nipple, and he did a little yelp.

"Good Lord, I'm going inside," said Sarah.

Reece couldn't take his eyes off Emma as she sashayed toward him in the shadows with a huge grin on her face. "God, that dress was killing me!" She took his hands and led. Reece stared down at her, her breasts swaying inside her bra, the panties cut really low. He couldn't decide if he was dreaming or not.

Sally was unbuckling Sammy's jeans and pulling them down. He tripped and fell, and she shrieked a laugh.

"Uh oh," said Emma. "You know what that means. Down with your trousers, big boy."

Reece wanted to panic, but steadied himself. He was living for the first time in his life and realized that he was getting naked on a carport in Hueytown with a beautiful woman.

"Need some help?" asked Emma. She didn't wait for a reply and jerked his pants down, but he was still wearing his shoes. Heather was taking off her top, and she was braless with nipples the size of dinner plates. Reece fell back into a chair and kicked off his shoes, then his pants. He realized he didn't have an erection and was thankful. Now Sally's bra was off, and she hugged Sammy close, dancing slow and laughing.

They danced to the end of the song, and then there was a car dealership commercial, which slowed things down.

"This is crazy," said Reece. He held Emma close, feeling her skin on his, and he felt like he was made of iron.

"We are crazy," said Emma, looking up at him with wet eyes.

The radio guy was taking requests, and up came "Sweet Home Alabama," and they all let loose with yee ha's and whoops, and the frenzy reached a tipping point with the refrain, which they sang in unison as loud as they could. Heather'd had second thoughts and put her shirt back on.

"Want me to take it off?" asked Emma. She pressed into him. "One of mine hangs lower than the other." She ran her hands up and down his back.

Reece didn't want her to under the circumstances, but didn't say anything. He was content to just be near her. "You're perfect the way you are." He leaned down and kissed her.

Sally saw them kissing and yelled. "You go, girl! Get it on!" And they did, and Sammy and Sally did, dancing and necking until they were covered in sweat and panting for breath. And then "Hotel California" slowed them down, and soon they were just holding one another, cooling down, slipping back into their clothes, and talking and drinking for another hour.

On his way home, Reece had the radio cranked, the wind howling through the cab, worried that he would get pulled over for drunk driving, and he felt that a new chapter in his life had opened, and wondered what would happen next. Should he call Kristin? What would he say?

Reece slept like the dead and woke to hear Dora and Horace getting ready for church. His head pounded, and he briefly relived the night before. There was a knock on his door, and it opened.

"You going to church, son?" asked Dora.

Reece groaned. "Not today." He pulled a pillow over his head.

"Well, alright. Biscuits on the table," and she closed the door.

Reece slept for another two hours and sat up in bed, wanting to call Emma. He wanted her to go to church with him that night. He stood, wavered, and held his hand to the dark paneled wall. He found his running shorts and went to see about coffee. The Sunday paper lay strewn around Horace's recliner. There was no coffee in the pot, and he boiled a cup of water on the stove and made instant. He felt sick but also alive and walked outside into the warm morning. He took in the monkey grass growing alongside the driveway, the yellow bells, and the huge elephant ears between the garage and the house. There was a hosta as big as a barrel. He glanced at the Sykes' house and wondered how Elbert was doing in the hospital, how Rodney and Mrs. Laramore were doing.

He took his coffee and walked shirtless to the metal swing, the slabs of marble cool against his feet. A car passed by on the road in front, and he waved, not sure who it was. There was the hammock between two pines, and he decided to lie there and look up through the trees. He tried to manage his coffee but spilled some on his stomach. "Damn," and he laughed.

The tops of the pines swayed but just barely. A squirrel was devouring a pinecone, sending down shards through the branches. Above the tree was a bright blue sky. The cicadas were quiet, and there was near total silence. He thought he heard an airplane, but then the drone turned to loud music, and a car that he couldn't see passed the house. He could tell that it had pulled into the Sykes' driveway. He listened, and a car door slammed.

The night before, Kristin had drinks with Brad, hers all nonalcoholic. They'd met on Green Springs at a small bar in a strip mall. The entire CCU staff seemed to be there, and she had felt dismal, but cheered to see so many people she knew. She'd driven herself and left the bar before most, telling Brad thanks and good night.

She was up early enough to make the Sunday service and wondered if Emma had come to the lake the night before. She dried her hair with the blow dryer and put on her makeup, feeling lost. She hoped her friend Amber would be at church. Gert and Edwin had already left for Sunday school. She surveyed herself in the mirror, criticizing her look. Her hair took so long to dry, and it was too wild, crowding her face with curls. She decided she could do with a new look and pulled her hair back, exposing her ears.

She wanted to cry and put on her brightest lipstick, getting some on her teeth. She wiped it off with tissue paper, concentrating on her eyes and then her eyelashes. Maybe she would meet someone at church. Maybe she would sleep with Brad. She wasn't a virgin anymore, thanks to Reece, and her stomach churned.

"Reece!" and she began to cry, throwing her mascara at the mirror. She had to walk through the quiet house twice, stopping to play a melody on the piano each time, but then she gathered herself and finished getting ready. God, he was an idiot. Didn't he know what he was losing? Didn't he know she had stood by him, had flown to godforsaken Ethiopia to be with him after he'd been shot? But Emma had been there too. She had been hovering over him when she entered the ragged unit with its dim lights and smell of urine. She wondered what the sermon would be about. Maybe it would hold a revelation for her. Maybe God would swoop down and make everything right. Edwin kept saying that whatever happened was God's will, and not to try to understand everything, but she found that impossible to do.

Wearing a pretty lavender dress with a belt at the waist from Laura Ashley, she pet Walter, put him in the back yard, and then drove to church, listening to a tape of classical music. She wondered if she should call him afterward, but bit her lip and shook her head no.

Emma slept in late with Sally beside her. They'd talked till three, and she was exhausted but jubilant. She dragged herself out of bed with her hair askew, a big cowlick on the side, and remembered the night before. She knew that Sally had orchestrated the whole thing, but knew that Reece had a great time. He'd said so and wanted her to go with him to church. She checked her watch, and she had just enough time to get ready, but decided she would just take it easy. Maybe she would call Reece, or perhaps he would call her.

She slipped into a scrub top and shorts and went downstairs to the smell of bacon, coffee, and cigarettes. Sammy snored on the couch. She knew that her mom would be outside, probably weeding the flowerbed, and she was right. She walked outside, enjoying the cool feel of concrete beneath her feet.

"Hey, Mom."

"Well, hey yourself, baby girl." She pulled a dandelion. "Y'all had quite the party last night. Sorry I didn't stick around."

Emma laughed. "Yeah, margaritas with Sally are always a good time. Probably best that you went to bed."

"I don't like those sweet drinks." Sarah moved from squatting to her knees. "What did Reece think? I hope you didn't scare him off. He's a nice boy. I can tell he's not used to wild girls like you."

"Wild? Well, maybe so. He had a good time. I had a good time."

"That's all that matters." She picked at individual blades of grass between her snapdragons.

"You're the best, Momma."

"I hope so."

Emma surveyed the green lawn that Sammy cut and the light traffic on the road beyond. She took a deep breath, smelled the familiar air, and likened it to a clean pillowcase. In Ethiopia, the air had been somewhat biting and had an edge to it, as if it were responsible for the daily suffering there. She stepped back inside and ate bacon off a plate lined with a paper towel. She drank a glass of water and then fixed herself a cup of coffee, wondering how Charles Rickers was, wondering if he would warm to her over the next few days.

She felt drained and imagined that she was running a fever, and went inside to check.

Reece had every reason to think it was Cindy who had pulled into the Sykes' driveway, but stayed put in the hammock, pretending to be asleep. He somehow knew that she would find him in her own time and just relaxed, drinking in the Sunday silence. Always, Sundays felt off and strange. He hung one leg off the hammock and pushed himself back and forth. Had he really danced in his underwear with Emma? She was curvier than he'd ever imagined in her bra and panties. He laughed and wondered if he would ever tell Dora about it. He doubted if she would find it even faintly amusing. He closed his eyes and took a deep breath, and soon found his eyes very heavy.

"Hey!"

Reece sat up, spilling cold coffee on his lap. "What the?" It was Cindy.

"Were you dreaming about me?" She laughed and sat on the swing. "Man, you were out. Sorry to scare you."

"Oh wow, I was dreaming hard, but can't remember what." He threw his legs over the side, feeling conspicuous without his shirt.

"Man, you've got the life. Do you even have to pay any bills here? God, I work my ass off, although my man friend pays the rent. I buy a lot of weed." She laughed. "I've got some in the car."

Reece put his head in his hands. "Gee, maybe not right now. I've got a pretty bad headache." He didn't want to tell her that he'd never smoked pot.

"Been drinking?" She pushed herself in the swing,

making it go as high as it would go.

"Had a bunch of margaritas last night." He took a good look at her, smiling like a little girl. She had braids pinned to her head and wore khaki shorts with a colorful blouse. All she needed was a hat. "What're you doing out so early?"

"What? Aren't you glad to see me?" She pushed harder, and the swing's legs lifted.

"Sure. Just didn't expect to see you."

"Grandparents at church? Don't tell me you've stopped going, being a missionary and all." She let the swing do its own thing, holding her feet straight out.

"Yeah. I just couldn't make it. Stayed out too late. Going tonight, though." He played with the coffee cup in his hands.

"Does Kristin, your fiancée, drink?"

"Not really. I was with my friend Emma. The nurse."

"Well, well," said Cindy. "Branching out. So, who are you in love with? Me, Kristin, or this Emma?" She put on a serious face.

"Oh, brother," said Reece. "Maybe I love everybody."

"You can't love everybody. It's against the rules."

Reece thought about that. "Then I'm a rule breaker. Technically, I'm still engaged, but it was you coming up at the counselor's that has me in a deep pile of manure."

"You mean our little quickie? That was exciting, especially when Maybell came in and you freaked out."

Reece pushed himself in the hammock. "Yeah, I broke down and confessed. I was feeling guilty."

"So, is the engagement off? If it is, we can hang out more." She adjusted her blouse.

Reece sighed. "According to her, it is. I just want to do the right thing, I suppose."

"Love has nothing to do with doing the right thing. Boy, you got to grow you some and use 'em. Life is short, or so I've been told. She can find another man in a heartbeat. I know I can. Got any more of that coffee?"

Cindy was sounding perfectly reasonable. "It's instant. You want me to make you a cup?"

"Instant? Gross, but sure. Why not?" She hopped off the swing and pulled him out of the hammock. "Ohh, let's drink coffee on the pier. I hate Sundays. Do you hate Sundays?"

"I don't like Sundays. Church more or less ruins Sundays, but I still go." He wondered how much longer that would last. Reece opened the door for her and followed her in. He put the pot of water on to boil. Cindy threw herself onto Horace's recliner. "We could do it in the recliner. I could sit on top of you." She gripped the armrests.

Reece was dumbfounded. "Do what?" He dropped in a heaping teaspoon of instant into two mugs. He felt that sex was in the air, and he felt a rise in his shorts.

"You heard me, Colonel. But first, you could give me a massage. That would be nice."

Reece fumbled in the drawer for a clean spoon. He tried to envision Kristin and then Emma, but all he could see was Cindy's naked behind staring him in the face. "What if I rub your shoulders down on the pier?"

"I meant a real massage, butt, tits, and all." She reclined and spread her legs. "Hey, I put out for you. It's the least you can do. I won't beg, though. Jeez."

"It's just that I'm trying to do the right thing. Like I said."

He poured water into the mugs.

"Forget the coffee. Come on. In your tiny bedroom, there. I've been thinking about what it would be like in there." She stood and walked up to him and put her arms around his neck.

Reece was paralyzed. His engagement did seem to be off, but what about Emma? Did he owe her something? He wasn't sure. She had saved his life, but they weren't a couple yet. He should be having sex three times a day if the opportunity arose. He felt her mouth next to his and kissed her. He let his hands rise to her waist, and she pulled him in close.

"That's more like it." She kissed him deep and hard and clutched at his shirt. "God, I'm horny. I'm on birth control, by the way." She raced her tongue back into his mouth, and he squeezed her butt. "Mmm."

Reece pulled back a bit. "I just feel so guilty, but you're so good-looking. I swear you're just about perfect."

"Just about? You can do better than that. Come on." She led him into his bedroom. The bed was a mess. "Undress me."

Reece paused but then undid the top button of her blouse. She leaned in and kissed him. He lifted the blouse over her head, and she tossed it onto the floor. She took his hands and moved them to her shorts. He undid the button and zipper, and they fell to the floor. She was curvy and tan, her thighs just touching. Her breasts filled her bra. She did a slow turn for him, and her panties were bi-kini cut.

"The massage, Colonel," and she lay on the bed on her stomach.

Reece climbed on and straddled her just below her butt. He touched the tan lines there and let his fingers drift across her back. She squirmed and giggled.

"You can unhook the bra."

Reece unfastened the bra, and she lifted up, pulling it off. He started at her neck and with his fingers massaged deep and slow, anticipating her naked body, his member sliding into her. He massaged down her spine, and she moaned, her face buried in a pillow. At her panty line, he pressed in with his thumbs.

"God. That's great. Keep going. I'll do anything you want."

"We need a condom," said Reece. His heart thudded in his chest.

"I have one. In my purse, but it's in the car. I don't think I can wait for that. I'm disease-free if that makes you feel better." She turned over, covering her breasts.

"Yeah," said Reece. He watched as she removed her hands, revealing her perfect nipples. He let her put his hands there, and he leaned down to kiss them, circling with his tongue. She arched into him, and he groaned and massaged her chest and stomach. He smelled electricity, gunpowder, and iron. He knew what he wanted to do and kissed her stomach, tickling her.

She put the pillow behind her head and reached for his shorts and unbuttoned them. He stood on the bed, bumping his head on the drop ceiling, and let them fall to his ankles.

"Take 'em off," she said, as she slid down her panties and spread her legs.

Reece was naked and, on his knees, staring at her wonderment, blonde hair and pink. He scooted back and then went in, licking her there, inhaling the sharp odor, his tongue seeming to have a mind of its own. And soon they were rolling in the sheets, Cindy raking her nails down his back, raising welts.

When they were finished, Reece lay on his side, sweating and feeling more guilty than ever, but God, the sex was so good. She wanted to do it again, and she put her mouth on his cock, but he pulled away.

"What? You hear something?"

"No, I'm just feeling so damn guilty. I could have sex all day long with you, I think."

Cindy laughed. "Yeah, if you could just keep Kristin off your mind. I've never been with someone so reluctant." She put his hand on her breast, and he let it slip away. There was a big wet spot on the sheet.

Reece took a deep breath and looked around for his underwear. Cindy got the message and began dressing. Reece wanted to tell her thank you or something, but nothing would come. It wasn't Kristin that he was worried about at the moment. The more he thought about Emma, the more he thought maybe he was in love with her.

"You're killer," said Reece. "I'm just a late bloomer. I... danced with Emma last night, and her sister and brother-in-law. I just might be falling for her. I'm sorry."

Cindy smiled. "Oh, the poor Colonel tied in knots. I didn't come out here to get married, just to have some fun. Things get boring with the old man, with Clarence. I think I love him in a way, but it's kind of like he's my dad sometimes. Creepy, huh? He's coming out after lunch. Y'all should hang out, have a beer."

Reece brushed his hair to the side. "That would be weird, for me anyway."

"He knows. He doesn't care. He tells me he loves me just about every day, regardless."

They moved back into the den and wound up with the two cool cups of coffee.

"Let's go to the pier with the coffee. I don't care that it's cold." Cindy picked up a mug from Reece's church. "But first, I need to visit the ladies' room."

"Sure." He wanted to call Emma, but Cindy was back again, and they were walking through the pines.

"Which pier?" asked Cindy. "I brought my bathing suit, but I'll put it on later."

"Either one," said Reece, and he followed her onto the Sykes' pier, the wood groaning beneath them. He watched minnows scattering at the edge of the thick cattails and then looked up at the bright sun. He imagined a phone ringing inside its hot nuclear oven.

Reece sat beside her, envisioning the people at church in their suits and ties. Maybe if he had gone...but what? What did it matter that he'd had sex with Cindy? He looked at her tan legs, stretched out in front of her. He thought about dancing with Emma in her underwear, and he longed to see her. He wouldn't even need to explain what had happened. Maybe she would just laugh him off. He smelled the lake and took a breath. He gazed at his feet, promising that he wouldn't have sex with Cindy again.

"What are you brooding over?" asked Cindy. "Not mad at me, are you?"

"Oh, no, just thinking. I think I'm in love with Emma."

"Have you banged her yet? Damn, I need a cigarette."

She sipped her coffee.

"No," said Reece.

"Well, keep it that way for as long as you can...to see how much you love her. I'm sorry I was so forward, but I guess I'm a nympho."

Reece laughed and sighed. "It takes two to tango."

"Yeah, but don't let love be a one-way street. Listen to your heart, boy. Listen to your heart." She squeezed his thigh.

Reece knew she was right and wondered at the source. But he still needed to talk with Kristin. They needed some kind of closure, some sort of resolution. Maybe they would go to the counselor and work it out. Maybe his crush on Emma was just a lark, brought on by tragedy. Something had to give, but no one deserved to be hurt, and he felt a welling of something akin to shame.

"You're pretty amazing, sister," said Reece. "Clarence is lucky to have you, regardless."

"Well, thanks. And the sex was pretty good by the way." A pair of dragonflies darted after one another, skimming the water.

"What you said," said Reece. He stared across the lake.

Emma shook down the thermometer and walked downstairs with it under her tongue. Reece hadn't said when he would pick her up for church, and she decided to call. The phone rang, and she walked into the kitchen.

She mumbled a hello but then pulled the thermometer from her mouth and looked at it. 99.5. "Hello?"

"Hey," said Reece. "Didn't wake you, did I?"

"Well, hey, and no. I was about to call to ask when you were coming."

"Starts at seven, so how about I pick you up at five. If that works."

"Well, sure. How's your head? I've got a headache and a fever, but I feel okay."

"Do margaritas give you a fever?"

Emma laughed. "I don't think so. I wasn't feeling too hot last night, but didn't say anything. I had you to distract me."

"Don't push yourself. You have to go to work in the morning."

"Don't worry. I'm fine." She poured herself a cup of coffee. "Mom's taking a nap. She worked in the flowers all morning."

"I'm glad she went in last night before we got in our skivvies. That whole thing was magical. Your family is a hoot."

"Yeah, it was. I think she knew things were gonna get weird."

"The weirder the better," said Reece.

"I'm just glad Sally didn't want to play spin the bottle."

"Maybe some other time," said Reece.

"Yeah, so pick me up at five. Mom made some killer lentil soup and cornbread if you want to eat here before we go."

Reece said that sounded good, and they talked for another half hour.

Reece pulled into the long driveway. He wore shorts and a pullover, but would change before church. He'd started off sweating in the truck, but the wind had cooled him. His face felt sticky, though. He hit the parking brake out of habit and hopped out.

"Hey, Mrs. Sarah." She was sitting on the carport, smoking.

"Hey, Reece." She waited for him to get closer. "None of that Mrs. for me. Makes me feel old. Sarah is just fine." She laughed and coughed.

"Okay, will do." He put his hands in his pockets.

"She's inside. Go on in."

"Thanks," and he went in, passing through the kitchen into the spare living room. She wasn't there, and he went to the bottom of the stairs. "Hello!"

"Hey! Getting ready. Come on up."

Reece wondered at that but went up the carpeted stairs. He turned into the hall, and Emma popped out of the bathroom, wearing a yellow sleeveless summer dress. She was brushing her hair. She looked strangely beautiful at that moment, a kind of lost soul waiting for the door to heaven to open.

"Wow, that's a nice dress." The hall seemed narrow and

too small for them, the ceiling like a lid. Family portraits lined the white walls, none of them with her father.

"Thanks. I've had it for a while. It was an Easter dress, but it's still so warm out. You wearing shorts to church?" She tilted her head, brushing and brushing, as if there were something there that needed to be eliminated. She tilted her head the other way and brushed.

"No, I'll change. It's so hot in the truck." He examined a portrait that seemed to be a school picture of Emma. "That you?"

Emma laughed. "Yeah, look how big my teeth are, like my mouth was too small."

"Cute, though. You want me to wait downstairs?"

"No, come in here with me. You can sit on the john."

Reece stepped into the pink-tiled bathroom. The pink was old and had an undertone of brown. Instead of the white toilet, he sat on the edge of the pink tub. "Lots of pink."

"Yeah, but I'm used to it. You don't mind if I brush my teeth, do you?" She gave him a look that dared him to say no.

"Heck no. Brush away." He watched her squeeze a tube of cinnamon Close-Up onto her brush. "That stuff is good enough to swallow."

Emma nodded and watched herself brush in the mirror. She spat in the sink and ran water into a small green plastic glass. She swished and spat again. "Real ladylike, huh?"

"I like it," said Reece. He tried to remember if he'd brushed his teeth.

"Take it or leave it, right? Now here goes the deodorant." She popped the lid from a stick and rubbed it on her smooth armpits.

"So, what's next?" He shifted his butt on the tub's edge, feeling his leg going to sleep.

"One last thing, a little lipstick. I don't wear much makeup." She took a tube of light pink lipstick and then smacked her lips, spreading it around. "There, how do I look?"

Reece fumbled for words. "Looking good."

Emma brushed her hair for another minute. "Now, done. Want some soup?"

"Sure. We have time. I got here a little early, I think."

"Couldn't wait to see me, right? Come on."

Reece followed her down the stairs to the kitchen and was soon eating a bowl of lentil soup at the table. She had already eaten. Sarah walked in, and he told her how good the soup was. She just smiled and said to eat as much as he wanted, that lentils were cheap. He thanked her again before they left and promised to have Emma back at a reasonable hour.

Back at the lake, he changed, and they still had about half an hour to kill, so they walked down the road and then to the long public pier. The water was deeper there. There was a bench at the end, and they sat admiring the view of the lake.

"Have you talked to Kristin?"

Reece admired her bare arms. "No, not since the last blowup. I keep thinking I should call, but she was so mad. I think she hates me now."

"Well, if I had been her, I would've freaked out too, being engaged, of course."

"Yeah, I've screwed up, but to be honest, maybe it's for the best. Maybe I'm not ready to get married." He felt better having said that.

"I'm not looking to get married," said Emma. "But I'm definitely in need of a boyfriend. Sally is convinced that we should get together." She nudged his foot with hers. "No pressure, right?" She laughed.

Reece decided to just be honest. "I'm very attracted to you. If it weren't for Kristin, I'd throw myself in front of a bus for you."

"Really, well, that's a weird thing to say, but I like it." She snuggled her shoulder into his. "You do have to end it, though, officially with Kristin, to get everything above board...and wean off of Cindy."

Reece found it hard to believe that he was talking about ending his engagement with Kristin, and with Emma no less. He felt a kind of freedom and relaxed at the thought of having everything settled, of everyone knowing what their fate in life would be. The tangible reality of being able to pursue Emma was within reach. Maybe he wouldn't have to go back to the counselor after all. He imagined Kristin putting her heart in a bowl of ice water, cleansing herself of him, unshackling him to be whatever it was he needed to be. The sky was blue with ragged clouds high above the earth.

"I mean, I still love her in some way, or maybe care is the better word. We had some great times together." He put his arm around her and smelled shampoo. "I think I asked her to marry me because I was leaving for Ethiopia, and I felt guilty for leaving. It was my way of patching things up."

"Damn, that's heavy, Reece. You never did seem excited to be engaged when you talked about it. But don't go asking me to marry you, because I'll say no."

"Thanks for the heads up. I just want to enjoy life, not be tied down. And right now, I want to enjoy you. I like your family, and I feel like they like me. Kristin's parents never liked me for whatever reason. I guess that maybe now they feel justified."

"I'd venture to say that you're already like family. Sally has never warmed up to anybody like she has to you and Sammy, too. He's such a manly man. And I can tell Momma likes you."

Reece felt like skipping stones. He wanted to tell her that he loved her, but not love in the binding sense, but rather bonding. She just made him feel good, and he craved that. "Maybe we should head back," and they did, walking hand in hand as if spending the last day of their life together.

They got to church a few minutes early, Emma in her yellow dress and Reece wearing black slacks and a pullover. He greeted people as they sat near the back on the right side. Horace and Dora had decided against coming, preferring to rest. With the overhead lights and the sunlight, the auditorium was overly bright, and Reece squinted as if he needed a hat. Cool AC blew over the gathering congregation, and Reece felt a peace of things familiar yet unseen. The elderly woman in front of them turned and spoke. She was a lifetime member of the church, predictably a widow, and had that bluish white hair of her generation. Reece introduced Emma, and there were smiles all around. On his way to the pulpit, Pastor Scoggins patted

Reece on the back.

There was a small choir, and Brother Dodds in shirt and tie got the service going with "Bringing in the Sheaves." There was another song, announcements, a prayer request for a family whose son had drowned, and then the offertory. As the plates were being passed, as the piano played, there was a latecomer who slipped in the back door and sat on the back row. It was Kristin, and right away she spotted Reece and Emma sitting together, but they hadn't noticed her come in.

Pastor Scoggins tugged at his collar and took the podium. He'd noticed the latecomer and asked if any visitors needed to be recognized. He cast his gaze toward Kristin, who raised her hand.

"We have one visitor tonight," and he gestured toward the back and asked her to fill out the visitor card with the little pencil. Reece didn't turn to look, but Emma did, and she poked him in the ribs.

Reece didn't understand, and she whispered to him, and he froze, afraid to look, but he did anyway. She was looking at him with sad brown eyes, and he felt that he would die. He wondered if maybe she planned to shoot him from three rows back. He knew that Edwin kept a pistol in the house. He had planned to put his arm behind Emma, but changed his mind.

Pastor Scoggins read a verse from the Book of Matthew and began his sermon on stewardship and the parable of the talents. Reece had heard the story a thousand times and couldn't focus on anything new that might be said. Emma was scribbling on a bulletin.

What do we do? she wrote.

Reece shook his head, feigning interest in the sermon, imagining being shot for a second time. He figured if there was justice that this bullet would kill him. He deserved it and imagined himself slumping, the last words on his lips, "I'm sorry."

For thirty minutes, that passed like individual hairs on a camel's back, Reece sat immobile and afraid. He imagined her coming forward at the end of the service, proclaiming her sorrow and righteous indignation. And when the service ended in prayer, he was at once relieved, but now he had the task of facing her, with Emma at his side. He turned, hoping she had slipped out, but she was there, Bible in hand, waiting.

"I have to say something," said Reece.

"Should I come with you?" asked Emma.

"Might as well." He stepped into the aisle, and it was just two paces to reach her.

"Surprised, aren't you?" asked Kristin. She wore the same Laura Ashley dress she'd worn that morning to church.

"Look, I'm sorry," said Reece.

"Hey," said Emma.

"Oh, don't be sorry, but you do owe me some explanations." She stood there as if backed by a large army of tanks and spears.

Reece paused to say hello to a departing member. "Can we go outside?" He glanced at Emma, who seemed on the verge of defiance, her arms folded.

"Sure, better yet, why don't we go somewhere and hash this out. Wendy's? It's on my way home, and I'm sure it's on your way back to Emma's house." She said Emma like dried syrup.

"This is kind of like stalking," said Emma. "I'd rather just go straight home."

"But you're such an important part of this," said Kristin. "I'm sure this will be the last time the three of us meet. So, what are you afraid of?"

They walked as a huddled threesome, held together by a toxic glue.

Reece looked to Emma for support. "Maybe it's best?"

"I have to go to work in the morning," said Emma.

They were outside in the cooling but still warm air. Orange streaked the sky.

"We all do," said Kristin.

"Okay, we'll go, but not for long, just long enough to sort this out." Reece felt he was being reasonable and looked to Emma.

"It's just the rest of our lives, right?" asked Kristin. "Thirty minutes sounds reasonable, right?"

They reached the bottom of the stairs.

"Okay, let's do it," said Emma. She stood close to Reece.

"The Wendy's in Roebuck," said Reece. "We'll meet you there."

"Fine," said Kristin, and she walked away.

"Reece, I don't know about this," said Emma.

"I owe it to her, plus it's on the way. Thirty minutes, and then I'll drive you home."

"I feel like a criminal. But, oh well, let's see what happens. The saga continues."

They drove in relative silence through Palmerdale, then Pinson, then Center Point, then Roebuck. Churchgoers filled the parking lot, come to have their last Sunday hurrah, and Reece had to make space beside the enclosed dumpster. Inside, the noise was appreciable and the line to the register long. Reece saw her in the back at a table for two, but there was only one chair. On his way there, he stopped at tables asking if chairs were free and took two more to the table where Kristin sat. He took a deep breath. He knew what the first words from her mouth would be.

Kristin cleared her throat. "Emma, you do know that he's having sex with Cindy?"

Reece winced. She didn't know about the latest rendez-vous.

Emma laughed. "Yeah, he told me. He's single, right?"

Kristin blushed. "No, he is engaged to me."

"I thought you called that off, after he told you." Emma was all business. "So, regardless, he's single. He can do what he wants, and it sounds like this Cindy is very aggressive."

"Look," said Reece. "I apologized. But you did call off the engagement."

"You're free to do what you want, huh? Free to date and have your good times regardless of your commitment to me."

"Yeah, he's free," said Emma. "Let the man be for Christ's sake."

Reece cringed.

"I'll let him be when I'm good and ready," said Kristin, her voice rising. "I need to know what he's thinking. Is it over? Has he just jumped ship and that's that?" She made a fist.

"You just need to let go and leave him alone. Christ." Emma was slouched in the small chair, but then sat up straight.

"I just need some time, some time where I'm not engaged. I think maybe we...dove in too fast. So much has happened. Everyone needs a break," said Reece. He wanted a shot of tequila.

"Does everyone include Emma or just me? Do you know how that makes me feel? Like something rotten, like a bad apple, and that's just not fair." She fought back tears and pushed the saltshaker.

"I guess I mean us. I'm willing to go to the counselor again, if you think it will help." His face felt sticky and warm. "I want to do the right thing, but don't exactly know what that is."

"Are you attracted to Emma?" Kristin wiped her nose. She'd brushed her hair back, putting hair clips so her ears were exposed.

Reece nodded. "I am. It's complicated."

"Either you are, or you aren't. But you've said it. So, do you still love me?"

Reece felt like a pincushion, each question piercing him. "Maybe I need some time to sort that out. I could still love you, but not want to get married."

"You need some space?" Kristin looked small and tired, ready to resign her fate.

"I think he needs some space," said Emma. "Maybe from me too."

"I didn't ask you," said Kristin.

"Hold on, sister—"

"Yeah, space. That's a good way to put it. I mean, we argue all the time. Every time I see you, we argue," said Reece.

"Because you keep wanting to do things, like have sex with other women!" The loudness of her voice surprised her. "I mean, who knows, I could be pregnant. Does Emma know that we've had sex? I guess she knows everything by now."

"I'm sorry. I'm always saying I'm sorry." Reece gazed through the window into the parking lot, a couple embracing, leaning against a red Mustang. "I guess you should take a test, to see, right?"

"And what if it was positive? Would you forget Cindy and Emma? Would that change things? I mean, it would be your duty." The surrounding tables had gone quiet, everyone listening with pricked ears.

"Yeah, that would change things, but I'm not sure what we would do. We would have to figure that out. Let's not go there until we know."

"How embarrassing. Now I have to go to the drugstore and buy a pregnancy test." Tears had begun to trickle.

"Hey," said Emma. "I'll go with you if that would help. I'm sorry that I'm in the way of whatever."

"Heck, why don't we all three go?" asked Reece. "Would that help? I don't want you to feel abandoned."

"It's too late for that," said Kristin, but she had brightened. "I'll let you guys go with me. Maybe we could go to Walmart, and I could do the test in the bathroom. I can't do it at home."

Reece looked at his watch. "Super. Let's do it. We'd better go before it closes, though. You okay to go now?"

Kristin blew her nose into a napkin. "Yes. Let's go."

Walmart was just down the road, and they parked in the vast parking lot and walked in silence. The greeter said, "Hey there, young folks!" and they turned left, headed to the health aisles.

"I think I know where it is. Should be next to the condoms, right?" She led the way.

The three of them stood there side by side, staring at the kits. There were two kinds.

"Which one?" asked Kristin.

"Maybe the most expensive one," said Reece. "I'll pay for it." He pointed to the one that was $12.94.

"You folks need any help?" asked a large woman in a blue vest. She held a box of fungus spray.

"No," said Emma.

The woman looked hurt and walked away.

Kristin reached for the kit and held it like a feather. "Okay, so now what?"

"Let's pay for it." He put his hand on her arm and led her toward the registers.

The cashier eyed them with a look of glum but glee. She was very dark and had a nearly shaved head. She scanned the item. "Thirteen eighty-five." She bagged the kit and held it out to Reece with a bored grin. He took it.

"Now, to the bathroom." He put his hand on her shoulder and said, "This way."

Kristin seemed to be moonwalking, as if she were about to encounter alien life. Emma took the bag from Reece and ushered Kristin into the bathroom.

Reece felt exhausted and looked out over the vast store. It was cool and bright. A man was buying a buggy-load of bottled water. He imagined the man had a well, that the pump had broken, and he needed clean water. The man paid and pushed the buggy. It had a spinning wheel on the front and made a noise. Reece realized he needed to pee and went to the men's room. An employee was washing his hands. He nodded. The man nodded. There was an odor of farts in the air, and he tried to take shallow breaths as he relieved himself. He walked back out and waited some more, checking his watch. What if Kristin were pregnant? He imagined a wedding at the courthouse, a quick honeymoon to Gulf Shores. He wondered what the child would look like.

A mother with a little girl of six or seven passed him. She had tattoos on her shoulder and was dragging the child, who was whimpering and sulky. The woman stopped and scolded the girl. "C'mon now. We ain't got all night. Daddy's waitin' in the car." She jerked the girl's arm. "Mommy, don't pull me." She planted her feet and resisted. The mother jerked her again. "I wish you would listen. Let's go. You know I need coffee beans and pork chops." The little girl relented and set her feet into motion.

Reece checked his watch and began to feel warm. What was taking so long? He paced down and paced back and put his hands in his pockets. He hoped it would turn out to be a girl. He couldn't imagine raising a boy. Boys were mean and did stupid things. He remembered jumping into piles of sawdust from a tall ladder inside a vast warehouse and wondered that he hadn't been killed. And then they came out, Kristin weeping and Emma with her arm around her. Like that, they walked out of the store with Reece following. He watched Kristin and Emma hug, and Kristin got in her Toyota and drove away.

Reece was about to explode. "Well?"

Emma frowned. "It was negative. I think she wanted it

to be positive. Maybe it was a bad idea for you to have sex with her. I feel sorry for her."

Reece exhaled. "Well, but we did."

"Okay, let's go. I'm tired," said Emma. "We've got our own test to do." She opened the truck door and got in.

Reece hustled on the unit. He had Mrs. Laramore in a chair, eating breakfast, and there were new orders for Rodney. He noticed a nursing assistant step into Rodney's room and went to check.

"What the heck?" Rodney lay on his stomach and looked like he was swimming across the English Channel. "Mr. Lasseter, you okay? We need to get you flipped back over. You'll suffocate like that."

"Lord, Lord," said Rochelle. "You got yourself in a mess. What you want to do?"

"Let's use the draw sheet to get him turned," said Reece.

"I don't want to fly in no airplane," said Rodney, gasping for breath.

Reece and Rochelle positioned themselves.

"There's no airplane, Mr. Lasseter. You're fine and safe here. Nowhere to go today, okay? Let's do it on three. One, two, three," and he grunted. Rodney was a heavy man even without his legs. Rodney rolled against the rail and then onto his back.

"They gonna drop me out, fly me up, and drop me out." His eyes were wide, and he seemed to be holding his breath.

"Take you some deep breaths," said Rochelle. "Nobody gonna hurt you here." She laughed. "He's something."

"Can you get his breakfast tray set up?" asked Reece. He patted Rodney on the arm. "You're fine. No worries."

He walked out and took Rodney's chart from Laronda's desk to check the flagged orders. He and Emma were going to the public health clinic for HIV screening on Friday. He was petrified that he'd be positive and have to tell Kristin and Cindy. He sat and charted for a while, chatting with Glenda. Rodney's doctor wanted him up in the chair three times a day and had changed him to a low-salt diet. Reece stopped writing and collected his thoughts, remembering that he needed to visit Mr. Sykes next door. He dreaded seeing Kristin there, but hoped he would anyway. Sheila, that morning, had told him that Kristin had gone to another party with Brad, and he wondered if it was true. He felt a pang, a cross between guilt and jealousy, and wondered if he had a right to feel that way.

The morning went quickly, lunch alone, and soon he had a break. He walked through the automatic door to CCU and didn't see Kristin. Mr. Sykes was in eight, and he went there. Elbert was sitting in the recliner beside his bed, MTV playing. He looked a bit glassy, but had good color.

"Hey, Mr. Sykes."

Elbert rumbled out a distorted greeting and tried to smile, his face drooping.

"You look good. I'll bet they get you out of here soon and onto the floor." He walked around the bed to the chair. "Need anything? Juice, water?"

"Naw, boy." Reece listened and deciphered his words. "How's my gar-en? My tomatoes?"

Reece cocked his head. "Your garden?"

Elbert nodded.

"Yeah, Horace is taking care of that for you. Don't worry. He'll keep it picked for you. I know you'd love to be back there." He saw Kristin peek around the curtain. "Hey! He yours today?"

"Yep," said Kristin. "He's doing better, aren't you, Mr. Sykes?" She surveyed the room. "Okay, I'll be back to check on you." She left.

Reece was stymied and lost his train of thought. He chatted with Mr. Sykes for a few more minutes and left. On his way out, Kristin was talking with a doctor he didn't know. She seemed calm and was smiling, as if the doctor were describing a favorite recipe to her. He paused to see if she would notice him and then walked away.

Emma arrived at eight and helped Darlene give Charles a serious bath in the walk-in shower. He had spluttered and cursed, and she had started laughing and couldn't stop. Her head ached, and she felt nauseated, and she wondered if her fever was back.

"Okay, highlight of the day," said Emma. "How about we get outside in the garden?" Darlene was downstairs eating a snack of chocolate pudding, the kind from a little tin can.

Charles scowled. "You nearly killed me in the shower. I haven't been to the garden in months, so no!" He was reclining on the bed on three pillows, his face red and angry. He looked to Emma like a scrawny old man rescued from the Grand Canyon.

"Oh, you're a pistol. Well, how about this? You go to the garden, and just see how you like it. If it doesn't suit you, we'll bring you back in. I'll get Darlene to help." She planted her hands on her hips.

"Dear God," said Charles. "Is my wife here? She'll put a stop to this nonsense."

"You mean your ex-wife. She's not here. She came on Friday and dropped off groceries."

"Where did they dig you up anyway? Nobody else wants me to go to the garden, let alone go downstairs. I'm perfectly comfortable right here."

"What about the sun on your skin? It'll do you good." She tidied up the bedside table and dropped an empty can of Ensure into the garbage can.

"The sun...can go to hell." He coughed, and his sunken cheeks flailed. He raised up and coughed some more. Emma put her knee on the bed and wiped his mouth with a tissue. "I can wipe my own mouth, dear. Where's Trish? I need to see Trish. Get me the phone."

"She your girlfriend?" asked Emma.

"Yes, nosy, she's my girlfriend."

"You sure are sassy today."

"This is my house, right? I can...be sassy if I want." He folded his hands in his lap. "So, are you just going to stare at me?"

Emma laughed. "I'm sorry if I'm bugging you, but it's my job to make you better, right? Look, just rest for a while and then I'll come back, okay? I'll let you be for now."

"That would be super," said Charles.

"But I want you to drink some water before I go." She poured ice water into a plastic cup and held it out to him.

"Oh God, it never ends." He took the water and drank two sips. "There, are you happy?"

"Can you drink more? You need to pee more."

"*You* need to pee more." He took another sip and handed her the cup.

"Good job. Okay, I'll be back. Holler if you need anything."

Emma joined Darlene downstairs, who was on her third cup of pudding.

"What did he say?" Darlene licked the spoon and dropped it into the sink.

"He said no, of course, but he can't fight us. He'll loosen up once he gets outside." She took a glass of water from the tap and drank. "Check my back, would you? I'm itching all over."

Darlene walked over, and Emma sat in a high-backed chair of walnut.

"Honey, you've got a rash for sure. Looks like it goes all the way down your back."

"Damn. I knew it," said Emma. "I'm just not feeling well these days."

"Maybe you should have that checked out. You don't want to compromise Mr. Rickers." She walked to the large window and watched the birds at the feeder.

"I don't think I'm infectious," said Emma. "But I wonder what it could be. Maybe I'm allergic to Charles." She laughed.

"I think a lot of people are allergic to Mr. Rickers, including his children."

They talked for a few more minutes and decided that it was now or never and ascended the stairs to undertake an enormous task.

By the end of the day, Kristin was tired, but she had two date proposals, one from Brad and another from Blake, Dr. Shelfwise. She told Brad maybe, but accepted Blake's invitation to have lunch on Saturday in Homewood. He was tall and sandy-haired, his thick hair looking as if a turbulent wind had caught him. She was all smiles as she reported off, having had a pretty easy day. She'd transferred Mr. Sykes out to the seventh floor and had not had a new admit, a rarity.

Back at home, she changed clothes and couldn't wait to tell Gert about Blake. She'd had serious thoughts of taking Brad up on his offer, but was glad that she hadn't. He was just too institutional, too dry. Gert was thrilled.

"Honey, he sounds like a real find." Gert wrung a dishtowel into the sink. Why settle for a nurse when you could have a doctor? "Gosh, I want to meet him."

"We haven't even had lunch yet." She dropped onto the sofa and scrubbed Walter's head. "You're a good boy, a good boy."

Robyn came in. "What's all the excitement about?"

"Oh, nothing," said Kristin.

"Yeah, something. You're grinning like a clown." She wore a blue leotard and shorts.

"She's got a new boyfriend," said Gert. "Now she can forget about that other guy."

"What? You mean Reece?" asked Robyn. "Who is this new boyfriend?"

"Stop. He's not my boyfriend. He's a doctor from work, is all. I've seen him around. He's a tall, blond, and handsome resident. We're having lunch on Saturday."

"Well, well," said Robyn. "You have ditched Reece. Not that I blame you." She stretched and palmed the carpet.

"Yeah, I saw him today." She looked a little sad. "Maybe I can hook you up with the other guy who's always hitting on me, Brad."

"Ooh, two doctors," said Gert. She was making quiche Lorraine.

"You said he's short, though," said Robyn. "That could be a problem."

"Well, it's up to you," said Kristin. "Beggars can't be choosers."

"Hey, that's not nice." Robyn went to the floor to stretch her hammies.

"Suit yourself," said Kristin. "But Blake is mine for now. And if he comes over, don't come prancing out in a bikini." She smiled.

Emma and Darlene walked into Charles' room expecting a battle. Darlene took the lead. Charles was dozing, sitting up.

"Mr. Rickers?" asked Darlene. "Mr. Rickers?" She reached over and squeezed his shoulder. "Hey there."

Charles opened an eye. The other one was stuck together. "Whu, what?" He gazed at them. "What do you two want?"

"We want to take you outside," said Darlene.

"To the garden," said Emma.

"Oh, hell no. I've already said no." He grimaced as if scolding a child for playing with matches.

"You need the fresh air and sunlight," said Emma. "Good for your immune system."

"Poppycock," said Charles.

Darlene frowned and looked to Emma. It was Emma's idea.

"Okay, we're going to help you slide to the edge of the bed and then walk you downstairs. We'll put the belt around your waist to help us hold you up. You can rest in a chair, and then we'll head out back." Emma used her hands to tell him this.

"Just drag me down the hall by my feet, why don't you?"

"Oh, come on. Your doctor wants you up and not just sitting in bed." She had one knee on the bed. "Just slide you over." She motioned for Darlene to help her.

Charles was too weak to resist and felt his body moving. "Do not drop me! I will have your skin if you drop me. For God's sake, what I want doesn't seem to matter." His legs slid off the bed, and they sat him up. Emma put the cloth belt around his waist.

"Here we go," said Emma. "One arm around each of us, and we'll grab this belt. You have to take steps, though, as big as you can. You ready, Darlene?"

"Ready." She was on his left, Emma on his right.

"Push up, Charles, on three. One, two, three."

"Goddamn," said Charles. He hung between them like a cooked lasagna noodle.

"Doing good," said Darlene.

"You're light as a feather," said Emma.

They moved forward, and Charles' feet lifted just a bit, but mostly his feet dragged.

"Good work, Charles," said Emma, and soon they were at the bedroom door and moving down the hall. Darlene huffed a bit for breath.

It took a full two minutes to get to the curved stairway, and there they rested, letting him sit on the top stair.

Charles looked around. "This is lovely."

Then they were ready again and went down each step and paused, down and pause.

"Halfway down," said Emma. "You can do it."

"How the hell am I going to get back up? You'll have to carry me."

"We'll cross that bridge when we get there," said Darlene. Her forehead and lower back were sweating.

And then they were at the bottom of the stairs, all three winded.

"Need to rest?" asked Emma.

"Yes, please," said Charles. They placed him in a wing-back chair beside a large potted ficus.

The quickest way to the garden was through the kitchen, onto the marble porch, and then down a short flight of stairs. It took them a good ten minutes, but then Charles was resting again in an outside chair in the shade of an elegant elm tree.

"I feel like shit," said Charles. "You're going to kill me."

Emma laughed, and they let him rest.

The garden was circular with four entrances that led through sculpted shrubs to the center, planted with irises and fitted with a square of padded benches. More or less dragging him now, pushing his feet forward with their feet, they placed him on a bench in full sunlight.

"Great!" said Emma. "You did it."

"Well, I hope you're happy, and I'm ready to go back," said Charles.

"Oh, no sir," said Darlene. She sat beside him. "This is too nice, and I'm bushed."

Emma squeezed in between them. "This is super. You want me to get you anything? A drink? How about a shot of bourbon?"

"That might not be a good idea," said Darlene.

"Whiskey with some ice. He deserves it."

"Well, the thought nauseates me, but why not? Now you're talking my language." He put elbows to knees, watching a large black ant crawl onto his house shoe.

"Tell us a story about the savings and loan outfit you were in," said Emma. "We'll get bourbon when we get back inside."

Charles craned his neck at Emma. "You're kidding."

"No, I'm not kidding. I bet you have some interesting stories."

"I was the boss until we had to close shop. The RTC shut us down. I could have borrowed our way back to solvency, but the feds stepped in and shut us down anyway. I got out just in time, I suppose. Damn feds."

"Didn't seem to hurt you much, judging by this house," said Emma.

"This house was paid for long ago," said Charles. "The business was exciting, but we were paying too much interest. I had three secretaries."

"Were they good-looking?" asked Darlene.

"Why do you think I hired them?" Charles managed a feeble laugh and sat up straight. "My primary secretary was Astrid. Man, she was something. Legs up to her armpits. Plus, she was bright, which was a bonus. I hate that everyone lost their jobs." He slumped his shoulders. "I was protected, and they weren't."

"At least you feel bad. I suppose there was nothing you could do," said Emma.

"Nope, not a damn thing."

"How about we sit here for another ten minutes and then head into some shade?" asked Darlene, and they did that.

Charles told them another story about his cat Whiskers that he'd had for fifteen years. She drank antifreeze in a neighbor's garage and died, and then they just sat, everyone sweating until it was time to go back inside. They walked and dragged him to the oversized half-circle couch and let him rest there for half an hour, flipping through a *Cigar Aficionado* magazine.

"Here's that bourbon you wanted," said Emma. She handed him a tumbler with mostly ice and a shot of the amber liquid.

He took the tumbler and gagged, but collected himself. "I can tell what bourbon this is just by the taste."

"Really?" asked Emma. Darlene was in the kitchen making sandwiches.

Charles took a tiny sip, swished it around in his mouth, and swallowed. He grimaced. "Pappy van Winkle, twenty years. Family Reserve." He looked at Emma to see if he was right.

It was actually Wild Turkey, but Emma said, "You're right! That's amazing."

Charles smiled. "Just need a good cigar, if I could hack it. I've got a walk-in humidor downstairs. Maybe tomorrow we can go outside again, and I'll smoke."

"If that's what it takes, sure. Should I just pick one out for you?"

"I think I'd like one of my Cubans, Macanudo. I'll tell you where to look tomorrow. Thanks. I mean it." He took another sip of bourbon and barely got it down. "Damn. It rots my gut that I can't drink like I used to. That was my pleasure. That and pretty girls." He winked at Emma.

Emma winked back.

Darlene came in with a tray. "Want to eat lunch where you're at? Turkey sandwich with sweet pickles."

Charles stifled a gag. "No bread. Just the meat and the pickles."

"Now you need some carbs," said Emma. She stood and watched Darlene place the tray on his emaciated lap.

"I know what I need." He stared at the plate and picked up a pickle and put it into his mouth. "Oh, pretty good. Didn't make me gag."

"Maybe you always need a taste of bourbon before you eat," said Emma.

"Maybe so." He ate another pickle and then ate them all, plus half of the sliced turkey.

Friday came, and Reece hadn't talked with Kristin since Sunday night. He'd seen her a couple of times in the cafeteria, eating with the same blond doctor. Reece was scheduled to pick up Emma at Charles's house and then run down to the public health building to get their HIV tests. He changed his shoes in the break room and hurried to the truck. He had directions written on the back of an envelope and soon found himself in Mountain Brook, driving down a tree-lined street. He pulled into the driveway and went to the door. It took a minute, but Emma opened up.

"Hey there, stranger."

Reece smiled. "Hey there, yourself. Man, this is quite a place." He walked through the entryway. "You ready to go?"

"Yeah, but I want you to meet Charles. He's a real hoot. He's upstairs in his chair."

Reece followed her up the sweeping staircase, admiring the paintings. One painting caught his eye. It looked like someone had been angry and smeared paint onto a canvas. He read the card below. "Yves Klein. I like it."

"Yeah," said Emma. "Me too. It's a mess, just like Charles." She topped the stairs with Reece behind her, and they soon passed through the oversized doorway. Charles dozed in the chair, reclined. At his side was a small table with an ashtray and a cigar.

"Charles!"

"What the hell?" He focused and saw Reece. "Who's

this? The guy you been talking my ear off about?"

Emma laughed. "Yep, this is Reece. He worked with me in Ethiopia."

"Nice to meet you, sir," said Reece.

"Rice?"

"No, Reece. Like the peanut butter cup."

"Well, Reece like the peanut butter cup. Emma is my girl now. I hope you don't mind."

Reece nodded his head. "I guess we'll have to share." He tried to laugh, but fell short.

Charles grinned and looked up at Emma. "I guess he'll do. You like bourbon, son?"

Reece had never had bourbon. "I'm sure I do. I've heard you like it, though."

"Hey, you can't tell him stuff like that. Patient confidentiality." Charles looked serious.

Darlene came into the room, and Reece was glad for a break. Charles made him nervous.

"I'll bet you're Reece," said Darlene. "It's nice to finally meet you." Her eyes went straight to the scars on his head. She shook his hand.

"Nice to meet you."

"How about us men have a drink before you get off to your magnificent life?" Charles put the unlit cigar in his mouth and blew pretend smoke.

Reece looked to Emma for help.

"We have an appointment to catch," said Emma. "Maybe next week, when I'm sleeping over."

"I like the sound of that," said Charles. "But we know who's in charge here, right? Boy, you're gonna need some mighty big suspenders to stay even with this one."

Reece nodded. "Next week sounds good. Sounds like fun." He felt he should shake Charles's hand and walked over to him. "Nice to meet you, sir."

Charles took his hand and pumped it once. "Enchanté très heureux."

Emma laughed. "There he goes, speaking French again. Okay, we have to go, Charles, and I'll see you bright and early on Monday."

"Bon voyage," said Charles, and they left.

In the truck, they drove toward UAB Hospitals and the public health clinic on Sixth Avenue South. Reece was lucky to find a space on the street, and they walked to the odd building with its pyramid of glass. Inside was cool, and they walked to the reception counter to get a number. In the crowded waiting room, a recording on the TVs was playing, and Reece stood transfixed, watching it.

"It's a VD video," said Emma. "To educate us." She laughed and pointed to two vinyl-covered chairs.

Most everyone was black, except for a young Hispanic woman with two children. A door opened. "Eighty-three!" A tall and lanky man checked his number twice and stood. He hitched his designer jeans studded with sparkles and walked with his head down, as if about to be carved into tiny pieces.

The video highlighted genital warts caused by human papillomavirus. There was an illustration of brownish raised lesions and then an up-close image of a vagina.

"Yuck," said Emma. "Don't watch that." She poked him in the ribs.

"I'm getting educated," said Reece in a low voice. He looked around at the faces and wondered what had brought them here. His eyes fell on what seemed to be a mother with her teenage daughter, who was very pregnant. The woman dressed formally, and the daughter wore a tight red dress that accentuated her stomach and large breasts. And then on the TV screens, there was a penis with warts on the foreskin.

"Just look away like everyone else."

Reece looked away, the video moving on to herpes. "How much bourbon is Charles drinking? Maybe I should buy some to get used to it."

"He barely drinks any. He just wants to taste it. I had a little drink with him today, and Darlene about died. I hope she doesn't report me. He needs some of his old life back."

"Eighty-four!"

The Hispanic woman and her children stood. She showed the number to a plump woman sitting next to her, and the woman nodded and pointed for her to go on.

"I guess that's a good move, the bourbon." Reece folded his hands, crossed his legs, uncrossed them. "How long do you think we'll have to wait?"

"I'm not sure. I'm a hundred and ten. That means I'll go first."

"Why? Because I'm a hundred and eleven? What's the logic?"

"Shut up, dummy."

Reece laughed a quiet laugh, and they waited for nearly an hour before Emma's number was called. She left her wallet with him and disappeared through the double doors. The nurse led her to an empty room and then proceeded to ask her questions and check off boxes on a form.

Emma answered and explained about the rape in Ethiopia, which didn't even raise an eyebrow as the nurse prepared to draw her blood. It took about ten minutes, and Emma reappeared with a wad of cotton taped to her arm. "You're next, Colonel. Isn't that what Cindy calls you?"

It took a few minutes, but Reece was called back, and he acknowledged having unprotected sex with two different women. He didn't mention that one was his fiancée. The nurse explained they should come in for testing too, even if he were negative. Reece nodded and watched the needle slide into his antecubital fossa. It didn't hurt, but he winced. The nurse wrapped his arm and sent him on his way, saying it would take about ten days to get the results back. They would call him.

Emma was perusing a beat-up *Highlights* magazine when Reece came back. "We look like twins," said Emma. "Want to go to McDonald's? It's next door, practically. I'm hungry."

After McDonald's, Reece drove her home, catching rush hour traffic. "What if one of us comes up HIV positive?" asked Emma.

He drove with one hand, slowing and accelerating behind a minivan with a Reagan sticker.

"Let's not think about that right now. We're just being safe."

They rode in silence until the exit.

"It's Friday night, so you want to go out?" asked Reece.

"Maybe not. I'm bushed. How about tomorrow night? Maybe go to the Seafood Box. I'll bet Sally and Sammy would be up for it."

"Okay, that sounds good." He glanced at her, her brownish blonde hair stirring in the wind.

"Maybe hang out at my place for a while tonight? Maybe there's a good movie on."

"Yeah, that sounds nice," said Reece.

He turned left, headed down her road, and then turned left into the driveway. Sarah was standing in the middle of the yard, and she waved. They jumped out, tired from the day, and joined her there.

"What in blue blazes are you doing, Momma?"

"Hey, Sarah."

Sarah held a tube of ant killer. "Killing these damn ants. Sammy runs 'em over with the lawnmower, but they come right back." She sprinkled some more. "Y'all doing alright?"

"Yep, just going to hang out," said Emma. "Don't get bit."

"Y'all go on and relax. There's a couple more of these near the road."

They walked to the house, Reece right behind Emma. He admired the way her hips moved inside her scrub pants and wanted to grab her and throw her on the grass.

"Let me go change," said Emma, and she turned toward him. "Thanks for going with me today. I really appreciate it." She stood very close to him, and he let his arms draw her near.

"No problem," he said, leaning down to kiss her, and she kissed him back, her eyes filling with something.

"Tag, you're it," and she broke away from him and ran laughing into the house.

They ate some leftover chili and hung out on the carport,

talking with Sarah until it was good and dark. She excused herself and went up to her room to read the latest Stephen King novel. A silence ensued, and Reece realized he was alone with Emma, that she was all his, and he wondered what to do. He was out of things to talk about and felt sleepy. He would have been happy to just sit there and look at her, but they wound up in the living room with the TV on, sitting very close to one another. *To Kill a Mockingbird* played on a movie channel.

"I'll bet you were like Scout when you were a kid," said Reece. "Probably even looked like her."

"That's funny, I was thinking that you were kind of like Dill." She passed him a bag of potato chips. "I can't stand that courtroom scene with Tom. It just creeps me out."

"Hard to digest," said Reece. "Can I put my arm around you?" A dandruff shampoo commercial was on.

"I was wondering when you would." She snuggled into him and looked into his eyes. "I wrote some letters today to the folks in Ethiopia. Wrote Dr. Guthrie and Afewerki. I'm dying to know what happened to Misrak. I just hope she made it back home."

"I haven't written anyone. I should, though, just to say thanks for getting me back home. Is it bad that I haven't already?" Reece played with her hair, running his fingers through it.

"No, but I bet they'd like to hear from you, especially Afewerki, which reminded me today that I promised to help him come and study here in the States. I have no idea how to go about it. Ooh, that feels good."

"Gadsden State has an English as a Second Language program. I know they take international students. Maybe you should check there."

"Huh, that's not too far away. He said he wants to study agriculture, which is fitting. I guess he could just get his associate's degree there and then possibly move on." She was flexing her neck and guiding his hand around her scalp. "I'll do that Monday. But how the heck am I going to pay his bills? That's the real kicker, if he comes."

"Maybe your church could sponsor him. I'll bet they would." He moved his hand to her neck and massaged her there.

"I had thought about that. It does sound like a good idea. I'll just have to run it by Pastor Tom. But first, I'll have to get him accepted into a program. It'll work out one way or another. Right?"

"Yeah, I'll help where I can. Maybe my church could co-sponsor him. One could pay his room and board, and the other could pay his tuition."

"That sounds like a good plan. I just can't imagine him here, though. He'd freak out. I mean, he would be freaked out. The first place I would take him would be the mall to get him some clothes."

"I'll bet he would go nuts over KFC. He said he'd never had fried chicken, just boiled." He pulled her close. "He could be like our adopted son."

Emma laughed. "Here's the scene with the old lady who turns out to be a morphine addict."

"I'd forgotten about that." He was thinking about kissing her. He slid down to her level and caught her look.

"You know, the night you were shot? I'd been racking my brains to find a way to be alone with you. Do you think I'm partly to blame?"

"Heck no." Reece moved in for a kiss, and she gave him one on the lips. "Nice."

"What if we'd never met? What if neither one of us had gone to Ethiopia? I wouldn't have met you, even though we live just an hour apart. I think about that." She kissed him again.

Reece felt thrills running through his body. "It is weird and strange how things happen. I guess if I hadn't gone, I'd be married already." He kissed her on the neck.

"You had to go there to figure it out. You had to get shot. I had to be...attacked. But it's turning out nicely."

She grabbed him and pushed on top, kissing him deep. He fell back and soon they were side by side on the couch, going at each other like teenage lovers.

Reece had moved to night shift, but he couldn't sleep before heading into work and felt like a robot walking into the bright glare of the unit. Andrew was the charge nurse and gave him Mrs. Laramore and Rodney, even though that meant switching around usual assignments, and Reece appreciated it. The day before, out of the blue, Kristin had called him at the lake. She had sounded calm and collected and had a proposition for him. If he really wanted to try and work things out, and she thought they should try, he would meet her at the counselor's office. But she had added that Cindy and Emma had to attend as well. There would be a great hashing of issues and a final conclusion reached. Otherwise, they were done.

Reece had already concluded that they were done, but felt bad that there was not an official closure as she was suggesting. He warned her that Cindy and Emma might balk at the proposal, and there would be nothing he could do if they did. She said he had to at least try, and he said he would, feeling the whole time that he was making a huge mistake. He was sure that Cindy would say yes, hoping for high drama. She would somehow derive pleasure from it, he was sure. Emma, he thought, would flat out say no and tell him to man up.

Reece introduced himself to the night-shift unit secretary, Gloria.

"I been hearing about you." She wore cat-eye glasses and had a permanent surprised look. She surveyed the scars on his head, and Reece reached up to touch one as if the hole might still be there.

"Yeah, good to meet you. Maybe it'll be a quiet night."

"Huh, no such thing as a quiet night around here. You got Mr. Lasseter, don't you?"

"Oh, Rodney? Yeah."

"He's a creepy one. You need to keep that curtain closed so he can't see me. I make him paranoid. He told Stella that I was going to poison him."

Reece laughed, knowing it was true, and then he said hey to the monitor tech sitting behind Gloria. She nodded, appraising him from head to toe, and then went back to watching the green-screen cardiac monitors. For now, all seemed quiet.

He went to six and peered around the curtain into the dimly lit room. Rodney sat in bed with his eyes wide open, and he flinched at the sight of Reece. Reece stepped in.

"Hey there, Rodney. It's me, your nurse. Reece. You look good. How do you feel?"

Rodney held his sheet with both hands. "Hello. I need a sandwich." His face was blank, but his eyes bored into Reece as if to discover his true identity.

"We can do that. How about a turkey sandwich?" He glanced at the monitor. Rodney's nasal cannula was off, the oxygen bubbling through sterile water behind him.

"Are you a nurse?"

"Yes, your nurse tonight. I've been taking care of you on day shift. I need to take a look at the bandages on your legs and listen to your heart. Is that okay?"

"They took my legs so I can't run." His mouth twitched. "I need to go home."

Reece lifted the sheet and surveyed his stumps. The

dressings looked clean, wrapped in elastic bandage. He pushed the call button, and Gloria answered.

"Who that?" asked Rodney. He raised up and looked around. "It's a ghost."

"No," said Reece. "It's just the intercom. Hey, can you order Mr. Lasseter a turkey sandwich?"

"Will do," said Gloria.

"Is the light in here okay for you? I can turn them off if you like, so that you can sleep." He washed his hands and took his stethoscope from around his neck.

"Leave the lights be, please." Rodney leaned forward and tried to look around the curtain. "Who out there?" He raised his sheet and bit it.

Reece backed off a foot. "No one, just the other nurses working, taking care of the other patients. You're in Birmingham, in Alabama, at the hospital."

"Oh," said Rodney. "I thought I saw somebody."

"Just the nurses and some doctors are all. You're safe here, very safe. Can I listen to your chest?"

"No, please don't."

"The doctor wants me to listen. It'll just take a few seconds. Okay?" He moved closer.

"Okay."

Reece listened to his heart, lungs, and belly, counted his respirations, and then pulled the blood pressure cuff off the wall. "Need to check your blood pressure and then your temperature, and then I'll leave you alone. How's that?"

"Are you a nurse?" Rodney whispered.

"Yep, a nurse. I work here, at the hospital." He wrapped the cuff around Rodney's arm as he watched with large eyes.

"Do they pay you?"

"Yes, they pay me. This is my job. Now hold the thermometer under your tongue."

Rodney opened his mouth, and Reece slipped in the glass thermometer, letting him hold it there. He finished the blood pressure, tidied up the overbed table, and checked the water pitcher.

Rodney mumbled and then shouted, sending the thermometer shattering onto the floor. He cringed and sank into the bed.

"Rodney, what is it?" Little balls of mercury on the floor.

"They gonna poison me."

"Who's that?"

"That lady. You see her?" He peered at the curtain, his cheeks bunched.

"No, nobody there. No poison." Reece tried not to laugh. He felt giddy and wondered what he would feel like the next morning. "I'll have to get another thermometer. Did you think it was poison?"

"Yes."

"It's not poison. I'll let you look at the next one. Maybe turn on the big light so you can see it better."

"Okay, Mr. Rice."

Reece laughed and let it go. He could be Rice for the right people. "Okay, I'm going now. Be right back," and he slipped out onto the unit.

Gloria peered at him through her cat-eye glasses. She looked crazier than Rodney did. She made a cuckoo motion with her hand. The other nurses streamed back and forth, filling little cups with pills, filling water pitchers, and answering alarms. There was a dull buzz to the unit, which seemed to belong exclusively to night shift.

Reece peeked in Mrs. Laramore's room, and she was snoring. He nodded to the resident on call that night and fetched a new thermometer. It seemed the empty room was going to be filled with a new patient for Andrew. Lifesaver, the helicopter, was flying in a critical MVA. The nurses called it Lifescraper.

The night passed in relative calm, broken only by the arrival of the new patient. Her neck was broken, and she couldn't feel anything below her waist. She'd been on a motorcycle headed the wrong way on the freeway. The driver had died. Around three, though, the monitor tech called out that six's heart rate had jumped to 140.

Reece ran in, and Rodney was in bed, struggling for breath. Reece reapplied the nasal cannula and turned up the oxygen. He feared that Rodney had thrown a clot to his lungs, and he was right. He called out to Gloria to call the resident stat and raised the head of the bed.

"Rodney, you're okay. Does it hurt when you breathe?" He glanced at the monitor, a normal sinus rhythm, but at 160. Rodney groaned and seemed about to pass out. His shallow breaths took on a ragged quality. He held Rodney's hand and told him everything would be okay.

The resident, Dr. Flag, had piled out of his bed across the hall and walked into the room, his hair one big mess, followed by Stella. Just then, Rodney converted to V-tach, and his heart rate flew to 240. His eyes briefly bulged and then closed. "Call a code," said Flag.

Code Blue ICU went out over the intercom as Stella pushed in the crash cart, flipping on the power to the paddles. Rodney's breaths had dropped to nearly nothing. Flag called out for an ET tube and then manned the cardioverter. "Clear!" and Rodney's upper body jumped. The monitor went wild and then settled back into V-tach. Rodney had stopped breathing, and Reece was at his side with the ambu bag, giving him breaths. Stella gave the Lidocaine bolus, and Flag removed the headboard, tossing it on the floor. Reece kicked the bed's code latch with his foot, and the bed went flat. The room was filling with people.

In went the laryngoscope, and Rodney was intubated. Reece removed the mouthpiece from the Ambu bag and attached it to the ET tube, giving Rodney deep breaths.

Flag moved back to the paddles and bumped the voltage to three hundred joules. "Clear!" Rodney heaved.

Everyone watched the monitor, and there were only huge waves at a rate of about ten per minute.

"Fuck," said Flag.

"Damn," said Reece.

And they did everything to try to save Rodney, but he passed, lying there dead. No one spoke, and Reece began the task of preparing Rodney for the morgue, his face pale, his heart racing.

"I'll get the cart restocked," said Andrew. "Sorry, man. I know you liked him." He put his hand on Reece's shoulder.

"Can't believe it," said Reece. "His damn paranoia killed him." He walked out to Gloria and ordered a morgue kit, which she ran down to fetch from central supply.

Reece turned off the overhead light and surveyed the wreckage. Everything was askew, as if there had been an earthquake. He peeled the gel pads from Rodney's chest, followed by the monitor leads. His eyes were open slightly, and he tried to close them, but they wouldn't. He wondered what Rodney's family would say. Would they miss him, and he was sure that they would. He sat in the chair and stared at Rodney's dead body.

It was another day before Reece could bring himself to ask Emma about Kristin's proposal. He'd slept off and on that day and awoke with a headache around seven. He ate a plate of corn and okra with tomatoes that Dora had kept warm on the stove. Finally, around eight, he called.

"Hey," said Reece.

"Well, hey. I was hoping you'd call. We're on for Saturday night with Sally and Sammy at the Seafood Box."

"Oh, cool...that'll be fun."

"You don't sound so good. What's wrong? Night shift messing with you?"

"It is kicking my butt. I forgot how disoriented it makes you feel. Hey, guess what?"

"What?"

"Kristin called me on Sunday."

"Really. What was that about? You're not engaged again, are you?"

"No, but she wants to meet at the counselor's one more time."

"Huh, you gonna go?"

"She wants you to be there and Cindy, too." He was talking at the table with his head in his hand, a perspiring glass of sweet tea in front of him.

"What? You're kidding. Man, that would be some session. Gosh, I don't think I need to be there. Y'all need to work that out."

"Maybe think of it as an adventure. I did call Cindy yesterday, and she's up for it. She wants to meet Kristin and see 'what she's all about,' as she said."

"Wow, you don't think she'd bring a pistol and shoot us, do you?"

Reece laughed and winced. "I did think about that, but she wouldn't do that. She's too gentle for that."

"Lord, let me think about it, okay? When does she want to do this?"

"As soon as possible. This week, maybe? Maybe Friday would be good."

"What would you say? I mean, what would she say?"

"I don't really know. She just wants closure, and I do too. Maybe this will be the end of the situation."

"You're not going to confess that you're in love with all three of us, are you?" She laughed. "I guess we could arrange a threesome."

"It would be a foursome with Cindy's sugar daddy, Clarence." He glanced back at Dora and Horace in their recliners. Dora was reading her Christian romance, but was all ears, and Horace was deep into a *National Geographic*.

They talked for another half hour without reaching an agreement, but she said she would let him know the next day. They said goodnight, and Reece headed to the bathroom looking for the Tylenol.

"You okay, son?" asked Dora. "I heard you say that Kristin called. You didn't tell me that. What did she say?" She wiggled her toes in her stocking feet.

Reece let the two capsules fall into his hand. "Not much. Well, she wants to meet with the counselor one more time. Wants to meet with Emma and Cindy, too."

"Cindy? Have you been messing with Cindy again?" She peered at him over her bifocals.

"Good Lord, so many questions. She's just jealous of other women. I don't know what will happen. But anyway, that's what she wants."

"What's that?" asked Horace. He looked up and smiled.

"Nothing, honey. Reece is going to go back to the counselor with Kristin."

"A counselor?" He pushed the volume up on his hearing aid, making it squeal.

"It's nothing," said Reece. "Girl trouble."

"Fiancée trouble," said Dora in a scolding voice.

"Sort of true," said Reece. "I guess I'll start getting ready for work. I don't think I can sleep anymore, but I feel so tired."

"I don't see how you do it," said Dora. "Only possums and raccoons stay up past midnight."

Reece laughed and gathered his things for a shower. He left at ten to get there by ten-thirty for shift change and report. He checked with Andrew, and he had Mrs. Laramore and a new patient, a young man who'd fallen thirty feet from a scaffold and had his hand catch in a cable, cutting it clean off. He also had a fractured skull and a broken hip, but was alert. He'd already undergone surgery to pin his hip back together. After report, Reece went to his room first.

Chuck was his name, and he eyed Reece warily, pulling the sheet up over his chest. "Evening."

"Well, evening," said Reece. He introduced himself and asked him how his pain was. Reece glanced at the stump on the end of Chuck's right arm and remembered Rodney.

"Got a damn headache from hell. I basically hurt all over. When can I get some of that morphine again?"

"You had your last dose at ten, so it'll be two before you can have it again. Let me turn off this overhead light. Help you get in the mood to relax and sleep." Reece did a head-to-toe assessment, and Chuck seemed clear except for the pain.

"Not gonna stick me anymore, are you?"

"Not by me. I imagine you'll have some labs come morning. Sorry about that." Reece checked the IV pump. It was KVO at 30 ccs an hour, primarily for the antibiotics every six hours.

"Damn, that'll be a great way to start the day."

"Yeah, but man, you're lucky. To be so clear-headed after cracking your skull like that and losing your hand. I know that must have been a real shock."

Chuck shuddered, thinking about it. "Just cut it off like butter. Nobody even thought to get it and put it on ice. I guess it's still hanging from the wire." He shuddered again, as if an icy chill had passed through him.

"Okay, Chuck. Well, you need anything? Food, drink?"

"You could get me some of that juice, grape, if you have it." He sat up and looked out onto the unit. "A queer came in here earlier. I thought he was gonna be my nurse."

Reece laughed. "That's just Andrew. He's the charge nurse. He's great."

"Yeah, great at you know what." He grinned and looked at Reece for affirmation.

"Okay, I'll get you that juice. It may be a few minutes. I have to check on my other patient," and he walked out to see Mrs. Laramore. "Hey there. Wide awake?"

"Lord, Mr. Reece. It's good to see you." Her voice was still hoarse from the ET tube. "That evening shift nurse, forget her name, she was a mean one. Roughed me up getting me on the bedpan."

Reece nodded. "I'm here to help any way I can. Gonna check your vital signs and listen to your chest, okay?" He noticed little sores on her nose where the nasal cannula rubbed, and made a note to put some antibiotic ointment there. "Okay, you're in good shape. You need anything? I'll get you some fresh ice water."

"I sure could use a sucker to put in my mouth."

Reece nodded. "Don't have any suckers. I think Gloria keeps some peppermints on her desk. Will that do?"

"That sounds real nice."

Reece checked her IV pump and glanced at the cardiac monitor. "Give me about five minutes, and I'll be back." He left to get the juice for Chuck and ran into Ingrid in the clean utility room. She looked haggard, and Reece knew she'd been working night shift for the entire span of her five years as a nurse.

"How's it going?" Ingrid pushed her thick glasses up on her nose. She was on her second cup of coffee for the night.

"It should be quiet tonight. I hope. Got the new patient in six, the guy that lost his hand." He bent down and retrieved two small cups of grape juice. "How's it going with you?"

"Just the same old same old. I'm first admit. That'll be fun, if it happens." She was staring at the scars on his head. "Andrew gave me the guy in one, though. He's a mess. Gotta give some blood in a few minutes."

"Yeah, well, let me know if I can help." He sauntered to six, giving Chuck his juice, and then to the main desk to review Chuck's chart. Andrew was next to him, and beside him Dr. Flag. He dropped the peppermint off to Mrs. Laramore.

The night passed slowly, and Reece looked at the round clock over and over, watching the minutes tick by. Every fifteen minutes or so, he went to peek in on his patients, who were asleep. Mrs. Laramore woke up and had to go to the bathroom. Instead of the bedpan, he put the bedside commode in her room, her mighty breasts swaying and threatening to throw her off balance. Chuck had his morphine right at two and had rested well after that. When he got home that morning, Reece felt as if he'd swum through an ocean of Vaseline and collapsed in bed without eating breakfast.

He slept till noon, caught in a sweaty dream, and tried but couldn't go back to sleep. He remembered it was time to cut the grass again, and he forced himself out of bed.

"You up so soon?" asked Dora. "You need some more rest."

"No, I'm fine." He surveyed the electric stove, a pot there simmering with Dinty Moore beef stew. He could smell cornbread baking in the oven. He figured that was why the house felt so hot. "Guess, I'll cut some grass." He sat at the table, thinking about nothing.

"You can do that later. Go back to bed." She peeked in the oven, letting out a yawn of heat.

"It'll do me good to get some sunshine. Don't want to turn into a vampire."

"First, you have to eat, okay? And you can go fetch Horace from you know where." She picked up a potholder and opened the oven again, retrieving the hot iron skillet.

"Not a problem. I'm hungry," and he went outside. He could hear rain crows calling in the trees and felt the prickles of pine straw against his bare feet. He reached down to scratch his ankle and nearly fell. He'd done well to recover from the shooting, but had dulled moments that made him wonder about permanent damage to his brain. He crossed the road, stepping quickly across the hot pavement. In the distance, the lake shimmered, and a big yellow sun lorded high in the sky. Horace was in his chair, his hoe propped against his thigh.

"Hey, boy!" said Horace. "You working hard at the hospital?"

Reece drew up, enjoying the coolness of the grass beneath the black walnut tree. "It's inside with air conditioning, as you say. So, I can't complain. Lunch is ready." He propped his hand on his hip, gazing at the dry stalks in Mr. Sykes' garden, heavy with corn.

"I'll be up directly. Let me start that pump again. It's been dry."

Reece walked around the garden to gather his bearings and headed back to the house. Dora stood on the driveway waving, and he trotted back across the road.

"It's Emma on the phone."

"Really?" He pushed into the house. The black phone was on the table. "Hello?"

"Hey, man," said Emma. "Your granny said you were awake. Can't sleep?"

"Yeah, night shift's got me upside down." Reece sat, admiring the cornbread cut and on a paper plate in the middle of the table. "You with Charles?"

"Yep. Got him outside in the garden again with his taste

of bourbon. Got the cordless phone. He's a new man."

Reece laughed. "Good for you. He's lucky to have you."

"Damn lucky," said Emma. "I like him. Well, I'm calling about that meeting with the counselor."

Reece held his breath, worried about either answer. "Yeah?"

"I'll go, but she has to understand that I have the right not to say anything. You think she'll go for that?"

Reece thought. "Why not? I guess that's your right. I'll call her today and let her know that the party is on."

"Party, my foot," said Emma. "Could be a bloodbath."

"That won't happen. I imagine that the counselor, Calvin's his name, will do most of the talking. He talks in riddles. He seems pretty intent on working things out, though."

"Huh, well, that would be good, I suppose. It'll be a strange get-together, that's for sure. I wonder if Cindy's man will come with her. What's his name?"

"Clarence. He seems pretty low-key. Maybe it would be good to have him in the waiting room, but maybe not. Oh heck, anyway, we're on for Friday unless she schedules something for next week. I'll get back to you."

"Yeah, do that. You can call me from work if you ever need to. I'm staying up pretty late. I've had this damn headache for days and can't sleep."

"I did think about that last night, calling you. But I didn't want to disturb Sarah, wake her up."

They talked for another ten minutes, Horace and Dora at the table.

Reece hung up, crumbled a piece of cornbread into his bowl, and dug into his stew, eating a waxy potato. He finished off two bowls and then excused himself to cut grass. On the mower below the road, sweat greased his head and lower back as the mower vibrated his body. He watched a killdeer swooping and landing in the neighboring vacant lot, soaking in the energy of the sun and the lake. Embedded within the roar of the mower, he wondered what his fate would be.

Friday came in a hurry, and Reece picked up Emma and drove with her to the counselor for the two o'clock appointment. He eased into the tight deck and parked.

"Here goes nothing," he said, and they walked to the elevator and hit fourteen. "Nice elevator."

"Yep," said Emma. She had her hands in her jeans' pockets, her shoulders stiff.

The elevator stopped on ten, and a man in a blue-purple suit and a yellow silk tie entered. He punched sixteen. Everyone nodded and looked at their feet. Reece identified the music playing as "Hell's Bells" but in Muzak. He muttered the song title.

"What?" asked Emma.

"Oh, the music, nothing." He spoke in a whisper.

"Yeah," said Emma. She blew her hair from her face.

Fourteen, and they walked into the deathly quiet carpeted hall. His stomach bubbled with helium. They reached the door with a rectangle of glass and peered inside. Kristin was there, reading a magazine, but not Cindy. He looked at his watch, 1:55.

Reece cleared his throat and opened the door, holding it for Emma. Kristin looked up, and she seemed to be trying to smile.

"Well, look what the cat drug in." Kristin went back to her copy of *Southern Living*. She wore a blouse covered in purple pansies and seemed poised for a careful attack.

Emma looked at Reece. "What's that supposed to mean?"

"Hey," said Reece. He glanced at the receptionist behind her tiny desk. *Who should sit by who?* "We're here." There were two chairs opposite Kristin, and he caught his toe on the coffee table, walking there with Emma on his heels, her arms folded.

Kristin ignored them as they sat, turning the pages as if searching for an important recipe or Bible verse. Two minutes of solid silence ensued.

Calvin's door opened, and Reece jumped. He watched a middle-aged woman with a frowsy haircut emerge, her eyes wet. Calvin had his hand on her shoulder, as if holding her to the ground. The woman went to the receptionist's desk and fumbled in her large purse embroidered with a cross. Reece watched her pull out a checkbook, tears dripping from her chin.

"Well?" asked Calvin. "I'll be right back," and he glared at Reece on his way to the bathroom.

Kristin looked up from the magazine and held it on her lap like a stone. "Well, where is Cindy? You said Cindy would come. I've already met Emma. Hello, Emma."

Reece stuttered. "Uh, she said she would come. Probably late is all." He averted his eyes and glanced at Emma, who seemed to be taking measured breaths.

Soon, Calvin reappeared and stood there with his hands on hips. "Shall we?" He motioned toward his office.

"One person's missing," said Kristin.

"She can join us when she gets here," said Calvin. "Let's just go ahead and try to get comfortable, get our p's and q's in order."

They stood. Kristin took the lead and went in first. There was a love seat and three chairs. Kristin sat on the love seat, and Reece and Emma took the chairs. The over-head fluorescent light buzzed.

"Tea, anyone?" asked Calvin.

Everyone nodded no.

Calvin went to close his door, and a noise came from the waiting area, a loud voice. Calvin looked out, and a look of alarm crossed his tan face. He wore dark slacks with a thin, off-red sweater.

"Hello, friends!" and it was Cindy. She barged into the room and stopped short as if hit in the solar plexus. "So, this is real? Who is who?" She was very drunk. Clarence had taken a seat in the waiting room, stroking his short red beard.

Kristin's mouth opened, but nothing came out.

"You must be Sydney," said Calvin. "Here, have a seat." He tried to hold her arm, but she pulled away and plopped down beside Kristin.

"I'm Cindy. And who are you? Are you Kristin?"

They were practically on top of each other, and Kristin scooted to the side.

"Yes, Kristin. We met at Wendy's and in the ER. I guess you know Reece," and she pointed at him.

"Yeah, Reece. Hey, Reece! We had sex, and I'll bet you want to talk about that. Am I right?" She blew out a deep breath, as if suddenly fatigued.

Calvin was still standing, assessing the group dynamics. He hadn't counted on anyone being drunk.

"I'm Emma." She looked perplexed, her half-smile making an appearance.

"Oh, Emma! I've heard a lot about you. You're a missionary like Reece. Gosh, God bless you." Cindy smiled and swung her pigtails back and forth. She wore tight skinny jeans and a white men's shirt with long sleeves.

"We have the proper introductions," said Calvin, forgetting about his tea. He grabbed his clipboard and sat in his wheeled chair. "Let's get the ball rolling. As you know, Kristin wanted to meet as a group. There are some questions she'd like answered, which I think she deserves under…the circumstances." He almost said mitigating and had meant to look up the meaning the day before. "Kristin?" He leaned back in his chair, holding himself there with his toes.

Kristin was still in shock at the sight of Cindy. "First, I want to know if he still loves me, and if he does, what will he do to show me?"

"Reece?" asked Calvin, serving as the line judge.

Reece wanted to die. He'd imagined she would ask that and tried to remember what he'd planned to say. "I still love you, but things have changed. I know I haven't behaved as if I do love you—"

"You're gosh darn right," said Kristin. "And the proof is in this room. How can you say that you still love me?"

"Hey, love is relative," said Cindy. "He loves the whole world. Is there a problem with that?" She smirked and reared her head back at Kristin as if trying to focus.

"Are you engaged to Reece? I don't think so." Kristin's bile was up. "He made a commitment, and in God's eyes."

Emma sighed.

"I'm sorry," said Reece.

"Well," said Cindy. "Sorry don't pay the bills. I can see where she's coming from."

Emma cleared her throat. "But you called off the engagement, right?"

"Yeah, because of you and, and, Candy here or Cindy, whatever her name is," said Kristin.

Calvin scribbled, trying to keep up. "So, let's wash one car at a time, okay? Let's focus first on Emma."

"He's in love with her," said Kristin. "It's obvious. They bonded over there in that godforsaken place."

"Reece?" asked Calvin.

Reece squirmed. He was in love with Emma. He looked at her. She'd been through hell, and so had he. "Okay, yes, I'm in love with Emma. It happened." He put his head in his hands.

"Is that why you had sex with Cindy?" Kristin glared at him.

"Hell, yeah. He's a great lover. A little skittish, though. You'll be lucky to have him," said Cindy. "Well, whoever gets him." She winked at Reece.

Reece was paralyzed and then spoke. "Okay, I've had sex with everyone in this room, except Emma...and Calvin. I can't say why other than it just happened. Love is a process. It has to run its course." He had no idea what that meant, but it's what he said.

"You go, boy!" said Cindy. "If neither one of these gals wants you, then I'm always available."

Calvin frowned. "Cindy, if you could withhold comment for a minute. This is a house of cards we're dealing with."

"Yeah, maybe we should just play cards instead," said Cindy. She looked defeated. "Or naked Twister."

Reece looked at Emma, who seemed to have shrunk. "I really do love you. I've been falling for you since the first day we met, but it's not until just recently that I could verify what I was feeling." He wanted to say that Cindy had seduced him, but didn't.

Kristin had begun to cry and put her hand over her eyes. "This is just awful, just absolutely awful."

Like lightning, Calvin handed her the box of tissues. "Okay, we're at 'just awful,' and we need to get to a better place. How can we do that?"

"It's over. It's over," said Kristin.

"There, it's okay," said Cindy. "Cry it out. I'm sorry I had sex with your fiancée." She put her arm around Kristin.

"Don't touch me, you bitch," and she pulled away.

Emma stood. "I don't think I'm contributing."

"No, wait," said Kristin. "I want to know if you love Reece. You have to tell me that. You have to be honest."

Emma sat back down. "Well, yes. You can say that." She turned toward Reece. "We were tested for HIV together."

"HIV?" asked Kristin. "Oh my God, Reece. Why would you need that?" She glanced at Cindy, putting two and two together. "That means I need to get tested and all because you're a sex maniac!"

"I'm not a sex maniac," said Reece. "It just seemed like the right thing to get tested."

"What?" asked Cindy. "Because of me? You think I'm infected, Colonel? That's a real laugh. Besides, I've been tested twice." She let out a laugh.

"No offence to anyone here," said Reece. "I did it for Emma. She had to get tested, and so I went along. That's all."

"I guess I should buy you a box of condoms," said Emma.

"Well," said Calvin. "At least we're working toward a resolution, getting our ducks in a row."

Kristin took a deep breath and shrugged. "This is pointless. They're in love, and what can I do? By the way, Mr. Myers, you have to pay for this session and the last session. Just think of it as money well spent. I'm leaving. I'm done." She stood and walked out.

Calvin called out to her. "Kristin, are you sure?" but she was gone. He'd once again forgotten to open with prayer and chastised himself.

"I guess we should go," said Emma.

"Y'all want to come back to my place and smoke a joint?" asked Cindy. "I need one bad."

"Maybe another time, I mean, if Emma wants to," said Reece. He felt like a watermelon cut in half. "I mean, I guess we're done. Thanks for coming." He turned to Calvin. "I can't pay today, but when I get my check, I'll drop by, if that's okay." He looked like hell.

Calvin touched his index fingers together. "Yes, under the circumstances, that would be fine. Shall we end in prayer? And everyone was so drained that they just bowed their heads.

"Dear Lord..." started Cindy. She raised her hands to the ceiling.

After the session with Calvin on Friday, Reece had taken Emma home, a long, quiet ride. She'd not been in a mood to hang out with him, and he'd left with a deep hole in his being. Had he lost everyone? Had Emma joined Kristin in her loathing of him? He'd called to make sure they were still on for the Seafood Box, and she'd said okay, but still sounded down. She didn't ask him any more about Cindy, but he knew that was what was bothering her. He dressed in jeans and a brown short-sleeved shirt, wearing his nice walking shoes, said bye to Horace and Dora, and headed to Hueytown.

He arrived at six-thirty, a few minutes early. Sammy and Sally were already there, and he knocked on the door.

"Come on in, pardner," said Sammy.

"Thanks." He wondered if Emma had told Sally and Sarah about the incidents with Cindy and prayed that he wasn't walking into an ambush. Sammy slapped him on the back and laughed. Reece lurched, turned, and shadowboxed him. He thought that it would feel good to hit somebody. "Back at you."

"There he is!" said Sally. She jumped off the couch and walked toward him with open arms. She squeezed him, pressing her breasts into him. She grabbed his butt and laughed.

"Whoa," said Reece. He was a bit confused. "Yeah, well, here I am." He wondered if Sammy was a jealous man or if he was just used to Sally's forward nature.

"Have a seat, cowboy," said Sammy. "Want a beer?

Brought some PBR."

"Well, sure thing," said Reece, and Sammy went to the kitchen.

"Sit by me," said Sally. "Emma's putting on the finishing touches. She doesn't just wear makeup for anybody, lucky boy."

Reece sat on the couch and saw the magazines on the coffee table, the TV that was off, the clock, and the bare walls. Sunlight streamed through the window, a haze of dust motes caught in the beams.

"Where's Sarah?" asked Reece, and he took the beer from Sammy. It was a tall boy. "Didn't see her car."

"She's out gambling, playing cards with her outlaw friends," said Sally. "She usually wins some money. They have a paid dealer and everything."

"Is it legal?" asked Reece. "Like in a casino?"

"It's illegal, just like dog fighting, but people still do it," said Sammy. He took the space next to Reece and grabbed his knee.

"Ticklish," said Reece. He felt like a book in the wind.

"He's ticklish, Sammy," and Sally lit into him, going for his armpits while Sammy grabbed his knee again.

Reece squirmed and went to the floor, laughing. "I spilled my beer!" He sipped the foam from the lid. "Damn, y'all are crazy." He struggled up, and then Sally pulled him back down. "You're mine until Emma gets here. Got that? You got that, Sammy? You're both mine."

Sammy laughed and chugged beer. Reece took a sip, feeling the sexual tension rising with Sally. She was older but good-looking with curvy hips. He let his mind wander and pinched his thigh.

"So," said Sally. "Emma was telling us all about the to-do with the counselor. Said you had a lot of confessing to do." She was in light-blue jeans and a frilly top that was cut low in front and in back.

Reece thought. "I didn't get to say much. It was very strange."

"Especially with the drunk woman there. What's her name?" asked Sally.

"That's Cindy." He looked from Sally to Sammy.

"Yeah, I'd like to meet her," said Sammy. He made a lewd gesture.

"You know that your iniquities will be visited on your children," said Sally, and she laughed. "I guess that's why Heather has such a hard time in school."

"Yeah, where's Heather?" asked Reece. He still had a vivid image of her dancing topless on the carport.

"She's home. She's a big girl now," said Sally. She hooked her arm into his.

"Sally," said Sammy. "Don't smother him." He was wearing his work pants with a clean t-shirt and leather boots.

"Hey, y'all," and Emma appeared. "You making sure he doesn't get away?"

"Heck yeah," said Sally. "He'll float off like a dandelion seed. Gotta hold on tight." She hardened her jaw. "I think he needs to be punished, though, for his iniquities."

Emma blushed. "Reece, you okay there?"

"Oh, what am I thinking?" Sally stood and led Emma to her seat. "Sit, girl, and acknowledge this handsome man."

Emma slipped onto the couch between Reece and the end. "Yeah, how could we punish him?" She grinned.

"Maybe we should tie him up and cover him with mustard."

"That sounds like a plan," said Sally. "Maybe maple syrup would be better."

"Hey," said Sammy. "Don't forget about me."

Sally came over and sat in his lap. "I can think of plenty of ways to punish you." She kissed him on the lips.

"You look great," said Reece, turning to Emma. She was in old, comfortable jeans and wearing her favorite blouse that was a light pink and gathered toward the middle.

"Well, thanks, Colonel," said Emma. She let him put his arm around her.

Sally laughed. "Yeah, we heard about the Colonel. I think that's what we should call him from now on."

"That would be strange," said Reece. Despite their craziness, he felt that he was falling in love with an entire family. "I may not answer." He sipped his beer.

"Emma, you want a drink?" asked Sammy.

"No, I'm fine," said Emma.

"Instead of the Seafood Box," said Sally, "why don't we go to the Mexican place. The Seafood Box don't serve alcohol, and I'm craving a Dirty Sanchez and maybe some margaritas."

"I'm in," said Sammy. "I like the fajitas. Reece?"

"Sure, sounds good to me. Emma?"

Emma gave a thumbs up, huddled beneath Reece's arm.

They all stood in unison and headed outside, without locking the door, and piled into Sammy's twin-cab pickup. Within five minutes, they were at El Sol and wandered in. It was packed, and there was a ten-minute wait, so they stood beside a plaster statue of Pancho Villa.

"There's that Watkins woman and her good-for-nothing husband." Sally pointed. "He beats her silly. I feel sorry for their kids."

Sammy clenched his fists. "Maybe he'll do something, and Reece and I can shine his shoes."

Emma rolled her eyes. "No fighting, boys. We can pillow fight when we get back to the house."

They stood there, shifting from leg to leg, and soon were seated in a booth right beside the Watkins. Sally had touched Mrs. Watkins on the shoulder, drawing a startled glance.

Emma and Sally slid in first, and then Reece and Sammy. The pretty waitress was over in a flash and went for their drink orders while they perused the giant menus.

"What'cha having, honey?" asked Sally.

"I think I'll have the wife beater," said Sammy. He glanced over at Mr. Watkins to see if he had heard and felt an elbow in his ribs.

"Sammy," said Sally. "Easy."

Reece caught on. "I guess I'll have the drunk bastard." He looked to Sammy for approval.

"Hey, settle down, you two," said Emma. "Maybe he'll choke on a bone." She laughed and whispered something to Sally.

Four margaritas, and they dove in, drinking them in a hurry, except for Reece. He wanted to savor the tangy sweetness, and it was refreshing. All eyes turned to the next table as Mr. Watkins stood and headed to the bathroom with big watery eyes.

"Hey!" said Sally. She waved and caught Mrs. Watkins' eye. Her name was Terry, and she brooded with slumped shoulders. "Y'all out for a date? Got a babysitter?"

Terry fiddled with a string of beads around her neck and looked toward the bathroom. "Yeah, sort of. Kids are with the grandparents."

"Call me sometime," said Sally.

Terry looked toward the bathroom again. "Okay, about what?"

"Just to talk. Been thinking about you is all." Terry had a girl Heather's age.

Terry watched as her husband walked back to the table. He seemed a little unsteady and gazed at the party of four next to his table and scowled at them.

Reece took notice that Sammy had taken notice.

"Drinking in the bathroom, brought his own hooch," said Sammy, and he was right.

Reece dipped a chip in salsa, and the waitress was back to take their orders. "Let's have another round before we order," said Sally. Both Sammy and Sally ordered big ones, and the waitress scooted off.

"So, let's talk about Cindy," said Emma. She took Reece's arm and draped it over her shoulder.

"Sounds good to me," said Sammy. "So, she just pulled her top down? What did her tits look like?"

"Ha," said Reece. His mind had drifted off to Ethiopia, to Godo, to the man with the rotten leg that had taken his bed the night he was shot.

"Careful now," said Emma.

"You know, just average, I suppose. But it was a shocker. Nothing like that had ever happened." He wanted to say that Emma had nice breasts beneath her blouse, but he'd never seen them, just imagined them.

"You can't blame a guy for looking. So did you do it on the pier?" asked Sally. She wanted the details.

Reece looked to Emma for help, but she just smiled. The drinks arrived. The Watkins had begun to bicker. Reece had just finished his first drink, and he took a deep drink of his second, hoping that Cindy would just go away.

"Reece?" asked Sally. "Are you deaf?"

"Uh, she wanted to do it in the boathouse, but then I said no. It was later that we did it in her grandparents' house." He felt he was discussing the weather. His thoughts scrambled. Why had he even told Kristin? He remembered where they'd done it the second time. "Look, what can I say? She was aggressive, and I caved. It'll never happen again."

"Why not?" asked Sammy. "Was she good?"

"Yeah, why not?" asked Sally. She was trying to dip salsa without looking, her chip catching air.

Reece thought. "I've got Emma, I think, to think about." He hugged her close to him. She had said she was in love with him.

"You're just a damn bitch," came from the Watkins' table.

Sammy held up his hand as if channeling the words their way.

"Hon, stop it," said Terry. She glanced at Reece and then at Sally and then at Sammy, then looked away, a sour look on her face. Their check was on the table.

"Don't mouth me," said Mr. Watkins. He ate the last crumb from his plate and looked around. His back was to Sammy.

"Uh oh, the tiger is pissed," said Sammy. He directed

his voice at the Watkins' table. Terry looked petrified.

Mr. Watkins had his elbows on the table and wiped his mouth with a red cloth napkin. He turned and glared at Sammy, then back at his wife. "Just keep your mouth shut, if you know what's best." He was a big man with a ruddy, flushed face.

"Looks like his mouth needs a knuckle sandwich." Sammy darted his eyes at Reece, as if conspiring to double-team the wife beater. Sally tugged his arm to calm him down.

Reece took another gulp of his drink. Emma had that half-smile, nibbling a chip, and he wished for the waitress to appear to distract Sammy.

Mr. Watkins turned his chair toward the booth. "I guess we know each other well enough. What's with the lip?"

"I don't know you from Adam," said Sally. She was hiding behind Sammy.

"I wasn't talking to you, bitch—" and Sammy was on him in a flash. Reece jumped up and watched them separate and face each other. Terry had her face in her hands.

"Sammy," said Sally. "Don't. He'll just hurt her when they go home." She glared at the big oaf.

"You apologize to my wife or apologize to my boot," said Sammy. He had both fists clenched, and all eyes were on them.

Mr. Watkins, in the dry-cleaning business, looked from Sammy to Reece. "Rot in hell," and that was the last he knew as Sammy slugged his chin, catching him with a perfect uppercut. Watkins slumped to the dirty carpet. Terry screamed.

"Well, I guess we best be going," said Sammy, reaching

for his wallet, pulling out a hundred, and throwing it on the table. He saw a large man coming from the kitchen.

They hurried outside and hopped in the truck.

"Seafood Box?" asked Sammy.

Charles passed the weekend in quiet dismay, looking forward to having Emma for three days running. She arrived with a small suitcase and arranged her things in a large guest bedroom with a four-poster, king-size bed and a view of the front yard and driveway. Sandy had reported off, and Emma knocked on Charles' door with gusto. He was sitting in bed, leaning back against two feather pillows, his breakfast of oatmeal with strawberries on a tray beside him. He'd barely touched it.

"Hey, man!"

"Oh, it's just you," said Charles. He tried to hold back a smile.

"It's not just me. It is me. You sly devil." That got a genuine laugh.

"Don't drag me out to the garden."

"I'm dragging you," said Emma. She was at his bedside with a knee on the mattress. "What's wrong with your breakfast?"

"I'm just so damned nauseated." He smoothed back his graying hair. "Need a shave."

"Let's tackle the oatmeal just a bite at a time. Take one bite now and then another in ten minutes. Can you do that? And get a strawberry in there before I eat it."

Charles reached for the spoon and, with a sour face, took a bite and swallowed. "Oh God." He put the spoon down.

"Good work, cowboy," said Emma. "I'll get that bathroom ready for your shower and a shave."

"Just give me five minutes, please." He took a deep breath and coughed.

"Not a problem." Emma went into the bathroom. There was only one clean towel left, and she noted that she'd need to do laundry. She took a small plastic tray of shampoo, shaving cream, and a razor into the marbled shower. She turned on the water, retrieved the handheld, and waited for the water to warm, testing it with her hand. Already, the hems of her scrubs were wet. All seemed ready, and she went back for Charles in his silk pajamas.

"Let's get naked here on the bed," she said.

Charles widened his eyes. "Gladly."

"You're just a dirty old man, aren't you?"

"Yes, I am."

Emma threw back the comforter and crawled onto the bed. She unbuttoned his top and slid it off. He had an inch-long scar beneath his left armpit. She'd noticed it before.

"Where'd you get that scar?" She worked his pajama bottoms down.

Charles' expression changed from one of bewilderment to one of history. "That's from the war, the Korean War. A little kid stabbed me with a knife. I wouldn't let him shine my boots." A look of worry came over him.

"Down come the undies," and she pulled them off. "Naked as a jaybird." His family jewels were tucked between his legs.

She helped him to the side of the bed and let him gather his bearings.

"Dizzy when I stand." But he stood with as little help as possible, put his arm on her shoulder, and let her walk him to the chair in the shower. He sat, breathing heavy.

"You're the first one who's asked about that scar. I don't really see it. God, it was cold in the winter. I hated it."

"Here, hold onto the sides, and I'll soak you. Did you shoot anybody while you were there?"

"Nope, not that I know of. But that little boy caught hell, and I felt sorry for him. They banned him from the camp and fired his daddy, who helped unload injured soldiers. I should have let him shine my boots, but I had just shined them."

Emma trained the warm water on his head, wetting his body. "Here, hold this and don't spray me for God's sake. Yeah, I guess you were probably under a lot of stress over there."

"Damn straight." Charles sat up, drawing his shoulders back.

Emma continued to chat with him about the war as she washed his hair and ran a washcloth over his body. Her shoes were wet, but her socks were still dry. She turned off the water and dried him with muscle.

"Hey, don't rip my skin off."

"Sorry. Now stand, and I'll get the rest."

Charles did as he was told, letting Emma dry him from top to bottom.

"There," said Emma. "All done. Now sit back down and I'll shave you." That took a few minutes, and she wiped the shaving cream from his ears. "Looking like a million dollars."

Charles muttered a thank you and ran his hand across his smooth face.

"Let's get you back in some clothes, and not your PJs. Alright?" She wrapped the towel around his waist and walked him to the chair. "Can I pick something out for you? Your closet is as big as my house."

"Just don't put me in a suit and tie. We're not going to church."

Emma laughed and entered the walk-in closet that was half-filled with clothes and shoes. She picked out a pair of slate trousers that had an elastic waist and a light-yellow pullover. She fetched some underwear and soon had him dressed.

"Feels good to be in regular clothes."

"Yeah, and you look good too. Let's go ahead and get you downstairs. What do you say? I'll bring the oatmeal."

"I'd rather not. Let me rest."

"Okay, five minutes rest," said Emma. "I have to wash your dang towels today, and I'll put clean sheets on your bed. You'll look good sitting at the kitchen table. I brought the paper in, and you can read it there."

She tidied up the bathroom and then began the slow journey with Charles down the stairs. He seemed a bit stronger and put one foot in front of the other. It took a few minutes, but soon they were in the kitchen, Charles at the table, looking like he was going to the golf course.

At the hospital, both Mrs. Laramore and Chuck, the man who had lost his hand, had transferred off the unit. Mrs. Laramore was on the sixth floor, and Chuck had moved to Spain Rehab across town. Reece spent a few minutes talking with Andrew and then dove into his night's assignments, a gunshot to the head and a hit-and-run.

The kid was only sixteen years old and had been shot at a park, a drive-by. He was on a ventilator, unresponsive, his pupils sluggish to light. There was no response to pain when Reece poked his knuckles into the boy's chest.

"Cecil, I'm Reece, your nurse. I'll be taking care of you tonight." The ventilator cycled, and the boy's chest rose and fell. Reece did his assessment and told Cecil that he'd been shot, that he was at Carraway, and that he seemed to be doing better even though he wasn't. Only his mother had been by to visit, but she held three part-time jobs and could only come once per day.

Reece dripped saline into Cecil's eyes and swabbed his mouth with glycerin sticks. He checked the catheter bag. "I have to go now, Cecil, but I'll be back to check on you." He washed his hands and headed to the next patient, the hit-and-run.

A frail man in his twenties with a cast on his arm and a chest tube draining blood-tinged fluid greeted Reece with a wary look. His name was Larry Sizemore.

"Hey," said Reece. "Mr. Sizemore?" He walked up to the bed rail and glanced at the cardiac monitor and IV pump. "I'm Reece, your nurse tonight."

"Is it night?" Larry spoke with a lisp, and Reece could see the scar of an old cleft palate repair.

"Yep." He looked at his watch. "Eleven-thirty. You need anything right off the bat?"

"I'd like a book. Do you have any books?" Larry's eyes were small for his head. "And maybe some..." He winced at the chest tube. "Some ice cream."

"Yeah, we're good with the ice cream. Not sure about the book. There's a Bible in the drawer. Will that do?"

"If that's all you have. I can't sleep unless...I read."

Reece took off his stethoscope. "Gonna check you out,

make sure your vitals are fine, okay?"

"Okay," said Larry. He shifted his heavy arm with the cast. "Did they ever catch who hit me?"

"Hmm, I'm not sure." He checked his blood pressure and then listened to his chest. Breath sounds were diminished on the right, where the chest tube entered between his ribs. The dressing was clean. "Looking good." He went to the small nightstand on wheels and retrieved the black hardback Bible. "Here you go. What do you like to read? Maybe I can bring a book tomorrow."

"I prefer science fiction," said Larry. He winced as he breathed.

"I'll do what I can, okay? I'll order the ice cream for you. Chocolate or vanilla?"

"Chocolate, please."

Reece stepped through the curtain back onto the bright unit. He was gradually adjusting to night shift, but still couldn't resist checking his watch. The minutes seemed to drag by, swarming the air like a cloud of gnats.

He wound up at the desk, talking with Ingrid and her thick glasses. She was twice his age, married, and had kids in college. She had a habit of clicking her pen.

"I hope Andrew doesn't run you off." She lowered her voice to a whisper.

"He's alright," said Reece.

"I think they let him be charge nurse because he's gay. Special treatment, if you ask me."

"It doesn't matter who the charge nurse is, just that there is one. I've never wanted to be charge. So, you think he gives you unfair assignments?"

"Almost always. He knows I like the women patients,

and he gives me old men." She made a face.

The other nurses were scattered along the big tables, charting. Andrew walked in from the break room across the hall and saw Reece talking to Ingrid. He moved along to check on his patients.

"God, it's just the way that he walks that irks me," said Ingrid.

"Mmmhmm," said Reece. He opened a chart, writing up his initial patient assessments. He felt that Ingrid would slug Andrew because he was gay.

Reece watched Ingrid step away and checked his watch. A young lady from dietary brought in the ice cream and took it to the room for Larry. "Thanks," said Reece.

Larry had dozed off but opened his eyes. "Is that my ice cream?"

"Yep." Reece peeled the lid off for him.

"What flavor is it?"

"Chocolate, like you asked for."

"Well, vanilla would be better, come to think of it." His small eyes peered from beneath his overhang of hair.

"Okay. I'll order some vanilla." He picked up the chocolate and the spoon, intent on eating it himself.

He walked over to Gloria and had her call for more ice cream. "He changed his mind about the chocolate. Wants vanilla."

Gloria frowned. "Maybe that's why he got hit. Couldn't make up his mind about crossing the street." She put her hands beneath her breasts and lifted. "Hot in here to you?"

Reece laughed. "No, always kind of cool to me." He heard an IV pump beeping and went into Cecil's room. He needed a new bag of normal saline, and Reece went to get it. Andrew was in the supply room.

"You getting the skinny from Ingrid?" said Andrew. His short blond hair was very neatly combed. He tapped his long fingers on the counter.

"Well, getting something. Does she want to be charge nurse?"

"Ha, there's no way in hell they'd let her be charge. She can barely do her job as is. She just strikes me as so bitter." He adjusted his black frame glasses. "Did she say she wanted to be charge?"

"No. Just complaining about you being charge. I blew her off. You're right about the bitterness." He imagined Ingrid washing her long hair in the shower, wringing it with two hands like a wet towel.

"That's what I thought. Just watch her, though. She'll never volunteer to help you, but she'll always ask you to help her."

Reece felt a creeping annoyance at the pettiness of Ingrid, and she wasn't the only one. Very few people seemed to be happy doing their jobs, even the doctors. He figured a lot of it had to do with stress, with people dying all the time. His other major beef was the amount of time he had to spend writing up care plans and charting. He sometimes gave his meds late, trying to keep up with the paperwork. Andrew took a urinal from the cart and left, and Reece walked with the bag of IV fluid. He remembered the cool Icelandic IV bottles in Ethiopia that had served so many purposes after they were used. He bumped into Stella.

"Oops, sorry."

"Eyes on the prize," said Stella. She was as tall as he was

and had shiny shoulder-length black hair. She was fairly flat-chested but had a prominent rump.

Reece wasn't sure what she meant, and he thought of Calvin, the counselor who spoke in riddles. He rigged the new bag of fluid. "Hey, Cecil, gonna turn you and then suction the tube that's in your lungs." He turned him, stuffed two pillows behind him, and placed one between his knees. Cecil's face and forehead bulged as if a mighty pressure was inside. Reece took the Ambu bag down, prepared his suction catheter, and popped open a tube of saline. "Okay, gonna make you cough." He unhooked Cecil from the ventilator and sprayed saline down the tube. Like gas on a fire, Cecil began to cough, and secretions shot up the tube. Reece suctioned and then gave him a few deep breaths with the bag. He hooked up the vent again, which was alarming with a piercing squeal. "All done for now, Cecil." He imagined that Cecil was cold, so he adjusted the sheet and the blanket. He remembered the chocolate ice cream and went out to the desk to eat it, but someone had thrown it away. "Dang."

Reece checked on Larry, eating his vanilla ice cream in tiny bites with a spoon. He had 100 ccs of bloody fluid in his chest tube drainage container, and Reece drained it. "Think you can sleep?"

"Well, I'll read some in the Bible, I guess." He seemed to be a kind of helpless soul, someone who things happened to that were always beyond one's control. He coughed and winced.

"We have pain meds if you need them. Percocet. How are you doing with the pain?"

"I'd rather not take them, if you don't mind. I want to

heal on my own."

"Okay, well, just holler if you need anything." The room was tidy, the chest-tube drainage box hooked to suction, making an aquarium noise.

"Okay," said Larry. "I might need you to empty my urinal." He spoke in soft tones as if explaining an ancient text to a child. Reece did that and washed his hands.

He stepped out and checked his watch, just after midnight, and all was well. He walked across the hall to the break room to pee, and two nurses were there gossiping. Standing over the commode, he wondered how Emma was doing, imagining that she was asleep. He decided to call her as soon as his shift was over, feeling a tiny bit better. He could hear the two nurses, Tiffany and Suzanne, talking about Ingrid. He flushed.

"Hey, Reece," said Tiffany. She was married and buxom with perfectly coiffed hair. She seemed to be the perfect Southern belle. "You haven't talked to us. We're not going to bite." She flashed a dazzling smile.

"You caught up? Have a seat," said Suzanne, smoking a cigarette. She looked very professional and had a man's haircut.

Reece leaned against the wall, his arms folded. "That's my fault, not being social. What's up?"

Ingrid walked in just then, and Suzanne grinned at Tiffany.

Ingrid waved her hand at the smoke. "Really? You could take that outside." She hitched up her scrub bottoms, which were too big for her. She mumbled and went into the small bathroom, just a sink and commode, no mirror.

Suzanne rolled her eyes. Reece was more or less looking straight down into her cleavage and sat, worried that he was staring.

"We heard you were engaged, but now you're not," said Tiffany. Her makeup was perfect and extensive. A huge diamond ring.

"That seems to be the case," said Reece. He fiddled with a styrofoam cup on the small table.

"You're single is what you're saying," said Suzanne. "There's plenty of bait around here." She blew smoke over her shoulder and winked at Tiffany.

"Well, maybe not single," said Reece. "I guess I'm seeing someone. Everything is happening so fast."

"Wow, that didn't take long," said Tiffany. She took a tissue and pressed her lips to it.

"I've known her for a while," said Reece.

"Was she your backup?" asked Suzanne. She laughed.

"Uh, no. She's a nurse, of course. We worked together in Ethiopia."

"Oh yeah, we heard about all that," said Tiffany. She reached over and brushed Reece's hair aside to look at the scars there. "You poor boy."

Reece blushed. "I'm fine. She saved my life over there. We bonded."

"That's romantic, I guess. You were engaged to Kristin on day shift in CCU. We know Kristin, sort of."

"Oh, really," said Reece. He checked his watch.

"I hope you didn't break her heart."

Reece wasn't sure which one said it. He was gazing at his hands. "She called it off."

"Because of the other woman, right?" asked Suzanne. "Oh, that's juicy."

"Well, yes, I suppose so. You guys worked here long?"

"We're veterans, and that means at least six months," said Tiffany. "People come and go like it's a carousel, especially night shift."

"Except for Ingrid," said Suzanne. "I think she was born here."

"I would like a day shift when I can get it. I feel like I'm floating on nights, like we're on a rocket in space."

Tiffany smiled. "You're cute." She glanced at Suzanne. "I bet you couldn't handle this, though." She stood, did a twirl, and then bent over and touched Reece's nose.

Reece tried to laugh. "Well, let me get back and check on my patients. One's brain dead and the other is reading the Bible." He stood.

"Bye, Reece," said Tiffany. She fluttered her eyelids, and Suzanne laughed. "We'll talk more."

Reece bumped into Dr. Flag coming into the break room. The room where he slept was next door. He passed by Reece, and Tiffany and Suzanne were inviting him to pull up a chair.

Reece did his rounds and settled in for the long night, thinking of Emma, Kristin, and Cindy.

Emma awoke at seven, bleary-eyed, and stumbled to the bathroom. She'd gotten up once during the night to check on Charles, but he had been asleep. She brushed her teeth, combed her wonky hair, and went to his room. He was just where she'd left him, but the sheets were tied in knots as if he'd been swimming in them.

She dressed and headed downstairs to make coffee and have something to eat before she tackled him. There was an apple in the fridge that she'd put there the night before. She poured herself a glass of orange juice and imagined that Reece was finishing up his shift. She bit into the crisp red apple and chewed, listening to the crunch inside her mouth. She wondered if she should shower and decided to wait till later. She looked in the fridge and saw butter and maple syrup, so she fixed two pieces of toast and made ersatz pancakes. She sat at the table, taking her time, gazing toward the windows over the sink. The phone rang, and she jumped.

"Rickers' residence."

"Hey, it's me."

"Reece, you still at the hospital? You're not pulling a double, are you?" She took the cordless phone back to the table where the apple core sat balanced on end.

"No, just calling you before I leave. Didn't wake you, did I? You sound sleepy."

"No, just eating. Gonna get old Charles up in a few minutes. What's up?"

"Just wanted to call. I'm so ready to get home, though,

and get to bed."

"Night shift will kick your butt for sure. Feel free to drop by here anytime. I think Charles likes you, plus you have to drink some bourbon with him."

"Yeah, maybe I'll do that tomorrow. I'm whooped, even though it was a slow night."

"Yeah, get home and sleep." Emma watched a fly land on the apple core and brushed it away, but it came back.

"Yeah, I will. Just wanted to say hey, so I guess I'll go. Good luck with Charles."

"Well, that's sweet. Okay, talk to you later," and she hung up.

She stood and felt a little dizzy, and she still had a headache, and the rash on her back was worse. She was about ready to go to the doctor, but her employee health insurance hadn't kicked in yet. She washed her plate and fork. She felt it was too cold and went in search of the thermostat, which took her a few minutes to find in a hallway. Below the thermostat was a large glass object on a pedestal.

Upstairs she went, holding to the rail, wondering what surprises lay ahead. Charles was awake, his eyes fluttering as if he was on the edge of a dream.

"Hey, you sleep well?" asked Emma.

"Hey." Charles lolled his head and focused. His face looked sweaty, and his forehead was oily. "Are you real?"

Emma stood beside the bed. "Yeah, I'm real. Are you real?"

"I guess we're both real." He grinned, showing his stained teeth, his receding gum lines.

"Got a big day planned for us," said Emma. "I think we need to plan an outing, where I take you to a restaurant or something. The garden was just step one. Maybe we could go to the zoo. You've got that fancy wheelchair."

"Lord help us," said Charles. "You do want to kill me. What would I do but just get nauseated and probably barf on the monkeys."

"I'll give you some nausea medicine before we go."

"It makes me sleepy. I'll fall asleep."

"I'll make a big pot of coffee before we go, and we can take a cup in the car."

"Then I'll have to pee. I'll pee myself."

"I'll put a diaper on your bad self."

Charles shook his head. He was stymied. "You just want to drive my car, don't you?" He owned a black 1985 Mercedes-Benz 500 SEC AMG.

"I haven't even seen your car."

"It's in the garage. It hasn't been started in six months, though."

"Heck, that's good news. I was wondering if we would have to take a taxi. Give me a key, and I'll check it out for you later. But today we walk to the mailbox!"

"What, can't you get the mail? Did you sign me up for a marathon, too?" He coughed and turned red.

Emma waited for his breath to return, and then she laughed. "Don't get shook up now. I'll help you. I'll be right there with you. I'll put the wheelchair halfway to the mailbox so you can rest."

"I guess I better have a big breakfast. We going to the garden too? I kind of like going to the garden." He looked ashamed to say it.

"That's what I like to hear," said Emma. "We'll do your shower first and then head down to the kitchen. Maybe we could watch a movie in that big room in the basement, the theater, just to kill time, instead of sitting on the bed."

"Does my doctor know that there's a madwoman in my house?"

"We tied him up," said Emma. "You don't need a doctor. You need a nurse to make you feel better, right?"

"Maybe not, if you wind up killing me." He brushed back his thin gray hair. His sunken cheeks gave him a chiseled look, almost handsome beneath the wasting.

"Okay, bath first."

She readied the water and supplies and soon had him scrubbed from head to toe, running the washcloth between his toes and giving his backside a vigorous scrub. He protested off and on, but he took it. When it was time to head downstairs, he staggered to the doorway of the bedroom by himself with Emma holding his elbow, but then he tired and began to sink. She caught him with the belt around his waist and helped him to the end of the hall and the top of the stairs, where he sat for five minutes gathering his bearings.

"Damn, this is such a big house. I need a little cabin in the woods." He rested with his elbows on his knees. The marble stairs hurt his tailbone, and he shifted from one butt cheek to the other.

"That's an understatement," said Emma. "Gives you lots of room to walk, though. You ready?"

"No."

"Well, I say you're ready. Let's get to the bottom."

He held to the walnut rail, and she supported his right side, taking one step down every ten seconds or so, and soon he was downstairs and sitting at his kitchen table,

The Birmingham News ready for him to read.

"Consider this the throne of your kingdom," said Emma. "How about some fruit, maybe a banana, and then a piece of toast. How about some eggs?"

"Emma, slow down, let me think. I guess I'll try a banana, but only half. You eat the other half. How's that?"

"Deal." She gazed at her handiwork with pride and peeled the banana, slicing it and putting it on a small saucer of expensive china. She did the same for her half of the banana and poured him a glass of orange juice before sitting down. "You don't need a fork, do you? Eat."

Charles smirked and said, "No, do you?" He put a banana slice in his mouth and chewed as if it were a piece of steak.

"Good for you," said Emma, and she watched him eat the six slices one by one and then drink half of his juice. "You're the man."

"I don't feel much like it."

Emma went to the toaster. She dropped in a slice of sourdough bread his ex-wife had brought. "Eat this toast, and we'll call it a day." She waited for it to pop up, then spread on a thin layer of butter and cut it into four pieces. "Here."

"I guess I'll get fat eating all these carbs."

"That's the spirit," said Emma.

"Here, you eat one piece. He handed it to Emma."

Emma tore a piece and popped it into her mouth. "Good bread. Your wife has good taste."

"Ex-wife."

"Yeah, ex-wife." She watched him muddle through the toast without gagging. They sat there and talked, as

Charles perused the front page of the paper. "Young waitress was killed near the Cahaba River. Looks like they got the psycho."

"Yeah, read about that. He sounds crazy."

"More than crazy. Lunatics everywhere you look."

"Any lunatics in Mountain Brook?"

"Throw a rock and you'll hit one," said Charles. He laughed, rattled the paper, and then coughed, turning red.

"How about some coffee? I forgot to get you some coffee. Got a fresh pot."

"No, I don't think so."

"Half a cup." Emma poured into a plain white cup and pushed it in front of him. "You need your caffeine, and your bourbon."

"And don't forget the cigars." He gave her a quick grin. "You're a pretty thing. Too bad I'm so old. We could hit the town." He sighed and looked her in the eyes.

"Not so fast, slick." She gave him a soft punch in the arm.

They talked a bit more, and soon Emma had him on the oversized couch in the vaulted entryway. She put the wheelchair halfway to the mailbox and went back for him. He managed to walk to the door and caught himself there, breathing deeply.

"Slow down, girl."

"Here's where I help you." She put her arm around his waist and his arm over her shoulder."

He grunted with each step and broke into a sweat. The sky was overcast, but the light was bright, and a steady breeze blew against his blue tracksuit. A line of head-high hedge bordered the circular driveway, and a colossal oak dominated the central grassy area, casting a great shade across the house and yard. How many dinner guests had parked there, bottles of wine in the crooks of their arms?

"Doing great," said Emma. She backed him up to the wheelchair, and he fell into it out of breath.

"You know...the mail hasn't even run yet."

"That's just our goal." She was perspiring, and sweat trickled from her eyebrows.

A Jaguar drove by, and then a Land Rover, followed by a lawn-care truck. No one was on the street walking, and the neighborhood was tranquil.

"You ready for the mailbox?"

Charles looked at her. "Just roll me back in the house. I think I'm done. Plus, I have to pee."

"Not so fast," said Emma. "Let's get this over with and back in the house so you can pee. Or you could pee on the mailbox."

That got Charles laughing and then coughing deep. He coughed up a wad of phlegm and spat it to his side, but it caught on the back of the wheelchair.

"Gross," said Emma. She laughed and leaned in, putting her leg between his knees and circling his torso with her arms. "Up on three. One, two, three."

Charles stood, just off balance, but Emma had him by the belt. "Ho now, soldier. Steady now."

They walked to the stonework mailbox and turned back, walking on acorns. Emma didn't let him stop at the wheelchair, and he struggled to make it to the open front door.

"Damn, girl." He was sweating.

"Inside, inside, to the couch. You can do it."

Twenty paces later, he collapsed on the black leather couch.

"Look at you!" said Emma. "Well done."

"Thanks," said Charles. He took deep breaths, but then got a cramp in his calf. "Oh, shit. Got a cramp." He leaned back and tried to straighten his leg. His big toe pointed down.

Emma squatted, took his foot, and pushed on it until the cramp was gone. "Better?"

"Yeah," said Charles. "I need to lie down."

"You were in bed all night. You've got to get used to staying up during the day." She sat beside him and hooked her arm through his. "We're buds, right?"

Charles rolled his eyes.

Dora and Horace flew into Dallas/Fort Worth and then took an American stumpjumper to Killeen Municipal Airport. Reece was to meet them, and they hurried off the plane. It had been forty-eight hours since the massacre at Luby's.

Reece stood near the gate in generic jeans and a Crimson Tide t-shirt. He'd spent the night at his pastor's house. The pastor had insisted on his coming, even though he had not wanted to go. He hadn't showered since the killings and felt grimy. Before he knew it, Dora was hugging him, and Horace was rubbing his back. He didn't want to, but he began to cry and sank into Dora, who was as tall as he was.

"Reece, you're safe," said Dora. She wore a light-gray windbreaker over her knit pants and blouse decorated with sparkly sequins.

"Yeah," said Reece.

"Have you eaten, son? Have you slept? You look a bit ragged," said Horace. He'd forgotten his glasses and squinted. He wore stretchy dress pants and a long-sleeve shirt with his Sunday shoes.

Reece wiped his eyes. He felt like he would explode. "Yeah, I've eaten breakfast at the preacher's house. He wanted to come, but I told him not to."

"I'm grateful to him," said Dora. She had her dark hair cut short, too short, she thought.

"What should we do?" asked Reece.

"Well, drive us back to the house. I need to look for

insurance papers. Have the police been in contact with you?"

"No," said Reece. "I left before anybody talked to me. I couldn't stand to be there."

"Son, you poor boy," said Dora. "I can't believe they're gone. We'll have to find out where they're at. Do you know?"

"The preacher said they're at a funeral home. I have it written down." He turned to walk back to the car.

They hadn't even packed a suitcase, catching the first flight they could.

"I'm just sick, just absolutely sick, Reece," said Dora. She took his hand as they walked.

"So, the shooter is dead, is what we heard," said Horace. "What did he look like?"

Reece tried to think. "I don't know. Tall and skinny is all I remember."

They walked into an overcast noon, a stiff wind blowing nonstop, rustling their clothes.

"What a wind," said Dora. She put her hand on top of her head as if her hair were a wig.

"It's always like this," said Reece. "The wind never stops blowing. It makes it hard to play basketball outside."

"How far is the car, son?" asked Horace.

Reece stopped at a curb and looked into the parking lot. He couldn't remember where he'd parked. "Over here, I think." He led the way, and it took them a few minutes to locate the homely Bobcat hatchback. He opened his door and leaned over and unlocked the passenger door.

"You okay to drive, son?" asked Horace. He ducked in behind the front seat, squeezed himself into the back, and sat on a bottle of lemon-flavored water. "Lord, what a small car."

"Why would they buy such a thing?" asked Dora, her hand still on her head.

Reece sat behind the steering wheel and laughed. He laughed a bit too long, but knew that it was all they could afford. He soon pulled onto Roy Reynolds Drive, headed to Veterans Memorial. It was only a five-minute ride to the tiny pink brick house on Zephyr Road. They drove in silence for a minute.

"Sure is dry here," said Horace.

"Are we going to go by that restaurant?" asked Dora.

"You want to? I don't want to," said Reece. "It's not on the way."

"No, I was just asking," said Dora. "Wanted to be prepared. Horace, do you think we'll have to go and identify the bodies?" Her voice caught, and she kept her eyes on Reece.

"I forgot to ask," said Reece. "Have you eaten. It's lunchtime." He glanced at Dora and saw her staring at him.

"If you like. We could use a hamburger," said Horace. "We missed breakfast in Dallas."

"There's a Jiffy Burger near the house." Reece hit the blinker and turned to hook up with Zephyr Road. He drove. "There's the house." He pointed as they passed.

"Lord, what a tiny house," said Horace. He craned his neck to keep looking.

The Jiffy Burger wasn't crowded. Reece recognized the cashier. She went to the same high school, but they had never spoken. Reece had spent the last three years of his life, since the move from Huntsville, in silent mourning.

The high school had been his thirteenth school, and he had just given up. They ate their burgers and fries and headed back to the car, the warm wind blowing.

Soon they were back at the house, and Reece opened the fence gate and pulled into the short driveway. "I need to let the dog in. I left him outside." He walked to the front door and realized he'd left the keys in the ignition.

Once inside, Dora and Horace gazed with blank looks at the bare walls. They recognized the furniture from years and years ago. Horace took a short tour of the two-bedroom house as if to make sure that his son and his daughter-in-law weren't there. Dora sat on the hard, golden couch.

The dog, Floppy, came inside, his head down, his stubby tail wagging. Reece crumbled two Gaines Burgers into his food bowl and watched him sniff them with disinterest. "Good boy," and he rubbed his head. He glanced at the sink with its dirty plates, the last meal with his parents.

Reece showed Horace the cedar chest where his parents kept all of their important papers, and Horace began to sift through the various envelopes mixed with photo albums. Reece found the paper with the name of the funeral home on it, handed it to Dora, and sat on the golden chair that matched the couch. He remembered standing on it to catch the warm air from the single vent in the Army apartment back at Fort Knox. He'd worn the same pair of green canvas tennis shoes for the entire two years they lived there, and he remembered his feet freezing as he walked through snow and ice to school. He went to check on Horace and saw papers spread across the thin quilt on the bed.

It took an hour or so, but Horace managed to find an insurance policy for ten thousand dollars and a burial policy. They had bought their burial policies just after they were married, as if there was a hurry.

"Son, we need to call the funeral home. Do you want to go with us?" asked Horace.

Reece thought. "No, I'll stay here." He was glad that his grandparents were there. He watched them leave through the front door, then stood behind the heavy curtain to watch them back out of the driveway. He realized that he'd be going back to Alabama and felt a little thrill. He walked into his bedroom and looked at his messy single bed with the flattened foam mattress. The middle had scooped out and hurt his back. He turned on his stereo and listened. It was "Take the Long Way Home."

Two hours passed, and the Bobcat pulled into the driveway. They had gotten lost and had to stop for directions both going and coming. Horace helped Dora out of the tiny seat and held her elbow as she walked with her head down. Reece met them at the front door.

Dora wiped her face with a tissue and let Horace guide her to the couch.

"Well?" asked Reece.

"It was them, son. It was them," said Horace. He put his hand on Reece's shoulder and stood there as if Reece would disappear.

"Well, what do we do?" asked Reece. He put on his coat, but he didn't know why. The house was warm and stuffy, serviced by a single unit in the front window.

"We got it worked out, son," said Horace. "You're coming to live with us. We'll get this house up for sale as soon as we can."

Reece didn't even know that they'd bought the house. He assumed it was rented like always. "When do we leave?"

"Well, gosh, son, it would be nice if we rest here tonight and catch a flight back tomorrow. Will that be okay?"

"Sure," said Reece.

"What's the church you go to? I want to call that preacher and let him know what's happening."

Reece thought. "It's the Baptist church on Skyline Drive. You need the number?" He reached for his mom's Bible on a TV tray and pulled out a bulletin. "The number's here." He held it out like a fish.

Horace took it and squinted. He handed it to Dora. "You dial for me. Where's the phone?"

"In the kitchen, on the wall," said Reece.

Horace spoke for a few minutes and hung up. "Well, I think that's got us covered for now. There's got to be somebody on base that we need to talk to, though."

"First and ninety-second, second armored division," said Reece. It was all he knew of his dad's job at Fort Hood.

"We can take care of that later," said Horace. He paced, as if trying to walk away the confusion.

"You're coming home with us, boy," said Dora, and she burst into tears.

Reece was into his second week on night shift and still exhausted. He just couldn't sleep past noon and felt compelled to sweep the driveway or do another chore. Today, Thursday, he was picking up pinecones and small limbs after a short rainstorm. He filled the bucket and walked to the burn barrel, which was already blazing. He was shirtless and in shorts, probably his favorite outfit. He'd run around the lake and was feeling a surge of adrenaline that pushed him through the yard, picking up debris. The sweat that had dried from his run now melted back onto his body like butter, making him glisten.

He thought about the tequila in the RV, how he hadn't touched it. He wondered how long it would keep. He'd been composing letters to Ethiopia in his head and planned to get started on those right away. He was embarrassed that he'd waited so long, but felt that everyone would understand. He picked up a pinecone and tossed it into the bucket. For a few minutes, he pitched cones from a variety of distances, making his way farther up in the back toward the yard of a brick home that housed a very nosy widow. She'd seen Reece peeing off the roof of the garage one day and called his grandmother to give a full report. Reece remembered her grandson, Greg, who had lived on the same street in North Birmingham when he was just four. They had been in the same daycare together, Reece's dad in Vietnam for most of the time. Unknown to the parents, the daycare was run by prostitutes who used the back rooms of the old colonial-style house as their rooms of business. Every morning, after the parents left, a young, pretty girl would make them sit in chairs and open up. She came by each child, holding a beaker of yellow liquid, and squirted the liquid into waiting mouths. The stuff tasted horrible, and then the kids slept till lunch, ate, and then went back to bed for another couple of hours. It had never occurred to him to tell his mother or his grandparents, not even when the pretty ladies had taken him into the basement and told him they would hang him in a bag from a hook if he didn't behave. The place was eventually shuttered and torn down.

Reece had to pee, and for old time's sake, he stepped behind a tree in full view of the brick house and gladly let his full bladder empty onto the pine straw. Relieved, he went back to the sticks and cones.

"Reece!" He heard Dora calling him. "Telephone!"

Reece dumped the bucket into the barrel, sending up a flash of embers and smoke. He trotted to the back door and went inside.

"It's Emma," said Dora.

He hurried. "Emma!" Sweat dripped from his nose and trickled down his back. Dora handed him a couple of paper towels.

"Hey, I'm at Charles'. Did the clinic call you?"

"The clinic?"

"Yeah, where we had the tests. The public health clinic."

"No, not yet. Are the results back? It's been about ten days." He wiped his face with the paper towels.

"They called the house, and Mom called me. They said for me to come to the clinic tomorrow for my results."

"We can go together. Mine should be back, too."

"Why didn't they call you? I'm worried."

"Maybe they will. Don't worry."

"Reece, I've got this rash on my back that's getting worse, and I can't shake this headache, plus I've had a low-grade fever."

"Huh," said Reece. "I guess that's worrisome, but don't jump to any conclusions." Dora was asking him if everything was okay, and he nodded that it was.

"Jesus, what if I wind up like Charles, somebody giving me a bath and feeding me? I'm in knots."

"Look, I'll go with you, alright? We can go after I get off work in the morning. Maybe let me get a shower at the house, and then I'll drive down and pick you up. We can have lunch."

"I appreciate that. But what would I do? Surely, I haven't gotten anything from Charles. I mean, it's primarily transmitted sexually. But those soldiers in Ethiopia. I remember the one who looked sick. He smelled horrible, like a rotten potato."

Reece sat down, careful not to put his sweaty back against the chair. "It'll be fine. We'll go together. We'll both get our results. I'll call and see if mine are back yet, although I'm sure they are." He drummed his fingers on the table, worried.

"That makes me feel some better. I appreciate it."

"Yeah, no problem. So, how is Charles?"

"He's fine. He can almost walk to the mailbox by himself now. He keeps asking when you're gonna come and smoke and drink with him. I'm working the extra day this week, but I'm off tomorrow."

Reece laughed. A banker wanted to consort with him. "He's a character. Next week, I promise I'll come by, maybe after work. Alcohol before noon, but why not?" He looked around to see if Dora had heard him, and she had. She was wagging her finger at him, sitting in her recliner.

"But this rash and the fever and the headache. And I swear I've been nauseated a few times. You know Charles is nauseated most of the day."

"You could have some kind of virus that you brought back. Not HIV, but some kind of bug. That's pretty common, I think. You had dengue fever while you were there. Maybe this is some kind of relapse."

"I did think about that," said Emma. "Well, thanks for making me feel better, but I'm still worried. I thought about making a will, not that I have anything, just some savings."

"Just put that out of your mind. Think positive."

"Okay, I will. I'll do that. Did you sleep better today? Dora said you were working in the yard."

"I woke up at noon again." He looked at the clock on the stove, and it said three o'clock. "I have these awful dreams I can't remember and wake up in a sweat."

"I hate that. It could take you months to adjust. Well, look, I'll go. Charles is on the couch listening to some music. He likes jazz. I still have to get out to the garden."

"Yeah, sure. Tell him I said hey."

"Will do. Thank you, Reece."

Reece hung up the phone. He hadn't told Dora or Horace about the HIV tests, but he knew he was about to.

Dora put her Sunday School book down. "Now what's happened? I swear you get into the most pickles."

"Nobody is in a pickle." He told her about going to get tested, that it was just a smart thing to do. He'd not told them about the rape, but now Dora knew.

"For Pete's sake, Reece. That poor girl. I just pray that the tests are negative. I don't think I could take it. Lord, Lord. I thought it was just the homosexuals that got that?"

"No, anybody can get it." Reece stood in front of the cool air from the window unit.

"Wait till your granddaddy hears this. Lord, Lord. I'm getting you two on the prayer chain right now. I'll call Doris Satterfield. She'll get it going. She reached for the ragged address book beside the lamp. "What's gonna happen next?"

"What happens next is that I pick up some pinecones." He stood and didn't wait to hear how Dora would phrase it. He wondered what he would do if Emma were positive. He shivered. He supposed he'd just be there for her, and that's all he could conjure.

Back outside, the warm air greeted him. A thin trail of smoke from the burn barrel twirled straight to the sky, passing first through the pine branches. He resumed the monotonous task, but kind of enjoyed it. He liked repetition. He liked mowing grass. He put two pinecones in the bucket and went to the far side of the back yard next to the Sykes'. Their side was choked with limbs and pinecones. Mr. Sykes would be home any day now, and he imagined that he'd run into Cindy. He hadn't used protection with her, and that ate into his mind, but she was as healthy as a horse.

He labored in the yard for another hour, picking up the smallest of branches, twigs. To take a break, he walked to the garden and sat in the chair beside Horace. They chatted for a while, and soon Dora was calling them up for a supper of fried catfish and cole slaw. The house reeked of hot oil, and after eating, he lay down for an hour and then got up, unable to sleep.

That night at work, Reece had Larry Sizemore again. His patient, Cecil, the kid with the gunshot to the head, had died. Larry's chest tube was out, his damaged lung fully re-inflated. He had been running a fever, which was mysterious, keeping him on the unit, even though he could probably be admitted to the floor. No train wrecks had come in to push him out.

"Hello," said Larry in his lispy voice. He was sitting in the chair, reading. Reece had brought him *The Martian Chronicles,* and another nurse had brought him *A Confederacy of Dunces.*

"Hello," said Reece. "Doing okay? You look good." He checked Larry's IV, through which he would be giving the antibiotic, and then checked his vital signs. He held up the thermometer to the light. "Ninety-nine-six. Gonna listen to your lungs." He did that and then pressed on Larry's fingernails to make sure he had circulation in the broken arm.

"Thank you again for the book. I don't feel so well, to be honest. I think it's the fever, and my leg hurts. I hope I can sleep tonight." He darted his small eyes at Reece.

"Yeah, the docs need to figure that one out, the fever. I can give you some Percocet at midnight if you need it." He pulled the overbed table closer to Larry. "Get you some fresh ice water too."

"I do think I'll need that," said Larry.

"They ever figure out who hit you?"

"Not that I know of. I don't even remember what kind of car it was. Oh well."

Reece checked his watch and washed his hands. "Okay, keep reading, but call if you need anything," and he left to see about his other patient.

He said hey to Tiffany in her crisp scrubs and perfect makeup and headed to room eight, a young woman with pericarditis, contracted after having a tooth pulled. Tiffany was thin and attractive, like a librarian is attractive. He peeked behind the curtain, and his second patient was awake.

"Hey there, Mrs. Biggs."

"Just Lola, please." She worked in medical records at the hospital.

Reece chatted with her as he did his assessment. She had no fever, which was great. The antibiotics and aspirin seemed to be doing the trick. She complained of some mild chest discomfort, but that was all. Reece brought a fresh pitcher of ice water and went to chart at the long desk, thinking nonstop about the HIV tests. He was sitting next to Andrew, who was on the phone with ER. A new patient was coming up soon. He charted on both of his patients and found himself cornered by Ingrid in the clean utility room. She complained to him about Andrew. She was first admit and would be getting the MVA. Reece just listened and nodded.

"At least he's not black," said Ingrid, catching Reece off guard.

"What?"

"Oh, nothing," said Ingrid. She seemed to be the most miserable human being on the planet. In her baggy scrubs, she left with a cup of coffee.

Reece wandered into the hall and peeked in the break room, sipping a cup of cranberry juice. Andrew was there, charting. He looked like a doctor with his black frame glasses. Reece said hey and stepped back on the unit. Ingrid was in twelve, getting the bed ready.

"Hey, Reece, can you give me a hand?"

"Uh, sure, what do you need?"

"Can you get me a suction setup?" She pulled down the sheet and blanket, then placed a blue pad across the bed.

Reece soon returned with a suction canister and a suction wand. He dropped the canister into the holder and attached the tubing to the pressure gauge.

"Anything else?"

Ingrid paused. "You could help me get him on the bed when he gets here."

"Okay," said Reece. "Will do."

"Hey, Reece," said Suzanne with the haircut like a man's. "Phone." She hit the hold button.

Reece could only imagine that it was Kristin and answered. "Reece speaking."

"I'm not bothering you, am I?" It was Emma.

"Oh brother, I thought maybe you were Kristin, calling to bless me out."

"No, it's me. Reece, I just can't get settled, thinking about that damn test."

He could picture her curled up on the couch, the phone cord bobbing across the living room. He almost forgot to speak. "Like I said, don't worry about it. Tomorrow will come and go, and then we can laugh about it."

"Gosh, I sure don't feel like laughing right now. You're not busy, are you? Sorry, I'm calling."

"No, no worries. It's pretty slow. A new patient is coming up from the ER, but he's not mine. He's Ingrid's. She's just a little bit crazy. She doesn't like gay people or blacks, or so she says."

"Maybe her new patient will be a gay black man." She laughed.

"One can only hope, but not for their sake. I wouldn't want her to be my nurse. She's always cornering me and complaining about one thing and then another."

"Don't you hate that?"

"Yeah, I do." Reece could see her, her half-smile, her bouncy short hair parted down the middle.

"So, I shouldn't worry, right?"

Reece laughed. "No, don't think about it. We'll go out for lunch. Want to go to your mom's barbecue place?"

"Sure. It'll probably be on the house, as usual."

"I'm not trying to get a free lunch."

"That's not what I mean. Charlie, the owner, just looks out for Mom. He's sweet."

"Well, we could do Mexican."

"No, not after Sammy plowed that Watkins dude. Let's go to Duck's. Surprise her. I won't tell her we're coming. Of course, I'll have to invite Sally."

"Yeah, the more the merrier."

The double doors swung open behind him, and in came the new patient on a stretcher with two ER nurses, followed by Dr. Flag.

"Here comes the new patient. I need to go and help."

"Okay, but thanks for listening. I feel better."

"See you tomorrow around ten."

"Right, around ten. Bye."

Reece hung up and walked to twelve, the stretcher lined up with the bed. Reece went to the far side, where Ingrid was standing. One, two, three, and they pulled the man onto the bed, bringing with him his endotracheal tube. The ER nurse gave him breaths with an Ambu bag, while Ingrid got him connected to the ventilator that had just arrived.

The man was thirty-three, black, and his head was bandaged. He'd been on a motorcycle without a helmet. The endotracheal tube was taped to his swollen mouth, his eyes just slits. Reece took the catheter bag lying on his legs and hung it on the bed frame. There was an IV in his neck. He watched Ingrid switch the IV fluids from the stretcher pump to the room pump. She knew what she was doing, but he felt bad for the patient. He nodded to Ingrid and stepped out of the room.

"Hey, Reece." It was Selena, the monitor tech dressed in dark blue scrubs. Her long black hair had a purple sheen to it. He'd noticed that the fine hair on her arms was blonde.

"What's up?"

Selena pointed at the monitor for six, Lola. "She's started to have some PVCs, some landing on the T wave. Kind of worrisome."

Reece watched the monitor for thirty seconds and saw two jagged PVCs. "Let me peek in at her."

He looked around the curtain into the dimly lit room. Lola appeared to be asleep. He wondered if he should ring the doctor on call and decided to wait a few minutes.

"Hey, just let me know if they increase," said Reece. He took a peppermint from the bowl on Gloria's desk.

Gloria loomed her eyes at him through her cat-eye glasses. "That'll be a nickel," and she laughed.

"I get paid in a week." He walked the perimeter of the unit and then sat down across from twelve, watching Ingrid bustle in and out. The man had begun thrashing, and she was tying his wrists to the bed with soft restraints.

"V fib in six!" shouted Selena. "Now V tach!"

Reece jumped and hurried to the room. Lola was sitting up in bed with a confused look on her face. Reece asked her to lie back and then apologized for what he was about to do. He raised his fist over her sternum about six inches and brought it down hard. Lola groaned, and he looked at the monitor. Andrew was behind him. She had converted back to sinus rhythm.

"Whoa, good job," said Andrew, but I'll let the doc know." He left.

Reece stood beside Lola, pushing the button to raise her head. He readjusted the nasal cannula, feeding her low-dose oxygen. She rolled her head and looked at him as if groggy.

"You okay? I had to thump your chest. You were in a funky heart rhythm."

"Jesus. I thought...I was dying." She slurred her words.

"The doctor's coming, just to check you out, okay? I'll stay here with you." He proceeded to straighten the sheets, and the doctor walked in. Reece explained what happened.

Dr. Shelfwise took a stethoscope from his back pocket and listened to her chest. He said a few words, pushed back his rumpled hair, told Reece to start a Lidocaine drip, and went out to write the order. Reece didn't know that Shelfwise had been on two dates with Kristin.

"So, can I go back to sleep?" asked Lola. "I'm afraid to. Afraid I won't wake up."

"I think you're fine. I'll get the new med going, and that will help. Don't worry, we're keeping a close eye on you."

"Thanks, but you hit me."

"Well, I had to. The next thing would have been the paddles, you know, to shock you. But you're good." He watched the room monitor, which was still showing an occasional PVC.

"I still can't believe you hit me, but thanks, I guess. That was scary."

"You're welcome," said Reece, and he went back to Gloria's desk to check the flagged order for the Lidocaine drip. "Well, that was a close one," he said to Gloria and Selena.

"Yep," said Selena. "It's like the writing was on the wall." She leaned forward, and he could see a cool tattoo of the zodiac on her lower back.

After work, Reece showered, slept a couple of hours, and then drove to Hueytown to pick up Emma. She wore a blue cotton dress and sandals with low-cut socks. If she did turn up HIV positive, she didn't want to be in an outfit that she liked. Reece parked on the street and held her hand as they walked toward the modern building. He opened the door for her. They approached the desk, took their numbers, and sat in the half-filled waiting room. An educational video was playing: breastfeeding. She looked at the screen and couldn't believe how large the woman's breasts were. One was bigger than the baby.

"Hey," said Emma. "That's just for the ladies."

Reece kept looking. How the baby was holding onto the giant nipple, he couldn't tell. It seemed to be a work of magic. "Okay, I'll quit looking." There was a novel in his chair with a torn cover, a romance of some sort called *Barstool Babe*. He held it out for Emma to see.

"Huh," said Emma. "Reece, I'm so freaked about this. You just don't know. Check my pulse."

Reece put his fingers on her neck and looked at his watch for thirty seconds. "Wow, hundred and ten. You are worked up. How can I help you relax?"

"Just talk to me. Tell me a story."

"Okay." He thought. "Well, one time I was at the lake during the summer. I was probably twelve. I was outside and could hear this faint sound of an animal. I walked down to the lake and kept listening. It was a kind of yipping. I figured it was coming from near the pool, so I walked that way. The noise got louder and louder. I walked past the public pier and then through some high grass. Whatever it was, it was in distress. Then I saw a beagle, a momma dog, and she was whining, staring at the water. I got closer and closer, and then I saw it. It was a puppy in the lake, trying to get up the bank. It was only a foot or so, but its little feet were just slipping off the mud." He paused for dramatic effect and looked up at the pyramid ceiling.

The door opened, and a man in slacks and a cardigan sweater called out a number. "Sixty!" They were sixty-eight and sixty-nine.

"Well? What happened next, silly?"

"I went over and scooped the poor fella out of the water. He ran to his momma, and she licked him all over."

"You saved its little life. That's sweet."

"I guess I did. I've always liked animals. I hate to see a dog chained to a tree, especially when it's cold." He examined his hands and put one on her knee.

"Tell me about that girl who burned the house down, the one up in the woods." She put her hand on top of his.

"Oh, that. Well, she wasn't too bright. She was good-looking for sure, but that was about it. Her grandmother was in the house at the time, upstairs. Her parents were at work. Her name was Kim."

"Go on."

"Sixty-one!" A heavyset black man wearing a Rasta hat stood and groaned.

"Kim decided to put some gas in her dad's motorcycle. I guess she was planning to ride it. Anyway, she spilled gas on the basement floor. To suck it up, she took a shop vacuum, and the thing burst into flames. She panicked and ran."

"And then the house burned to the ground, right?"

"It did, and the grandmother barely got out. Caught the woods on fire too, but the fire department kept it from getting too far."

"And they rebuilt the house, right?"

"They did. Reminds me of the time I burned my grandparents' barn down, my mother's parents." He withdrew his hand and put his arm around her.

"Sixty-two!"

"Really? You haven't mentioned that before. How old were you?" She shifted in the hard chair.

"I was eight or nine. I can't remember."

"How did you burn the barn? You were a bad kid."

"Yeah, I was wild. My dad was overseas in Germany, and I was living with my mom in Cullman. One day, my mom takes me and the neighbor's boy, my friend Bob, out to my grandparents' house, an old farm with a huge red barn. We played for a while, but then we got bored. So, we walked down the road about half a mile to this little country store and bought some gum and two Hav-A-Tampa cherry-flavored cigars. They cost a nickel apiece."

"They sold them to you?" asked Emma.

"Yeah, no questions. Anyway, we get back to the house and sneak into the barn loft to smoke the cigars. We were used to smoking cigarettes, but not cigars. Outside, it was in the nineties, and in the loft, it was probably over a hundred degrees. The loft was filled with dry bales of hay. I remember that neither one of us liked the taste, so we just played with them, making little fires out of piles of straw. We'd make a fire and then stomp it out."

"Oh no," said Emma.

Sixty-three stood and disappeared through the wooden

door.

"Of course, we get bored with that. It's after lunch by now, and we go inside to watch TV. My granny was in her recliner by the window in the dining room, and my mom was in the house too. We turned on the TV and found *I Dream of Jeannie*. It had only been a few minutes when my granny yelled out, 'Barn's on fire! Barn's on fire!'"

"Did you run and hide?"

"I should have, but I wheeled around on the green vinyl couch and threw back the curtains. Flames poured out of the barn loft door. I nearly died, but then Bob and I ran outside with my mother. All I could do was just watch."

"Did the fire department come?"

"Not right away. But cars were stopping. Someone got a hose and stretched it to water down the corn crib that was next to the barn. There was an old guy, and he got the cows out. The whole thing was on fire up top, and I was sitting in the grass like it was a movie without sound."

"God," said Emma. She poked him in the ribs.

"All of grandpa's farm equipment was in the barn along with his old Ford pickup. They managed to get the tractor out and a few other things, but already burning wood and hay were falling into the bottom of the barn, and the whole thing was on fire, a huge pillar of white smoke."

"Sixty-four and sixty-five!"

"Seeing the truck in the blaze took me in. I figured it would explode, and then it did, sending up a fireball. Everybody ran back, but I was still sitting in the grass. I couldn't take my eyes off it." Reece paused, piecing it together. "I remember dreading the second my grandpa would get there. I thought for sure that he'd shoot me. I saw him shoot a stray dog one time."

"Did he show up?"

"Yeah, he came flying up in his Chevy and hopped out, but the barn had collapsed by then. He never once seemed to look my way. Well, the fire just burned and burned, and by the time the firetruck got there, it was too late, but they sprayed more water on the corn crib."

"Sixty-six!"

"Jeez, that makes me sweat just to tell it. It was one of the worst days of my life."

"So, it burned, and then what happened?"

"Well, believe it or not, no one even suggested that we might have had something to do with it. Talk revolved around how hot it was that day and how that could've been what caused it. But my mom did get me and Bob out of there and back home. No one has ever asked me if I did it, and sometimes I wish they would, so I could confess. But back then, there was no way I was going to fess up. I was too scared and considered it some kind of divine intervention on my part."

"They just let it go, just like that?"

"Ha, funny thing was that my grandpa, who had never really liked me, would drop hints sometimes about the barn. One day, I asked him if he had fishhooks, and he said, 'Nope. I guess they burned up with the barn along with everything else.' I never asked for fishhooks again, that's for sure. But they knew I did it."

Sixty-seven answered the call and stood, gathering her giant purse and pulling a five-year-old by the arm.

Emma squeezed his thigh. "I'm next. Oh Lord. Why am I so dang nervous?"

"You're fine. Everything's fine." He scoured his brain for another story, maybe one with a happy ending. "Oh, there was this time in Germany, when we all lived together over there, near a little town called Nelligan. It was the day before Halloween, and my parents decided to buy me a costume. We went to the base PX, and the entire shelf was empty except for one outfit. An O.J. Simpson Buffalo Bills outfit."

"Oh God. Reece, I'm so nervous."

"You're fine. Everything's okay. Anyway, the costume had a brown face mask, pants, and a shirt made of silky material that was a kind of baby blue. I was O.J. Simpson, and that was that."

"Sixty-eight!" Emma stood and walked that way, looking back.

Reece sat hunched over and began flipping through the torn copy of *Barstool Babe*. He wondered if he should have gone with her, but he was waiting for his results. He would be next. Everything would be fine. The breastfeeding video on the TV ended in a hiss of white noise, clicked, and then automatically rewound, leaving a black screen and "Rewinding" in red.

He glanced to his right at a man in his fifties and wondered what had brought him to the health department. The man's brown slacks had hiked up his legs, showing a thin pair of grayed white socks. Reece read a short passage from the novel and put it down, looking to his left at a young woman with a pained and bored look on her face. She seemed to be pregnant, but he couldn't tell for sure. He glanced at his watch. Emma had been gone for nearly fifteen minutes, and a trickle of panic eased up and down his spine.

Another five minutes passed. Reece kept looking at his watch. He saw the door open, and it was her with a man in slacks following her. He stood. Her face was blank, and then she smiled when she saw him. When she was standing beside Reece, the man put his hand on her shoulder and walked away.

"What?" asked Reece. "You okay?"

"Yeah, okay."

"Well, what happened?"

"Sixty-nine!" It was Reece's number. He looked to the nurse standing in the open, didn't know what to do, and waved.

"Emma, here, have a seat. I'll be right back. They called my number."

Emma sat and looked up at him. "Yeah, go ahead. I'll be here."

"You sure?" He waved at the nurse again, who looked impatient.

"Yep, positive."

Reece wanted to take that as a good sign and followed the nurse into a small office where the man in the slacks was sitting at a desk piled high with manila folders. He reminded Reece of his dad, seriously balding with flakes of dandruff in his hair.

"Just have a seat." He opened the folder in front of him and cleared his throat.

Reece sat.

"Mr. Myers, you're negative, I'm happy to say."

Reece started to stand, but the man asked him to answer a few questions first about his risk factors for HIV. He explained that Reece should always use condoms when having sex and asked him to sign a form showing that he had received his results and post-test consultation.

Reece scribbled his name. "Is that all? I need to get back out there with my friend."

"Yes, that's all. Be careful."

Reece nodded and hurried back to the waiting room. Emma was just as he had left her, but her cheeks were wet with tears, and his stomach dropped. He sat beside her.

"Emma, tell me." He held her hand.

Emma cleared her throat and wiped at the tears. "I'm positive. They drew blood again to re-test me, but I'm positive. Reece, I'm positive. What will I do?" She broke down and put her head to his chest, sobbing.

Reece held her. "Oh, God, Emma, I'm so sorry." He held her and let her weep, wetting his shirt with tears.

Emma tried to bring her tears to a halt. "Reece? What do I do? There's no cure, not even a treatment. "I'm going to be like Charles, dying slowly."

"Hey, I'm here with you. We need to get you home, right?" They had planned to go to Duck's for lunch, where Emma's mother worked.

"Seventy!" The old man stood and walked toward the nurse.

"I can't believe it, Reece. Those damn soldiers. They raped me. They gave this to me." At that, her tears halted, and she sat up straight. "Damn them to hell."

"Yes, damn them to hell. But it could have been a dirty needle when you were in the hospital."

"That was six months ago. I would've started getting sick sooner. Now it makes sense: the fever, the headache, the rash. Have you seen the rash?" She pulled up her shirt. "Look."

Reece looked. He saw a smooth red rash. "Wow. I had no idea. I mean, you told me about it. Wow. I can't believe it." He ran his hand over her back. "Let's get you home, okay? Here. Still want barbecue?" He stood and held out his hand to her, and she took it.

"I still have to eat. But not Duck's. I don't want to ruin mom's shift." She took a deep breath and wiped the tears from her face, smearing mascara.

"How about the Waffle House?"

"The one where we danced."

"Yeah, that one."

"Okay," and she walked, Reece guiding her to the glass door and outside. The sky was clear, the sun hot. There was no breeze, and Sixth Avenue was crowded.

Reece ushered her to the old truck, and there was a ticket on the windshield. He opened the door for Emma, closed it, grabbed the ticket, and shoved it into his back pocket, cursing. He turned the key, and the starter was trying to spin, but made an awful groan. "Fuck." He reached under the seat for a heavy wrench, got out, went to his knees on the hot pavement, and hit the starter as hard as he could three times. He jumped back in the truck and tried it again. It turned, stopped, then turned, and the engine cranked.

"Impressive," said Emma. She laughed.

"I'll get a new car soon," and he pulled into traffic, forgetting his seatbelt. Briefly, he was lost and couldn't remember which street he needed for the interstate, then remembered it was Fourth Avenue. He was driving too fast, as if speed would help.

"Hey, slow down," said Emma. "It's okay. No hurry."

Reece drove onto the interstate and then battled his way across two lanes to take I-59 South toward Hueytown. It was hot in the cab, and he rolled down his window, sweat pouring down his back, his forehead. They rode in silence, Emma staring straight ahead.

"This could have been a false positive, you know," he said. "The re-test could be negative."

"You know, I'm in love with you."

A knot formed in his throat, a desire to wail and smash something made of glass. He glanced at her, and she was unbuckling her seat belt and scooting toward him with a half-smile to die for.